Catherine Texier

VICTORINE

Catherine Texier is the author of three previous novels, *Chloé l'Atlantique*, *Love Me Tender*, and *Panic Blood*, and a memoir, *Breakup*. She was the coeditor of the literary magazine *Between C & D*, is a regular contributor to *The New York Times*, and has written for *Newsday*, *Elle*, *Harper's Bazaar*, *Cosmopolitan*, *Marie Claire*, and *Nerve.com*. Texier lives in New York City.

VICTORINE

Catherine Texier

ANCHOR BOOKS

A Division of Random House, Inc.

New York

FIRST ANCHOR BOOKS EDITION, APRIL 2005

Copyright © 2004 by Catherine Texier

All rights reserved under International and Pan-American Copyright Conventions.
Published in the United States by Anchor Books, a division of Random House, Inc.,
New York, and simultaneously in Canada by Random House of Canada Limited,
Toronto. Originally published in hardcover in the United States by Pantheon Books,
a division of Random House, Inc., New York, in 2004.

Anchor Books and colophon are registered trademarks of Random House, Inc.

Grateful acknowledgement is made to Yale University Press for permission to reprint
an excerpt from *The Tale of Kiều* by Nguyen Du, translated by Huynh Sanh Thong.
Translation copyright © 1983 by Yale University. Reprinted by permission
of Yale University Press.

The Library of Congress has cataloged the Pantheon edition as follows:
Texier, Catherine.
Victorine / Catherine Texier.
p. cm.
1. Aged women—Fiction. 2. Runaway wives—Fiction 3. Women teachers—Fiction.
4. French—Vietnam—Fiction. 5. Reminiscing in old age—Fiction. 6. Parent and
adult child—Fiction. 7. Vietnam—History—1858–1945—Fiction. I. Title.
PS3570.E96V53 2004
813'.54—dc21
2003054860

Anchor ISBN: 0-385-72126-9

Book design by Dorothy Schmiderer Baker

www.anchorbooks.com

Printed in the United States of America
10 9 8 7 6 5 4 3 2 1

In memory of Paule Texier, my mother

De la tête jusqu'au nombril
Femme était moult belle et gente
Mais en dessous était serpente
Serpente voire vraiment:
Queue avait, burlée d'argent
Et d'azur, dont se débattait
Tant que l'eau toute troublait

> *—La Légende de Mélusine*

From head down to navel
She was woman, fair and graceful
But below that she was snake,
Snake, if ever snake there was:
Tail she had, with bars of silver
And azure, that thrashed about so
The water was clouded through and through.

> —The Legend of Mélusine

VICTORINE

There are families of gamblers, families of leftists, families of womanizers. My family has its share of wayward women. Women who have a streak of wildness and rebellion, who balk at the yoke of married life. Maybe it's a kind of recessive gene or personality trait, like blue eyes. Once in a while it skips a generation. My grandmother didn't get it, but my mother did. And so did my great-grandmother, Victorine.

In the big white villa where I grew up with my grandparents and my mother on the outskirts of Paris, the villa with the weeping willow and the blue cedar and the swing that hung from the branches of a chestnut tree, the enigmatic shadow of Victorine hovered over us. She died before I was born, and her name was rarely mentioned, or if it was, it was with a disparaging shrug or snort. What she had done was unspeakable.

All I was able to piece together was that Victorine had left her husband and children—one of them my grandfather—in the little village in Vendée where they lived, in the late 1890s. There were rumors that she had gone off to Indochina with a customs officer. She returned in 1900, at the latest, since she was back with her husband and gave birth to her youngest son, Maurice, on May 30, 1901. There was no account of the time in between. It's as though she had fallen into a hole, and those years had been erased.

PART ONE

September 8, 1940

11:15 a.m.

THERE'S BARELY enough time to go to the beach before Maurice comes to pick her up for lunch, but she doesn't want to miss seeing the ocean for the last time. The rain, which has poured down for the past three days, has finally stopped and washed the sky a deep, spotless blue. She hurries through the bungalow, impersonal now that most of the furniture has been moved, folds a blanket into her tapestry bag, and puts on rubber galoshes over her soft woolen slippers; the sand might still be damp.

The old steamer trunk stands in the middle of the empty parlor, where the movers have left it, after having brought it up from the basement the day before. The trunk is smaller than she remembers it, its leather scuffed and scratched from years of use. She runs a finger through the dust. It's been forty years.

She struggles to slide open the locks. A heavy smell permeates the old clothes: sandalwood. Her hands fumble along one side of the trunk, then the other. She had slipped in the diary afterward, hastily, she remembers. She pulls out a copy of *Madame Chrysanthème*, a novel by Pierre Loti, then a catalogue of the 1900 World Expo. That one, too, she must have put in the trunk later. Has she misplaced the diary? She finds a few more books, a photo album with a red leather cover, a blue ledger filled with a list of items: white handkerchiefs, pillowcases, tablecloths with *point lancé* or Valenciennes, each priced in piastres. Finally, her hand feels a rectangular object at the bottom of the trunk. She pulls it out. Yes, it's the brown notebook. It smells damp and smoky. Without opening it she puts it into her bag and quickly walks out. Drops of water festoon the latticework running under the roof of the bungalow. In the garden, she notices, the hollyhocks, which have grown tall and wild over the summer, are fading to pale lavender and watery pink, as if their colors were running with the late summer rain.

Her joints are swollen with arthritis and her fingers a little twisted at the knuckles. She's carrying her big tapestry bag by the handle. She's tied an apron over her dress as if she were going to the backyard to pick a head of lettuce or chard for dinner, and put on a cardigan; it's cool by the ocean. The dress is navy blue, printed with tiny white birds or windmills. The cardigan is hand-knitted in a shade of lilac or puce, or just plain gray. Her legs are covered with thick, white cotton stockings. On her feet are the slippers with soft soles and gray pom-poms, and the rubber galoshes over them.

The dories are leaning drunkenly, pastel blotches in the morning sun, their masts teetering low above the wet sand. Just as they had that day when he had come up to her, in his big black overcoat, holding his hat over his chest, bowing. When she was a young bride, before the birth of Daniel, Armand had taken her to Paris and they had gone to visit an exhibition of paintings everybody was talking about. The canvases were covered with tiny splashes of color that blurred when you came up close. But if you took a step back, the scene quivered to life. People said it was sloppy, not good art, and yet now, the beach in the late morning, dotted with the hulls of the dories, mottled with the flickering shadows cast by high, wind-swept clouds, reminds her of those paintings.

She spreads the blanket at the foot of the dunes, sits down, removes her rubber galoshes, and takes the notebook out of her tapestry bag. Forty years, she thinks again. Forty years that she hasn't seen it or even opened that trunk. It had remained closed through all her moves, from Velluire to Maillezais, from Maillezais to Le Gué de Velluire, from Le Gué de Velluire to Villa Saint-Claude, here, in La Faute.

The brown cardboard cover, she remembers, was originally embossed with arabesques in a Moorish style, probably to imitate Moroccan leather. She opens it. A few letters and yellowed newspaper clippings slip out on her lap. Some of the pages are stuck together. She separates them carefully in order not to tear them. The faint blue lines are barely decipherable now, and the original violet or blue ink has turned a pale umber.

Several pages are covered by foreign words dotted with accents.

Cám ơn
Chào
Chào tạm biệt
                    biệt
chúc ngủ ngon   *dạ*
CÂY BÀNG bún riêu   *phía nam*
CÔ CHIÊN   *Chan doo*   *cái màn*
làm gi   *đóng cửa*
ời đâu   *nha quê*   *buổi tối*

She reads the words slowly one after another. Most don't mean anything to her anymore.

A loose page in a thick paper, folded four times, reveals several rows of Chinese characters. One of them, she recognizes, spells out her name.

維克特琳

The others are indecipherable to her now.

She leafs back to the beginning of the diary and reads the first entry.

4 avril 1898

Saw A. on the beach yesterday. They say things always happen for a reason. Do they?

April 1898—she was not yet thirty-two.

La Faute

APRIL 3, 1898. She was lying on her stomach, chin resting on folded hands, her stockinged toes digging into the sand, an open parasol next to her, and watching her son, Daniel, a gawky boy who had just turned twelve.

It was at La Tranche. Palm Sunday. After lunch at Tante Emilienne's, Daniel had carried his fronds to the beach to see if they had been cut from the reeds growing on the dunes. They had. He brandished them victoriously to show her he was right, dropped them in the sand, and ran off toward the ocean.

She had a dog-eared copy of Balzac's *Eugénie Grandet* open in front of her but she wasn't reading. The pages were covered with sand, the grains had gathered in the crack of the book. And, just like that, he had walked into her sun and squatted next to her. His hat was in his hands, between his knees, his face in deep shadow.

It was the same beach. Only a few kilometers up the coast. With the same wide-open horizon, a horizon of the end of the world. The only sound, the squeal of the seagulls, tearing at the cottony peace of the morning, now as then.

He had moved sideways so that the sun had suddenly flashed into his blue eyes.

Don't you remember me? he'd said. And she'd said, No, not looking at him.

It was too unexpected, a ghost from another life. This man

in the big black overcoat and the black fedora and the waxed black shoes, what did he have in common with the slender, blond boy running barefoot in the sand, carrying crates of mussels? He crouched and looked into her eyes and smiled. She saw the tiny chip on his front tooth. He was looking into her face so intimately that in spite of having two children and a husband, she blushed like a girl.

No, she insisted, stubbornly, she didn't remember him. She made her eyes blank, sat up and folded her legs under her. If she denied the past, then it would be as if it never existed.

I don't see . . . I don't remember . . .

She lowered her eyes to her book and closed it.

He read the title upside down.

Eugénie Grandet, he said.

Yes. Have you ever read it?

Yes.

It was awkward. Ridiculous even. They were alone. She could see Daniel, by the jetty, his tiny silhouette bending over or squatting, she couldn't tell.

Your son, he said.

How do you know?

He shrugged. It's not hard to guess. When did you get married?

Monsieur . . .

He nodded. He traced the figure eight in the sand with his finger. What happened to you? he said.

But Daniel was already running back, his pants rolled up on his skinny calves, holding his shoes in his hands in front of him, like a present. Dropping to his knees next to them, he upended one of the shoes. Small pink-and-white shells tumbled out of it.

He had gotten up then. Brushed the sand off his overcoat, off his hands, put his fedora back on. He looked tall, taller than she remembered, and wider across the shoulders. He had grown into a man.

Now that he had his hat on she couldn't see his eyes anymore. He was standing against the sun and hesitated for an instant. Daniel looked up from the heap of shells he had gathered and watched him silently, not saying anything.

He touched his hat and bowed.

Au revoir, madame.

Au revoir, monsieur, she replied.

Later, after he had left and they were walking toward the road, Daniel would ask her, with a sulky look on his face, Who was that man? And: Does Father know him? And she would say to her son, perhaps a little too testily, *Mêle-toi de ce qui te regarde.* Mind your own business.

She counted the years on her fingers. She was thirty-one then. They had met for the first time fifteen years earlier, when she was sixteen. It was the summer of 1882. Or was it '83? She was losing her bearings. Once thing she knew for sure: she hadn't passed her *brevet* yet.

It was low tide, the same golden time in the late afternoon as it is now. It was already a little chilly. The beach was dappled with conical shadows made by the little peaks and valleys of fine sand, stretching as far as the eye could see. On this part of the Atlantic coast the ocean can withdraw as far as a mile out, and roll back up, as they say, "as fast as a galloping horse."

She is headed toward the little group of boys, toward the open sea, her long braids flipping against her back. In those days there were reeds growing on the dunes, but no casino, no wooden cabins, and certainly no bathers. Holding her long white muslin skirt up with her fists, she is running in the damp sand, leaping over the puddles of sea water. Her fine leather boots are wet but she doesn't care.

The boys are coming back from the mussel beds, unloading crates of shells from a dory, stacking them up. All tan legs and muscular arms and a dusting of mustache on their upper lips. Her cousin Jules is among them, helping out for the summer, still white as a turnip under his long-sleeved shirt. She's come with her sisters, Bertha and Angelina, to tell Jules the carriage is waiting to take them back to the farm for dinner. But it's Antoine whom she wants to see.

He's the tallest one. The blond with the blue eyes. His pant legs are rolled up on his calves. His shoulders are square and deeply tanned. The fine down on his arms is almost white from the sun. He's watching her run toward their little group. As if he knew something about her she doesn't know herself. She won't speak to him, only to Jules. Doesn't even look at him. But he knows, she can feel it.

He steps right into her path and she almost trips and falls into his arms. She pretends to be angry but she giggles. He pulls on one of her braids.

I want to show you something, he says, but first you've got to take off your shoes.

She hesitates, then bends over to undo the tiny buttons.

Her feet are naked in the warm sand now, her pink toes look like pale worms. Embarrassed, she digs them deep in. The sand coats her ankles. Her stockings are unrolled, her unbuttoned boots lie on their side, abandoned.

Come on! Hurry up!

He's running ahead of her. She lifts her skirt up to her knees. Her ankles and her legs are free, her knees knock against each other. She's excited by the freedom of her bare skin. Tumbling, stumbling in the sand, now dry and loose, now wet and packed hard, now submerged and sucking her in, way out toward the open sea.

Wait! Wait for me!

But he's already by the mussel poles, tall sentinels standing up against the upcoming tide.

Look at this, he says.

The mass of mussels clutching the wooden posts are a deep, blackish purple. The thick cluster of them, glittering black diamonds in the setting sun, immobile masses, dripping sea water, look silently, stubbornly alive.

Touch.

She hesitates. Her hand stops in midair.

Go ahead, touch! They aren't going to bite you.

He takes her hand and brings her fingers into contact with the dark shells.

They are hard and sharp like knives, yet furiously hairy, a tangle of little beards. She removes her hand quickly as if she has just been burnt. He laughs. He places both his hands, wide open, on the mussels, traces their sharp outlines with his thumbs, to show her he's not scared.

I'll bring you some for dinner. A whole crate.

She looks at her feet sinking deeper into the wet sand.

We're leaving, she says. We're leaving La Tranche.

When?

The day after tomorrow.

Your sisters too?

Yes, all of us. It's a whole day's journey back to Cholet. We've been here a month. She turns on her heels. We should go. The tide's coming in.

Wait. Don't leave yet. Do you see the island, over there?

She puts her hand over her eyes. You can barely see the island for the sun, melting in apricot trails along the horizon.

Yes.

Do you know what it's called?

Ile de Ré.

And farther?

What do you mean? There's nothing farther.

What's beyond the horizon, way, way over there?

America?

He nods approvingly.

Excellent geographic knowledge. Congratulations!

Don't talk down to me, she thinks.

I'd like to go there one day, he says. Or . . . He flips his chin toward the Lay estuary, inland, to the east. Over that way.

Where?

To the colonies.

The colonies?

Yes, you know, overseas.

Which colonies?

I don't know yet. Will you go with me?

She laughs. You don't even know where you want to go!

But he's looking at her seriously. Not laughing at all. There comes that look in his eyes again. Challenging, as if he can see through her childlike, easygoing mask to a core of fear and longing. She turns her face away.

And just when he's about to crack a smile, they feel the water sloshing around their ankles. The tide is coming in, fast. He grabs her hand.

Come on. Let's go back. Hurry!

She remembers the pressure of his fingers, the warmth and weight of his hand as he pulls her back toward the shore. And the softness of the wet sand sucking her feet in. The sand, which has suddenly turned cool, now that the sun is dropping into the ocean. How fast they had to run back, arriving breathless near the others. How Angelina, who was waiting by the carriage, had looked at them holding hands.

The following summer, she comes to the beach sometimes in the afternoon with Angelina and Bertha. Tante Emilienne's horse and buggy drops them off and picks them up in time for dinner. They spread a blanket at the foot of the dunes and take off their stockings and shoes. Bertha and Victorine read, while Angelina, the youngest—she's just twelve—plays in the sand. She's been building a castle with elaborate turrets and a minaret, in an audacious mix of architectural and period styles. Occasionally, Bertha lifts her head from her book and gives her suggestions. Victorine is making her way through Balzac that summer, or is it Stendhal? All she remembers is that her attention wavers. She's waiting for the boys to come back from the mussel beds.

After the crates of shells have been stacked, she gets up as nonchalantly as she can—I'll be right back, she says over her shoulder—and strolls over to where the boys are tying up the dories.

Antoine sits next to her on the jetty, their thighs touching, their legs hanging against the stone wall, their toes skimming the surface of the ocean. She knows her sisters can see them, but she doesn't care. She isn't doing anything wrong, is she? They are only talking. Antoine is different from the others. He's from Nantes, for one, he's not a village boy. He seems more mature, a little aloof, although he is only a year or two older than she is. They say his mother died, that he's an only child, that his father was not from around there, that he's been raised by his aunt and uncle. That he's been to the capital. To Paris. These are rumors. He doesn't say those things to her. He doesn't speak much about himself. But she notices, that second summer, she notices that hint of *accent pointu*—which is how the Parisian accent is perceived in the provinces where they still roll the *r* and sprinkle their speech with patois—his vowels shortened, slightly nasal, and his *r* flat. He sits on the jetty with her and tells her about his dreams. He's only interested in the future. He takes her wrist, up under the delicate muslin of her camisole, and confidently presses her hand to his thigh.

She glances at her sisters. Bertha has her nose deep in her book. Angelina is kneeling in the sand, shaping a crenellated mole, without looking at her hands, her eyes fixed on the jetty. When she notices Victorine looking at her she turns her head away and pretends to be absorbed in her sand castle.

I know where I want to go, Antoine says, as if their conversation of the previous summer has barely been interrupted.

And where is that, she asks, ignoring Angelina, not removing her wrist from the circle of his fingers, acutely aware of the rough texture of his pants.

In-do-chi-ne, he pronounces slowly, separating each syllable. Do you know of it?

She rolls her eyes, trying to hide the turmoil she feels under her self-confidence, arrogance even, as a student who's just graduated with honors at her *brevet*, who's about to turn sixteen on August 11, and about to start teaching in September—the youngest schoolteacher in France! Does she know of Indochina? Of course, and for that matter—

But something in his eyes stops her from teasing him. His blue eyes, in the late afternoon light, look right into hers. They are so clear, so intense, something in her crumbles. His fingers, laced through hers, tighten. His face leans toward hers, his full lips, his chin with the shadow of a blond beard, his lips are on hers, lingering at first, then pressing softly, insistently, and then they hear Angelina's voice.

Victorine, the horse and buggy's here. Come quick!

But he holds her back. Not a kiss, now, no—she's pulled away ever so slightly hearing Angelina calling her—but her hand still pressed hard against his leg, his eyes still in hers, his look more passionate, more tender, more naked, more troubling even than a kiss, not letting her go.

And yet, two years later, it is not Antoine who will wait for her at the altar of the cathedral of Cholet as she walks down the aisle at Victor-Paul's arm, but a dark-eyed schoolteacher named Armand Texier, who teaches at the boys' school in Velluire, a little village at the edge of the marshland.

THE BEACH is wide and pristine, entirely empty save for the rows of footmarks delicately imprinted in the damp sand by the seagulls, and the heavy human footprints left by the Germans who patrol the beach every morning.

You can't step out of the door without running into them now, with their gray uniforms and bean-shaped caps. Like those two she saw earlier on her way from the bakery, on Main Street, stiff like a couple of rods, practically falling into goose step. The tall one, with his blond hair, his pale blond eyebrows, the sharp line of his chin, was shocking in his beauty. How can she even think about him that way? A *Boche*! They never called the Germans by any other name. So those two were heading toward her, and just as they were about to cross her path, they politely stepped off the sidewalk to let her pass. The tall one looked right at her and nodded imperceptibly. He had pale gray-blue eyes. The color she imagined of a cold, northern sea. Blue eyes are not so common in Vendée. People have hazel or brown eyes, sometimes green, like hers. At least she thinks that he nodded. But maybe he didn't. Maybe it was the cold intensity of his gaze that got her heart racing.

She stares at the curb of the ocean, her end-of-the-world horizon, and lets the journal slip from her lap. The sun is high, the shadows are brief. Near the dunes, protected from the wind, it is still warm enough for her to do without her cardigan. It must be close to noon. She takes out her knitting and from the open mouth of her bag a blue yarn unrolls with a tiny, soothing jerk with each click of her needles. She's a fast knitter. One day it's a baby camisole. Another day a pair of socks, knitted seamless with four needles crossed at right angles. Or a white *brassière*, a heartwarmer, whose flaps cover the chest and tie up at back with two satin ribbons. Sometimes she stays on the beach all afternoon. When the pewter of the ocean turns to copper, she folds her knitting and rolls her yarn into her purse and does her rounds of the fishermen's houses. She knows when this one has just had a baby, when that one has gotten married, when this other one is stuck at home, crippled with a broken leg. She knows how old the kids are, how much they've grown, how big the toddlers' feet.

In their whitewashed cottages, the sailors welcome her, their skin tan and leathery, their eyes even more faded after a week or two at sea, their hands cut and blistered and rough from the handling of cordage and riggings. They invite her to sit at their kitchen table and offer her a glass of mirabelle or cognac and sometimes she asks just for a cup of coffee. And then she takes out the cardigan she's just finished or the socks or the camisole, and they sit and talk around the table. And after a while, the wives come, and then the children, their canvas pants rolled up on their calves, smelling of seaweed, carrying buckets of small crabs, trailing gray, wet sand behind their feet, and they all sit and talk until it's time for dinner and they invite her to stay over. She's always carefully, even elegantly dressed when she visits them, she makes a point of wearing a freshly pressed dress, a Sunday dress, and her curly gray hair is combed neatly, with the left part straight, and there's her ring on her finger, which is now twisted with arthritis. Not her wedding ring, it's been a long time since she's worn it, but the tourmaline set in gold, the one she says is an engagement ring when they ask.

Don't forget I want to be buried here, she reminds them, and as she points toward the open sea the tourmaline flares at her hand.

Right in the cemetery by the shore, so that you can come and visit me after I'm gone.

They laugh. They say, *Bien sûr, Madame Texier.* They don't know, these sailors and their wives and their strings of children, some born barely a year apart, what it means to her, to be buried by the seashore.

All they know about her is that she has been married, then separated, and she has raised her youngest son by herself after the first two children were grown. They see him, Maurice, he drives over on Sunday with his wife and their little boy, and sometimes he comes by himself and takes her out for lunch.

She was a good woman, they'll say after she passes away, she went to mass, she gave to the parish, she cared about the poor. She had a passion for the ocean.

Armand

JULY 5, 1884. It is late, past midnight, a warm evening in Cholet, where the evenings can turn sultry, away from the ocean breezes. Victorine is hurrying back home through the tiny, narrow streets flooded with the white light of a full moon, the only sound the sharp click of her heels on the silvery pavement.

She pushes the heavy wooden door. The Jozelons occupy the first floor of a Renaissance townhouse built around a pebbled courtyard in the heart of Cholet. At the left of the courtyard is her father's shop—Victor-Paul Jozelon is a master craftsman by profession, a painter of coats of arms on carriages and coaches—which is set up in the old stable. The combined smells of paint and horse manure are so familiar she barely notices them. The gas sconces cast trembling funnels of light up the walls. The flagstones echo. The horse neighs, hearing her steps. She takes off her shoes. She's supposed to give *le bon exemple*—be a good example for her younger sisters. Instead, she is the one who errs. In a few years, people will say in town that the Jozelon girls are *légères*, fun-loving, easy. And it will be her fault. She's the one who started it all. But that summer, she doesn't think about those things.

Where were you?

Her father's voice booms from the shadow of the foyer. She's startled.

Papa?

Do you know what time it is?

She cannot see him at first. He must be standing by the stair-case. Then she sees his reflection in the big mirror hanging on the foyer wall. His shirt glows a bluish white.

Answer me!

She tightens her shawl around her shoulders.

Midnight?

She freezes in front of him, her knees trembling but her head tall.

Twenty past midnight!

He grabs her arm.

Where were you? Who were you with?

She pulls her arm back.

Adèle, she lies. Adèle, Armand's sister, who is also spending the summer in Cholet and whom she sometimes visits in the evening. She keeps her voice low and calm. She will not show him her fear.

He pulls her back by the shawl.

It's the third time this week you're coming home late. Do you know what they call girls like you?

But she drops the shawl into his hands and flees down the hallway.

In their bedroom Angelina and Bertha are still awake. She sits down between them. The three heads gather; long dark curls drape over white nightgowns.

Has he been drinking? Victorine asks.

Not particularly.

Don't worry. He will have forgotten it tomorrow.

Were you with Armand?

She nods.

Do you love him?

Will you marry him?

Why doesn't he like Armand? Angelina asks.

He's jealous, Bertha says.

He doesn't know about Armand, Victorine says. It's me. It's because of me. I work. I go out at night. I do what I want. It makes him angry.

The other two heads nod. Hands caress Victorine's hair soothingly, remove the pins from her bun. Strands of hair are pulled off her face. A white handkerchief is proffered to wipe off her tears. But she's not crying. She is folded around herself like a fist.

August 1919. My little sunbeam, her father says. She hasn't heard that in a long time. She's sitting by the side of his bed in the old house in Cholet. His voice is halting. He has to catch his breath every other word. The approach of death is softening him, making him sentimental. It's during the annual ox fair, the first one after the end of the war—*la Grande Guerre* they called it because of the million and a half French soldiers who died in the trenches. They can hear the rumble of the crowd and the auctioneer's chanted screams, barely two streets away, on the square. They have to raise their voices to hear one another. It's exhausting him.

We used to call you that. Sunbeam, Victor-Paul repeats. It was not so long ago.

She feels like an imposter. As though she had fastened a sunny mask over her real face to fool them.

It was a long time ago, she says. And anyhow, it was only you who said that. Not mother.

Your mother felt the same. She was just not very demonstrative. He sighs.

You were a happy child.

There's a scream outside. The crowd always screams when the best oxen are sold.

Not always, she says. I was good at pretending.

Don't say that, he says. Don't say that. You're making me sad. And then something happened, he goes on. You changed. When you left, you remember? You were never the same after you came back.

Oui Papa. I remember.

A deafening clamor rises in the crowded square.

It must have been a damned good one, Victor-Paul says. He closes his eyes, exhausted.

Yes, she says, taking his hand.

One day, he had stopped calling her Eléonore, which was her given name, and switched to Victorine, her middle name. She was five or six. She had brought home a painting of a tree she had done at the little school. The tree was painted on paper, thin lines of white paint over a black background. It looked as if it had been caught in a snowstorm in an eastern or northern country, not a tree from their parts. He had whistled with pleasure when she had brought it to him. *Elle est douée, cette petite!* he had said. Takes after her papa, doesn't she, Marie-Louise? They were standing at the door of the workshop, in the courtyard. Very nice work, her mother had said, and she nodded toward the house. You didn't finish washing the mushrooms, Eléonore. You left them on the kitchen table. Run along inside. Victor-Paul pinned the painting on a wall of the shop, and showed it proudly to his assistants. After that, Victorine would come to the shop sometimes in the afternoon and paint on pieces of wood she found on the floor. We should have named you Victorine-Eléonore, Victor-Paul joked, not the other way around. Eventually, the name Victorine stuck. Only Marie-Louise, for a long time, insisted on Eléonore.

He built her the swing the following year. The courtyard in Cholet led to a small cherry orchard enclosed between the walls of the adjacent houses, where Marie-Louise grew cabbage and lettuce and strawberry patches. The cherry trees bloomed in a halo of pink in May, and when they fell, their petals covered the wrought-iron bench half-collapsed along the back wall, a bench that Victor-Paul always promised to repair, but never got around to. He was whimsical in the work he did in the house or the garden. He'd prefer to build something from scratch rather than tinker and fix. He built them a dollhouse, the year after Angelina was born—

hand-painted with exquisite details of flowers and gold moldings—but that was later. The swing came first. He had fashioned it out of elm, the same wood he used to repair the broken axles of carriages, and tied it to the oak with two ropes. Meanwhile, the old bench rotted and rusted. In the spring and summertime, when her homework was finished, Victorine would slip out alone to the orchard and swing by herself, or sit on the bench under the cherry trees and read. At the end of the afternoon, Marie-Louise's voice would carry all the way over the wall, Eléonore! Eléonore! She wouldn't move, stayed quiet, until Marie-Louise would give up and switch to: Victorine! Victorine! Victorine! Then she would get up and go inside to help with dinner or look after her sisters.

As far as she could tell, there would have been nothing wrong with Armand, if her father had known about him. When she met him, the first year after her *brevet*, they were both teaching at Velluire's district school, Armand at the boys' school, Victorine at the girls'. He was six years older than she was—a perfect age difference by all accounts. He came from a family of elementary school teachers and farmers. She was staying with an aunt who lived in the village. He was a boarder in the mayor's home. It was natural that they would meet. She didn't like him at first, at least not as a potential suitor. He had a handsome, strong face, but he was a bit short and he was dark, with jet-black hair, olive skin, and a beaked nose. He looked like a Basque, they said. Armand was funny, always in high spirits and joking. He would wait for her at the gate of the girls' school and walk her back to her aunt's house. He played a little dance around her, telling her the names of all the trees, which animals lived in the woods, making her laugh. He seemed to have an encyclopedic knowledge of nature. He brought pheasant hens that he had shot, pieces of fresh venison as presents for her aunt to cook, the occasional hare. He would pull it out of his satchel by the neck, its body still soft and warm. When he found her bent over a history book, studying the chapter on the Hundred Years' War, or choosing a little-known Ronsard poem to teach in class the following day, he gently teased her.

You're the smart one, the brainy one, I barely passed my *brevet*, and I was older than you when I took it. If I had my choice I'd hunt all day long instead of sitting in front of those simpletons teaching them the history of our ancestors *les Gaulois*! But she wondered if those praises were not really backhanded compliments, as though so much erudition and love of learning gave her a secret advantage over him, a man of the land, almost elevated her to a higher social class, and he needed to belittle her accomplishments.

She saw him with other girls, sometimes, girls who wore rouge and showed their ankles and laughed too loud. Girls he picked up at the stagecoach stop when they came back from the Sunday market in Niort, the nearest town. He called them *catins* and *goyots*, crude, disparaging words men used for easy women. She didn't mind. She even found it exciting, a whiff of a life she was forbidden to live. That's what men did, that's how men talked.

Anyhow, she wasn't thinking of Armand that way. She was still thinking about Antoine, the tall, blond boy on the beach, that first year. But she hadn't heard from him again since that summer. He had vanished. And she hadn't gone back to La Tranche.

The second year, when Armand came to meet her at the arrival of the stagecoach, as he did with those other girls, when he took her hand and helped her get off the high step, she found him more dashing and spirited. She liked the way a strand of his black hair had escaped the pomade and fell over his bright eyes, and he was easy to talk to. She laughed louder than she had before, she felt giddy and joked with him on the way to her aunt's, and when he pressed her a little too tight in his arms she didn't pull away. The hunting season had just opened and the following Sunday he brought a bottle of Chinon and a quartet of quails he had killed the day before and her aunt sautéed them with a handful of chanterelles in a cognac-and-cream sauce and they ate all afternoon long. A neighbor stopped by and they played luette, the card game everyone was playing then and which was hilarious, because you were not allowed to talk, but had to announce the cards with winks or nods or funny faces. Armand sat at a right angle to her and their arms occasionally touched and she did nothing to avoid him. They hadn't talked about marriage, but later that day he said he wanted to introduce her to his parents during the summer.

That's how it started. She was seventeen. Even though he was only twenty-three, he had been with quite a few women before, he didn't hide it—he even boasted about it. And secretly, she liked that, that he was experienced with women. With her, he didn't press his luck. She was a respectable girl, the kind of girl a man marries. He went to pick her up after class, at the school gate. The children whispered among themselves when they walked away, arm in arm. It was a relief to see him after school. Sometimes, during the day, she felt as restless as the little ones. It was Armand who suggested she should enlist the older children to help teach the younger ones reading and simple operations, like adding and subtracting. By Easter of that year, her younger pupils, who were five years old, had all learned to read at the second grade level, and she told Armand that she thought she would be a good teacher.

And then it was the end of the school year and the Saint John's dance. There was an orchestra set up behind the church and pear wine was served on long tables under the willow trees. The hawthorn hedges were in bloom and the air smelled of lilac and hyacinth. All the girls wore the *quichenotte*, the big headdress that came out on both sides of the face like blinkers on a horse, she thought. Later, when Armand tried to kiss her, she told him the headdress had been devised to discourage English soldiers who'd invaded the coast from kissing the local Vendéennes. In English they say "kiss not." That made him laugh. He said he wouldn't be discouraged as easily as those lame *English* and pulled the head-dress off her head, tossed it into the grass and pressed his lips against hers. She didn't resist. It was a hot, moonless evening. She felt naked, the breeze in her hair. The orchestra played well into the night, and they all danced in the dark.

They ended up with another couple in a field of beets behind the church, at the edge of a little wood. They stood against a tree.

He lifted her skirts and touched her with his fingers, then pressed himself against her. Afterward she didn't feel any shame, but on the contrary a certain pride to have been wild, not a prudish girl. And anyway, they hadn't even taken off their clothes.

A few weeks later Marie-Louise was leaning into the steam rising from the tub of boiling water like a witch over her cauldron.

Isn't it your time? She glanced at Victorine over her shoulder. Her forearms were red, coated with soapsuds.

I washed them myself, maman, Victorine said.

Marie-Louise gave her a look.

I didn't see them on the line.

Victorine didn't say anything.

Marie-Louise wiped the soapsuds off her arms.

I'm ironing tomorrow. With this heat, by the time you finish hanging the last piece of linen, the first is already too dry and wrinkly to be ironed properly. Put them on the pile of clean laundry while they are still damp, will you?

After everyone had gone to bed, Victorine tiptoed to the washroom and wetted a week's worth of clean towels and hung them up to dry on the line.

When she crossed the courtyard back toward the house, there was a light at their bedroom window, and a shadow behind the shutters. She wondered if Angelina had woken up. The gas lamps were on and she might have seen her. Victorine tried to think of a plausible explanation for what she had done. She wasn't sure whether she could confide in Angelina. And anyway she was still so young, barely fourteen. But when she got back upstairs, the bedroom was dark, and her sister seemed asleep.

She lay down in her bed and listened for a moment to her uneven breathing.

Angelina had always been a troubled sleeper. Victorine remembered coming back to their bedroom, years ago, when her sister was tossing in her bed and moaning, her legs kicking to free herself from the tangled sheets. Maman! Maman! she was crying. Bertha went on sleeping. Victorine sat down on Angelina's bed. Angelina woke up with a start and put her arms around her waist and held her tight. She was sobbing. Her face was wet with tears.

Victorine took a handkerchief out of her pocket and wiped her gently.

Angelina shook her head like a cat and rested it against Victorine's shoulder.

Don't leave, she said frantically. Please stay with me.

Shhh . . .

Victorine picked up her skirts and lay down next to her.

Tell me your dream, Angelinou, she whispered, but her sister had already fallen back to sleep.

Every Sunday Marie-Louise and the three girls went to mass together. Victor-Paul stayed home. He wasn't actively antichurch, but he wasn't a believer and he teased his wife for being a *calotine*—a pejorative term for a devout Catholic. They stood on line to receive the communion at the altar. You didn't have to go to confession, as long as you hadn't sinned. Small, venial sins were acceptable. On the way to church, the girls debated which sins required confession, if they had to be mortal or capital. Angelina, who loved dessert, thought gluttony was acceptable. Maybe jealousy too. Bertha, who was the theorist of the three, said they were all mortal, gluttony, concupiscence, adultery, lust, jealousy, anger. I thought mortal was if you committed murder, Victorine said. Bertha said mortal didn't mean that you had killed someone, it meant that you were condemned to die and burn in hell. But if you took the communion and you had done a capital sin and you hadn't confessed, that was a mortal sin and you'd burn in hell too.

They still hadn't resolved the issue by the time mass had started. The Agnus Dei came, followed by the Confiteor. Victorine stood in line behind Angelina. They all kneeled and opened their mouths, one after the other. They went to church, but Victorine was teaching at the district school, not at the nuns', and in Vendée that was tantamount to being anticlerical. Angelina got up and winked at her, making a show of sucking on the host. Victorine frowned. She kneeled. The marble step felt cold and hard even through the layers of petticoats. It was the old parish priest, the one whose breath smelled of cheap wine. He mumbled the prayer while making the sign of the cross with the host. She stuck her tongue out and tried to hold her breath. The host was light as paper. She pressed it against the roof of her mouth and walked back to the pew. If she didn't salivate, it could stick to her palate for a while without disintegrating. She'd have to wait until the *Dominus vobiscum et cum spiritu tuo* and the *Ite missa est*, hoping the host would stay in one piece. Finally it was the Deo Gratias and they all stood up. The host was beginning to melt. She tried to push it on the tip of her tongue to keep it aloft until they got out onto the church parvis. But they ran into their neighbors and the two families stood greeting one another and she had to wait again before she could excuse herself. She strolled away from the group, toward the cemetery. Half of the host had melted and what was left of it had turned into a tiny, rapidly melting glob of pasty saliva. She spat it into her hand.

Victorine, Victorine, wait for me! Angelina was running behind her.

What are you doing, following me?

Are you ill?

Angelina looked innocent, with her hair braided and tied with pale blue ribbons and her freshly starched petticoat, smelling of violets. But her eyes were inquisitive. At thirteen she knew more than she let on.

No! I was just taking a walk.

Is something wrong? Angelina's eyes were probing.

Nothing, Victorine said. She wiped her hand on her skirts. Let's go back.

And yet, in the end, Angelina was the first one she told. Even before Armand. The two of them were alone in the kitchen heating a pair of irons over the hot wood stove.

Promise you won't tell anyone, Victorine said.

Angelina opened her eyes wide in anticipation and crossed herself. *Croix d'bois, croix d'fer, si j'mens, j'vais en enfer.* Wooden cross, iron cross, if I lie, I go to hell, she chanted.

But when she heard the news, her little face turned pale and she dropped the iron she was holding. The burn mark on her thumb never completely went away. Victorine regretted having said anything.

A tentative, fresh sun dusts Niort's stone façades with a golden glow when they emerge from the noon mass at Notre-Dame. Armand is wearing a brand-new felt hat with a black ribbon and a black cloth jacket, and Victorine a white linen dress with a pleated bodice and a high collar. Niort is so much more lively on Sunday mornings than Cholet, but this time Victorine doesn't enjoy their walk, hand in hand, in the market, wandering between the baskets of potatoes and radishes arranged on the bare ground amid a flurry of carts and horses and frantic poultry and bleating sheep.

Along the Sèvres, the river that meanders through town like a little Seine—its two arms embracing an old mill built on an island—the trees are creeping with ivy, the birds are singing. It's a carefree summer day. They sit down on a bench by the river under a pergola dripping with grapes. A man and a woman, tipsy, arm in arm, steadying one another, stagger toward the little bridge.

Look at these two, Armand says, putting his arm around Victorine's shoulders, not even lunchtime and they are already drunk. Victorine gently pulls free.

What's the matter? he asks.

She presses her hands together between her knees and takes a deep breath. The excitement and defiance of the Saint John's night party are long gone.

I am going to have a baby, she says.

What?

Armand's thick, black eyebrows arch high, then he blows through his lips—not a whistle exactly, and not quite a sigh.

Are you sure?

She nods.

Briefly, his head drops between his hands. But he quickly straightens up.

We'll get married, he says, his tone resolute.

He glances at her, then looks away. She can't tell whether there is love in his eyes. She only sees his determination, his capacity to make a quick decision and to take his responsibility. Perhaps he is trying to impress her. If only the baby had come later. But it's too late already. There is no time to talk of love. And the relief that rolls into her heart is mixed with a distinct chill—like a sudden gust of wind slamming a trapdoor behind her and propelling her into a long, black tunnel. At seventeen she is the right age to get married. But not like this. Not this hasty marriage without even a courtship or a honeymoon . . . She tries to remember those lines from Flaubert she had learned by heart. Something about traveling for your honeymoon toward countries "where, at sunset, you can stand on the gulf's shores and breathe the scent of lemon trees." Well, hardly. Just this sad little mill in the middle of the river, that she has seen dozens of times. The carts pulled by mules, piled high with unsold fruit and vegetables, peasant women sitting on top of mounds of soiled potatoes, and then later the ride back to Cholet in the familiar coach, the old percheron horses dragging their hooves as though they were half-asleep, moving through a fog.

What are you thinking about? he asks her.

Nothing, she says.

He picks up her hand again, this time chastely, not fingers entwined but his palm laid flat over her hand, warm, protective, reassuring. He could be a good husband, she thinks.

We'll have a family. I love you, Victorine, I've loved you ever since I've met you.

You do?

She pulls her hand from under his. Gently. He shouldn't think that she's rejecting him.

Are you scared? he asks her.

She doesn't know. All she feels is that heaviness in her stomach, deep down, as if her blood was about to come but couldn't be released, and her breasts, a bit fuller in her corset.

I will talk to your father, he says.

So, this is it, he's taking over. She imagines the two of them, Armand and Victor-Paul, who have never met, the two of them in the Jozelons' parlor, talking man to man—she watching silently—debating her fate. Her handing over. She sees herself walking down the aisle of the Cholet church at the arm of her father in a corseted wedding dress, her long veil carefully arranged to hide her swollen belly in its folds.

Let's not do it, she says suddenly.

What?

Maybe there's something we can do.

What are you talking about?

You know, Josephine Joliette, the one who lives in the thatched house in the woods by Gué de Velluire?

Who?

The one—you know, the healer?

What are you talking about? His face shows utter incredulity.

She looks away, wishing she hadn't spoken.

It's just that . . . we shouldn't be forced to get married because of . . . because of this. Her hands are tightly coiled in her lap.

You shouldn't have done what you did, he says sternly, in the tone of a father talking to his daughter. It's too late. We'll do what we ought to do.

I shouldn't have done what I did?

We shouldn't have done. You're not a virgin anymore.

In profile, his face is hard, his mouth bitter. His hands resting on his legs, one on each knee, like a peasant, she thinks.

What are you saying?

I'm sorry—he's still not looking at her—I'm not judging you. But it's true. That's what happened.

The chill comes back.

It's so . . . harsh the way you say it, she says. She gives him a quick glance. What about you? Weren't you part of it?

He pauses for a moment and turns toward her, softening.

Me too. You're right. Both of us. But let's not take it too tragically. We were going to get married anyway. He smiles and playfully pulls on the ribbon tying her collar. The baby is just a little ahead of schedule. His dark eyes are warm now. He laughs, merrily, it seems. His laugh is almost unbearable to her, as if it is a false attempt to hide the harshness he's shown before.

Were we? she says.

Were we what?

Going to get married?

Sooner or later we would have.

I wish . . . , she says. Her voice breaks a little. I wish it wouldn't . . . have happened like this.

He places his arm around her shoulders again and this time she doesn't pull away. His arm feels solid. She rubs her forehead on his shirt. They have talked about meeting the families. Would they have gotten married? She will never know. The question of love and the question of marriage, of marriage for love, is forever rendered moot.

He runs his finger over her cheek. Victorine! Look at me. It will be fine.

A month earlier, in the room that he had rented in a Cholet pension for the summer, she had lain down with him one afternoon, and he'd said, I love you, his face buried into her neck. It was warm, the shutters were half-closed, bands of light stretched across the sheet he had pulled over her naked body. She had said *je t'aime* back in a joyful melting of her limbs. But did she love him? What was she doing there, in his narrow iron bed, in defiance of all the social rules she had grown up with? She couldn't resist Armand's desire. And maybe—she realized much later—maybe she was thumbing her nose at her father, at his authority?

. . .

Later, at dusk, after the return trip to Cholet in the afternoon coach, Armand and Victor-Paul are sitting at either end of the sofa, a glass of port in front of each of them, Victorine at the edge of an armchair, to the side.

Armand has been masterful, a worthy opponent to Victor-Paul Jozelon. Assertive beyond his years and taking the matter into his hands.

We were planning to get married, Armand says, simply, brilliantly, she thinks, staring at him. We just got ahead of ourselves. With a sly smile he adds, I take all responsibility for our actions. Victorine, you must know, Monsieur Jozelon, is a modern young woman. She works, she is free. Our generation is changing the rules.

Victor-Paul takes his pipe from the table and stuffs it with a pinch of loose tobacco, then lights it, taking his time, pulling on it slowly until the tobacco starts to burn and releases a plume of smoke.

Victorine shifts in her chair and wonders, if she is a modern young woman, why isn't she the one talking to her father right now?

Papa . . .

Jozelon Père lifts the hand holding his pipe. It is between the men. His face is a mask of reprobation. He moves the bottle of port toward Armand's glass, then, noticing that it is half-full, pulls it back and fills up his own glass, which was empty.

Has it ever occurred to you, young man, that my daughter, who is, as you were saying yourself, a remarkable young lady—and, make no mistake, I am extremely proud of her, proud that she is working, extremely proud, indeed, I encouraged her to pursue her studies, to teach—such a remarkable young lady that she is the youngest schoolteacher in the whole of France—no small feat, you will admit no doubt. Has it ever occurred to you that perhaps she was destined to a bigger future than to marry a schoolmaster like yourself? That what you did, in effect, ruins her chances to have a future befitting her accomplishments with a man more worthy of her than you are?

Papa. This time she won't speak for herself but to defend Armand who surely doesn't deserve such an attack. Papa, it's unfair.

Again, the pipe lifted, stopping her.

Has it, Monsieur Texier? Has it occurred to you?

Armand clears his throat. He is the picture of poise and self-control. He's ready to measure himself man to man. Until now he has been leaning forward, his elbows balanced on his thighs, but now he pulls his chest up and crosses one leg over the other, his right ankle resting over his left knee.

Monsieur, Armand says, his voice tightly controlled. I want you to know . . . my intentions were good . . . I never intended . . . I love your daughter. We intended to get married. I am convinced that the two of us can build . . . a solid and happy future.

Transfixed, a spectator at her own fate, Victorine watches Armand.

Victor-Paul Jozelon drains his second glass of port. Takes his time to put it down. Upends his pipe into an ashtray, empties it. They wait for him to be done. Then he stands up. He's not a very tall man, rather on the slender side. But his face is imposing, framed with a pair of brown mutton chops, his mouth fleshy, firmly set.

No, he says. Plain and simple no.

Victorine's heart leaps. Confronted by her father's punishing command, she forgets her terror of marriage.

She gets up too.

You can't do that, she says. Her legs shake under her. You can't stop us from getting married.

I certainly can, he says, and without a word he walks out of the room.

But in the end he didn't stop them. In the battle between his power and his expectations for his daughter, and Victorine's honor, honor won. Marie-Louise, to Victorine's surprise, warmed up to Armand immediately. It was as though she were conveniently overlooking the circumstances which led to the marriage, in her relief at seeing Victorine settling down.

It'll be good for her, she told Victor-Paul. *Ca lui mettra un peu de plomb dans l'aile.* That'll put a little lead in her wings.

They were alone in the parlor after Victorine had walked Armand to the street, and didn't realize she had come back into the house and could hear what they were saying.

She watched the profile of her mother, the fine beak of her nose framed by the severe bandeaux of her black hair, the mouth characteristically pinched after having delivered a definitive statement, her hands folded together in the lap of her black dress, her back straight as a pin—as though carrying the weight of three unruly daughters demanded an inordinate tension of all her muscles and a fierce vigilance.

We'll see about that, *ma chère mère*, she told herself. She walked past the parlor door without stopping and went straight up to her room.

As for Armand's parents, François and Augustine Texier, they had made up their mind about Victorine before meeting her, it was obvious. The day of the engagement, which took place in Cholet at the Jozelons' home, at a small lunch party on a Saturday in September, they shook her hand stiffly, as if they were entering a rather unpleasant but inevitable business arrangement with her, rather than welcoming her into their family. The Texiers were certainly not bigots, they kept a reasonable distance from the Church and never missed an opportunity to mention that the family had been pro-Revolutionary when Vendée, a bastion of Royalists, had been the only French province to oppose the French Revolution. Perhaps that is why they hadn't opposed the marriage. But they were *bien-pensants*—conventional. Victorine always felt they turned up their nose at her, in particular Marie, Armand's older sister, who was already married, a teacher herself, on her way to becoming a headmistress, and who never missed an opportunity, it seemed, to make Victorine feel whimsical, if not downright unstable and odd. She lived and taught in Vouvant, a village north of Fontenay, and had recently opened a little storefront off the church square where she sold medicinal herbs. Even without yet knowing that formidable personality, Victorine felt the impact of Marie's piercing and inquisitive eyes when she first met her at the Texiers' house. They had politely kissed. Marie, then, had taken a step back and looked at her, as an adult sometimes looks at a child, a stare, really, probing her, and Victorine had seen a flash of surprise or suspicion in her eyes that quickly dissipated. Armand joked later that Marie claimed to be able to see the future. Not that anybody can confirm it, he said. Still, the look Marie had given her that day had made her uneasy. Adèle, Armand's younger sister, on the other hand, who was two years her junior, had spontaneously offered her friendship. Adèle was the first one of the Texiers, at the end of the wedding, who came up to her and kissed her, throwing her arms around her and wishing her good luck.

Anyway, by the time the final arrangements were made, Victorine was three months pregnant, and she was passing into that peaceful state in which whatever life throws at you is met with equal serenity. It was as though she had forgotten, in those short months, as she got plumper and her energy slowed down, her fear of marriage and motherhood, her romantic longing for passion and adventure. The alternative, finding herself with child and alone, was impossible to confront. There was now something oddly reassuring in fitting in and fulfilling the fate that was dealt to her, like cake dough lazily spreading into the mold. It was a relief not to have to shoulder the burden of life by herself. Maybe she was a coward, but at least she was accomplishing her destiny as a woman. While a hasty wedding was planned—a simple family lunch following mass at the Gué de Velluire chapel—she stopped seeing the long, dark tunnel of marriage she had imagined earlier. In its place spread a wide, perfectly sunny clearing. When the school year started, in early October, they rented a house in the

little village of Maillezais, where they had both been hired—
Armand at the boys' school, Victorine at the girls'—in the area
of Vendée called the marshlands. The village stood in the middle
of an amphibian maze of canals almost entirely shaded by vaults of
willows and alders, like transepts in a cathedral. When the road
dipped under the dark canopy of trees Victorine felt that she had
entered a magical land of dappled light and rippling shadows. The
house was typical of the area, whitewashed with royal blue shutters, its roof hanging low, and stood at the top of a slope of grass
bordering on a canal. A bush of golden gorse blazed in the milky
light. They had their own canal boat, a *yole*, tied at a pontoon, with
the *pigouille* or pole lying at the bottom, and a weeping willow
whose reflection danced with the duckweeds on the surface of the
water.

APRIL 1885. Upstairs, in the bedroom under the eaves filled
with heavy oak furniture, lace, doilies, and precious bibelots, clutching Angelina's hand on one side and Bertha's hand on the other
side, Victorine is moaning and panting. Marie-Louise, her mother,
and Augustine, Armand's mother, take turns walking up and down
the narrow stairs, carrying pots of hot water and laying fresh towels on the bed, ready to receive the baby. Clearing the way for
the women, Armand has been gone since dawn, hunting. When
he comes back, in the afternoon—Merlin, their pointer, sensing
something, sniffing at his boots, chasing his tail like a whirling
dervish—Daniel is already born, cleaned, and swaddled, sleeping
in his mother's arms. His face is shut close and swollen, his miniature fists curled tight, like a tiny boxer.

The spitting image of his father, Armand says, cracking a
smile. The small skull, covered with a wet down, disappears into
the cup of his hand.

Mon fils.

Serene, relieved, Victorine watches Armand from her mound

of pillows. How awkwardly he places the tips of one finger to the delicate mouth, to the button nose, to the transparent eyelids, how his face is melting in surprise, in delight, in tenderness even.

When he puts the baby back down in Victorine's arms, the tenderness lingers in his eyes and he kisses her lightly on the cheek. Well done, *ma chérie*, he says, but already his mouth tightens, perhaps a reaction to what he feels might be overindulgence or excessive softness, a shadow quickly obscuring the momentary delight. Victorine catches that painful split for an instant, before he stretches up.

I'm hungry, he says to his mother. What's for dinner?

Victorine hears the kitchen buzzing down below, fire crackling, pots banging, chairs scratching the stone floor, voices muted. Safely above, she sings a lullaby to the baby. *Do-do-l'enfant-do, l'enfant dormira bien vite. Do-do-l'enfant-do, l'enfant dormira bientôt,* over and over, lower and lower, until they both fall asleep.

Two years later Madeleine is born in the same room, which is now even more crammed with Daniel's little bed, soon to be moved to the other bedroom, which they already call the children's bedroom. Petite, pink, with light brown curls, she's the image of her mother, and a vivid contrast to Daniel, who has Armand's jet-black hair and darker skin. The tenderness fades faster from Armand's face when he sees the baby that January afternoon. The shadow overtakes him again. Another baby, but not another son.

CHRISTMAS 1887. Victorine is twenty-one, at home in the Maillezais house with her two babies. Daniel, on all fours, is running around the dark kitchen pushing a wooden wagon with the words *Paris–Orléans* hand-painted on its side by Victor-Paul, and Madeleine sleeps in the brand-new cradle with the swan neck, from which hangs a flowing, lace curtain. In western Vendée, so close to the ocean, the winters are never really frigid; they are damp and chilly. And yet Victorine is always cold in those early winters of her marriage. She says that her house is colder than the school, because their only heat comes from the fireplace. But there is always a fire roaring and the small kitchen warms up fast. The days are long, taking care of two young children. And when they sleep a deadly silence falls upon her. If she hadn't known another life before—the pupils' eager faces in the first row, their excitement when they could read a whole sentence on the blackboard, their hands impatiently raised when they knew the answer, *Moi, Madame, moi!,* the faded colors of the old map of France on the wall, the human skeleton in the corner, always good for a fright the first day of classes—would she feel this emptiness, this coldness of the soul? She wonders if there is something amiss in her heart, that she seems to love taking care of other children rather than her own.

In the huge fireplace flames lick the blackened bottom of two cast-iron cauldrons hanging low over the fire. Water is boiling for the laundry and the dirty dishes in one, a bean soup simmering in the other. Cloth diapers are soaking in cold water in the sink.

Victorine is sitting at a little desk. On the wall in front of her hangs a tiny oil canvas painted by her father. It portrays Alexandre Dumas's three musketeers, Athos, Porthos, and Aramis, and D'Artagnan, the fourth, in full seventeenth-century dress, flowing shirt sleeves in bright colors, billowing pants, thick mustaches, long hair, big floppy hats, swords at the ready, and a general martial air. The details of the scene are painted with the same precision of line and clarity of color as the coats of arms her father paints on carriages. Pupils' papers are strewn in front of her.

She has offered to help Armand grade his students' finals before Christmas.

Don't consider it a favor, she has told him in the morning. I'll be glad to help you.

He accepted, grateful, and took the afternoon off to go to Fontenay to buy a new pair of rubber boots.

And it's true, it's for her own need, really. She is missing her work. But after correcting a dozen papers, she realizes what she really misses is the classroom, the children's hands going up, eager, their eyes bright with excitement.

Daniel whines and pulls at her skirt asking to go pipi. She takes him to the outhouse, behind the vegetable garden. The outhouse door has a kind of porthole carved at eye level which Daniel is constantly intrigued with. So intrigued, in fact, that she suspects he asks to go just for the thrill of sticking his face through the hole. He immediately climbs up on the soft, worn, wooden bench and stretches up on his toes until he can look through the porthole and hold his tiny hand out. Outside, as the afternoon wanes, a fine mist falls, sure to turn into rain during the night.

Sky make pipi, Daniel says, laughing hard at his own joke, feeling the rain on his hands and letting it drip from his fingers.

Victorine smiles, hurries him back to the warmth of the kitchen. Madeleine is stirring for her evening feeding. The white-bean-and-pork soup gives off a smoky aroma, Armand will like it, she hopes. The rectangle of gray, at the window, darkens. The fire crackles. Soon it will be time to set the table.

The portrait of a happy family. She picks up Madeleine and puts her at her breast, making herself comfortable in the deep chair by the fireplace, her feet up on a carved bench made especially for her by her father. Everything as it should be. A solid, good life ahead of them.

So how is it that when Armand comes back and takes off his wet galoshes at the door and slips on his felt slippers and asks, as ever, What's for dinner, little mother?, distractedly ruffling Daniel's hair, and sits down at the table, elbows planted wide, and pours himself a glass of Anjou rosé, how is it that while Madeleine's head drops off the breast, beatific little mouth still half-open, drooling pearly milk, how is it that no peace and quiet descends into Victorine's heart but instead that strange, dull feeling?

FEBRUARY 2, 1888. They are all gathered at Cholet for *la Chandeleur*, Candlemas. Marie-Louise is in the kitchen, making crêpes. Madeleine is sitting on Victorine's lap, pulling on the cameo that hangs from a ribbon of black velvet tied around her neck.

Arrête, Madeleine, she says, trying to hold back the little hand that keeps yanking at her neck.

You look pale, Victorine, Victor-Paul suddenly says, looking at her from across the table.

It's nothing. I'm just tired.

She can feel her father looking at her, perhaps waiting for her to say more, but she keeps her eyes down, focused on Madeleine. Victor-Paul thinks it's staying home and not working that is making his daughter restless. For such a conservative and old-fashioned man he occasionally has progressive ideas about women, or is he just making an exception for Victorine? He thinks such a good brain should not go to waste and that perhaps going back to teaching would benefit the whole family in the long run. He's proposed this to Armand and to Victorine several weeks ago, the last time they were in Cholet, but Armand said no, he was opposed to it. He believed that Victorine would get used to not working.

The little ones give her a lot of work, Armand says. Especially being so close in age.

Madeleine cries, tries to free her hand.

Hush, Madeleine, Victorine says, showing more impatience than she would like.

Put her down, Armand says. She'll be calmer in her chair. His voice is cutting.

Victorine flashes an angry look at him.

Armand, Victor-Paul says, hardly hiding a hint of sarcasm, I think you should let your wife out of the house sometimes.

They all know he's talking about teaching. Victorine looks at Armand, who doesn't take the bait. It's clear he's avoiding the subject altogether.

But Angelina jumps right in. She says she's thinking of applying to teach at one of the new, state, nonreligious schools which are opening all over Vendée. Bertha looks dreamy, barely listening. She's about to be engaged to a young man from Niort. Working must be the farthest thing from her mind.

It wouldn't be a bad idea, Victor-Paul says. They all know he is worried about his capacity to provide his two younger daughters with a decent dowry. The old-fashioned horse-drawn carriages, the beautiful *calèches* are being retired, or not as well maintained and repainted as in the past.

Victorine listens to them and says nothing. She has made her decision already. She puts Madeleine back in her high chair and sets clean plates on the table. She's pleased but not a little surprised that her father is suggesting that she should go back to teaching. One of Victor-Paul Jozelon's maddening and endearing contradictions is that he will take one side of an issue and then will flip around and argue its opposite. That's his way of shutting off his opponent's arguments. *L'exception confirme la règle.* The exception confirms the rule, one of the golden phrases of French grammar books—a way for a Cartesian mind to make room for conflict and exception without losing its sense of order or losing face.

Victorine makes her announcement as she's carrying in a fresh platter of crêpes from the kitchen.

I've decided to teach the little school next October, she says. I've already talked to the headmistress.

When? This time Armand doesn't stay silent.

Victor-Paul picks up a crêpe from the platter and whistles appreciatively. The crêpes are golden, glittering with butter and sugar, with just a few brown spots here and there. Why not, he mutters, chewing on a piece of crêpe, might do her some good.

Marie-Louise puts the bottle of pear liqueur and the pot of coffee on the table.

What are you talking about? Her face tightens. Angelina and Bertha look at each other.

What about Daniel and Madeleine? Armand says.

Hearing his name, Daniel, who's perched on his own high chair and intent on fingering and banging the painted wooden beads strung in front of his tray, stops kicking the legs of the chair and stares at his father, then at his mother standing next to him.

I'll find someone to help take care of them, Victorine says.

Don't stand up like this, Armand says. His voice is sarcastic. Won't you condescend to join us at the table and sit down like us mere mortals?

Daniel starts kicking again, alarmed.

Maman, he says. Maman!

I am not condescending. I'm standing because I just came from the kitchen. She hates that tone he takes when he gets angry.

She sits down next to Daniel and cuts a piece of crêpe for him to eat. He stops kicking immediately and stares at her, his eyes wide.

Armand puts down his cup, causing the coffee to splash on the saucer.

I can take care of her, he says, turning to Marie-Louise. What does she need me for, if she's going to work?

Marie-Louise shakes her head. She is on her son-in-law's side on this one, but will keep her mouth shut.

I do need you, Victorine says, holding a fork to Daniel's mouth.

Oh yes, but what for? Armand asks.

Armand, Victor-Paul says. Shut up. Please.

Armand is the husband, granted, but it is Victor-Paul's house, and she is Victor-Paul's daughter. He looks weary. He seems to have grown old suddenly.

Madeleine gives a sharp cry. Bertha emerges from her day-dream and picks her up, rocking her in her arms, singing softly, *Do-do-l'enfant-do, l'enfant dormira bientôt.* It's obvious she can't wait to get married and start her own family.

Victor-Paul is flushed. He's gone through a couple of liters of red, Victorine doesn't need to count the empty bottles on the table to know that. His fingers are curling in and out in an attempt to keep control.

Papa, Victorine says.

Marie-Louise gets up, wipes her hands on her apron. *Eh be,* she says, disapproving but noncommittal. With a wave of the hand, she motions to Angelina and Bertha to help her clear the table.

Armand wipes his last piece of crêpe in the sugar at the bottom of his plate.

Fine, he says. It is between her and me, anyway. Victorine, we're going home.

In a while, Victorine says. I'm not done. She finishes her own crêpe, then gets up and joins the women in the kitchen, Bertha carrying Madeleine in her arms, leaving Armand and Victor-Paul alone. She imagines them pointedly avoiding looking at each other, silently listening to the noises of dishes being washed and put away in the kitchen.

Back at home in the evening, Victorine sits down in the rocking chair, suckling Madeleine before putting her to bed. Armand stokes the fire, carefully pushing the logs over the burning twigs, then stands in front of it, his back to the leaping flames.

Tell me, Victorine, why does it matter so much to you? he says. His voice startles Madeleine, who lets go of Victorine's breast and moans in protest.

Shhh, Victorine says.

We have children. Who's going to take care of them?

She puts Madeleine back into her cradle and for a moment looks at the baby's tiny hands, which rest like porcelain miniatures on either side of her face. Then she turns toward the fireplace and pokes a log to push it back into the flames.

Victorine, don't you think I can provide enough for the four of us?

She straightens up and adjusts the curtain around the cradle, aware that she's avoiding him.

Of course you can. It's not that. It's just . . . well, sometimes I'm afraid I'm not such a good mother.

What are you talking about? He studies her face. What's wrong?

She leans against the mantel of the fireplace and looks away.

Nothing really. Sometimes I think—I think I would take care of them better if I went back to teach.

How is that possible, Victorine? I don't understand. Aren't you happy?

I'm happy.

He looks at her and shakes his head.

You're just not used to being a mother, that's all. But if you want to teach, well, all right. All right. Maybe if it's a couple of afternoons a week. Come.

He uncorks a bottle of plum brandy, fills two shot glasses, and brings her one. He puts his arm around her waist.

To us, he says. He lifts his glass. We have a good life, don't we?

He's right. They do. She clinks her glass against his.

To us. She smiles at him.

OCTOBER 1, 1888. In the bright and crisp early morning, Victorine pushes the school gate open, her hair done up in a chignon, her feet tightly buttoned in fine kid leather, hay-yellow flounces at the edge of her skirt, and a ruffled umbrella of the same color under her arm. The girls are already standing in two straight lines, one for the younger class, one for the older class, in front of the gray building, waiting for the headmistress to pull on the bell. She crosses the yard quickly, waves at Madame Perrin, who teaches the older class. Inside, her classroom is unchanged, with the same smell of chalk and fresh ink in the inkpots, of paper from the pile of new notebooks on the side of the desk, the board washed and wiped to a glossy green. Long rectangles of bright light run up and down the pupils' desks in broken patches almost all the way across the room. The same old map of France is hanging on the wall, with the same frayed edges, maybe an extra rip or two on the right-hand side. Another map, brand-new, hangs next to it now. It's a map of the world, this one, showing the French colonies and protectorates in bright yellow. It is titled *The French Empire*.

She is sitting at the desk, her waist arched in a corset, her chest swelling the ruffles and pleats of her blouse of starched cambric, when the children come in and sit down. Here they are, in their flax linen smocks, parallel rows of forearms resting on the slanted desks, staring at her in silent anticipation. They don't know what to expect from a pretty teacher who is younger than their mothers. And she is nervous, she hasn't taught in four years. They are getting restless already, fingers fidgeting, chairs scratching. She recognizes them, of course, most of them, anyway, from the village.

The younger class is difficult to teach, because the children range in age from five to nine or ten, and their levels are vastly different. She separates the class into two groups: the older pupils, who already know how to read fluently, on one side, and the little ones, who are just beginning. To the older ones she gives a page from Pierre Loti's new novel, *Madame Chrysanthème*, a story about Japan, which has just been published. Loti is certainly not part of the curriculum—he is a young sailor turned journalist from southern Vendée who travels extensively in the Orient and has just started publishing books—but she wants to expose them to another reality than the provincial life they know. Meanwhile, for the younger pupils, she writes simple words on the blackboard: *CHAT* and *chat*. She draws a cat, its head resting on its folded paws. The children laugh. They repeat in unison: *CHAT! CHAT!* Underneath, she writes *CHIEN* and *chien*. She draws a dog next to the words, its ears pricked and its tail pointing up. She draws white spots with the chalk all over his body.

It's Merlin, one of the little girls in the first row says. The girl, Berthe, is her neighbor Jean Lucien's younger daughter.

They all laugh again.

Shhh, she says, putting her index finger across her mouth. But what about the word? She points to it with a wooden stick. Can you read it?

CHIEN! They all repeat.

The ice is broken. She has their attention. It is that moment she likes the best about teaching, when a bond is created and the children finally enter the game.

At the end of the period, she has a few of the older girls read a summing-up of the Pierre Loti page out loud. By the time the lunch bell rings, in spite of some resistance from the back rows—the back rows, she remembers, being always more sullen, often opposing a wall of silence, or just a façade of boredom—she feels the class come alive, engaging with her. Some hands shoot up spontaneously to answer or ask a question. When she stands up to dismiss the children and they walk out in one file, she realizes her hands are moist, the underarms of her jacket dripping with sweat. She breathes deeply. She's made it through the morning.

And she remembers now what she has missed so much: the spark in the children's eyes—some of them anyway—their thrill when they master a new task, when they hear a new story about the world.

In the village, she knows people call her La Parisienne. In their opinion, she's a little too much, her opinion of herself is a little too high. *Pète plus haut que son cul*—farts higher than her ass—they whisper at the butcher's and the baker's and in the kitchens. She shouldn't leave her two little ones with that girl from La Villette—she knows that's what they say behind her back. But she's twenty-three and she doesn't mind that they think that way about her, she secretly relishes it, in fact, and walks with her chin up, sways her skirts with a self-conscious bounce, and carries her umbrella at a rakish angle.

When she was Madeleine's age, a new series of children's books was launched by the publisher Hachette. It was called *The Illustrated Pink Library,* and its most popular books were written by a Russian émigrée married to a French nobleman, the Comtesse de Ségur. Whenever Victorine received one as present—for her birthday, for her saint's day, or as a prize at the end of the school year—she invariably devoured it in a day or two, then placed it next to the others on the bookcase beside her bed. She was proud of the growing row of reddish pink spines. The books' covers were decorated in gold leaf; the text was illustrated with woodcuts. The boys in the prints wore gaiters and waistcoats over their shirts. The girls had on voluminous skirts and modest scarves tied over their long, corkscrew curls, and belts of satin ribbons. They ran after their hoops or spun them with a stick. Her favorite was *Les Malheurs de Sophie*, Sophie's Misfortunes. Naughty and mischievous Sophie was not beautiful but had "a big mouth always ready to laugh." Her mother let her play outside without hat or gloves, rain or shine, and she was always getting into trouble. One day, for instance, she got the idea of sprinkling salt over her mother's tiny pet fishes and chopping them up for lunch—not quite realizing she was killing the poor fish. Another time, worried that her doll was too pale, she put it out in the sun, and returned later only to find that its head—which was made of wax—had melted and its eyes fallen off. Her mother always forgave her for her naughtiness, but when she died, Sophie's father remarried and Sophie was beaten by her stepmother. Yet she always managed to bounce back with the same irrepressible spirit.

Unlike Sophie, Victorine was not particularly inclined toward risky natural science experiments. But she loved to play in the rain and she secretly envied Sophie's nerve. What would happen to Sophie when she grew up? she wondered. Would she tame her rebelliousness and curiosity and settle down? Would she live in a little house by a canal with a husband and two children? Girls like Sophie, even if they had had a miserable childhood, always lived in castles like that of Monsieur le Comte de La Bretonnière in Pouzauges. They married noblemen and had enough servants to take care of their children while they did whatever struck their fancy. The life Victorine knew wasn't like that. Her mother was fond of making a pun about Monsieur le Comte de La Bretonnière, who owned a dozen carriages—all maintained and repainted every year in Victor-Paul's shop—and lived a life of magnificence in a sixteenth-century Renaissance château surrounded with a thirty-six-hectare hunting preserve. *Ce n'est pas un comte,* she'd scoff, *c'est un conte de fées.* He is not a count, he is a fairy tale. The pun summed up her mother's philosophy of life, which combined her awe of the nobility with her deep suspicion of any flight of imagination, literary or otherwise. But Victorine never missed a chance to accompany her father whenever he delivered a refurbished carriage to the Pouzauges castle. When she walked the park's perfectly manicured alleys, and ran her hands over the mossy sculptures standing guard along the pond, she knew there was another life than the one she lived, that it wasn't a fantasy.

The books, their spines turned dark red now, sit on a shelf in the children's bedroom, waiting for Madeleine to be old enough to read them. Victorine hasn't opened them in years. She has given up dreams of nobility. But not dreams of other worlds. She is still a voracious reader, but she has moved on to another kind of literature. When Armand chides her for reading *Le Rouge et Le Noir* or *Anna Karenina,* she opens her eyes wide and acts mock-naive. Those books of yours are an evasion of reality, he says, sounding like her mother. Evasion is not a word that Armand uses as a compliment. He means that she has her head in the clouds.

So when she has changed from her schoolteacher clothes, and the soup is simmering, when Madeleine is finally asleep, and Daniel plays quietly with his wooden train, she sits down by the fireplace and reads a few pages of a novel. But if Armand walks into the kitchen, she puts down the book and slips it under a stack of homework or a book of pastry recipes, like a schoolgirl caught cheating.

THE SUN, rising high above her, is drying the damp sand. Maurice should be here any minute now. Couples and families are strolling along the dike, behind the reeds. The eleven o'clock mass must have ended. She hasn't been going to church lately. Fatigue. A sense of discouragement since Pétain signed the armistice. How could he? The hero of Verdun! But then, were the French prepared to send a few more million men to be butchered again by the Germans? They went right around the Maginot Line. It happened so fast. Sometimes she even forgets which day of the week it is. Without her weekly lunch with Maurice, Sunday mornings would feel like any other day.

She puts away her knitting, the blue baby bonnet barely touched.

Although Vendee was in the occupied zone, at the very beginning, in June, along the coast, you could make yourself believe that the war was taking place far away, that France was still eternal France. By the ocean you could forget the occupation. The gulls didn't know any better. They dived and fed and squawked. The tide came and went, same as always. They had butter and milk and meat and potatoes and still all the fish and seafood the fishermen could bring back to shore. The letters from Daniel, who had started producing metals for the arms industry in his factory outside Paris, seemed to come from another world. But now, even at the shore, the illusion of normalcy is getting harder and harder to maintain. England, which has refused to surrender, is on its knees with the nightly raids on London. German is spoken in Paris. German! People are saying the winter will be hard, that there will be a meat shortage, that they'll have to live on rutabagas and topinambours. Those odd names. They joke about them. Everybody is back on bicycles. Thank God she still has a stack of wood for the fireplace. The worst is that they've started to patrol the beach day and night.

3 mai 1898

Do we choose our fate or do we submit to it? When we studied the outcome of novels like The Idiot *or* La Princesse de Clèves *in school, we said that fate was character. If I teach high school one day, I will try to explain this to the children. Would they understand it? They know, without having the words for it yet, that character is the sum of largely uncontrollable forces. Zola's characters, programmed by social and psychological forces beyond their will; Dostoevsky's characters, powerless, possessed by their fate.*

But no. It was just a chance encounter. Meaningless.

It's all a fantasy.

Victorine

Saigon, February 15, 1898

My dearest sister,

It's been so long since I have seen you. I miss you, I miss Bertha and our parents, but I especially miss you. But Vendée is so far away and so different that sometimes it seems to belong to another world altogether.

I fear the "yellow disease," that's what they call here this mysterious inertia or melancholia, caused by the constant heat and humidity. Especially when the monsoon rains come. It's so strange, Victorine, did I ever tell you about the monsoon? I don't remember. The rain falls like clockwork every afternoon at about the same time. It's a little like a violent summer storm, and when it clears up, it's as though nothing had happened. But the sky is always heavy and full. Thank God we still have two months of dry weather until the rains start again. But I can feel that languor of the body and the brain already. Not Jules, he's up every morning at dawn, and gets to his office at the Department of Defense before the heat becomes unbearable. He is our pillar of morality. I can't say as much for myself. Thank God we have some help, a cook and a boy to run errands. By the way, you might be interested to know they are in dire need of teachers here. Pierre Perrin, from Fontenay,—his wife used to teach the older class at Maillezais, years ago, remember? Anyway, he is *teaching at the Collège Chasseloup-Laubat even though he only has a* brevet. *If you and Armand ever thought of coming to join us, how happy it would make me and Jules, but oh—I don't know if Armand would want to leave his beloved Vendée?*

Kisses to all of you,
Your sister,
Angelina

She's always so eager to see her sister's handwriting, with its long, curly loops. Angelina has been in Indochina for more than six months, and Victorine devours every detail of her letters. This time she has sent a postcard along, showing a market street with women in wide-legged pants sitting cross-legged on the ground, surrounded by flat straw baskets full of fruits or vegetables Victorine doesn't recognize. She tries to imagine that languor Angelina is talking about, how the heat can affect you. These women, in the market, look placid, indifferent to their surroundings. But of course they would be used to the climate.

A series of notes mistakenly played in the minor key instead of major bring her back to reality. For a brief moment, she had forgotten she was sitting by the fireplace in Maillezais, listening to Daniel practicing a new Chopin nocturne—a very difficult one, in B flat major, that he has just started to learn.

The left hand now, Victorine tells Daniel.

He leans forward over the piano, his unbuttoned shirtsleeves dangling on his wrists, focused but still hesitant. She remembers playing that same nocturne herself on this same upright, in Cholet. He has talent, she thinks, heart, but not much patience. It's almost impossible to keep him at the piano an hour every day, as the teacher requests.

When will I play this, maman, Madeleine asks from the big tapestry armchair, where she is reading, on the other side of the fireplace. Her feet in their little lace-up boots swing above the ground. At ten, she is a bit fragile, a thin girl with pale skin and delicate features, a catlike face framed by wavy, reddish brown hair, always carefully plaited in two long braids. Pretty, but secretive. Just as Angelina used to be, it suddenly occurs to her.

Not yet, *ma chérie*. You're not quite ready.

A day like this, in the early spring, the rain and the wind won't let up. It feels as if you're tossed on a boat. A real boat. An ocean boat. Not like the *yole* Victorine can see from the window, gliding flat and silent across the canal, its boatman standing upright and poking the water with the long paddle, like a gondolier, except its load is more mundane, bags of potatoes and a pile of wood logs. No, the boat she is thinking about is an ocean liner, heading east across the Mediterranean. Soon it will reach Alexandria and the Suez Canal. At night its decks are illuminated, music can be heard faintly, escaping from the grand ballrooms.

Daniel has picked up the melody again, with both hands this time. He runs it through without a single mistake.

Much better, this time, *mon chéri*, Victorine says. She slowly folds Angelina's letter. Miraculously the ocean liner is now already pulling into the Saigon harbor under the gusts of a tropical rain.

SUNDAY, MARCH 27, 1898. It's still pouring rain. Madeleine is still reading her book in the tapestry armchair. Armand and Daniel have been out hunting since the early morning. The lamb shank sputters and crackles on the spit and the *mojette* is simmering in a cast-iron pot hanging in the fireplace. The table is set on the white tablecloth that Augustine, Victorine's mother-in-law, has embroidered herself in Point d'Alençon lace, with the Limoges set of plates from their wedding. It's an ornate set, with a cluster of pink roses in the center of the plates surrounded by garlands of pale green leaves and a gold trim. Victorine finds it a bit gaudy. But it's a wedding present from Armand's parents, and she feels obligated to use it on Sunday. Certainly, Armand expects as much.

Ah! Quel temps!

The rain whips in with Armand, as if a bucket of water has been dumped from the top of the door.

He takes off his rubber boots. The dog sniffs them, whipping them with his tail, and, in three leaps, knocks Madeleine's book out of her hands.

Arrête Merlin! Madeleine says. And she wraps her arms around the brown snout of the pointer.

And now Daniel follows Armand. Same shock of black hair loose on his forehead. Same rubber boots, same Macintosh, in a smaller size. He's a skinny boy, *le gringalet*, his father calls him. Perhaps lovingly, but the repeated tease burns.

One after the other, they hang their rifles on the rifle rack.

Not like that, you idiot. What did I tell you? Always make sure the safety is on.

Victorine and Daniel exchange a glance.

Did you come on Jean Lucien's *yole*? she asks.

Yes, Daniel says. He gave us a ride from the bridge.

Armand's Macintosh is dripping on the floor, where the door-step stone is worn smooth and the water gathers into a puddle in the hollow of the stone.

Damn weather!

Victorine says nothing. Her whole body tensed up when he walked in. He's always provoking, teasing, testing.

In a minute, he'll talk about the wild boar he's spotted down in the little wood of Velluire. He'll say that he has to go back tomorrow. That this time, the pig won't get away. And then later he'll do the evening hunt, when the woodcocks fly out of the woods into the open fields at dusk, and he won't come back until the middle of the night.

Daniel, coming with me tonight?

I've got schoolwork to finish for tomorrow, Daniel says.

Victorine looks at him. He glances at her and lowers his eyes. It's not the schoolwork. She saw the new Jules Verne he was reading, *Around the World in Eighty Days*.

Armand shrugs. Schoolwork should come first. Still. It's not a good thing for a man to be too bookish. The boy takes after his mother. Well, Merlin, it will be just you and me at the *passée*.

The dog vibrates from ears to tail at the word *passée*.

Down, Merlin! Armand's voice booms threateningly. He's energetic with his gestures, powerful. Sharp gusts of wind always seem to be blowing around him, the air never quite still.

Merlin collapses immediately, stretches his snout on his master's feet, grunts, then flips over on his back, giving his brown and white freckled stomach to be scratched.

Victorine watches them for a moment, then turns toward the fireplace to unhook the pot of beans.

What's the matter, *p'tite mère*, cat got your tongue?

Lunch is ready, she says.

She brings the *mojette* to the table.

I got a letter from Angelina yesterday, she says.

Yes? Armand says, sitting down and unfolding his napkin. What does she say? Still with the savages in Saigon?

There's something in his voice, an undercurrent of frustration, which perhaps explains his testiness. She wonders if he too, sometimes, has secret fantasies of escape. But his face doesn't betray anything. He pours wine into their glasses, and a little in Daniel's too, which he mixes with water.

Me too, Madeleine asks.

Say please, Victorine says.

Please.

You're too young, Armand says.

Daniel makes a face at Madeleine.

They are still enjoying it there, Victorine says. Except for the heat of course. But they have a cook and a helper.

Armand lifts the lid off the pot and sniffs in, stirs with the long wooden spoon.

Hmm . . . smells good. Your sister was never such a great cook anyway.

Why don't we go too? Daniel asks. Across the ocean!

Victorine glances at him but doesn't say anything. She watches as Armand brings the spoon to his lips, careful not to burn himself, and shakes his head.

You overcooked it. Look. He points the spoon at her, then tips it over the pot. The beans stick to the spoon instead of flowing smoothly. Look at this: it's like purée. Not to criticize you, mind you. Just a bit of advice.

I like it better this way, Daniel says, unrolling his napkin.

Victorine's heart fills with gratitude. Daniel is always the one who's caught in the crosscurrents, who feels the subtlest shifts of mood.

You, you couldn't tell the difference between a truffle and horseshit.

Madeleine laughs.

Armand looks at Daniel, who's making a point of savoring the beans, his face down.

It's a joke, *petit bonhomme*!

Madeleine giggles.

Look at me when I'm talking to you!

Leave him alone, Victorine says. He thinks he's just being witty, she is convinced of that. Wit at the expense of others, as when one pulls a child's ear, pretending it's all in good fun. She stares at Armand for an instant, defiantly, then she averts her eyes so that he won't be able to read in them what she herself isn't sure they might reveal.

You married a Texier, he says, responding to her look. You'd better get used to it! That's the way we are. And Daniel, don't be such a crybaby. Toughen up!

The paper-thin slices of lamb roast curl off the carving knife, and Armand delicately straightens them as he lays them down on the platter, pressing them, one by one, with the tip of the fork.

Très bien, he says to Victorine.

Relief sweeps over her, along with a sense of pride, which shames her; how is it possible for the two opposite feelings, shame and pride, to coexist?

Daniel, to answer your question, Armand says, it's not so easy to get up and go, uproot your whole family. And why would we do that?

Madeleine holds her plate out.

Look at her little face, so intent on showing her goodwill. Does she realize that she's taking sides with her father? Yes, of course she does. She will always side with him. Each child is sitting at the end of a seesaw: every time Daniel withdraws or silently rebuts his father, Madeleine twirls her pretty petticoat or flips her braids at him.

He serves Madeleine first, then Victorine, and Daniel last. Daniel nods no, but the thin slice of roast glides on top of the *mojette* anyway.

We could go there, Victorine says. As a matter of fact, they are looking for teachers. The Perrins are there.

The Perrins from Fontenay?

Yes, they left six months ago. Angelina met them in Saigon.

Armand shrugs. To each their own.

And again Victorine wonders if he is as satisfied with his life as he says he is. His eyes are veiled, absent. Perhaps he too has become restless.

Mange, he says to Daniel, more gently this time. Make a man out of you.

But Daniel won't touch it.

APRIL 3, 1898. The following Sunday was Palm Sunday, the day she has replayed so many times in her mind, with the slightest shifts of details, illuminating one moment or another, depending on her mood.

The whole Texier family had met at Tante Emilienne's at La Tranche for lunch. It had been a long lunch, as those family lunches always were, and it was threatening to last until the middle of the afternoon, what with coffee and *pousse-café*—the various brandies and spirits—still to be served. Victorine got up from the table, her plate of *île flottante* still half-full in front of her. To this day, she has no idea why she suddenly felt like taking a walk on the beach. Perhaps it was the memory of those summers of long ago? It had been years since they had visited Tante Emilienne.

Too cold for the beach, in my opinion, Armand had muttered, but *à ta guise*, my dear. And Daniel's voice had emerged from the other end of the table. May I go with you, maman?

It's a beautiful day. The weather has abruptly changed, as it so often does in April, right around or before Easter, from winter to spring, and the afternoon is quite mild and sunny. They walk the few blocks to the beach in silence, Daniel holding his Palm Sunday fronds in his hand and concentrating on kicking a rock with his shoe without losing it all the way to the dunes. On the beach, Victorine puts down her parasol, unties her shoes, and lies down at the foot of the dunes, while Daniel runs off toward the ocean. Behind her is a curtain of reeds shading her from the wind. Her eyes closed, she feels the softness of the sand under her stomach, the warmth of the sun on her back.

Victorine.

The voice startles her. It's too confident to be a question. Yet it also hesitates.

Victorine?

She lifts her head and squints. There's a man in a black overcoat and a fedora, squatting close to her, a pose too intimate for a stranger, suddenly robbing her of the sun.

Don't you remember me?

She squints some more. She sees his knees, and his hands hanging between his knees, the soft blond down on his wrists.

You should be careful with your skin, he says. The sun can burn, even this early in the season.

She rubs her palms together to shake off the sand from her hands.

Excuse me?

We met before. Don't you remember? Insisting, this time.

You must be mistaken. I have not seen you here before. She funnels sand out of her fists. One fist on top of the other.

I often come to this beach, he says, when I do my rounds.

Rounds? she asks, scooping up more sand and letting it spill out again.

I work with Customs, now, he says. Victorine—is it you?

She can't see him well; his face is shaded with the sun behind him. But the voice is familiar. And then he moves a little to the side and she sees his eyes.

You're mistaken, she repeats, a little coldly.

For a moment, she'd thought . . . but no . . . Antoine would be a man now, of course. It was just his eyes. The same clear blue eyes . . .

But just then, Daniel runs back to her and she folds her legs under her and sits up.

She shakes her head. She closes her book. She sweeps the sand off one foot, then off the other, slowly puts her boots back on and starts lacing them carefully, picks up her parasol. She knows he's watching her. But she doesn't look at him.

I don't know what you're talking about. I've never seen you before in my life, *monsieur*.

She opens her parasol in a sharp movement.

Viens, Daniel.

When they get back to Tante Emilienne's house, Bertha sees them in the hallway and asks, What's wrong?

Nothing. Why?

You look like you've seen a ghost. Either that or you're with child.

Victorine sits on the bench and leans her head against the wall.

Are you?

She shakes her head. Do you remember that boy, on the beach, who used to work on the mussel beds, his name was Antoine?

Bertha sits on the bench next to her.

Antoine? Of course. I told you I saw him a few years ago, remember? I heard he got married.

I just saw him. On the beach.

Oh, Bertha says. He hasn't changed, then.

Why do you say that?

Bertha laughs.

Because of the way you look.

Why did she pretend not to recognize him? Lying alongside Armand at night, she sees Antoine's legs, his trousers taut over his knees in the opening of his overcoat and falling loose over his shoes. His arms with the fine, blond down. His hand which encircled her wrist years before, when they sat side by side on the jetty at L'Aiguillon. In the dark of the room, she feels his fingers slip under her sleeve, run up her arm, up the inside of her elbow, he kisses her, his hands on her shoulders, on her breasts.

He leans over her and, one by one, undoes the buttons of her camisole. She hears his voice: Do you want to see the world with me?

Unable to sleep, unable to lie quietly, she gets up and walks down the stairs to the outhouse.

She shivers on the wooden bench, she clutches her knees with her crossed arms. The moonlight, shining through the round porthole, plays silver circles on her naked arms, piercing the shadows with a cold brilliance almost as bright as daylight. It's as though all those years she has kept the feeling of his fingers on her wrist buried under the smooth surface of her life, like those insects caught in clear amber she once saw in a Russian souvenir shop in Paris. The insect—it was a wasp, she thinks—was perfectly preserved, intact under the smooth veneer of the resin. If the amber had been shattered, the wasp might still have stirred and flown off.

She rocks with her knees pressed against her chest. Back and forth, back and forth, in a soothing motion. She knows what the feeling is, of course. It's desire, which, no matter how vigilant she has been, how vigilant she always is with other men, cannot be totally suppressed. She desired Armand that way when she first met him, or in a similar way. She feels relief. It's simply desire for a man. A man who has come back from her youth—almost her childhood. Nothing more natural, after all. Any woman, in her situation, would have been unsettled. She just has to let the feeling pass. With time it will fade and she'll remember it fondly one day—a secret she'll keep like a precious memento in a souvenir box. Knowing that it's there, that she can hold it and look at it now and then, will fill her life with a glow.

When she comes out of the outhouse, the moon has reached its zenith, a white disk pouring a hard light through the leaves of the willows. Everything is the same, the grassy slope leading to the canal, the *yole* pulling on its rope and hitting the pontoon with a dull, muffled sound. It's just that for a moment the full moon brings everything into sharper relief.

At recess the next morning, she watches the little ones play in the backyard, the girls dancing a *ronde* in their pinafores, the boys kicking a ball and raising clouds of dust. After a while, she slips into the school office and takes a blank, lined notebook from the shelf. Alone in the classroom, she sits down at one of the little desks and dips her pen into the porcelain inkpot. The first word is slightly indented from the left margin, the way she instructs her pupils to start their homework:

4 avril 1898.
Saw A. on the beach yesterday. They say things always happen for a reason. Do they?
I did recognize him. I wasn't absolutely sure at first. But as soon as I saw his eyes, yes. It was a long time ago.
The year I turned fifteen.
But his eyes haven't changed.

His skin was brown, his pant legs were rolled up, his chest was bare. His hair was pale blond in front. It was from the sun, he said.

His eyes were so pale in contrast to his dark skin, it made him look almost feminine. He had the eyes of a pretty girl. She had never seen eyes of that shade of blue before. You could almost see through them. You could see what he saw.

Sex was secret in those days, especially in the provinces, and perhaps especially in straitlaced Vendée. When she read the novels of Colette, much later, she realized women had lovers, sometimes even female lovers, all they had to do was lift their abundant skirts and let their lovers unhook their corsets and unbutton their camisoles and fondle their bosoms and take them from behind. Once, years before, Armand had brought back naughty postcards from a trip to Paris. She'd stared at the fleshy, corseted beauties in garter belts, swaddled in yards of velvet, lifting up their petticoats for the salacious delight of well-endowed, mustachioed gentlemen. He'd teased her and then caressed her until she moaned. But these scenes were all taking place far away, in another world. In Vendée, if anything happened at all, it was all in secret. Doors double-locked. Sounds muffled. It was nobody's business.

On a warm Thursday afternoon in early May, when the children are off for the day, a few weeks after her encounter with Antoine on the beach, Victorine is catching up at the school office when she notices a tall man at the school gate wearing a straw hat and a flax-colored jacket.

At first she thinks he's a stranger, an official of some kind who has lost his way. She opens the front door and steps out.

Vous cherchez quelque chose, monsieur?

It's because he doesn't move that she recognizes him. And the way his face is shaded by the straw boater.

He must have been watching her from a distance for a while.

Leaning against the gate without moving, without saying anything. Not hiding, you couldn't say that, because he's in plain view. Waiting, waiting for her to come out. He is in no hurry, he knows that she will come out sooner or later. And suddenly, the intensity of his look is broken by a childish smile, revealing the tiny chip on his front tooth.

She is the one who moves toward him, crossing the pebbled courtyard.

When she is a meter away he touches his hat, briefly, without removing it.

He has a sardonic smile, one corner of his lips coming up. Do you recognize me this time?

She doesn't smile back. Yes.

Are you sure, now, Victorine? Why did you pretend you didn't recognize me?

I don't know.

Really? Did I change so much? You haven't, though.

She laughs. She knows it's not true.

He looks at her in silence, a long gaze taking her in, setting her in turmoil. Then he shakes his head.

It's not true. You have changed. You're beautiful now. You were a pretty girl.

Were you looking for me, the other day?

No, I wasn't looking for you. How could I? I had no idea you'd be there. I was doing my rounds, just as I told you. I work at Customs at La Rochelle. The shipping department. Once a month I check with the smaller harbors along the coast. I had stopped at La Tranche on my way to La Baule. By chance.

She nods.

The idea that it was nothing more than an accident reassures her, oddly.

He puts his hand on her arm.

Aren't you going to ask me in? I would like to see where you work.

She takes him to the little class, at the back of the building. They sit at desks too small for them, their knees touching. The wood of the desks is carved with the names of students and crude geometric shapes and equations solved long ago. In the upper-right-hand corner, a small inkwell of white porcelain sits next to a narrow groove holding a pen. She picks up the pen, dips it into the inkwell, and gives it a twirl.

I am married now and I have two children, she says, wiping the pen carefully against the lip of the inkwell and putting it back in its groove. I heard you were married too.

He's taken off his hat and placed it on the desk in front of him, covering the student's carvings. Now she can see his eyes, but in his eyes she doesn't see a wife and a family.

You heard wrong, he says. I am not married.

Relief sweeps over her. She picks up the pen again and stares at it. It's an ordinary school pen, the wooden handle soiled with dried blue ink.

Why did you come back?

He leans over and kisses her.

The sound of a ball, hitting a window, interrupts their kiss. Immediately afterward, a boy pushes the gate open and runs across the yard after the ball. Instinctively, she lowers her head, so as not to be seen.

We shouldn't be here, she says. I must go.

Ice-cold water splashes against the flatware, making Victorine's fingers stiffen, as if she has plunged them into snow. She fills the cauldron with water and hangs it in the fireplace to heat up. When the water starts to boil, she pours it into the enamel basin and mixes it with cold water. A sensation of pleasure comes to her from stirring the warm, soapy water, from rubbing the dishes with the washcloth balled into her fist. She's accomplishing a chore and nobody, least of all Armand, who's sitting at the little bureau correcting pupils' papers, can tell that she's actually enjoying it and secretly making it last. He has a red pencil in hand. Even without looking at it she knows his slanted, fastidious handwriting, the way he checks accurate statements in the margins, the exclamation and question marks he dashes off angrily when mistakes are made.

Where were you this afternoon?

Excuse me?

Merlin, stretched by the fireplace, growls in his dream.

Where were you this afternoon?

She picks up a cloth and starts to wipe a glass.

What do you mean?

Armand stacks the students' papers on the bureau.

Ready, Merlin?

The dog skids across the room and does a crazy dance by the door, clawing at it with its front paws, which makes Victorine cringe a bit.

Down, Merlin! Yes, we're going out. It's Thursday today. And you were at school. Jules, Robineau's little boy, saw you in the classroom. He said there was a man with you.

She picks up another glass from the draining board. With a very fine cloth, her mother has taught her, it is possible to wipe a glass so perfectly that not a speck of lint remains on it, not a smudge. She holds the glass to the light to make sure it is perfectly clear.

I was preparing the geography lesson for tomorrow. Jules must have seen the postman, he was delivering a parcel to the headmistress's office.

She carefully puts the glass down and picks up another one.

Ah bon.

Armand gets up and makes a whistling sound with his lips and cheeks, imitating the whoosh of a wild duck taking off. Merlin's long ears prick up. Victorine can't help but laugh.

This dog is more expressive, the way he twitches around, than a five-year-old!

Yes, he's a pretty clever dog.

You're going to do the *passée*?

Yep. I saw a couple of mallards at Velluire this morning.

What time shall I get supper ready?

Armand buckles the ammunition belt around his hips.

There's a *veillée* at Chaillé, he says. I'll stop by on the way back. Don't bother with supper for me.

He puts on his hunting jacket, the bulky brown moleskin one with the thick quilted lining. He has his back to her. When he turns, his hat comes down low on his forehead, hiding his eyes.

Too much trouble to come all the way back. Don't even know what time we'll be done hunting. Don't wait up for me.

She knows what those last words mean. It's a kind of code between them. It doesn't happen that often, but when it does, it feels like being stabbed. At least he always lets her know. Maybe it's better this way. And if she were to confront him, he'd say: A man is a man. It means nothing. Or: I'm honest, I don't do anything behind your back. You're the one I love, don't ever doubt that.

And she believes it. In case she starts doubting this, her sisters—well, only Bertha now that Angelina is gone to Indochina—remind her. She nods her head and makes little guttural noises, the minute sounds and gestures of mild reprobation and acceptance that women use to smooth things over. What's the point of getting yourself worked up about something you cannot change?

She's standing by the table, one hand on the back of a chair, leaning on it.

He goes to her, boots still wet from the morning, jacket smelling of wood and grass and wilderness, dog snapping at his heels.

He pats her on the behind, pushing his hand into the fold of her skirt.

She elbows him, but he grabs her by the arm, hard.

Hey, watch out, you! Come on, Merlin.

The door slams behind them.

Her hands grip the back of the chair so tightly the knuckles are white.

The frames of the windows shiver. The evening wind is picking up. Time to close the shutters. The sun, going down, hits the copper cauldrons above the sink. The whole room is briefly flush with a red, metallic glow, and then the corners, just as suddenly, sink into darkness.

YOU CAN'T come in. Someone saw us last time. The boy with the ball. He is in Armand's class.

He's at the school gate again, in his flax-colored suit, his straw fedora in his hand. Another Thursday. They can hear children playing in the square, the sound of their high-pitched voices piercing the quiet of the village.

Don't you have to go to work?

I took the afternoon off. Shall we go for a walk?

He points to the woods, toward the back of the village.

Without a word she walks out with him and closes the gate behind them.

There's already an unspoken complicity between them: he will come to see her and she will follow him.

They take the little path behind the school. *Chemins creux*, they call those narrow, leafy paths, banked up by hawthorn or broom hedges as if they have been hollowed out of the ground. This one sinks deep into the woods right behind the school.

Let's go to the *lavoir*, she says. The laundry is usually done on Mondays. There shouldn't be anybody out there today.

If someone sees them together, it will be as compromising as if she were seen talking to him alone in front of the school. Even more so, because of the obvious intent to hide.

Down below the *lavoir*, the canal glitters between the willows. The trees, spreading their leaves over the water, darken the afternoon light to a dark amber. A *yole* sways, tied by a rope at a wooden pontoon.

Let's not stay here, he says. Let's go for a ride.

It's Jean Lucien's *yole*, she says, we can't take it without asking him.

We'll bring it back. We're only borrowing it for a little while. No harm done.

Do you know how to paddle?

He pulls her by the arm.

Of course I do! Come. I'll be your gondolier. It'll be like going down the Grand Canal in Venice.

You've never been to Venice! How would you know?

How do you know I've never been to Venice? Here. Take my hand.

But she hesitates on the shore. She barely knows him, after all, she only has the memory of a summer by the beach when she was still a girl . . .

It's not a good idea. If someone sees us together . . . One of the children . . . I don't want to get into trouble . . .

We won't. I promise. Jump in. His voice is strong, confident.

Suddenly, the image of a reddish pink cover with gold letters comes to her mind: Sophie, up to no good. What mischief she created! Well, you can't think of the consequences of everything all the time, can you?

He helps her into the *yole* and waits until she sits down, then unties the rope before leaping on board. The little barge pitches sharply under his weight. She grips the edge of the wooden bench with both hands.

Don't worry. I'll catch you if we capsize. Do you know how to swim?

She laughs. No!

I'll have to teach you, then. There.

He steadies the boat and, standing at the stern, deftly maneuvers the *pigouille*, the long wooden pole that serves as both paddle and rudder, moving them slowly along through the film of duck-weeds that completely covers the surface of the water. He lets the boat glide under the little bridge and after a while he lets go of the pole and sits down next to her. They drift under the canopy of trees in the golden-green light.

Do you mind? He pulls a cigarette case from his pocket.

She shakes her head no.

He strikes a match and lights up. The smoke spices up the dank smell of the canal water, recalling the bonfires of dead leaves the villagers light up in the fall. She watches the smoke coil for a moment before dissolving in the opalescent light. A smoker. Her father occasionally smokes the pipe, Armand doesn't smoke. What does it say about them? A guttural croak suddenly breaks the silence. Then another one. And another.

What's that noise? he asks.

Frogs.

He laughs. What a racket they make!

She laughs too. And after that, for a long time, they remain silent. He tosses the rest of his cigarette into the water, where it floats and drifts like a cork through the leaves.

His hand comes to rest next to hers on the bench. She stares at his flat nails, at his long and wiry fingers, so different from Armand's.

Their two hands are separated by barely half a centimeter, and she desperately wants him to close that distance, to touch her. She is so focused on their hands that she is startled when he speaks to her.

Have you ever regretted anything in your life?

I don't know, she says. I've never thought about it. I think if you make a mistake in life, you learn from it.

He says nothing. His face looks pensive.

And you?

Yes, he says. Regret can be for what you haven't done as well as what you have done, can't it?

He leans forward, elbows on knees, letting his wrists drop between his legs, the same gesture he had made when he'd crouched next to her on the beach.

When I saw you the other day, for instance.

A thin layer of water sloshes at the bottom of the boat under their feet.

What happened to you after that summer we last saw each other? she asks.

I went to Nantes and studied engineering. And then I was hired on an ocean liner of the Messageries Maritimes.

Really?

Yes. It's easy to find work in the boiler rooms. Not that many men are willing to leave their families behind, not for very long anyway, and the journeys are long, six months away from home.

So you went far across the ocean, after all.

There's a flash of surprise and pleasure in his eyes.

You remember, then.

Yes.

Well, I did. I traveled for ten years on various ships, and when I came back I got a position at Customs at La Rochelle.

And you didn't get married.

He dips his fingers in the water and brings them back with a handful of duckweeds. He crushes them in the palm of his hand.

I could say I never found the woman I wanted to spend my life with. But that would be banal.

She glances at him.

Do you not want to be an engineer anymore?

I don't want to stay here. I want to get into business, import-export. I've been looking at fabrics. Linen, especially, in Cholet.

The famous Cholet handkerchiefs. I'm from Cholet, you know.

Then you must know the manufacture of linen is taking off. I've been told there's a future in the export of linen to the colonies.

Indochine, she says.

He smiles. You remember that too.

My sister Angelina, she's there with her husband. He's an officer. Did you go there when you were working on ships?

Yes.

She feels a sharp pain. Would it have been better if he'd been married with three children, three little ones with blond hair like him? She thinks of Daniel with his jet-black hair, of Madeleine, who has her father's eyes.

How about you? Are you happy, with your family?

No, she says, firmly, shocked not only by the conviction of her answer but by the lack of emotion in her voice.

He doesn't say anything. He doesn't ask her about her husband. He doesn't ask her if she loves her children. Maybe he assumes that she does. Don't all women love their children?

Maybe I shouldn't have come, he says. He takes her hand. His skin feels hot against her palm.

A group of boys dash from behind the grass, laughing, playing hide-and-seek between the trees, not paying attention to the lonely boat stationed under a willow, and run off as fast as they've appeared.

We should go, she says.

But instead, he presses her to him. His arms around her back.

I should have done this then, he says. I was an idiot.

His mouth is against hers.

Stop. Stop it. Someone will see us. Those boys are going to come back.

She pulls away, catches her breath.

The *yole* sways widely.

I told you I'll catch you if you fall.

I dreamed about you the other day, she says suddenly.

It's true. He was swimming in the ocean, his hair slicked back, his shoulders bobbing in and out of the waves. She was standing at the edge of the water, barefoot, watching him. She wasn't wearing a corset, only a nightgown that rippled lightly against her bare skin. He was swimming away from her, toward the open sea. Her dream was silent. You couldn't hear the roar of the undertow or the screech of the seagulls. She was trying to call him but no sound came out of her mouth.

That was your dream?

Yes.

She runs her fingers in the small hollow he has at the back of the neck where his hair is shaved close.

Oh God!

She doesn't know if he's laughing or sobbing.

Victorine, he says, I want to show you . . . I want to show you what the world is like. I want—

A muted scream or laugh, some distance away, pierces the silence. She pulls away. The boys could come back any moment and see them together.

Take me back, she says. Tears fill her eyes.

In the dimming light, as though caught in another dream, she watches his steady hands churn the pole back and forth in the stream, while the humid coolness envelops them.

WALKING AHEAD of her, carrying her bag and blanket the few hundred meters separating the dunes from the casino, Maurice looks dapper in his linen suit and straw hat. In the summertime a few tables are installed on the deck overlooking the ocean. Although the weather has warmed up since the rain stopped, there's only one other table occupied, a family of four having their lunch. Under the parasol the air is breezy.

I should have gone back home, she says, and changed these galoshes for proper shoes. My clothes don't do justice to yours.

You look perfectly fine, maman, he says. The sand is still damp. And this dress is pretty. You look like a young girl in it.

She shakes her head, uncomfortable with the false compliment. She hates those comments made only to appease an old woman, especially coming from Maurice. She expects more honesty from him, or at least more originality.

We will go back to the house after lunch, she insists, and I will change then.

As you wish, he says.

The seafood is still plentiful. You can find mussels and oysters and eels, all the fish you could wish for. They sit in front of plates piled high with periwinkles and crayfish, and a cold bottle of Muscadet. The tide is halfway in and the dories are floating, their masts pointing upward now, bobbing up and down like buoys.

My last time, she says. She crunches a crayfish leg with her teeth and sucks on it, closing her eyes for a moment as the brine washes into her mouth.

Maurice pours her more wine.

You're only moving five kilometers inland, he says. Don't be so melodramatic.

She nods. She knows better. She waves the crayfish leg at him.

At least the Germans can't take that from us.

You mean, the seafood?

Yes.

No, they can't.

Don't forget to take the seagull, she says. It's on top of the mantelpiece.

It's at that moment that he takes the picture. He bought a Leica—ironically, a German camera—in Paris, before the war broke out, and has become passionate about photography. He kneels in front of her, steadies the camera on one knee and snaps. In the photograph she is sitting on a plain wooden chair, with a row of potted plants behind her. A small, plump woman with a Peter Pan collar of white *broderie anglaise* over her dress printed with small white windmills or tiny white umbrellas. She looks young for her age, seventy-four, her gray hair cut short and wavy in a bob *à la garçonne*, wearing a pair of small, wire-rimmed glasses. Behind the glasses, her eyes are dreamy, large or childlike. But if you look closer, even a little malicious.

Ever since she's lived in La Faute, she's had lunch with Maurice on Sunday. Daniel is married and settled in Paris. Married to that Texier girl, his first cousin, Armand's niece. Back then—how many years now, twenty-five?—she'd been appalled by that marriage. Nothing against Anne, personally, but to marry a Texier, and not only that, but Marie's daughter! Marie, Armand's older sister, who had never missed an opportunity to offend her. No! She'd warned him, and asked, How can you marry into the family that did me so much harm? Her mother hates me. Not to mention that they had to ask for special permission from the Vatican because they were first cousins. But his mind was set. His wandering years were over. He wanted to settle down and Anne was the one. She was young and naive, *pure laine* as they used to say back then, pure wool—she had never left Vendée—but she had character and she was very pretty. And maybe he didn't care about hurting his mother. He'd never forgiven her, with good reason. As for Madeleine, she is married too, a schoolmistress in Fontenay. And, like Daniel, she has her reasons to stay away. Anyway, she is the daughter, and it's even harder between mothers and daughters. Whereas Maurice never left her. Maurice is the one who's here. Who's always been here. Of course, she's been there for him too. Just the two of them. People frown on boys raised alone by their mother. They say they're soft. And maybe she did overprotect Maurice. He was a bit of a sickly child. Not athletic like Daniel, who was a swimmer and later a boxer. Maurice had a certain indolence and fragility about him. Did she encourage it?

She remembers that time when he was grown up, but still living with her, way before his marriage, he was maybe eighteen or twenty. That day when he had come back soaked from a ride on his bicycle under the pouring rain and he was shaking all over, she was afraid he would catch pneumonia. She had prepared a hot mustard poultice and heated water to give him a warm foot bath. He still has such beautiful feet, she had thought when she had rubbed them with a dry towel and massaged them with camphor oil, the way she used to massage his feet when he was little, and Daniel's and Madeleine's and Armand's too, years before. That's what they did then, she remembers, to ward off colds.

Certainly, she had been more maternal with Maurice than she had been with Daniel or Madeleine.

Shall we go? he says.

She slowly comes back from her reverie and looks into her son's dark eyes.

Yes, yes, of course.

What are you thinking about?

She chuckles.

When you were little, she says. Your feet.

Maillezais

JULY 1876. It was at La Tranche, a little farther up the coast, that Victorine went to the seashore for the first time, the year she turned ten. La Tranche was a long way from Cholet, but her father had to deliver a carriage that he'd just finished painting with the azure-and-gold arms of the Comte de La Bretonnière. She had insisted on riding with him. She wanted to see the ocean.

It was disappointing at first. You couldn't even see it. It had shrunk to a gray line, at the end of a huge swath of sand, perhaps half a kilometer deep. Closer to her, shallow pools of sea water shimmered like mirrors.

The wind made her gasp, and then laugh. She ran ahead of her father, toward the water. Her skirt whipped around her calves and she had to hold it down with both hands. In Les Herbiers, where they had lived before moving to Cholet, the wind didn't blow like that. Even in Niort, which is closer to the shore, it comes on all nonchalant, bristling in the leaves, lifting them in lazy curls. Victorine liked the fierce wind of the ocean better. It was a wild, exciting wind.

If she let the wind blow out her skirt, could she ride it like a gliding bird?

On the way back, her feet felt gritty in her shoes; she kept wriggling her toes and enjoying the strange new sensation. When she got home, she carefully poured the sand from her shoes into a little Sèvres biscuit box that she kept on her night table.

THAT BOX is now on top of the rosewood bureau in their bedroom in Maillezais. The sand she brought back from La Tranche, years before, is long gone. She keeps her rings in it: an amethyst set in gold, a brilliant mounted in platinum, a pearl set in a circle of minute rubies. In the bureau drawers she keeps her lace handkerchiefs, her corsets reinforced with whalebone stays, her bloomers of peach silk, her light camisoles of white gauze. In a little pouch of dark blue leather fastened with a drawstring, two identical pairs of earrings of filigree silver and brilliants, an ivory and garnet locket. And on top of the bureau, a small vial of verbena essence, rouge, her loose powder with the puff made of swansdown in a box of blue china, her bottles of rosewater and cornflower water, her silver and ivory brush set, and her silver manicure set with ivory handle in a blue leather case. The cherry-wood chest inlaid with mother-of-pearl is filled with discarded buttons.

Every night before going to bed, she polishes and buffs her nails; she scrubs the heels and the balls of her feet with a pumice stone. She loosens her long brown hair and brushes it a hundred times before tying it in a single braid. But since her boat ride with Antoine on Jean Lucien's *yole*, those rituals have taken on another meaning, or perhaps they have finally found their true meaning. Each brushstroke, each motion of the file around her nail, each undoing of her petticoat buttons, is for Antoine. Each millimeter of her flesh feels infused by him.

In front of the rosewood bureau she is poised, her shoulders milky, her hair not yet braided, loosely waving down her back. The gilded mirror, pitted, reflects her eyes. *Pers*, they say in French about the changing gray-green color of her eyes.

Her body, still tiny, has barely changed since adolescence.

Her skin, still creamy white. Her narrow waist barely thickened by the two pregnancies.

She moves her hands over her chest. The peach satin of the corset feels perfectly smooth, taut between the whalebones, its structure encasing her waist and hips in a pure hourglass shape, her small breasts pushed over the top edge and blossoming like ivory globes. This garment, which she sometimes thinks of as a medical or orthopedic apparatus, with its skin-tone color and rigid architecture—as if her body couldn't naturally hold itself up without its support—this garment which she loosens at night with a sigh of relief, suddenly appears to her as an object of desire, dangerously intimate and precarious.

At the bottom of her Catholic soul, there's a yearning to take it off. The tight corset undone, she could easily tumble and come loose.

And when it is unhooked for the night and she's dressed in the long, white, chaste gown she buttons up to her neck, and Armand runs both his hands up the whole length of her legs, she doesn't mind, no, in spite of everything, she remembers liking it, even then.

> *May 20, 1898*
>
> *Chère Victorine,*
>
> *It was not right to come and see you again. I am the one, not you, who opened a possibility, a door. I am the one who came to disrupt your life. I apologize for that. I have been torn. Is it possible to go back to the way things were?*
>
> *Everybody has* un amour de jeunesse. *A love that, perhaps, wasn't meant to be. Your life took another turn. What is the point of regretting? Who's to say that it isn't for the better? Married life is married life, regardless of whom we're married to. That's what I've been told.*
>
> *As I am writing this, I am not entirely convinced myself. But*

I don't think it is right to take a path that might upset if not ruin your life and the lives of those who are dearest and closest to you. I would never forgive myself.
    A toi pour toujours,
    Antoine.

The letter was among the usual stack of official school business in manila envelopes and the brown-covered, blank notebooks printed with the Education Department letterhead. Opening the thick, off-white envelope with the stamp carelessly glued, unfolding the paper, already felt like a betrayal. She stared at the unfamiliar handwriting, the angular loops in black ink, the lines slanting upward to the right, the few words crossed out and rewritten (*amour de jeunesse*, regretting), the signature, underlined with a flourish. The words themselves seemed too dangerous to decipher. She walked out into the narrow courtyard at the back of the school, used to store tools and construction equipment, where she knew she would be undisturbed. She sat down on a wheelbarrow left behind by the handyman and forced herself to read. But again the words floated in front of her eyes. She couldn't make sense of them. She kept trying to find a hidden meaning between the lines, the nervous and hesitant handwriting belying the measured, formal style, as though what Antoine had written and what he really wanted to say were worlds apart.

They walked together after school, back to the little house by the canal, Armand in his dark suit and gray spats, Victorine in her long skirts sweeping around her ankle boots, side by side, as they did every day. It was a short walk, ten minutes from one end of the village to the other. She tried to maintain a normal conversation, wondering whether Madeleine might be coming down with influenza, complaining aloud about little Jeanne Robitaille whom she had to send to the corner for talking during dictation, suspecting the baker's wife to be with child for the fifth time. But the letter, tucked into her pocket, felt so vivid, so palpable through the light cotton of her skirt that she was startled when Armand's pants

brushed against her and he kept walking absentmindedly in silence, as though nothing out of the ordinary had happened. And
she felt a shameful pleasure at the idea that her secret evened out
the power between them.

IN THE NARROW path leading to the *lavoir*, her feet crush the
soft heather and the moss. She follows the towpath until the long
shadows of the alders engulf the mirrored surface of the canal.
The dimming light soothes her. She must hurry. If she doesn't get
back home soon to prepare dinner she will arouse Armand's suspi-
cions. Her time must be accounted for, like that of a child. But
instead of heading back, she leans against the pontoon where Jean
Lucien's *yole* is still tied and rereads Antoine's letter. They've only
seen each other twice since that day on the beach. And yet it feels
as though a bond has been established between them, which is
underlined by his very hesitation, his fear. Perhaps they've already
gone further than they allow themselves to believe.

The evening is long, unbearably long. A simple dinner of milk
soup and compote followed by the endless evening chores: washing up and cleaning up, correction of homework, mending by the
fireplace, Madeleine on one side, Victorine on the other. A wicker
basket sits between them, full of odd socks, camisoles missing a
button, a weft-worn sheet that needs to be turned over. At the bottom of the basket is the linen tablecloth they've been embroidering together since the winter. Victorine unfolds it carefully and
stretches the stiff, flax-colored fabric over their laps. Every night
they each work at opposite ends of the cloth, embroidering a few
centimeters at a time. Madeleine moves more slowly, even though
she's getting quite skillful in the art of Venetian stitches. Victorine
was also embroidering at her age, at ten or even younger, starting
out with *point de croix*, the easier cross-stitch. Her mother had
been serious about the girls' traditional upbringing, and Victorine

spent more time indoors, bent over napkins and tablecloths and learning how to iron and boil the laundry and stir cauldrons of quince jam, than she did outdoors, playing with a hoop and stick, or even on her studies. And now she raises Madeleine the same way, passing on the tradition exactly as she has received it.

Daniel, meanwhile, is pursuing his spring project of taking apart his bicycle and cleaning each piece before putting it back together, in spite of Armand's complaints that they are always tripping over screws and bicycle parts. His fascination with bicycles, Victorine remembers, disappeared as soon as the bicycle was put together again, and was replaced with a passion for the new vehicles he had glimpsed in Cholet and in Niort: the automobiles and the steam engine.

But that will be later, in the winter. At present, Daniel reluctantly stores his bicycle parts in the back room, and Victorine and Madeleine fold the tablecloth and return it to the wicker basket when it's time to go to bed. And Victorine still has to wait for the children and then for Armand to turn in upstairs. She waits for the last sounds—furtive voices, shoes dropping, drawers opened and closed—to die down. Until she can safely sit down and write the letter she's been composing all day.

> *Cher Antoine,*
>
> *I can't. How can you? You are right. Of course you are right.*
>
> *Why did you come then? Why did you come twice?*
>
> *Do you realize the door we have opened cannot be closed again? Never again.*
>
> *Do you think my life will go on as if nothing had happened? Maybe your life will. But mine . . . You might be right, to say that it doesn't matter whom you're married to, married life is married life. And even if you and I were married, it might one day feel just like another married life. Maybe. I don't know.*
>
> *We need to live. Are you saying that our wishes do not count when weighed against my responsibilities, the choices I've made?*

Are you saying it would destroy all around us? I think children are more resilient than that. They want their parents to be happy. And I think the ones who would risk the most would be us. Are you saying that the risk of love and passion isn't worth taking?

Ridiculous. Utterly ridiculous.

She crumples the page and tosses it into the fire. When it is thoroughly consumed, she scatters the ashes with the poker.

JULY 14, 1898. They are all gathered around the long table at the Sainte-Christine farm for the *Quatorze Juillet* lunch. Victorine sees the whole table reflected in the big mirror over the fireplace: the blaze of the candles, the porcelain plates and crystal glasses laid on the white tablecloth, the row of children on one side, grandparents on the other side—François and Augustine, Armand's parents, Victor-Paul and Marie-Louise, Victorine's parents, sitting next to one another, the younger couples at both ends. Everyone is married now and with their children—Bertha already has three and it doesn't look like she is done yet—except Angelina and Jules, who are in Indochina and are still childless. It's their second summer away. The older women have their hair parted in the middle and severely pulled back under the headdress, while the young ones wear their hair up, with loose strands playfully fluttering on the sides. Reflected in the mirror, the succession of lacey blouses pinned at the neck with a cameo and the men's dark jackets is striking. An hour or so into the meal, the men will doff their jackets, roll up their shirtsleeves, and plunder the reserves of Anjou and Bordeaux. The sun is slanting edgewise across the stone floor, from the small windows, the candles necessary because the farmhouse dining room is always in a half-light even at lunch in July.

Victorine sits between Armand and Lucien, Adèle's husband,

and starts passing the *charcuterie* around. Her glass is full. She dips her lips into it. It's a mellow Bordeaux, perhaps a Saint-Emilion, the bottle is too far for her to read the label, the bread is golden and crusty. The conversations, around her, blend into a light buzz. Armand's arm is draped over her chair. She leans against it, softly. His hand casually brushes her shoulder. She's with him, she's one of them. She is where she should be among their two families. For a brief moment she's filled with a pleasant sense of security. Maybe this is her reality, and the rest, Antoine, her dreams of escape, a fantasy. She smiles at Armand. He presses her shoulder.

It's summertime, the day is warm, the children are on vacation, starving after the morning spent following the Bastille Day parade. The hors d'oeuvre—*rillettes* and headcheese and *oeufs mayonnaise,* which are deviled eggs without the peppery or paprika topping, and *céleri rémoulade*—are avidly passed around. The *boudin noir,* in particular—homemade too, a fat blood sausage unevenly and roughly rolled into its own skin and pan-fried—elicits enthusiastic praise.

It's during the lull between the *boudin* and the eels that Lucien decides to stir up the waters.

So this busybody Zola is back on the stand again, did you hear that?

It's already more than an hour into the meal, and the meat hasn't yet been served—*boudin* doesn't count. But a dozen empty bottles already sit by the kitchen door, like stripped-down prisoners of war.

Rightly so, Marie, Armand's older sister, says, carefully laying her flatware, fork and knife, side by side on her empty plate.

I'm so tired of that story. Victor-Paul empties a bottle of Chateau-Latour so brusquely the wine spills out of his glass and stains the lace tablecloth a pale pink. By the way, did you see what's going on in Sudan?

We've just planted our flag in Fachoda, I know as much, Lucien says, wiping up *boudin* juice with his bread.

You haven't heard, then? Well, believe it or not, the English are already contesting our presence over there. *La perfide Albion* is once again trying to put a spoke in our wheel. They want to control the Nile. If you want my opinion, I'm afraid they will. Their Kitchener is supposed to be a brilliant general.

There would go our Djibouti-to-Dakar grand dream—a coast-to-coast French Africa, Armand says.

Victorine's mind is wandering away from the conversation. She stares with a slight disgust at the dish of eels Marie-Louise has just set in the middle of the table, gleaming and tangled in their sauce like a nest of dark rattlesnakes.

At least we've got a pretty strong foothold in Asia. They say you can make a fortune in two years in Cochinchina, if you're clever, François Texier says, from across the table. The comment jolts Victorine back to reality. Her father-in-law looks so much like Armand! His chin high, his mouth set, a lot of black still in his gray hair.

If you don't die of dysentery first, or the typhus, Victor-Paul grumbles.

Lucien lifts his glass in the direction of his wife. Adèle, another one!

How? Armand asks. Not by working for the French army, like Jules, that's for sure.

Heveas plantations, Marie-Louise says. Doumer, the new governor, has been importing seedlings from Sri Lanka and apparently they are taking marvelously to the Indochinese soil.

Victor-Paul turns toward her with mock-surprise. And how do you know that?

I read it in *La Quinzaine Coloniale.*

Seigneur, Marie-Louise, Victor-Paul says, serving himself more *boudin* and a generous helping of apples. *La Quinzaine* is the mouthpiece of the colonial party. Bet you didn't read about the Black Flags. Our troops are being attacked by bands of rebels in the North, in the Tonkin. It's heating up over there.

Marie-Louise shrugs. I've been reading it since Angelina left. It's informative.

I wouldn't put too much trust in it.

What's *heveas*? Daniel asks, his voice starting high-pitched and suddenly plummeting to an impressive bass.

Rubber trees. Do you know, Dany, the way rubber is produced? No.

The rubber tree is gouged, Armand explains in his school-teacher's voice, cut open, and a cup is attached underneath and a whitish liquid oozes out of the bark. That liquid is called latex. Then the latex is left to thicken and processed into rubber.

I thought rubber was produced in Africa, Daniel says.

You're right, Monsieur know-it-all, only some rubber plants have been shipped to Asia, and have taken remarkably well there. There's much hope that the rubber production will support the Southeast Asia colony.

Actually, from what I read in *Le Figaro,* Victor-Paul says, wiping his mouth, it's not rubber but opium that's supporting Indochina. A lot less noble, but apparently extremely profitable. It seems that we have taken over the opium production and distribution. What do you think of that, my dear Armand?

Armand drains his glass and puts it down.

The empire is going to do us in. Paris keeps pursuing dreams of grandeur. But look what happened in '70. We lost Alsace and Lorraine.

The '70 war had nothing to do with the colonies. We were trying to hold back Prussia. And we got a licking.

I hear Saigon is very beautiful, Victorine says dreamily, interrupting them. And she suddenly feels Marie, who's sitting across from her, staring at her, as though, with that one sentence, she had revealed herself. She blushes and turns her face away.

Bertha puts down the shank of *pré salé* on the table, done rare with *mojettes,* the way they all like it.

What, you too read *La Quinzaine Coloniale*? Victor-Paul teases Victorine.

Non, Papa. Victorine passes the dish of *mojettes* to Armand, relieved to have a chance to explain herself. That's what Angelina writes in her letters.

I wish everybody would stop talking about Indochina and the French Empire, Bertha says, sitting down. It's so boring.

La Perle de l'Orient, François Texier recites. Every other article on Indochina manages to get that little phrase in. Saigon: the most beautiful jewel of our colonial crown.

Armand, tasting the beans, whistles in appreciation.

Not overcooked, he says. Perfect in fact. Adèle, congratulations!

Victorine shoots him a look.

There's a silence while everyone digs into the lamb and beans.

This business of the colonies is foolish, Lucien says. I agree with Armand. It's going to suck us dry. And for what?

The glory of the French Empire. That's what for. We can't let the English and the Germans take over the world, Armand's father continues.

You're joking, right?

No. What's the alternative? Look at the ascent of socialism in Russia. *That's* the real threat. Mark my words.

After that a silence falls, as if the topic, although appropriate for Bastille Day, was too vast and too weighty to be pursued.

Madeleine, straighten your back, Marie-Louise says. Your face is hanging over your plate. What would your guardian angel say if he saw you like that?

Maman, please, Victorine says.

Marie-Louise looks away, unhappy to see her authority undermined.

What's for dessert? Daniel cuts in.

Still hungry, Dany?

But there's still the salad of *frisée* and *mâche,* followed by a tray of cheeses—mainly local goat cheeses, *chabichou* and *fromage cendré,* and a couple of Camemberts from Normandy, before the platters of *tourtisseaux* are brought to the table. And by then the conversation is safely drifting to the upcoming World Expo—

the huge exhibition that's already planned for the following year, to celebrate the new century, and Victorine's mind wanders off again. There is still coffee to be served, and white fruit liqueur— liquid gold shimmering through the glasses. The late afternoon sun will dapple the white tablecloth stained with wine, eyes will be dazed, conversations will die down as the shadows slant deeper into the room and be revived by fresh infusions of coffee and more liqueur, and then the day will fade into dusk and someone will get up and light the oil lamps . . .

Just then, Madeleine starts complaining of stomach cramps. She's holding her belly with both hands, bent over her plate, white as a pot of clotted cheese.

What's wrong, Madeleine? Marie-Louise asks.

Victorine watches her for a moment, unable to get up, as a mother should, to hold her daughter's forehead, fret over her. Maybe it's the wine, all that food, but a fog seems to have descended upon her, keeping her pinned to her chair, paralyzed.

Victorine, your daughter's not feeling well, Armand calls.

She rushes to help her up. Madeleine manages to stand up and walk out into the backyard, and then gets sick over a clump of dandelions by the kitchen door.

Victorine wipes her mouth gently with her napkin, and holds on tight to the shivering body.

My shoes, Madeleine says weakly.

Don't worry about your shoes, *ma chérie*, they can be cleaned.

Madeleine slowly picks herself up and leans into Victorine's arms.

What's wrong, maman? Why am I sick?

Something you ate, I am sure. It's just a little indigestion.

Stay with me, please, Madeleine says, gripping her hand.

Of course I will. Victorine kisses her temple, wanting to make up for the distraction she has shown at the lunch table. Let's sit down until you feel better.

On the bench under an elm tree, Madeleine lies down, her head on Victorine's lap. Her eyes closed, her face peaceful now, a cloud of pink coloring her cheeks, she seems more open, vulnerable, the way she was as a child. She has grown guarded lately, her nose always in a book, never missing her prayers at night, kneeling by her bed in her nightgown. Well, there was nothing wrong with that, of course, but she seemed almost too withdrawn.

The backyard, in the late afternoon, is cool and quiet, a rectangle defined between the vegetable garden on one side, the chicken coop on the other, and the green expanse of a clover field stretching at the back. Adèle comes out and tosses handfuls of seeds at the door of the coop. The hens peck at them with their quick, jerky, up-and-down motion, as if they had springs in their necks. Then she wipes her hands on her apron, gathers her skirt, and carefully locks the gate to the coop.

No eggs? Victorine asks her, from the bench.

We ate them all for lunch. Is Madeleine feeling better?

No, Madeleine says, but her voice is firmer.

Victorine laughs, because it's obvious she's feeling better.

I'll bring you some Ricqlès.

I hate that, Madeleine complains.

But when Adèle comes back with the little bottle of mint alcohol and Victorine shakes a few drops on her handkerchief, Madeleine sniffs it, takes a deep breath, and lies back on Victorine's lap.

Better now?

Yes.

Adèle sits next to them on the bench, brushing the seeds off her skirts. After a while Madeleine dozes off.

It's all that food, Adèle says. It's too much for them.

The air is still balmy, and the children are finally let loose outside, as the sun, going down, glazes the top of the hawthorn bushes. Daniel shouts something they can't quite make out to the others, his voice suddenly breaking in the middle of a word. They laugh.

He's growing up. Watch out, Victorine, if he turns out like his father . . .

Victorine shakes her head.

He won't. This child is going to go far.

Adèle looks at Victorine reproachfully.

Nothing against Armand. He's just got different ambitions. Armand loves it here. He is a true *Vendéen*.

A ball shoots into the farmyard and the children erupt after it. A pack of little wolves kicking dust, the girls trailing a hoop, their waist ribbons rippling high behind them like shiny tails, the boys blocking the ball and immediately charging back to the front yard. Daniel is hanging behind, an open book in his hands.

What's he doing? Adèle indicates Daniel, who's muttering to himself and suddenly pointing in a dramatic flourish toward the chicken coop.

Reading Victor Hugo. He's learning *Hernani* by heart.

He walks past them, without even acknowledging their presence, reciting a few lines from the play:

> *Ce que je veux de toi, ce n'est point faveurs vaines,*
> *C'est l'âme de ton corps, c'est le sang de tes veines,*
> *C'est tout ce qu'un poignard, furieux et vainqueur,*
> *En fouillant longtemps peut prendre au fond d'un coeur.*

> What I want from you is not vain favors,
> It is your soul, the blood in your veins,
> It is what a dagger, furious and victorious,
> Reaching far and deep, can dig out of the heart.

Adèle chuckles. What a romantic!

And for a moment, inexplicably, Victorine has an urge to tell her about Antoine—to tell anyone, really, her heart is so full, in a constant state of excitement, carrying a burden on the verge of exploding. But she wouldn't be that foolish. Adèle—Armand's sister!—would be the last person she could trust with her secret.

He's a dreamer like you, Adèle says. His head full of fantasies.

Victorine says nothing. It is the Texiers' opinion of her. Let them think of her whatever they wish. She won't argue with them.

August 2, 1898
Cher Antoine,
I wasn't going to answer you. It's foolish, maybe, to write now. But life has thrown you and me on the same path again and I believe there's a reason for that. That's all.

My children are at home for the summer. The days are busy with them around. Yet the summer is long without the classes, they stretch in a blur. My life doesn't feel quite real, do you understand what I mean by this? I do not know what is real or not anymore. I do not know what my life should be.

Je pense à toi,
Victorine

The sound of a door opening upstairs is followed by the shuffling of bare feet. Swiftly she hides her letter under her skirt. Daniel stumbles down the stairs, rubbing his eyes.

What are you doing, maman? His voice is sleepy. He yawns.

I couldn't sleep. It's a bit stifling tonight, isn't it?

He sits down across from her, elbows on the table, head in hands. He looks tired and not just because it's the middle of the night. Too skinny. Or maybe it's the shadow growing over his upper lip, this down that she cannot get used to.

Yes.

The moonlight sweeps silver across the floor. The crickets buzz.

What's the matter? Daniel asks.

Nothing. Why?

I don't know. You seem sad lately, maman.

She puts her hand on his. Her little boy. Not for much longer. He leans his head on her hand as though he was about to fall asleep on it. She remembers when he was a child of three or four, even older, how he used to press his cheek against her hand when he was tired at night. He would be full of life and energy, and then, suddenly, at the dinner table, before dessert sometimes, he would collapse like a baby.

It must be the summer, she says. It's a long summer. She draws her hand through his hair, lightly, almost shyly, the texture of his thick hair so familiar, and yet not sure how a mother is supposed to touch a growing boy.

He sits up, yawns again, and pulls his hand from under hers. He looks at her with his sleepy eyes and she sees that the old intimacy is still there. He smiles briefly, acknowledging it, but not lingering in it. He places his open palms flat on the table as Armand does and pushes himself up.

Bon. I was just going . . . He gets up and pours some water into a glass from the carafe they always leave at night by the sink. I was thirsty.

AUGUST 15, 1898. The halftime of the summer is *Le Quinze Août*, its high point and sultriest weather, after which it will slowly and surely unravel, spoiled by the thunderstorms that plague the latter part of the month. It's also the feast of the Assumption, when the Virgin Mary, ethereal in her long, blue veil and her vaporous halo, is carried by a flock of cherubs to her beatitude in heaven.

At the end of mass, right after the *Ite missa est,* the priest walks out of church with the choir boys and everyone gathers on the church square in the blazing sun, opening their parasols. If you were looking at the scene from above, the whole parvis would turn into a flower bed of white and cream and pale pink flounces twirling this way and that. And then, after a beat, the flower bed would shift into a narrow line and start moving forward in the streets of the village past city hall, past the school, past the communal line, all the way to the ruins of the old abbey.

Ave, Maris Stella,
Dei Mater Alma

Atque Semper Virgo
Felix Caeli Porta

Madeleine is singing at the top of her lungs. She even knows the Latin prayers by heart. Daniel mouths the words. It's obvious he doesn't know them and pretends. Armand is silent, ahead of them, his face closed. He doesn't even bother to pretend.

Victorine glances slightly to the side, toward Daniel, and immediately looks back ahead of her. Standing right behind them, with his straw hat and his linen suit, his hands in his pockets—a rather cavalier posture for a religious procession—is Antoine.

He's so close behind she could almost lean against him. Armand is walking in front, only separated from her by the butcher's wife. If he turned around he would see Antoine. Of course, he doesn't know him, has never seen him before in his life, but wouldn't he guess the closeness between them?

Madeleine's eyes are riveted on the prayer book. Victorine worries sometimes about her ability to shut out her surroundings; she seems to be turning more inward lately. Maybe it's her age . . . Victorine keeps walking, holding her parasol over her head, clutching Madeleine's small sweaty hand and keeping her eyes on the perfect, straight part in her brown hair, which is plaited in two long braids tied with white ribbons. She doesn't turn back.

At the Virgin's chapel, Armand crosses himself distractedly without bending down and moves on. Victorine kneels next to Madeleine and presses her hands tight. The chapel is tucked against an outside wall of an old abbey, in the open air, and yet a coolness emanates from the medieval stones. A vase of lilies set by a painting of the Virgin spills a heady fragrance. They both recite the beginning of the Hail Mary together, Madeleine staring at Victorine's mouth to read the words she has forgotten. When they get up, Victorine glances over her shoulder. Antoine doesn't kneel either. He slows down, lets a few people come between them, and follows.

After the chapel, the procession breaks up and Armand, Dan-iel, Daniel, Madeleine, and Victorine walk back to the village in a little group. Victorine lets herself turn around only once to look for Antoine, but she doesn't see him anymore.

I need to stop by at the *boulangerie*, she tells Armand, keeping her eyes lowered.

Ah yes, get us a *brioche* for dessert, he says.

I don't like *brioche*! Madeleine starts to poke at Daniel with a skinny finger.

Stop it, Armand says.

Madeleine quickly sticks her tongue out, then smiles demurely.

There's a line at the bakery, everyone stopping to buy baguettes and *bâtards* fresh out of the oven, *choux à la crème* and *brioches*. The parasols are now folded, held by a ribbon around the wrists.

The front door opens. Excuse me, a man's voice says, the door closes behind him with the sound of the bell, and he is standing right behind her again. After the baker's wife wraps up her bread and her *brioche*, he quickly asks for a *ficelle* and steps out of the shop with her.

Can we talk for a moment?

Her pulse is racing.

You have some audacity to come and see me right in the open like this . . .

She cannot think of any other quiet place, so she starts up the little street that climbs up to the cemetery.

I got your letter, he says when they arrive at the gate. I didn't want to write you back at home. And school is closed . . .

She was right, the cemetery is deserted, but for how long?

You shouldn't have come. Not like that, while I'm with my family, on a Sunday.

I thought it would be easier to approach you on a crowded day like today.

On a crowded day? Your reasoning leaves something to be de-sired. I mean—people talk, you know. They notice things like that.

We're just having a conversation, he says.

She doesn't say anything. Her legs are shaking.

I didn't want you to think I had just disappeared.

You came all the way here to tell me that?

He smiles. Not a full smile, but a smile that has so much in it, desire, guilt, seduction, tenderness, such a complex mix of feelings that she cannot sustain her anger and she turns her eyes away.

I wanted to see you, he says.

His hat is in his hand and the *ficelle* is awkwardly clenched against the hat, and she softens. She's standing in front of him, swinging the paper bag from the bakery.

I don't have much time—my family is waiting—

He drops his bread on the stone ledge of the railings, takes the paper bag out of her hands and pulls her to him, his arms around her waist, his lips unbearably soft, his hands unbearably tender. He traces the outline of her lips, pushes his finger gently into her mouth, inside of her teeth, around her tongue, she bites it softly she thinks someone's coming, she isn't sure, she thinks someone is bound to come and find them, his hands move down and around her waist, she hears her breath come faster, someone is going to come and see them, your heart is beating he whispers, he feels her heart his hand on her breast, I've got to go she says. Let me go. I can't he whispers, his voice normally a little raspy but in a whisper it flows so sweet, I can't he says his voice like a caress his hands come up around her breasts. No she says, I have to go. I know he whispers but I can't . . .

They're waiting, she says, I must go. And she steps out of his reach, picks up her paper bag with one hand, with the other smoothes her hair down.

He holds her back tight by her wrist.

Can I write to you?

If you want.

Where?

At school. *Au revoir.*

. . .

The two of them, Madeleine and Daniel, are waiting for her in the kitchen.

Maman, you were so long at the bakery, Madeleine says.

What did you get? Daniel asks, tearing open the paper bag from the bakery.

There was a long line and then I met Joséphine Dufour on the way back. We chatted for a while.

It's not a lie. She did meet Joséphine Dufour on the street, although she only talked to her for about half a minute. Armand is out in the backyard, so the lie, or the half-lie, is really for the benefit of the children. Daniel, satisfied that she did buy a *brioche*, is now deep into the reading of *Les Pieds Nickelés*, the comic strip, while Madeleine, standing at the foot of the staircase, is twisting a knotted loop of yarn around her extended fingers to play cat's cradle. But even though her eyes are intensely focused on her hands, she is bristling with awareness.

Your hair is funny, she says. And then she seems to forget what she has said and busies herself coiling the yarn in a complicated pattern around her fingers, slipping it off her thumbs and pulling it out.

Already the reality of her conversation with Antoine and the kiss is fading behind the alternate and quite plausible reality of an imaginary conversation with Joséphine Dufour about the children and the upcoming school year. She's surprised at the ease with which her small, original lie immediately blossoms into an elaborate story. She knows she's only buying time, a temporary lifesaver. It's familiar. It's the same way she lied to her father about Armand. She remembers the blurry, in-between land of fuzzy boundaries and split reality in which she lived then, where truth—already a shaky concept, vulnerable to the vagaries of memory—gradually gets corrupted, irremediably altered.

Only there's nothing more to lie about after their encounter. Antoine's letters do not come. Every morning she wakes up with anticipation, waiting for the moment when she can finally leave the house and walk to school and check the mailbox attached to the gate. And every day she walks back home, disappointed, her heart heavy, hoping that the next day will bring news. She tells herself that the mail is slow, that Antoine is protecting her, that he is cautious. There is no reason, after all, that he would rush into a correspondence that might endanger her. Perhaps he doesn't want to write, but will surprise her and appear one day in the village, as he did on August 15. He is busy with his business projects, she tells herself, he may have traveled to Cholet, or maybe to Paris, to inquire about Indochina. But wouldn't he write from there?

So the summer progresses in Maillezais. Madeleine brings back a basket of wild strawberries from the woods. The copper cauldron simmers all day long with the frosty bubbles. They take turns skimming the foam. The glass jars full of hot jam are lined up on the kitchen table, waiting to cool down and to be sealed. Then the cherries ripen, and another batch of jars wait, open-mouthed, on the table.

They are steadily working on the linen tablecloth. It's almost three-quarters done and Victorine has started embroidering the centerpiece with the entwined initials of their two families, *J* and *T*. Daniel sits on the grass and draws. Victor-Paul offered him a sketchbook at the beginning of the vacation and he has been filling it, day after day, with vivid landscapes and portraits. He takes after his grandfather, Victorine thinks with pride. After lunch, in the empty hours, she watches the barges glide on the canal in the torpor of the afternoon, carrying fruits and vegetables from the market, firewood, or sometimes a cow. In the afternoon, she cuts across to the schoolhouse and checks the mail, then stops at the baker's and the butcher's on the way back. At dusk, Daniel comes back from riding his bicycle and drops it in the alley, while Victorine and Madeleine are busy shelling peas, coring cantaloupes, snapping the threads of string beans, shaving the asparagus stems. Pools of scarlet light filter through the gauze of the overhung leaves and shimmer on the surface of the canal. The end of the summer stretches ahead like an endless bridge that will inevitably circle back to the same path: October 1, the first day of school.

In the dusky light of September, a quiet despair overcomes Victorine. She wonders if it's less painful to surrender to the pain than to fight it, if it's the same with all types of pain, the pains of the heart and the pains of the body.

ANTOINE'S LETTER is waiting for her in the office, the first day of school. She folds it into her notebook and can hardly wait for lunchtime to open it. She runs to the backyard at the end of the period and tears the envelope open.

> *Victorine chérie,*
>
> *Forgive me for my long silence. I didn't want to disrupt you and your family again, as you said I had when I surprised you in August. I am trying to respect your wishes, your family life. I've worked very hard the last few weeks at setting up the business I have mentioned to you. I have prepared a budget, but had to wait until the end of August for the Cholet factories to open and evaluate the possibilities of exporting our local linen and importing silk from Cochinchina.*
>
> *But this is not of much importance. I am writing to you because the memory of these too brief moments we had together is a constant pain that never leaves me.*
>
> *I cannot stop thinking about you.*
>
> *Antoine*

Victorine, *viens donc!*

Armand's voice echoes from their bedroom.

It's five o'clock in the morning. She is sitting at the kitchen table, drinking a glass of water. A shell-pink spindle of light floats beyond the willows.

What were you doing downstairs? Armand asks, not unkindly, when she climbs back into bed.

I couldn't sleep.

You've been moody, lately. Even when you sleep, you're restless.

Perhaps it's the summer, she says. She lies down on her side, her back to him. The heat wakes me up.

Here, I have just what you need . . . His voice is teasing, amorous. He wraps his arm around her. A little something to help put you to sleep. He lifts the nightgown and places his hand low on her stomach.

Non. She pulls the gown down her legs.

He fondles her gently through the thin cotton of the gown. I thought you couldn't sleep, he says.

Stop it.

Then, suddenly, his mood shifts. In one move he's pulled the nightgown up to her waist and entered her.

She tries to push him off with her elbow.

NON!

Ah, la râleuse. Stop whining and let yourself go. Where's the girl who couldn't get enough of it, where'd she go?

She grabs the bars of the bed with both her hands. She tries to raise her knees, but he pulls her legs straight back.

He's pushing himself into her and digging his hands into her shoulders. And now gripping her hips and going deeply inside her. The amorous mood is replaced by a rage as if he wanted to pierce her through and through. There's no letting go, this time, no turning her resistance into dark surrender, which then explodes into furious pleasure. Not this time. He must know, she thinks, but she doesn't care anymore. Her hands slip off the bars, clutch at the bolster; she buries her face into it, she's acutely aware of her teeth biting down in the fabric, her saliva wetting it.

Her breath comes quick and fast, raspy, but it's not from pleasure, she will not give in this time, she will refuse herself the pleasure.

. . .

A week later. Antoine's note is scribbled on a white Bristol card, and says only: Where can we meet?

The brevity of that line terrifies her. This time she won't be able to resist him.

In church, she kneels against the front pew, her hair covered by a mantilla of black lace. She is going to tell him they are mistaken, that what they believe is pure romantic love, a higher calling, is in fact no more than carnal temptation, that it's a test of her faith, of her marriage. Her face leaning into her folded hands, she recites *Ave Maria, gratia plena . . . Sancta Maria, Mater Dei, ora pro nobis peccatoribus . . .* She is sure of it, they are gullible, their attraction for each other is the work of the devil. You fool, that's exactly how the devil operates, under disguise.

September 8, 1940

3:00 p.m.

THE BLACK CITROËN QUINZE pulls up on the Maillezais square in a cloud of smoke. Victorine steps out of the car. She asks Maurice to wait for her while she walks around the village. A cool breeze has picked up. The wind whips the hair in her face and a colorless dust drifts across the street. She wraps her cardigan tight over her chest with her arms and walks across the church plaza. Sunday afternoon in Maillezais. The village is empty. There's a café, now, which didn't exist when she lived there. A handwritten sign inside the window informs potential clients "Will Reopen at 16 hours 30."

The school is exactly as she remembers it, a two-story, gray stone and stucco building, set back from the street behind an iron gate. The courtyard is deserted. It's the same gate, the one on which Antoine leaned one day, watching her come out of her classroom, his eyes squinting in the sun.

Down the street from the school, on the façade of the bakery, the word *BOULANGERIE* is still painted, exactly as it was, in curlicued script. The door is locked. She peers inside. A pair of curtains, embroidered with twin peacocks, still hangs in the window. The very same curtains, she could swear. But that's impossible . . .

The whole village looks like a theater set left intact, long after the actors have walked out.

Did you find what you were looking for? Maurice asks when

she climbs back into the car. His hands are steady on the wheel, as if he has been waiting in that position, without moving, the whole time she was walking in the village. She wonders if he has any idea why she wanted to come to Maillezais, other than to gratify an old woman's nostalgia. He looks at her. She doesn't see anything more than a simple question in his eyes.

No, she says, without looking at him.

He kicks the Citroën into first, second, and third gear in quick succession, raising two puffs of dust at the back wheels.

I told you. We should have come during the week.

No, she nods. It wouldn't have made any difference. Take me back to La Faute.

Antoine

10 Octobre 1898
This afternoon. In the abandoned barn in the alder forest,
behind Jean Lucien's house. It isn't too risky, the barn belongs to
old Monsieur Vernieux and he doesn't use it anymore since he's
had his stroke. In my heart, I feel strong. We have to stop.

It's a beautiful, clear Saturday afternoon. Victorine walks down
the slope of grass toward the canal and follows the towpath all the
way past the village; so as to avoid crossing the church square and
the main square with its two cafés, all the way to what they call the
lovers' bridge, which marks the intersection with a smaller, little-
used canal, and follows it till it reaches the forest on the other side
of Maillezais. She walks past the deserted *lavoir,* through the wood
of alders, and into the barn, leaving the door ajar. She's planned
their meeting carefully, at a time when both Armand and Lucien,
Adèle's husband, will be gone hunting for the afternoon at Sainte-
Christine's farm with Daniel and Madeleine. She told Armand she
had to stay in Maillezais to correct homework. She waits behind
the door, listening to the calls of birds, the furtive rustling of leaves
in the woods. And then, right on time, his steps, heading straight to
where she is standing.

He closes the door behind him and takes her in his arms in the
cool darkness of the barn, which smells of hay and manure and

wood shavings and oil from all the machinery parked in the dark like great, quiet beasts.

No, she says, pushing him away. It's a mistake. It's wrong. A temptation.

Is this a speech you've prepared? he asks. You sound like a priest. Come, let's sit over there and talk, shall we? Please.

He takes her by the hand and makes room for her on top of a bale of hay, and she sits down at a little distance from him.

We shouldn't be seeing each other. It's wrong, she says again. Her hands are clasped on her lap.

He is silent for a moment.

Is that what you really think?

Yes, we have to stop everything, the rendezvous . . .

He looks around the barn, at the gray light filtered through the windows covered with grime.

You asked me to come here to tell me that?

There's a trace of humor in his voice.

You wanted to see me, she says quietly.

Yes, I did.

He lights a cigarette and drops the match on the ground, among the hay. She presses her foot on it to make sure the flame is put out.

Watch out, she says.

He looks at her with an ironic look in his eyes. Yes, he says. It would easily catch fire, wouldn't it?

She suppresses a smile.

It's up to you, he says, his face turning serious. If that's what you wish, we will never see each other again.

She swings one leg over the other.

If that's what you wish.

She glances at him. Her hand is close to his. Her body leans toward him. Their shoulders touch, their arms. He weaves his fingers through hers. And then it's over. His arms are around her, awkwardly, his lips on her lips. The discussions she used to have with Bertha and Angelina about the nature of sins, what makes a venial sin, a capital sin; the memory of the blessed host she would try to spit out if she hadn't confessed; the prayers hastily mumbled after communion; the puffs of incense drifting above the altar: all forgotten.

She remembers lying with him at the very back of the barn. He had found an old blanket and laid it on the floor. It was covered with bits of hay that scratched her back and arms. She remembers how his hands had felt, warm and dry and strong, where he had bared her skin, on her breasts, between her thighs. She remembers his kisses in her neck, hard, voracious kisses, not letting go of her. She remembers how he had gently opened her legs and searched for her with his hand, then his lips. How he had held her, her legs folded against his chest, tucked under him, how her breath had come in quicker and quicker gasps, and he had put his hand on her mouth to smother her cries. She remembers the side of her leg hitting something hard, perhaps a wooden handle or a metal arm. She felt no pain. And then nothing. He held her for a long time afterward, they stayed wrapped in each other in silence. A hazy light fell from a round dormer window under the eaves. Her memory is blurry now, so many years later, but the smell of hay and oil, the patches of light, the deep shadows are still incandescent with passion.

It's very dark in the barn when they get up and dust themselves, except for a golden frame of light around the door. He walks to the window to read his watch. She remembers getting worried that it might be very late because of the darkness in the barn. But when they walk out, the sun is still bright although the air is cooler and the shadows are longer. She remembers thinking, the light is too harsh, and he says, Better let me go by myself, and he kisses her again, his lips pressed hard against hers. And then he is gone.

She walks back into the barn and tries to fix her hair and clean her blouse and her skirt of the little bits of hay caught there, but she can't really see anything. She crosses the woods back to the *lavoir* and stops for a moment to rinse her hands and try to make herself look the way she did before, but when she walks up the slope of grass along the canal, she hears their voices, the children and Armand. She tries to think of a story to tell, another lie, in case they notice anything suspicious, something about having gone to the barn, but for what reason? By the time she arrives at the door, the three of them are already in the kitchen, oblivious of her, except for Merlin, who growls when she bends over to pat his head and sniffs her suspiciously, and she's concerned that he might be giving the alarm that something's amiss. But Armand only says, Quiet, Merlin, without even turning around, pulling half a dozen pheasant hens out of his hunter's bag and displaying them on the table all bloody and already turning rigid and with a tender finger pokes their plumpness, the velvet of their feathers. I'll cook a couple for dinner tonight, she says, the rest we'll give to Jean Lucien.

They notice nothing about her, they don't even look surprised that she walked in after them, they ask no question. It's as if nothing has happened—Merlin, after a while, seems appeased, panting noisily by the fire—and she thinks that maybe it can all be erased. And when she sits down with Madeleine outside the kitchen door later in the cool evening to pluck the hens—Look at this pretty red feather, Madeleine says, can I keep it?—she is herself again, chatting and cheerful.

> *10 octobre 1898, minuit.*
> *Le mal est fait. Alea jacta est.*

The next morning, when she washes up, she notices the dark blue bruises on her left leg from her ankle all the way to her hip.

She makes sure to cover herself completely when she gets up and not to undress or dress in front of Armand. After a couple of days, the marks turn dark purple and yellow-green. Some are the size of a saucer.

But at the end of dinner, a day or two later, out of the blue, Armand asks her: What happened to your leg?

She pretends not to understand. She sweeps some crumbs with the edge of her hand and gathers them into her other hand. He insists. She says, Oh that? She has fallen in the basement a couple of days ago. She's tripped over the handle of the wheelbarrow.

He puts his fork and his knife on either side of his plate and wipes his mouth.

You're lying.

Excuse me? she says. She goes on picking up the dirty dishes. Goes to the sink. She tries to keep busy, moving about normally so that she doesn't have to face him.

Look at me when I'm talking to you.

In the same tone he talks to the children when they've done something wrong. Not mean, exactly, something else. She can't find the word. She has an urge to tell him everything. A confession followed by a couple of Our Fathers and that would be it. Run off and play in the garden. But she can't tell him. It would be the end of everything. He would have total power over her. She's entirely in the wrong.

She has to lie. Another lie. Once she's decided that there's no alternative, it's easy. She says she'd gone to pick up empty jars in the basement and while she had her hands full, she tripped and fell down the stairs and bruised her left leg. She couldn't believe how big the bruises were, she says, but they're going away now.

I don't believe you.

He points his finger at her neck.

And what about this? he says.

She puts her hand to her throat.

What? she says.

He snorts. You got *those* bruises falling down the stairs too? Fell head first, did you? And the step bit you?

She says nothing. She stacks the rest of the plates, balances the glasses on top of them, and carries them to the sink.

Even Merlin, he says. Look at him.

What do you mean?

Look at him!

She turns toward Merlin, who, hearing his name, is pricking up his ears and growling softly by the fire.

Haven't you noticed the way he's been around you? Slinking around?

No, she says.

She brings the white plum liqueur he likes to drink after dinner. She pours a finger's worth in a shot glass and places it in front of him. He sighs.

Sit down with me, he says, forcing his voice to be gentler.

She sits at the table across from him.

Aren't you drinking?

No, she says.

He drains his shot glass and fills it up again.

He swirls the liqueur in the glass and drinks it in one shot. Then he glances at her. There's not as much hostility in his eyes this time.

I know I'm not always a perfect husband.

She's startled by this admission of wrongdoing. In his loose white shirt, half-pulled out of his pants, one button opened at the neck, his arms resting on the table, his shoulders slightly hunched over, his jet-black mustache lately shot with gray, he looks sad.

But you know I love you. In my own way I'm faithful to you. What I do otherwise means nothing. You do know that, don't you?

For an instant she's overcome by a wave of guilt so intense that she too wants to lean over the table and drink the plum liqueur with him, touch his hand. Yes, Armand, I know, she wants to say. We are together, you and I. That is the truth. The rest doesn't matter.

But she doesn't lean toward him, she doesn't fill her shot glass. She doesn't drink with him. She doesn't move. The distance between them is not about his infidelities. Affairs are normal, perhaps, in the course of a marriage. They are to be expected. Anything, she thinks, could be forgiven to the person who touches you. The distance between them is about something as unfathomable as the color of the sky after the sun has set or the smell of gardenia in the spring.

She sighs.

Do you have nothing to say? he asks again. And behind the

shaky gentleness of the voice she senses his anger, rising again with her silence.

I know, she says. I know it means nothing to you.

He fills another glass, drinks half of it and sets it down deliberately on the table.

Look at me, he says, and this time there's no mistaking the threat in his voice.

She looks at him. There's no more sadness in his eyes.

You've been with a man. His voice is dark, threatening, barely contained. Don't lie to me. I know how to tell a woman who's been with a man who's not her husband. He puts his hand over his chest, right across the suspenders holding his pants up. I know, Victorine, because I've been with women like you!

He hits the shot glass so hard with the back of his hand the liqueur spills across the waxed tablecloth and drips on the floor.

You've betrayed me!

What?

You heard me.

I've no idea what you're talking about.

She feels white inside with terror.

He leans over the table and grabs her sleeve.

Sunday, when we were at Sainte-Christine and you stayed in Maillezais, what did you do?

She tries to pull her arm away but he has her in a tight grip. She tells him he is deluded. She reminds him she had stayed home to work that day, she finished correcting the pupils' papers. She tells him: You know what people say, that if you accuse someone of a sin it's because you have committed it yourself first. He lets go of her wrist, knocking over the bottle of plum liqueur, which shatters on the floor. She stares at the shards, glittering in a patch of light. The sweet and tart smell fills the room.

He points his finger at her. You're sneaky, he says. You're hiding something.

She can't stand looking at him.

Go clean up, at least!

She hears him get up from the table and then a crash. She turns to look. He's hitting the wall with the back legs of his chair, above the little desk, by the place where Victor-Paul's Three Musketeers painting is hanging, methodically going at the hard plaster, as if wielding a hammer, until the plaster starts chipping and falling in chunks and the painting crashes. His arm muscles are bulging under his shirt, his whole back tense with the effort.

When he's done, he tosses the chair across the room. It lands by the fireplace on its back and one of the bars snaps and pokes up, splintered. She watches him without moving.

You don't even have the honesty to admit it!

He climbs up the stairs. She hears his heavy steps and then the door to their bedroom bangs shut.

She gets a washcloth and quietly wipes up the liqueur. She gets a broom and a dustpan and sweeps up the shards of glass. She picks up her father's painting and carefully reassembles the broken frame around the canvas. Then she mops the whole kitchen. It takes her a long time, the floor is sticky. She has to clean it twice, using a bucket of water to rinse it off. She washes the dishes. She doesn't want to stop. As long as she is cleaning up, and sweeping and wiping and putting the dishes away, time will be suspended.

Armand replastered the holes he had punched in the kitchen wall and went about his daily chores in a murderous silence. Then, a few days later, he decided to build a tool shed in the backyard, between the outhouse and the vegetable garden. Victorine watched him from the kitchen back window, measuring and hammering, whistling gaily at times. His violence seemed to have vanished.

She didn't know what to say to Antoine. Her feelings were too conflicted. She wrote four different letters and threw them all out. Finally, she sent him a short note.

Something happened. Don't write to me. Don't try to contact me. Please respect my wishes.

After a week or so, sadness came over her, the way a serious disease suddenly declares itself after a period of incubation. She didn't recognize what it was at first. She would be going about her life, preparing for school, cooking dinner, when she would suddenly feel a loss of energy, a deep melancholy. She had to stop what she was doing and sit on a chair, or even lie down on her bed. After much hesitation, not knowing whom else to turn to, she went to see Marie, Armand's elder sister, in the shop where she sold healing herbs in Vouvant. The coach pulled up across from the church, and Victorine got off. Marie's shop was on a smaller square, a few hundred meters away, but she walked in the opposite direction. Vouvant was slightly bigger than Maillezais, but it gave her the same feeling: the somber façades of the houses, the wind blowing in sharp gusts in the narrow streets, the few people throwing inquisitive glances at her as she crossed the square—she knew what they meant: she was a stranger here, what was she doing? Both villages were coiled tight around the church, looking inward. They had no horizon.

The ruins of the Mélusine tower stood above the village, covered with a thick mantle of creeping vines. Victorine took a walk up to the old castle. The view there was more open, you could see across a small valley running parallel to the Mervent forest. Victor-Paul had taken her there once in his horse and buggy. She remembered it clearly. It was a hot summer day, and they had gone to the tower to feel cooler.

One morning, Victor-Paul told her that day, as they were walking up to the ruins of the old castle—this happened a long time ago, in medieval times—Raymondin de Poitiers was hunting the wild boar in the Mervent forest—the one you can see from here—when he got lost. After walking a long time, he stumbled upon a cascade where three beautiful nymphs were bathing. One of them had curly red hair that ran down her back all the way to her waist. She watched him come with a little smile on her lips. He fell instantly in love with her. Victor-Paul took Victorine's hand and pressed it in his. Mélusine agreed to marry Raymondin but on one condition: he would have to leave her alone in the castle tower every Saturday night until Sunday morning and promise never to ask her what she was doing. Raymondin accepted and they got married.

They came to the foot of the tower and sat down on a step. Victor-Paul patted the stone wall behind them with his hand.

This very tower, he said.

Victorine—she was seven or eight at the time—hung on his every word, mesmerized.

But, like Bluebeard's wife, Victor-Paul went on, you remember me telling you about Bluebeard, don't you?

Victorine nodded in silence.

Well, like Bluebeard's wife, Raymondin grew more and more curious about what Mélusine was doing behind closed doors every Saturday night. He became so obsessed that one night he couldn't help but open the forbidden door to the tower. Perhaps it was where we are sitting right now. Victor-Paul made a gesture as though he was opening an invisible door in front of them. No door opened, only the wind stirred the leaves of the ivy. Victorine trembled.

Do you want to know what Raymondin saw, Victor-Paul asked?

Victorine held her breath and nodded.

Victor-Paul's voice took on dramatic accents:

Mélusine was bathing in a basin of green marble lit up with tall torches. From the waist down, her legs had turned into the scaly, silvery tail of a snake, which rested languidly on the rim of the basin. Raymondin stood there, speechless, horrified. Mélusine screamed, and wings sprouted out of her back. She flew off through the open window and over the rooftops. That way. His hand showed the valley.

Victorine pressed herself against him, and he put his arms around her shoulders. As it happened, he went on, she was with child when Raymondin discovered her, and as punishment for having hidden from him her true nature, the son she was carrying in her womb was born with long, deformed teeth. He showed his own teeth to Victorine and she thought with alarm that they had grown abnormally long in the space of a few minutes. That son later came back to the village, Victor-Paul continued, alone, and grew up to be a quiet and perfectly decent fellow. Because of his big teeth he was given the name Long-Tooth Geoffrey.

What about Mélusine? Victorine asked with a small voice.

Mélusine, Victor-Paul said, was never seen again.

The tower hadn't changed. Half of it was collapsed. It looked more desolate than ever, especially on a windy day like today. It was all that remained of the Vouvant castle. Victorine tried to find the step on which she and her father had sat down that day, but she couldn't. Maybe it was overgrown with grass. She slowly walked back down toward the square where Marie kept her shop.

She told Marie she was tired, she didn't think it was anything serious but could Marie prescribe something that would restore her energy. Marie's dark brown eyes were prying almost, as if she could sense that Victorine was harboring a secret but couldn't quite figure out what it was, although she would, sooner or later. Then she took out several little glass bottles from her shelves and mixed their powdery contents into a tin box.

It's a tonic, she said. Cinchona, gentian, and rhubarb. She handed the box to Victorine. Take it to Dr. Hermon, the pharmacist on the square, and have him make little pills out of that. Take one before each meal.

But the herbs didn't help. Victorine would snap at Armand if he asked when dinner would be ready or asked her to mend a sock. Her rage would flare for a moment, then the sadness would come back and she would labor over the sock or the button to appease him. Or she would become irritated at Madeleine when she missed a stitch. Armand grew distant. He returned later and later and sometimes missed dinner altogether.

Antoine didn't write back.

And yet, during the whole month of October, she waited every day for the mail barge to pull up at the pontoon, as she had done a couple of months earlier, and every day, after the mailman had left without bringing a letter from Antoine, she swayed like a little girl on the swing to soothe her disappointment. She let her boots kick in the dust, past the edge of her skirt, and watched the sun peek through the canopy of elms. From where she sat, their house, perched on top of the slope of grass, glowed in the noon sun as on one of her father's miniature paintings.

Victor-Paul had taught Armand how to make the swing out of a wooden board and two ropes. It was an exact replica of the one he had made for Victorine in the orchard of Cholet. When the swing had first been installed, she remembers, her feet didn't touch the ground, and her toes poked, pointy and thin, from under her dress. When she swung, the ribbons of her belt floated behind her in the still summer air.

My three queens, her father called her and Angelina and Bertha. The rare times he paid attention to them. When he had been drinking just enough to make him happy and loose, but not enough to turn his face into a fist of rage.

One time—not the time they went to the ocean, but another time, perhaps five or six years later—he took her with him to the castle of Monsieur le Comte de La Bretonnière to deliver a carriage he had repainted. He was carefree and he sang *Guilleri, Carabi,* at the top of his lungs. The song always made him think of Monsieur le Comte, because Caraba, he said, was the name of a marquis. She sang along with him:

> Il était un p'tit homme qui s'appelait Guilleri, Carabi
> Il s'en fut à la chasse, à la chasse aux perdrix, Carabi
> Toto, Carabo,
> Marchand d'caraba . . .

> *There was a little man whose name was Guilleri, Carabi*
> *He went hunting partridges, Carabi*
> *Toto, Carabo,*
> *Merchant of Caraba . . .*

When they arrived at the castle gate, they went around to the back, straight to the stables, their horses' hooves slipping and tripping over the round, smooth cobblestones. The cook came out and sat her in the kitchen on a hard-backed chair and offered her a glass of milky white barley syrup. From the open window she saw the Comte's son in full riding outfit, shiny black boots and hard cap, guiding his horse by the bit. He had dark blond hair and a long, angular face. He seemed a little older than she was, perhaps twelve or thirteen. But his clothes and his demeanor, haughty and detached, made him look like a man. She had never seen a boy with that kind of poise before. It was intimidating. He stared at her with curiosity, but without a smile or any expression on his face, as if she was too far away to see him looking at her, and then pulled himself up on his horse with such sureness and lightness of step she was thrilled, and sad to see him go.

THE LETTER that finally comes is not from Antoine. The mailman turns it this way and that and upside down and whistles.

Ha-noi, he spells out, reading the round ink stamp. Must be from your sister. If you don't mind my being nosy?

Tucked into the envelope is a photograph of Angelina and her husband, Jules, standing proudly before a backdrop of luxuriant vegetation. Jules is wearing a jacket in the Asian style, with a stand-up collar, and Angelina a pale-colored summer dress, both of them looking like *colons,* the term they were using for the French established in one of the new colonies. A young Asian boy in a silk tunic and loose pants is squatting at their feet, their domestic, probably. Folded next to the photograph is the clipping of a newspaper drawing. It depicts a *colon* dressed in a black suit, followed by three Asian boys running after him, one armed with a huge feathered fan to cool him off, another carrying his pack of cigarettes and lighter, and the third holding an umbrella to shade him from the tropical sun. Underneath, Angelina has written her own caption: Jules and our three "boys." The caption is obviously meant as a joke, but, along with the photograph, it makes Victorine cringe.

There's no letter, but a postcard, captioned "Hanoi—Rue Paul Bert," showing a street corner with storefronts and a cart with oversized wheels and a leather hood—a kind of local vehicle, she guesses—pulled by an Asian man. She studies the postcard in detail. The whole street wouldn't be out of place in Niort, if chestnut trees were growing along the façades. There's even a dog, a brown and white pointer, smack in the forefront of the photograph. And yet the white clothes worn by the man, his bare feet on the street, the abundant leaves on the trees evoke a totally different world. On the back of the postcard these words are written:

> *We've finally moved to Hanoi. Jules couldn't wait. It's cooler than Saigon but less entertaining. Angelina.*

She flips the postcard back and runs a finger around its edges. What would it be like to walk that street?

Armand comes out of his brand-new tool shed, heading straight to her, his walk slow and deliberate. She slips the letter between the folds of her skirt. She doesn't want to talk with him—they haven't had an intimate conversation since his outburst a few weeks ago—and especially not about Angelina's letter. He stops a couple of meters from the swing where she sits. She looks at him in silence, holding her breath.

I shouldn't have done what I did, he says.

She sways silently, watching him.

You don't say anything, you see. It makes me angry.

He waits for her to say something, and when she doesn't, he goes on.

It's easy to imagine anything, even the worst. I don't know what got into me, that day. It was those bruises on you . . . Say something, don't look at me like that.

She looked at her father in that same blank way when he had had too much to drink. He'd get into a rage too, sometimes, in the middle of the night, sometimes all by himself. Nobody knew what triggered him. All the men drank a lot then. It wasn't particularly unusual. He'd curse and throw things around in the shop. The horses neighed wildly. The girls would wake up and sit together on Victorine's bed, talking in low voices, waiting for it to end. Marie-Louise would come in and tell them to go back to sleep. My poor little girls, she would say. My poor little girls. Hearing the inflection in her voice which managed to pity them and simultaneously accuse Victor-Paul was almost worse than hearing him go wild. It was as though she was condemning them to a life of being victims, victims of circumstances, as though she was telling them: the life that has been assigned to you is going to be your fate. Marie-Louise's voice, in those moments, was like a key turning in a lock. Victorine's silence was her only resistance.

Armand stops the swing with his foot.

Are you not happy?

I don't know, she says. Life is always the same. In the summertime, especially, it feels like we're trapped here.

He nods. Yes, he says, it's a small village. Not much happening. Sometimes I feel that too.

He pushes the swing back with his foot, not that hard, but hard enough to make her hold on to the rope with both hands.

You wanted to know, she says.

He says nothing for a moment. Kicks the swing one more time and releases it.

We can go to Paris. Remember that trip we took that summer?

Yes, she says. It was nice.

This is our life, he says. What more do you want? You wanted to work. You're working. We have two healthy children. He turns around toward the house. What more do we need? If you're never satisfied with what you have, you'll always be miserable.

Maybe, she says. I don't know.

He nods. He puts his hand over hers on the rope.

You like this swing?

Yes, she says. She laughs a little.

Your father taught me how to make it.

I know, she says.

He pushes her playfully and she kicks up her legs.

You like that?

Yes, she laughs again.

Higher?

Yes! She laughs, louder, the swing flying high, higher, her skirts uncovering her bare legs.

Hey, madame! Nice legs!

I got news from Angelina, she says at dinner. Armand lifts his eyes from the *rillettes* she's made fresh from pork from Adèle's farm, a tiny gherkin balanced at the tip of his fork.

Again?

They just moved to Hanoi.

Can I see the postcard? Madeleine asks. Can I see the postcard?

She shows it to them, the postcard with the big cart pulled by an Asian man and the dog crossing a street that looks like it could be in Niort.

Oh, Madeleine says, look at the dog. He looks like Merlin!

Do you think they'd let people go for free if they worked on the ship? Daniel wonders.

Yes, I think they would, Victorine says. She gives him a sly glance. But wouldn't you rather go in a submarine, like Captain Nemo?

Who's Captain Nemo? Madeleine asks.

Oh, you're such an ignoramus, Daniel says. It's in a book by Jules Verne. It's not for girls. You've got your Pink Library books.

Don't say that, Victorine says. She can read Jules Verne too.

I know what you are talking about, Madeleine says, with a pout. It's a book called *Twenty Thousand Leagues Under the Sea*. I saw it under your algebra book.

But Daniel ignores her and studies the postcard again. What's that cart for? Is it the kind of carriage they use over there? He laughs. Pulled by a man instead of a horse! Are there slaves over there, like there used to be in America?

No, Victorine says. But I don't think they are treated very well. Armand glances at the postcard.

That cart, Dany, is called a *pousse-pousse.*

Daniel looks more carefully. Should be called a pull-pull, rather, he jokes. He stares for a moment at the postcard. With a combustion engine you could transform this cart into an automobile. These poor people wouldn't have to work so hard.

Crazy to go there, Armand says. The latest cholera epidemic has taken hundreds of Europeans.

Let me see! Let me see! Madeleine cranes her neck to see better.

Armand hands the card to Madeleine.

And it's full of bugs! Ugh! she taunts Daniel, running her fingers round his neck, making a buzzing sound. Scorpions, mosquitoes, big, fat ones that bite you in the night while you sleep and they find you dead the next morning!

You're horrible! he yells.

Did you learn that with Madame Berger, Madeleine? Victorine asks.

"Our magnificient colonial empire," Daniel recites. That's what *we're* studying. He makes a face at Madeleine.

Stop it, children! Armand hits the table with his hand. Daniel, go out and close the shutters. Madeleine, help your mother.

If you don't catch the *cochinchinette* first—, Daniel says.

Stop it, Daniel!

—or the bubonic plague!

ALL SAINTS' DAY, 1898. The brush Victor-Paul is holding ends in a wisp of gold. He's drawing feather-thin lines of gold at the edges of a red-and-white-striped banner, regilding the crest of a coat of arms on a robin's-egg blue carriage. One brush stroke and it's done. He doesn't have to go back over it. Not a drop, not a smudge. The precision and swiftness of his hand is still astonishing, the unsteadiness of his life coming to a prefect poise at the point of a brush. He steps back and contemplates his work for a moment, then corrects a tiny dent.

His intense self-absorption used to fascinate Victorine when she was growing up. Walking into the shop on Impasse de l'Abbé Doisnaud, this place of skilled men, was like penetrating an enchanted cave. It was bustling from morning to night, even on Saturdays and sometimes on Sunday afternoons. Turpentine, leather, oil paint, the acrid scent of iron melting. There was sawdust on the ground and the constant crackling of the forge. The sparks flew off, a red rain. The iron was being worked over like molasses and shaped by hand on the anvil. The smells were intoxicating. She was mesmerized. The men didn't pay attention to her. The tools of the shop required total focus. One false move, she knew it, could cause a fatal accident. She never touched any of the tools, but she sometimes picked a brush and painted gold leaves or azure stripes on discarded pieces of wood lying in the sawdust. The men cursed and got drunk and swaggered and talked about women openly and crudely. There was no shame among these men. They wore pants held up by suspenders and sometimes no shirts on their torsos in the summertime. Their skin was tanned like the leather they tooled and tufts of hair sprouted on their chests. They were loose and rough and crude and raw. And they were proud of it.

May I try it? Daniel asks.

Victor-Paul hands him a brush and lets him practice on a piece of wood lacquered white, just as Victorine used to do. His brush strokes are firm, if a little wide. In a few minutes he has made a rather good replica of the coat of arms. Madeleine watches from a distance, careful not to get any paint on her brand-new velvet dress.

He's a good artist, you know. Victor-Paul turns to show Daniel's work to Victorine. Better than last time, son.

Runs in the family, Victorine says.

Just then a gas-powered vehicle, its cabin open to the air, pulls into the courtyard in a cloud of smoke, causing Victor-Paul's horses to neigh and wildly beat their hooves over the deafening sound of the engine.

Daniel drops the brush. An automobile!

He runs out with Madeleine and they stand in the courtyard, staring at the amazing machine, a shiny black coupé half-hidden in a cloud of black smoke.

Speak of the devil, Victor-Paul says. For the car is a devil to him: he knows that if automobiles take on, he'll be without work within a few years. He steps out of the shop to greet the new-comer. It isn't often that an automobile comes to Cholet, and even less often right into a carriage shop.

The cloud of smoke vanishes as the engine is turned off. Two men step out of the carriage in leather helmets and heavy glasses and scarves tied around their noses to protect themselves from the sun and the dust, making them look like medieval warriors.

One of the men introduces himself as Baron de Langlois, and inquires whether Victor-Paul would consider painting his family coat of arms on the front and sides of his brand-new Panhard & Levassor. The two initials, *P* and *L,* are entwined in the front, in the same style as the letters Victorine and Madeline embroider on the tablecloth.

A Panhard & Levassor, Daniel whispers, reverently. Maman, it's the car that won the Paris–Bordeaux race!

Maybe not the very same car, Victorine says.

They only made ten of them, or maybe a hundred, I'm not sure. Look, Madeleine, this is where they put the gasoline, under that hood. Don't touch!

Victor-Paul invites the baron into the shop and the children follow them in. The other man, the one who has been driving the car, unties his scarf and removes his glasses. It's Antoine.

His face shows astonishment when he sees Victorine, then he quickly regains his composure. She stares at him.

He comes to her and takes her hand.

Madame, he says, nodding politely. I didn't know—I had no idea you'd be here. I knew—

She turns around to see if the others are noticing anything, but they are in the shop, preoccupied.

What are you doing here? she whispers.

Monsieur le Baron requested my services to drive his car.

I didn't know you did that.

He is about to answer when Daniel walks over to the automobile and gingerly touches the side, as he would the flank of a horse, his face serious, making him look older than his age.

Isn't it hot? Madeleine asks. You said not to touch.

Not back here. In the front, under the hood, it's hot, that's where the engine is, Daniel says with authority.

My son, Daniel, Victorine says.

Daniel shakes his hand.

I believe we met, monsieur, Antoine says, a long time ago, on the beach of La Tranche.

Daniel looks at him blankly, either not remembering at all, or refusing to acknowledge him, and walks around the car to inspect it.

My daughter, Madeleine.

Madeleine comes forward and curtsies. *Bonjour monsieur!* she calls and then runs away, laughing.

What about your business projects? I thought you were traveling? She deliberately keeps her voice distant, as she had that day on the beach.

He tries to read her eyes but she looks down. He hesitates for a moment.

My plans are taking shape. I will leave sometime in the winter. Keeping the same distant tone she uses.

Victorine notices that Madeleine is watching them from a distance.

My sister Angelina is there, I mean in Indochina, with her husband. I told you that, perhaps?

Yes, you did. Where is she?

In Hanoi.

It's a nice little town, Antoine says. But it's not Saigon.

He climbs into the car and turns on the engine, which causes smoke to pour out and the two horses to neigh again, alarmingly this time.

Climb in, he says.

She shakes her head.

My children are here, she says. She turns toward the shop. My father . . .

Just for a short ride. Monsieur le Baron will no doubt give me permission. We'll be back in a few minutes.

She looks at him, hesitant.

He's my friend, Antoine explains. He just bought this car and doesn't know how to drive it.

Very short, then, she says.

She pokes her head in at the door.

Monsieur Langelot is going to show me the automobile, she says.

Maman, where are you going? Madeleine cries.

We'll be right back, Antoine says.

Just down the street. Victorine waves at her.

Madeleine doesn't wave back. Daniel stares at them with a stony, reproachful face.

I am taking you away from them, Antoine says, turning his head over his shoulder to maneuver the car. They don't like it. In profile she sees the straight line of his nose, his chin half swallowed by the strap of the helmet. There's sadness in his voice.

No, she says. They don't.

I'm sorry. It's my fault.

Let's go, she says.

He backs away from the front door and drives up the narrow street. The car jolts along on the cobblestones. Antoine presses the horn as frightened passersby flatten themselves against the wall. Watch out! Victorine says. He slows down. The street is so narrow there's barely enough space on either side.

He takes her around the old neighborhood of Cholet, Place

Travot, and down to the Mail, all the way to rue de l'Abreuvoir. Faster this time. People stare at them, some of them applaud and wave. Antoine waves back. Victorine holds on to the indentation of her door with both her hands when he makes a turn. He puts his gloved hand on her arm.

Don't worry, he says. You won't fly out of your seat. Why don't you tie my scarf around your face?

He takes it out of his pocket and hands it to her. Here.

She looks at him but she can't see his eyes through the goggles. She smiles.

I prefer to see where I'm going, she says.

He laughs.

I didn't mean over your eyes, madame! But over your nose.

She laughs with him.

No, that's fine.

You can keep the scarf anyway, he says, still looking at her.

Keep your eyes on the road, she says, smiling. But she tucks the scarf into her sleeve.

He drives along the river. The smells of the river, the wind whipping into her hair, make her think of that first time she went to the beach with her father, when she had imagined that she could ride the wind like a bird. In fact, frightened by the noise of the car, sparrows, which were pecking in the weeds, take off in front of them. Two boys playing by the river turn around and gawk at them. She holds her hair down with her hands and laughs.

Mon Dieu! They're going to wonder where we are.

He pulls up by the riverbank and stops the engine.

Victorine, he says. He looks at her for a moment, then: I can't stop thinking about you. I know you know this.

She looks away, toward the river. The two boys have resumed their game of tossing flat pebbles as far as they can into the river.

It was an accident, he says, my showing up at your father's shop. I promise you.

I know, she says, still looking at the boys.

I get used to not seeing you, he says. It becomes like a dull pain that I almost forget. But when I do, when I speak with you, like this, when I hear your laugh, it seems so—so natural to be with you. I—I hope I'm not offending you.

She turns to face him. His eyes look dark, almost a marine blue, as though the late afternoon shadows were reflected in them. His strong face is open, questioning. She's never seen a man showing so much emotion on his face. She's never met anyone like him, in fact. The men she knows—her father, and certainly Armand—tend to stay on their guard. Antoine, on the other hand, seems free and spontaneous, not only in his actions but in his feelings too. One of his hands is still on the steering wheel. The other one rests on the seat between them. An extraordinary feeling of happiness suddenly fills her. She places her hand on top of his and entwines her fingers through his.

You're not offending me.

A smile plays on his lips. Perhaps he has received the answer he was asking for.

She lowers her eyes. I feel the same, she continues. She puts his hand back on the steering wheel. Let's go back, now.

Antoine wrote to her and they arranged to meet at the *lavoir* on a Saturday, when he was off from work and Victorine could leave the house inconspicuously. Just to talk, she said in her response to him. Did she want to repeat the scene in the barn a few weeks earlier, or on the contrary, put an end to what had happened between them? She only knew that she had to see him. She put on her jacket of heavy wool and a shawl over her shoulders and kept her arms crossed over her chest all the way. The wind was blowing in sharp gusts.

He was there already, smoking. He crushed the cigarette when he saw her and took her in his arms. He smelled of wool and wood and smoke. He kissed her on the lips.

It was really very simple, he said, taking her by the hand and leading her to the *lavoir*. They sat side by side on the stone lip where, in the summer and springtime, the village women brushed and washed the laundry. He had been thinking and thinking about it. He had applied to be transferred to Indochina. He was pretty sure Customs would accept the transfer. They needed men over there. He loved her. He wanted to be with her. Would she consider going with him?

She was astounded by his question. She listened to him, fascinated by his self-confidence. It reminded her of the way he would talk to her on the jetty of La Tranche, years ago. He had the same look in his eyes that seemed to see beyond the plain reality of their life. He was telling her about the color of the Mekong River, the smell of the frangipani flowers, the taste of ginger. I will show you a world that you will fall in love with, he said. She thought it was outlandish, a wild idea. He was not talking about her leaving Armand and her family anymore, or betraying one man to follow another. He talked only of the Orient; he made Indochina sparkle like a jewel.

They agreed that she wouldn't see him on the sly, behind Armand's back. It was just something that she could never do. So they either had to put an end to the situation, or . . . Exactly, he said. It was the conclusion he had come to himself. Perhaps it was the very daring of the idea that was making it conceivable. It wouldn't be like leaving Armand to live with Antoine in another village, with all the rumors, the shame, the reprobation, her reputation and her life ruined. There would be nothing petty or sordid. It would be romantic: a leap into an enchanted world. She couldn't see leaving Armand and the children, but she could see herself with Antoine on the deck of a steamer, in the middle of the Indian Ocean.

And my children?

He pressed her hand.

We'll take them with us, if that's what you wish. I don't want to separate you. I'll take the three of you. His eyes searched hers.

She saw Daniel leaning over the banister, on the upper deck of an ocean liner, his hair blown into his face, Daniel laughing into the wind, Daniel visiting the boiler rooms and inquiring, with that serious look he took, about the power of the engines. Madeleine reading on a deck chair, her feet crossed at the ankles. It was a fantasy straight out of a novel. Perhaps later, yes, when they had settled into their new life, she could bring the children into it? But she couldn't see Antoine, who had arranged his life to be as free of responsibility as possible, facing Daniel and Madeleine every morning, hearing their squabbles, giving his time and attention to children's needs, no matter how undemanding they were.

It started to rain, a fine drizzle. They said goodbye, almost formally. She went back home, removed her boots, and dried herself in front of the fire. She was shivering, afraid that she might have caught a cold. I want to be with you. I want you to come with me. She repeated the words in her mind. Rolling them like a diamond in her hands. They made her drunk, light-headed. Deliriously happy. I want. I want you.

On a whim, a few days later, just to see, Victorine sent out for the forms to apply for a teaching position in the colonies.

The forms came in a manila envelope. They were a dull light brown, like all correspondence from the French government. They were asking for the usual, dates, diplomas, income, marital status. And finally, that line: if married, husband's authorization. *Signature du mari.*

THERE'S ALWAYS a priest involved in the affairs of a Vendée family. The curate you unload to, his face hidden in the shadows behind the wooden grid of the confession booth. Sometimes the priest is a sinister figure, abusing his power. Sometimes he is benevolent. The *confesseur* serves as confidant. He is supposed to be sworn to secrecy, but if the sin acknowledged is a legal crime, a murder, say, he is required to report it. Sometimes he agonizes, caught between competing loyalties, the confidentiality he owes to his flock, and secular law. Sometimes the priest talks. But even if he doesn't, he knows.

The priest who takes the confession in Maillezais is middle-aged and clean-shaven. He wears a pair of tortoiseshell spectacles and his thin, long mouth curves with suppressed appetite. It is the mouth Victorine stares at through the grid squares, the mouth that asks, Have you sinned, my child? The ritual question not really leaving room for a true answer, other than the litany of sins listed in the mass book: theft and greediness and jealousy and the bit about desiring your neighbor's wife or even full-blown adultery—although she doubts that anyone confesses to that. And Victorine usually picks a plausible assortment of venial sins to get it over with, and be assigned a penance of a couple of Our Fathers and Hail Marys.

She sees herself kneel, her head lowered under the black mantilla, preparing her words: *Mon père j'ai péché.* I have desired a man who is not my husband . . . I have desired another man . . . I have desired . . . I desire . . . I have committed . . . the sin of adultery. . . . Her face lowered, she wouldn't see the mouth twitch ever so slightly, in anticipation of the details.

Father, I have thought of leaving my husband to be with that man.

The monstrosity of those words.

I have thought of leaving my children to be with that man.

No. She wouldn't give him that pleasure. She wouldn't see him preen in the village swollen with the knowledge of her dirty secret.

This is what they do to women like her. They don't need to brand them with the red letter. They don't need to call them names, although they do.

There was a woman in Cholet whom they saw sometimes on market days. The woman's hair was blond streaked with gray. She let it fall loose on her back or simply tied it with a ribbon on her neck instead of knotting it on top of her head. Victorine thought she was strange, like a gypsy, but beautiful, in her way. She wore no corset, you could tell from the way her body moved under the fabric of her dress, and the leather of her shoes came apart. Poor women, she had observed, were often tightly buttoned, perhaps as a sign of embarrassment at their own poverty. Their clothes were just made of cheaper material and their skin was rougher. They made every effort to be inconspicuous. This woman was different. She didn't try to hide herself. Victorine didn't know her name, but she heard her mother once mention her as "that woman." Doesn't she have any shame? Marie-Louise had whispered. She obviously didn't. Is that what it was? That she didn't have any shame, as a good, proper woman was supposed to have?

Women like her, women who strayed, bad mothers, bad wives, it was all the same, women who didn't do their duty. *Femmes qui se laissaient aller,* who let go of their modesty, of their shame. You took one step off the path and *pffit!* One second you were there, one second you were gone.

She wakes up, breathing in the smell of Armand's skin, the wall of his back in her face. She feels the curve of his shoulder with her fingers, wraps her hand around it. The smooth thickness of a man's shoulder. She lets it fill her hand for a moment, rests her head against it. In his sleep, Armand shifts and brings his arm toward her to press her to him. Silently she slips off the bed. She tiptoes to Madeleine's bedroom. In the moonlight, the child's braids are streaked with silver. She's resting on her back, both her hands thrown on either side of her head, palms open, fingers curling softly. She used to sleep this way when she was an infant, except then her hands were closed tight. Victorine pulls the blanket up to her chin and Madeleine gives a faint moan. She touches the girl's cheek and lips with a finger. She feels the warm breath on the back of her hand. She stops at the door of Daniel's room. His blanket is thrown off and his body twisted, one arm flung across his naked chest, his pajama shirt on the floor. He must have been too hot during the night. She doesn't enter the room. It wouldn't be proper. He's almost a man. She strains to hear his breath. His black hair contrasts with the pale pillow. Then she walks downstairs and stands at the front window, watching a leafy branch of oak sway across the rectangle of glass.

He wrote to her again, at school. They had to meet urgently, he said. He had to be at La Roche-sur-Yon for some administrative business, the following week, and would go through Fontenay and Maillezais on the way back. Could she meet him again at the *lavoir* after morning classes on Friday? It was very important. He would be there at noon, waiting for her.

What could be so urgent? It was difficult to arrange, meeting like that on a school day. She would only have a short time, fifteen or twenty minutes, to see him. Classes ended at noon. They usually had lunch at home around one o'clock. She prepared salted pork and lentils the night before and ran off to the *lavoir* as soon as the bell rang for the lunch break.

He is already there, waiting for her. Instead of taking her in his arms, he hands her a brown envelope. She immediately recognizes the round ink stamp of Saigon. *Douanes Françaises d'Indochine* is printed on the left-hand corner. French Customs of Indochina.

Open it, he says.

> *Monsieur Langelot,*
> *In response to . . . we have the pleasure to inform you . . . that the position to which you have applied is open in Saigon. Your appointment is due to begin on February 15, 1899. Please make all necessary arrangements as pursuant below, for your passage to Indochina. . . .*

The *Tonkin* is leaving from Bordeaux on January 8, he says. They still have room, I inquired.

She sits down on the edge of the *lavoir* and drops the letter next to her.

I am happy for you, she says, and suddenly her heart drains of emotion. Her fingers grip the edge of the bench.

He sits down next to her.

I know it's terribly sudden. I didn't expect to be called so soon.

January 8, she says. It's in a month and a half.

He nods.

The misty journey through the Indian Ocean she had concocted from Angelina's postcards and letters is dissolving with the reality of a date in January.

I don't know, Antoine . . . I thought I'd have more time. I didn't tell them anything. I would need to prepare them . . . I would need to prepare myself.

The words sound empty to her, next to the terror of what she is about to do.

Of course . . . , he says.

She looks at him. In his eyes she can read her own confusion, her abject fear.

I cannot fathom . . . , she begins. He takes her hand. It's the—the failure, the failure to do my duty, do you understand?

She picks up the letter again, looks at the elegant typeface of *Douanes Françaises d'Indochine,* and hands it back to him. Her eyes hold his for a long minute.

But I couldn't bear to stay if you left.

I saw Madeleine alone in the village this afternoon, Armand tells her. He sounds stern. It was almost seven. All the other children were already back home. Where were you?

It's after dinner. He's sitting at the little desk, reading pupils' papers in the light of the oil lamp. Madeleine is knitting by the fireplace. Victorine is sitting across from her, mending socks. Daniel is reading. Armand has spoken without turning toward them.

I was delayed . . . , she says, slipping the wooden egg into a sock of Daniel's and stretching the toe over it . . . at the library, and then I stopped by at the butcher's and there I met Marie Mineau and we talked and I went to her place to get a ball of yarn of that gray I am using for Madeleine's camisole, because I don't have any left, and then I came back and . . . She wasn't alone very long. Her needle weaves in and out of the sock in a square pattern, steady. It's not true, anyway, what you're saying, there were still other children playing outside. There's no harm in that.

She's aware that all these excuses make her sound weak but she can't stop herself. She pulls the yarn out too hard and breaks it.

Something's missing in here, Armand says, touching his temple with his forefinger.

Madeleine looks up from her knitting. She lets the yarn slide off her finger.

You're not quite there, do you know that? he says, and walks out of the room.

Madeleine digs the needle into the looped yarn and resumes her knitting.

Antoine has already taken care of the passage. But there's information to gather. How to travel all the way to Bordeaux, for instance? Clothes need to be sorted or bought for the trip. Toiletries, books. Everything will be put aside in an old suitcase of boiled leather she hides in the attic, behind a trunk full of clothes that had belonged to her grandmother.

She is not preparing for a voyage but accomplishing a series of gestures that her mind separates from their meaning. It's as though she has received an assignment, with a precise list of chores, and once she has completed one, she sets about doing another. One day, alone at school after class, she comes upon the forms from the Education Ministry that she had sent for and put aside. She reads them carefully, and, almost as a game, starts filling them out, line by line. When she gets to the line *Signature du mari*, she dips her pen in the inkpot of her desk, and, on a piece of white paper, practices Armand's signature which she knows by heart. A whole row of *Armand Texier* with the flourish curling under. By the tenth or fifteenth attempt, she manages a reasonably convincing copy. But when she tries her hand on the form, she fudges it, and the signature looks as though a child had tried to imitate it. The officials would see right through it. She rips the forms into little pieces and tosses them in a trash basket outside. If she had sent them off and correspondence from the Indochina Education Department were to arrive in Maillezais, Armand would be immediately suspicious. Anyway, it's too late now. And what would be the point of applying for a teaching position? It wouldn't make her departure more acceptable. There are other, more pressing matters to attend to in preparation for the trip. The question of her traveling clothes, for instance. She is teaching every day, including Saturday morning, and has few opportunities to leave Maillezais, except to go to Cholet to visit her family, or to market in Niort, but only rarely. They usually do their errands in Fontenay, which is much closer. Market day there is Saturday.

She asks Madame Perrineau, who teaches the older class, to substitute for her on Saturday. She tells Armand she needs to buy wool and linen thread at the haberdashery in Fontenay. At nine in the morning, with a group of women heading for the market, she boards the stagecoach waiting in front of the post office, its two old Percheron horses grazing the weeds along the gutter.

With money that Antoine has given her, she buys a suit of blue linen in the only clothing store of Fontenay, and a dress of ivory cotton, hosiery, a pair of lace-up boots, and toiletries, as if she was planning a trip to Paris rather than to the Far East. She also buys a *chabichou* cheese from Poitou and smoked ham at the market, and enough balls of wool at the haberdasher's to cover the new suit and shoes she hides at the bottom of her carpetbag. She acts in a kind of feverish calm. In the stagecoach going back to Maillezais, she looks at the women loaded with food from the market, baskets at their feet. Perhaps, after all, she will not leave. Perhaps, once the suitcase has been filled and the ocean passage secured, once she is confronted with the reality of her actions, she will realize it was all a fantasy and she will resume her normal life. Perhaps attics all over the countryside are full of suitcases all packed and ready but never used.

It was like standing at the edge of a ravine: on one side the familiar village of Maillezais, and on the other side, an exotic post-card world of junks and opium smokers and *pousse-pousses* wheeled under a crushing sun. On one side her husband of thirteen years—not a bad marriage, not a bad marriage at all, considering. Her life. Her two children. Her work at school. On the other side, a man who makes her dream, a man who embodies freedom and adventure, a man who opens the world to her.

They stone women like you.

In the little Gothic church of Maillezais Victorine kneels on a pew in the late afternoon. An old woman lighting candles in a side chapel, an old, dried-up *grenouille de bénitier*—a "stoup frog," as they call these women who spend their lives dipping their fingers in holy water—is throwing curious glances at her. It is dark and cold in the church. The light floating down from the stained-glass windows is dull. *Notre Pére qui êtes aux cieux* . . . No. Not that. *Je vous salue, Marie, pleine de grâce* . . . There is no prayer for what she has done or is about to do. *Jésus, aidez-moi* . . . But Jesus has condemned adultery. He would not look kindly at what she is about to do. Perhaps, later, she can be forgiven . . . If she repents . . . If she accepts the punishment . . .

There's no answer in the church, only a deep silence echoing with a feeling of quiet despair and desperate hope left behind by all the worshipers who have been praying on these pews for six or seven hundred years.

ONE SUMMER, when she was ten or twelve, she had gone with Jules, the other Jules, her cousin, to the big pond at Sainte-Christine's farm. They were alone, hot and stiff in their Sunday clothes, in the tall grass at the edge of the pond, and he had said, I dare you. Jump! Jump! Victorine, I bet you don't have the nerve to do it. Jules had stripped down to his underwear and dived in one easy splash. She'd removed her shoes and her stockings and her skirt, and had stood there, in petticoat and camisole, staring at the thick water of the pond, feeling its muddy surface with one toe. He stood up a dozen meters away, his arms coated with leaves like a *fadet*, one of those mischievous Vendée sprites that are said to live in the woods of the bocage. Are you coming or not, he had asked her. She took one step, and the sharp stones at the bottom of the pond bit into the soles of her feet. Another step. Her foot slipped into a slimy hole and she almost lost her balance. He was watching her from the middle of the pond, water up to his chest. Don't walk, he said, dive in like I did. But she'd backed off and run to the house leaving her shoes behind while he had cried after her.

Trouillarde! Trouillarde! Coward! Coward!

She hadn't dared tell him she didn't know how to swim.

She woke up in the opaque light coming through the window white with frost. Armand was up already, tending the fire downstairs. There was still a bit of warmth in the bed where his body had been. She wrapped herself in the quilts and folded her legs against her stomach. She had to get up in a few minutes and wake the children. In winter, they all left together early because it was warmer in the school. She could hear Merlin downstairs, banging on something with his tail. Armand had opened the door for him. When she went down Armand was wearing his boots. He'd already been out.

It froze last night, he said. The first frost of the year. It's early.

Yes, she said. I was thinking, we should keep Merlin in at night.

Armand nodded.

Jean Lucien says the winter will be very cold this year. We'll have to be careful with the vegetable garden.

Yes, she said. Before we go from Cholet, we should cover it with canvases. I'm worried about the strawberries.

He squatted to give Merlin a bowlful of last night's beef leftovers.

I've made some plans for this room we talked about building on this side, he said, pointing toward the wall he had punched a few weeks earlier. To make a proper dining room off the kitchen. I'd like to show them to you.

Yes, she said. Let's start working on it.

She will not leave. Their life will go on even if in her mind she will dream of another one. She is like those alders shading the canal, whose roots reach so deep only a hurricane could shake them out of the earth.

She cannot imagine not setting out every morning for school at Armand's side, tiptoeing in the dewy grass, so as not to get her boots wet. She cannot imagine being anywhere else but here, in this house. She cannot imagine not seeing the sun stretch across the floor in the morning, bounce off the copper pots, and glow red in the late afternoon. She cannot imagine not smelling the vegetable soup or her *mojettes* simmering in the fireplace in the evening. She cannot imagine not closing the shutters every night, folding their house tight against the windy Vendée night.

> *15 décembre 1898*
> *It is Daniel I'd be worried about. But he will have his father. A son needs his father. As for Madeleine . . . Sometimes I wonder if this child loves me. Maybe it's her age. All girls stand up to their mother. Or this is what I tell myself about her.*

And the next day:

> *16 décembre 1898*
> *Would they follow me, if I explained?*

She would gather them one afternoon, while Armand was out, in front of the fire, or outside by the canal. My children, she would say, I have something to tell you. And she would look into their eyes. Their eyes, innocent, bored maybe, impatient, waiting to be told about a new chore, or some plans for the following Sunday, or perhaps Daniel, more sensitive, would question, What is it, maman? What is wrong? Yes, they would think something was wrong, an illness to be revealed perhaps, or even, yes, a move to another village. And that's the way she would say it: we are moving. We are going to move. Where, Daniel would ask, to Gué de Velluire, or to Arçais? And she would say, No, farther. How farther? To Niort? Madeleine would ask. Stop it, Daniel would interrupt. Are you crazy, Niort? And she would say, My children, no, farther than Niort. Angers? Daniel would ask. They would make a game out of it. Poitiers? Paris? And she would shake her head. No, much, much farther. Farther than Paris? Yes, farther than Paris. And they would be speechless, she would really have their attention by now. But Madeleine would burst into tears. I don't want to leave. Why are we leaving? Daniel would look at her, inquisitive: Where then? And she would say, We are going to go to Indochina, *mes chéris.* Indochina, Daniel would repeat. Indochina! Have you or papa been assigned there? Did papa change his mind? And she would say . . .

No, she couldn't say it. It was impossible.

She could only leave alone. And she couldn't imagine any goodbyes, any confrontation, any transition. One story ended, another one started. Magic; sleight of hand. That would be the only way she could do it.

I'm frightened, she tells Antoine in the little woods behind the *lavoir* where they have agreed to meet to discuss the final travel arrangements, on another Thursday afternoon because it's easier for her to get away. He's off from work until his departure. I . . . don't know if I can go through with it.

He lights a cigarette and inhales deeply.

Let's walk, shall we? We can talk about it.

She is surprised by his calm.

Now that we are so close to leaving, he says, it's natural that you would have second thoughts.

They are walking briskly, to keep warm. It's a few days before Christmas and the ground is frozen, the trees skeletal, the sky low. Their breath hangs in the air. An orange vapor hovers toward the west. They hurry in the cold. They don't have much time until nightfall.

What do you want to do? he says. You still have two weeks to decide. Your passage is booked. His voice is neutral, the emotion held back.

I'd like to think about it, alone, for a while. We're going away to Cholet for Christmas in two days, anyway, but I'd like not to see you until it's time to leave, and make my final decision, by myself.

He smokes silently.

You don't want to do it. Isn't that what you're telling me?

I don't know, she says after a while.

They are walking side by side in silence, not touching. She's keeping her hands tucked in the sleeves of her coat, as in a muff.

I want to be with you, she adds. Don't doubt that, ever. But— it's such a huge leap, and my— She cannot find the words.

He says nothing, just smokes in little puffs. They are reaching the bouquets of elms, and beyond that, the mossy clearing is spiked with frost, crunching under their feet.

Bien, he says finally. If that's the way you want to do it. But— Victorine. I have to tell you one thing, and I hope you don't misunderstand why: I'm going anyway. I want you to know this. No matter what you decide. I will be on the *Tonkin* on the eighth. I will not change my mind. I'm leaving. Whether you're coming or not.

What do you mean?

Just what I said. I'm going to leave. I want to be with you too. But I'm going.

His voice is soft but determined. He takes her by the shoulders.

I love you, Victorine, he says. As much as I know how to love a woman. But I will leave, even if you don't. It's what I have to do.

She tries to read his eyes but she can't.

He lets her go and pulls harder on the cigarette. Well. That was rather melodramatic, I'm sorry. I don't mean to threaten you. It's just that—this is the moment for us. If it doesn't happen, life will go on, who knows in what direction. I don't know. We don't control life. You would be here and I would be there. He pauses for a moment. Indochina is far, very far away.

He flicks away his cigarette. As if to illustrate his words it lands at quite a distance, in a bush of heather.

I understand, she says, trying to keep her voice steady. But this is the way I want to do it. I will either be in Bordeaux, at the ship. Or I won't.

On the twenty-second of December, Victorine, Armand, and the children took a hansom cab to Fontenay, and from there the night stagecoach to Cholet. It was a long trip in those days, she remembers. But that's what they did. Every year, they arrived at the Jozelons' on Christmas Eve and stayed until a few days after the New Year.

They didn't celebrate Christmas as it's done now, with the sumptuous dinner of foie gras and oysters. It was midnight mass that mattered. They were all bundled up at the back of the church, Victor-Paul and Marie-Louise and Bertha and her husband and children, Victorine and Armand, Daniel and Madeleine, and Marie was there too, and Armand's parents this year. The big meal was on Christmas day, the pâtés and terrines and the goose and the chestnut purée. The crèche was laid out on a bed of hay on the dining-room dresser. They were all sitting around the long Cholet table and lunch rolled on in a blur until Marie, who was sitting across from her, asked, her eyes bearing on her, Are you feeling better, Victorine? And Armand said, What's wrong with you, are you sick? And she said, I'm fine, I was just a little tired for a while. It's the beginning of winter, Marie-Louise said, everyone feels that way. When the days get so short and gray. It'll pass with spring. I have an announcement to make, Bertha said. She rarely saw Bertha now, since she had moved to Niort, and of course she knew what she was going to say before her sister opened her mouth. We're expecting another child, Bertha said, and they all broke into congratulations and little squeals of delight. Victor-Paul opened a bottle of champagne and passed around the flutes. That'll be our sixth grandchild, he said, and when Angelina gets going . . . He was beaming. This was what their life was about, one generation after another, the family as a clan, huddling together. It felt safer that way. Daniel and Madeleine would get married and have their own children, and she and Armand would grow old together, and then retire and wait for the decline . . .

After dessert Victorine walks out into the cobblestone courtyard. It's dark already. And quiet. The gaslights are lit. She sits on one of the stone posts used to tie up the horses. She can hear them shuffle and rattle in the stable. She's shivering, but at least she can see the sky, which has a dull white glow, as though it is going to snow. There's a dampness in the air. Perhaps if she strained hard enough she could hear the backwash of the ocean.

Maman, *est-ce que tu es là?* Madeleine's voice asks from the door.

Oui, Victorine says.

Coffee is being served.

I'm coming.

But she doesn't move.

You will always be their mother, she tells herself.

You will send for them, she tells herself.

They are almost grown, she tells herself.

You may never have another opportunity, she tells herself.

It isn't you, in this marriage, in this house. You have a right to another chance at life, she tells herself.

They still have their father, she tells herself.

You will be back, she tells herself again.

January 6, two days before the *Tonkin* is to sail from Bordeaux, is a Saturday, and after class is over, Victorine cooks blood sausage with stewed apples and mashed potatoes for dinner, a favorite of Armand's. For dessert she makes floating islands—egg custard topped with meringue—which Madeleine adores, and prepares a platter of *tourtisseaux,* those puffed pillow-shaped pastries sprinkled with icing, everybody's favorite.

Hmmm, what's the occasion? Armand asks, his mouth full. You've never made them better.

Nothing, she says. No occasion. Her voice, she thinks, is that of a murderer.

She washes the dinner dishes, as ever, wipes the glasses till not a finger smudge is left, as ever, and checks each and every one of them in the soft gaslight. She even washes Merlin's bowl with extra care and fills it with fresh water and takes it to him by the fireplace. He laps it sloppily, as ever, but when she extends a hand to pet his back, he looks at her deeply with his watery, pale brown eyes, as though he isn't fooled by her affection, like the others.

In bed, during the night, she lies with her face buried against Armand's shoulder, against the warmth of his skin, the sharpness of his smell.

She waits until breakfast is over on Sunday morning, until she's gone with the children to the nine o'clock mass, until Armand leaves to go hunting, until Daniel hops on his bicycle to meet his friend Jacques on the church square, until it's time to send Madeleine to get a dozen eggs and a baguette in the village— thirteen to a dozen, remember to tell the grocer! After they have all left the house, she climbs to the attic and changes into her traveling clothes; quickly, carefully, she carries the suitcase down the stairs and leaves it for a moment at the door. She puts away the breakfast dishes. She wipes the table one last time. On the smooth, shiny surface of the waxed oak table, she doesn't leave a note. She lays a clean lace doily in the middle. She lifts up the curtain from the window. There's no one on the path. She walks out with the suitcase in her hand as though it was a basket to go to market. She walks across the lawn toward the canal, she walks along the towpath until it forks away from the village and branches out along another canal. Three or four miles she will walk, along one and then another towpath. There will be a bridge over the canal, and from there a back road. Nobody will see her. Another four and a half miles and she'll be at the stagecoach stop, in another village. There, a group of people will be waiting on the sidewalk. Nobody will know her. She will be the young woman wearing the pale blue suit under a long gray coat, and a pair of gray gloves, carrying a suitcase, going on a trip to Bordeaux.

They will never see her again.

In the stagecoach, Victorine keeps her suitcase at her feet. In her gloved hands she carries her journal, but doesn't open it. Next to her a large man wrapped in a heavy black overcoat is dozing off and his head keeps slipping onto her shoulder, forcing her to lean against the coach window. The whole day and night, as they pursue their journey, she tries not to think how many hours it will take them to realize that she is gone. Gradually, in the early morning, images of the house, of the waxed table and the sun reflected on the copper pots, dissolve, until she falls asleep and the big man wakes her up in Bordeaux.

In the late afternoon, the white façades of the city glow a delicate pink, but she only has eyes for the huge hull of the ship that rises so high it blots out the sunset.

MAURICE PARKS the Citroën outside Villa Petit Claude. Victorine's bungalow stands a couple of blocks from the ocean, a gingerbread cottage adorned with a latticework of lavender wood under the roof and a lavender gate. Its neighbor, Villa Marguerite, is almost identical, except that its latticework and gate are painted periwinkle blue. Sometimes a visitor makes a mistake and rings the bell for Marguerite instead of the one for Petit Claude, or vice versa.

It was nine years ago that Victorine first moved to the little bungalow. She'd retired from teaching; she had to be by the ocean, she'd explained to Maurice. The sea air was excellent for her health. Every afternoon she leaves her three rooms full of books and magazines and the stuffed birds her friend the taxidermist has given her and takes a walk on the beach with her knitting bag.

Now all that's left in the kitchen are a table and two chairs. In the parlor, on top of the old worn trunk sits a silvery seagull, looking strikingly lifelike.

This is what you want me to take to l'Aiguillon? Maurice asks, pointing to the trunk.

Yes, she says. Will it fit in the car?

He says if another man can help him, he thinks he can fit it in. The owner of Villa Marguerite next door might be able to. He's always home on Sundays.

She makes them a tray of tea and brings out a dish of those long sugar cookies called cat's tongues and they sit at the wooden kitchen table, across from each other, both leaning on their elbows, like an old couple. When they spend time like this, the two of them alone together the way they used to be, she almost forgets that Maurice is married and has a son himself.

The house feels empty, he says, looking around. It sounds different. He clicks on the china teacup with the edge of the spoon. Hear? It's the sound of emptiness.

Yes, she says.

What's in the trunk? he asks, pointing at it with his chin.

She puts her teacup down without answering.

The trunk, he says, louder, as though she is hard of hearing. I don't remember seeing it before. It has a weird smell.

It's an old trunk. Full of old clothes and books. She pauses. It comes from Indochina.

Indochina? Really? From Uncle René? Wasn't he on the Board of Education or something in Saigon?

No, she says, not from Uncle René.

Well . . . , he says, after a moment of silence. You must be getting tired. He gets up to clear the dishes.

She shakes her head.

No, I'm not tired.

Don't you feel the chill? It was so warm at lunch. I'll make a fire for you in the fireplace in the other house, he says. You'll be warm for the night. I'll pick up some logs from the shed.

I'll miss the beach, she says.

You'll come back. The bus will take you back.

No, she says. I won't. Not with the *Boches* around . . . They won't let us move freely anymore. You'll see. It won't get any easier.

She gets up and knocks the sugar bowl off the table. The sugar spills into her lap but Maurice catches the bowl before it crashes.

Oh, sorry, she says. I'm so awkward. She brushes the sugar powder from her lap. I'm sorry. I don't know what came over me.

You're tired and upset, he says. It's normal. Why don't you lie down while I pack the car?

No, thank you, *mon petit*. I'm going back to the beach. I'd like to take a last walk before the sun sets.

She buttons her cardigan over her dress and a little *paletot* over the cardigan. The cardigan is hand-knitted in a shade of lilac or puce, or just plain gray.

When she arrives at the beach she sits down at the foot of the dunes, protected from the wind, and turns the pages of the notebook.

> *12 décembre 1898*
> *Do I not have this sense of responsibility? Not at all?*

> *18 janvier 1899*
> *He is the only thing in my life that I can . . .*

> *2 avril 1899*
> *The heat, in this room, is so suffocating we spread wet towels on the mattress at night and lie on them. Sometimes I dream wide awake, as if I had a fever.*

> *10 septembre 1900*
> *I do not regret anything, now.*

She closes the notebook.

She remembers how the rickshaws, the *pousse-pousses*, hurt her back worse than a horse.

Qu'est-ce que c'est tape-cul, he said. *Tape-cul*. Hard on the ass. The words made them laugh. They were on their way to town.

The world, outside the rickshaw, was swarming. The colors were so vivid, the crowds so quick and thick and the sounds so loud she felt like a butterfly bursting out of a cocoon.

She remembers how ethereal the blossoming of the cherry and pear trees was in the gardens, that spring of 1898—when he had appeared on the beach—those pale, fragile bouquets fading at dusk against the translucent blue of the sky.

How light the canopy of green, when you glided along the canals in and out of the quivering light. The green thickening, darkening as the barge sank deeper into the maze.

How sultry the classroom, during the third trimester tests, the children fidgeting in the front rows, the older ones daydreaming by the open windows, a fly buzzing, the pens scratching on the papers in the dusty silence.

How long the nights, lying awake next to Armand in the dark.

PART TWO

The Tonkin

JANUARY 23, 1899. She sees him from a distance, a tiny silhouette walking toward her on the quay, in the cold shadow cast
by the huge, curved hull of the *Tonkin*. Victorine! His face glows
with anticipation. But she's stiff, frozen. So you came, he says. She
shivers, puts her suitcase down. He takes her in his arms. His lips
touch her cheek. She turns her face aside. He steps back, confused,
picks up her suitcase. Their trunks are in the pile of luggage waiting to be loaded onto the ship. They walk side by side in silence,
as though they were strangers barely acquainted. He guides her
up the gangplank, up to the second or third deck, through the
crowd massed by the railings, alone now in the narrow hallways,
portholes on one side and lacquered cabin doors on the other
side, interminable hallways down several sets of stairs, each step
lined with a brass band, the hallways getting dirtier as they get
farther down, huge cockroaches zigzagging off their path. He
takes her hand and squeezes it tight. They stop in front of cabin
number 304. The number is affixed in brass on the door in loopy
figures.

Inside, in the dark, humid cabin, a rat scurries past them and
disappears out the door. She screams and jumps back.

Antoine sets their bags on the floor.

They don't usually jump on the beds, he says with a grin. Anyway, you've got me. I'll protect you in case of an invasion! I hear

they're usually more respectful of the first- and second-class cabins, though. With a bit of luck, they might leave us alone.

She laughs a little.

And I was imagining a journey in luxurious splendor.

Oh, the dining rooms and parlors and drawing rooms, no doubt, will be splendid, but I'm afraid the second-class cabins are a bit plebeian, although palatial compared to third-class accommodations.

Indeed, once their eyes are accustomed to the dark, the cabin is hospitable, if tiny. Two bunk beds, a banquette upholstered in dark blue leather, and a small toilet dresser on the side with a clean basin and towels. He closes the door behind them, opens his arms, and presses her to him. But again, she turns her face to the side. She is cold, rigid. This is not a romance, this is life, she is terrified, she could still walk out of the cabin, down the long corridors, all the way to the quay. The ship is still at dockside. She could still turn around and go back home. He takes her gently by the wrist. Let's not, she says . . . Does she even say those words? If she doesn't, it's all the same. They hang in the air. At the very least she wishes she had her own cabin. How can she, just like that, go from one man's bed to another's?

She turns her back to him, to the portholes. From up here you can see the ocean lap and swirl way below as if you were standing in the tower of a very tall cathedral. Rainbows of oily water quiver across the surf. He wraps his arms around her from behind, around her shoulders, narrow like those of a young girl, and he buries his face into her neck.

Victorine, he says.

She breathes deeply and leans against him, and then, without turning around, slips her fingers through his.

Later, before going to dinner, he sat on the bed next to her and gave her a little jewelry case of gray velvet. She opened it, holding her breath. In it was a tourmaline set with brilliants and two gold bands. She looked at him.

I still have my wedding band, she said.

She tried to take it off but her finger had grown around it and she struggled with it.

Let me try, he said, and twisted it off very gently.

I haven't taken it off since my wedding day, she said.

Allow me. He got down on one knee and took her finger. Madame . . .

She smiled. He slipped the gold band he had given her on her finger, and then the tourmaline.

It fits, she said.

I wish we could do this in a proper ceremony, he said.

She stretched her hand into the light and moved it so that the stone glittered. Then she took the other gold band and put it on his finger.

Well, Monsieur Langelot, shall we have dinner then?

In the dining room there are oysters on a platter between them, candles in silver holders. Candles on every table, and a grand piano. The sea is so calm—not even a hint of roll—they could be in a grand hotel in Paris; at least that's how she imagines a palace in Paris. If we pitch, she says, the candles will topple and start a fire. I hear these big liners are very stable, he says. A conversation about little things. Try the oysters with a dash of lemon. Hmmm, she says, yes. Hmmm. And, oh my God, look at this, as the rack of lamb is being carried by. Spinach? he offers. Please. Are you scared? he cuts in suddenly. Yes, she says, and looks away. But he cups her hand with his and she raises her head.

Finally, he says.

What?

You're looking at me for the first time.

To be seen in public with him, a couple to the eyes of anyone who'd care to look. A couple with him, while she's married to another, has children with another. Has abandoned her children. How can she? A stranger, that's what he is. A perfect stranger.

Don't think, he says, squeezing her hand. Don't think about anything. We only have one life. There's only now. Right here. Nothing else is real.

Vivez, si m'en croyez, n'attendez à demain; Cueillez dès aujourd'hui les roses de la vie, she quotes.

He looks at her with surprise.

Ronsard, she says. That was his philosophy of life. Live, don't wait until tomorrow to pick the roses of life.

He has a little ironic smile.

Exactly.

She looks at his blue eyes that can turn cold or cloudy in an instant, at his blond hair now trimmed military short—he's had it cut in Bordeaux, just before boarding the ship—his strong shoulders, strong hands, a bit rough, the hands of a man who can fix the engine of a ship, who can steer a boat and drive an automobile, the hands of a man who doesn't sit still. He's wearing an elegant pearl gray suit, of a good cut, and the suit looks good on him, the jacket hangs well on his shoulders, which are wider than Armand's, his body bigger, taller, a man from the North.

I can see everything on your face, he says. All your feelings. When you worry, when you're joyful.

Oh? For instance, what am I feeling now?

You're afraid. You're not sure of what you're doing. But you're ready to make mistakes.

You see all that on my face? Or do you just have a good memory for what I've told you?

Whichever you want to believe.

And suddenly his smile breaks, his face glows like that of a boy, the mask falling, warmth and tenderness enveloping her. He pulls her to her feet.

Let's dance.

The tables are being cleared. They drift with the crowd emerging from the first-class dining room. The dresses sweeping the carpeted floor are the color of melon or absinthe or amethyst, the latest fashions from Paris. Victorine, with her elegant reputation in

Maillezais, feels provincial in her simple dress of lavender voile. They follow the smell of face powder, the flowery fragrances. Houbigant, Coty, a new Guerlain fragrance that she recognizes from Niort's newly opened big store, tuberose notes, jasmine, musk, oppoponax, floral bouquets, crisp Cologne waters! Already the orchestra picks its chords, stumbles into the first notes. The first couple begins to glide across the parquet floor.

They dance. She hadn't thought he would be a good dancer but he follows the tempo of the waltz with ease. He presses her body to his, much closer than waltzing requires, it's indecent, she can feel him. She doesn't blush. She is beyond blushing.

What? he asks.

Why do you ask?

There was a mischievous look in your eyes. Just now.

She smiles into his eyes. She has just been thinking of that expression, loosening the moorings. Well, she is doing just that herself. She has created a scandal? Well, so be it! The tempo of the waltz picks up. They twirl faster and faster. This is what she has been looking for all her life, that feeling of pure joy.

And then suddenly, her head turns. The mix of fragrances, the dancing, and the roll of the ship makes her nauseated.

Are you not feeling well? he says.

No, she says.

Let's go to the deck, he says. You look pale. Fresh air will do you good.

The night is cold. Gusts of wind slap her. The spray of sea water wets her sleeves. She shivers. He takes off his jacket and puts it on her shoulders.

She leans over the railing. She's sick. She's sick for a long time, waves and waves of nausea that keep coming even after her stomach is empty. He holds her by the waist, gently removing strands of hair from her face. He wipes her mouth, her eyes. He takes her back to the tiny cabin, sits down by her side on the bunk. She is mortified, ashamed to have shown herself at her most vulnerable, repulsive even. She bursts into tears. I'm sorry, she says, I'm so sorry. *Allons, allons,* he says, wiping her eyes again, holding her in his arms, there's nothing to be sorry about. She opens her eyes. A dim light is flickering from the gas burners. She hopes that the light is too dim for him to see how red her cheeks must be, how swollen her eyes. She hides her face in her hands. Where is the carefree spirit that inflamed her in the ballroom? She would like so much to stand up bravely and freshen up her face and go back with him to the dance floor, to that waltz they were dancing, to celebrate their happiness, their love, their new life. Instead, this . . .

I'm sorry, she whispers, I'm so sorry, I'm ruining our first evening. But she can't help herself, she sobs, she hiccups. I wanted to dance with you. I'm such a killjoy.

Killjoy, he repeats with a soft laugh. Hardly. Everybody gets sick the first time, especially on the dance floor. You were not the only one, I can assure you.

He smoothes her hair with his open hands. *Allons,* he repeats. He takes a little bottle of Ricqlès and puts a few drops of it on a fresh handkerchief, as she had done just six months ago that afternoon at Sainte-Christine when Madeleine was sick. The sharp scent of the mint alcohol soothes her stomach.

One more time, he says. She breathes the mint more deeply. His arms are warm around her. Don't worry about anything. I'll take care of you. What matters is that we are here, together. You will feel better tomorrow.

She leans her head against his shoulder. Like a blind woman she feels the softness of his arms, the curve of his shoulders. Her fingers trace the contour of his chin, the tendons on his neck.

Am I so different from him? he asks.

Yes.

I am not him, he whispers. I want to love you the best way I can. I will not betray you.

But, she thinks, I am the one who cannot be trusted, I am the betrayer. I am the one who broke the rules, who created a scandal. But she doesn't feel guilty, this time.

Her head rests in the crook of his arm. She presses his hand tight. He lays her down on the bed and slowly undresses her, un-laces her corset and removes her petticoat and camisole, unrolls her stockings, then covers her with the sheet and lies next to her.

For a long time she cannot sleep, even after he has pulled his arm from under her neck, and moved to the edge of the bed to give her as much space as he can. The porthole gradually turns opales-cent, a pure relief after the oppression of the night.

When he wakes up she's already corseted and freshened up, her hair done up in a bun, the flounces of her cream-colored guipure lace perfectly positioned on the armchair. The colors have come back to her cheeks.

Feeling better?

Yes.

So they will come down to the dining room as a proper couple for breakfast. *Monsieur et Madame Antoine Langelot.* Perhaps as Madame Langelot she can let herself be Antoine's wife.

So they will sit for five weeks, every morning for breakfast, every midday for lunch, every evening for dinner, so they will introduce themselves to strangers. *Monsieur et Madame Langelot.* And do you have children? they will be asked, and she will wince at the thought of Daniel and Madeleine, she will say, no, and he, no, not yet. And this "not yet" will fill her equally with panic and with a bittersweet longing. As if in another world, the world where *Monsieur et Madame Langelot* are husband and wife, they could start another family, they could have a future together. And perhaps her past can be erased just by stepping on the deck of an ocean liner.

The wood on the dance floor is waxed. Every night they mix with the other couples, mostly young, army husbands, customs officers, civil servants and their pretty wives getting tipsy with the wine and the fruit liqueur, exchanging pleasantries, teasing one another, the returning veterans exciting them with tales of exotic dangers.

On the ship, she is free, she has no past, the present can always be reinvented. Madame Langelot is a different person from the serious Madame Texier. She laughs, she is vivacious, carefree, she wears ivory petticoats and pale green camisoles under her lace dresses, she laughs a little too loud, her neck tilted back, she drinks champagne. She is thirty-three years old, she still feels like a young woman, as young as when she was dancing on Saint John's night by the hawthorn hedges. She's living her first honeymoon, the one she never had with Armand. She will finally "stand on the gulf's shores and breathe the scent of lemon trees."

The weather turns when they reach southern Portugal. The Strait of Gibraltar is a blur in the rain. Half of the passengers are sick in their cabins. It will rain through a good portion of the Mediterranean Sea, way past Sicily, until one morning they wake up and the sea is calm and it will remain like this all the way to Crete, sky of azure and sea of blue velvet, and they will all lounge on the decks in the afternoon, sipping Martel in the shade of the parasols. And then, as they head toward the coast of Egypt, a storm rises in the middle of the night and the *Tonkin* starts to pitch violently and she is sick again. For nearly a whole week she doesn't leave the cabin. He brings her tea and chicken broth from the kitchen. She should take some nourishment, otherwise she will lose her strength. You're never sick, she says. I was, he says, the first time. I got used to it. You will too. He holds her head. He cleans up after her. I give you so much work, she says. You must love me, she says. He smiles. He says, Think what you want.

She had read that in the early days of the South Asia trade, more than thirty thousand Frenchmen had perished at sea on the Compagnie des Indes ships.

Her voyage was not fatal but was nevertheless debilitating. She can still recall the days spent lying pale and exhausted in the sweltering cabin or bending over the toilet, and then everyone hovering, complexions the color of paste, as she was helped from bunk to chaise longue and back. The gritty black smoke discharged by the stacks was unbreathable if it blew aft toward the cabins, and caused her eyes to itch and water, so that she had to tie a little veil of white muslin around her head (Antoine had brought his motorist's glasses, which encased his temples and made him look dashing, but didn't work nearly as well). Soot covered every surface on deck with a thin, greasy film.

At least the journey didn't take one hundred days, as it did before the opening of the Suez Canal, when you had to circle Africa all the way around the Cape of Good Hope and all the way back up the Indian Ocean.

It took a little over a month. You'd start off at Bordeaux, make your way through the Strait of Gibraltar, cross the entire length of the Mediterranean from west to east, stop at Alexandria, and enter the Suez Canal at Port Said. Then everything would slow down to an excruciating crawl. There was only one lane. You had to wait for the ship traffic from the other end to pass until you could make your way down to the Red Sea. The sands stretched on either side as far as the horizon. The heat was bone dry. You had Africa on your right and the Sinai and Arabia on your left, and eventually you rounded the coast of Yemen into the Gulf of Aden. Then on through the Indian Ocean, around India, to the Strait of Malacca. You'd make a final call in Singapore and then it was a straight shot north through the South China Sea to Cape Saint-Jacques, your first sight of Indochina. But it was still not over. The ship still had to be towed up the Saigon River. The nights were so hot, they sometimes spent them out on the deck, on chaise longues, in a kind of stupefied languor.

There's Victorine, in a pastel-colored camisole and petticoat, lounging under a parasol, ankles crossed, reading Guy de Maupassant's *Bel-Ami* or Dumas *Père's Le Comte de Monte-Cristo*. On good, calm days when her stomach is steady, she leans over a map of Indochina, and with a pencil circles the names of the towns they've talked about or are likely to visit. And she reads the booklet distributed by the Compagnie des Messageries Maritimes for the benefit of the French settlers.

"You should sleep on iron beds with a mosquito net, a kapok or horse-hair mattress, covered with one sheet and one blanket. Flannel belts should be worn at the beginning to protect the stomach from the climate."

Wouldn't that make you even hotter? she asks Antoine.

Oh, this is all nonsense, he says. This is just meant to spread terror among the newcomers.

The section on the "hydrotherapy" rooms, newly installed in some houses in the colony and copied from the English bathrooms in use in India, is particularly fascinating to Victorine, who didn't have a proper bathroom in Maillezais, but only the ubiquitous porcelain basin and water pitcher.

"You should not take showers when you arrive in Indochina," she reads. "You should start with quick applications of wet sponges over the whole body, except the stomach. After a couple of weeks, the skin is ready to stand the shower, which should not exceed one minute."

They both laugh. Not to worry, Antoine says, chances are we won't have any shower anywhere!

He's leaning over the railing of the second-story deck in a light-colored suit. Later, after dinner, he will be playing whist in the first-class lounge or drinking on the lower deck with the sailors.

Why, she asks him late one night when the *Tonkin* is crawling down the Suez Canal, why do you prefer the lower deck to the lounges?

How do you know I went there?

I know, she says, I saw you go down there earlier.

I don't prefer it, he says. But sometimes, I get tired of the first- or second-class lounge. They can be so stuck-up. For a brief moment, his voice has taken on a clipped *accent pointu*, the Parisian intonation, mixed with a hint of nasal vulgarity, as if he was himself a sailor scorning the upper class. It makes her uneasy, even though she can tell he is only playing, perhaps out of provocation. Coming from a craftsman's family in Vendée, teaching elementary school, she's acutely aware of her social position, *bourgeoise* by virtue of her education, but only *petite-bourgeoise*, and only recently—for one or two generations—elevated above the ranks of the peasantry.

You sounded like a Parisian, she says. Just now.

He laughs. He's lying on the bed, still dressed, smelling of cigarettes and alcohol. Well . . . that may be because I lived in Paris.

She leans on her elbow, embarrassed that he might have found her naive and perhaps even prejudiced.

What was it like, living in Paris?

It was hard at first, because I grew up in Nantes until the age of twelve, when my mother died, and in Paris everything was different, the school, even at home with my aunt and uncle. We lived in the Thirteenth Arrondissement, near Montparnasse.

What happened to your father?

I—I never knew him, he says, turning his head away.

I'm sorry. I shouldn't have asked, perhaps?

He turns back and smiles.

No. It's no secret.

So when I first met you, you'd already been living in Paris for a while . . .

I'd go to Vendée in the summer, work on the mussel beds, then I'd return to Paris for the school year. You know, he adds, on the ship, it's not the same as in France. People here are thrown together in a small space. They mix more. At least I do. I used to do that in Paris too, go to local bars in the Thirteenth. I felt freer. He looks at her quizzically. Does it bother you?

No, she says. Of course not. But in truth, she isn't sure. The freedom he's talking about is exciting, and yet a little frightening. Everything is so different here, already, the rules more slippery.

At first she kept trying to calculate the time of day in France, as their own clocks had to be adjusted in their slow eastward progress, and imagining what they must be doing at any given moment. Having breakfast, walking up the stairs, Daniel suddenly bursting through the front door, a breeze lifting the lace curtain at the window. The house as it looked from the canal perched on its slope of grass. And then, after a while, the image blurred to a shimmering mirage rising from the endless present. Past Aden, three and a half weeks into the journey, in the middle of the Indian Ocean, closing in on Ceylon, the humidity made the yellow sky implacable, the horizon a cocoon of gauze.

In the dead heat of the afternoon, in the middle of the ocean, all boundaries collapsed, there was only desire, a vertigo in which they tumbled. The sheets twisted under and around them. Sweat coated their necks, the inside of their thighs, the underside of their arms, the small of their backs. She forgot everything, her children, the smells and noises of Maillezais. The memory of another life.

The cry *Terre! Terre!* suddenly rouses them in the laziness of a half-sleep.

There's a rush out of the cabins, uncorseted women, men holding up their unbuttoned pants without suspenders, crowding the decks. Another cry: *Cap Saint-Jacques!* The tricolor flag is fluttering above a little lighthouse, surrounded by a few fishermen's cabins scattered along the shore.

In the humid dawn, the *Tonkin* still has to push for several hours through the thick yellow waters of the Saigon River, meandering between the mangroves. Here and there a flat barge passes, reminding her of a Vendée *yole*. It's invariably a woman who stands at the back, her face entirely hidden under a conical hat, not holding a pole but two oars crossed in the shape of an *X*. Farther inland, fields of bright emerald green seem to float, half-submerged in water—rice paddies, Antoine tells her.

And then, at last, a dazzling white building emerges like another mirage, above the stench of marshes and refuse.

Hotel des Messageries Maritimes, Antoine says. Beautiful, no?

Leaning over the railing of the upper deck, Victorine sees only the crowd on the quay, the clamor swelling to a shrill pitch as they make their way down the gangplank. She's overwhelmed by the pungent smells: ripe pineapple, dried cuttlefish, the sharp scent of cilantro, others that she doesn't recognize.

But more overpowering even than the crowd, the competing smells, more overpowering than anything, is the heat, the all-enveloping, inescapable, damp heat. As in the basement of the Cholet house when the laundry was boiling, the steam causing the temples, the inside of the thighs to sweat, the hair to curl and to stick damply to the neck, the feet and the hands to swell.

After just a few steps Victorine's feet in their tight boots are squeezed as if caught in two vice grips. The sweat drips from her forehead, from her neck, in sticky rivulets.

You'll get used to it, Antoine promises, as soon as you take these shoes off your feet and you change your clothes. Look at these two, he says, pointing to a couple walking in front of them, the woman stumbling in her patent leather lace-up boots, the man's black wool suit turned a sinister shade of blackish green from the sun. The French come here, he says, expecting to lead the same life they lead on the mainland, same clothes, same schedule. It's a serious mistake. The tropics are unforgiving, he adds in a mock-serious voice, if you don't learn how to adapt.

Down on the quay, they stand among the big-wheeled carts she had seen on Angelina's postcards—*pousse-pousses*, as they say here. They are lined up abreast; the men who draw them call out *Monsieur! Madame!* with a soft, lilting accent. Some of them are so small and skinny it's hard to imagine how they can pull these carts which carry one or two passengers just by the strength of their arms and back. They smile broadly, uncovering dark or black teeth.

It's betel, Antoine says.

Betel?

Yes, it's a kind of nut they chew on. Makes their teeth all black. They dip a betel leaf in quicklime and chew on it. A tonic, suppos-edly, to combat the effects of the heat. An ancient custom.

Like that old woman? Victorine asks, pointing with her chin toward a woman sitting on the side in a group of women and children, the few teeth in her mouth entirely blackened.

Yes, exactly. But she only looks old. Bet she's all of twenty-five. Come, let's get a *pousse-pousse*.

Antoine is not at all tired, it seems, but energized, his face full of excitement, his eyes brighter, his posture different, his voice taking a similar lilting inflection.

Victorine keeps staring at the women, who, she realizes now, are busy picking apart the children's hair and regularly clicking their thumbs and forefingers, probably looking for lice, the way she remembers poor peasant women doing in the back streets of Cholet.

Antoine has arranged for a *coolie-xe* to take them to their hotel. The man is dressed with torn pieces of cloth barely hanging on his emaciated body, just as his *pousse-pousse* seems to be held together with iron pieces roughly riveted over the original wooden frame. Another man follows, pushing the big mound of their luggage in a local version of a wheelbarrow. The luggage reaches higher than the porter. Victorine feels for the men, struggling and sweating in that heat to carry them and their luggage.

In spite of the driver's astute maneuvering—he moves as fast as the devil on his bare feet, deftly jockeying with other drivers to keep ahead, his rags trailing behind him—the road is a quagmire of potholes and rocks which jolts them around mercilessly. And they constantly risk collision with the myriad vehicles that compete for the road, rattan hansoms, tilburys, horses, all weaving about in total contempt of any rules.

Qu'est-ce que c'est tape-cul! Antoine says. Pretty hard on the ass.

A heavy, black, horse-drawn carriage passes them, forcing their driver to pull up to the side of the road.

We could have taken a proper carriage like that, he says. But I thought you'd enjoy the local transportation. Was I wrong?

No, she says. She puts her head on his shoulder. At each pothole she laughs, she holds on tight to his hand, she loves it. Under the leather hood sheltering them from the sun, she feels like a decadent queen.

I've certainly been on smoother rides, he says.

Like the Panhard & Levassor in Cholet, for instance? she says with a teasing smile.

For instance. You won't believe it when you see the hotel, after this. I have been told it's the best hotel in the whole of Cochinchina. That can be considered a business expense, wouldn't you say? He grins. No doubt the linen manufacturers would be glad to contribute to our stay, if they knew.

The Hotel Continental feels like a palace after the roughness of the ride from the docks. Pale yellow stucco on the outside, it's an ocean liner of dark wood and shiny brass inside. Their bedroom seems gigantic after the ship's cabin, but it is stifling, the dark furniture, with its carved fleurs-de-lys, oppressive. The mosquito net enveloping the bed doesn't stir; there's no breeze whatsoever. Yet from the window opening on the inner courtyard rises an exquisite smell.

It's jasmine, Antoine says. It begins to open up in the late afternoon, and by evening it gives off a lovely, full fragrance, like a perfume. He removes his shoes and jacket and lies down on the bed, sighing deeply with relief and fatigue, while Victorine hangs her clothes in the armoire.

Let's enjoy the Continental while we're here, he says. We're not going to have the same luxury in Cholon, in the Chinese town, I'll tell you that.

I know, she says, carrying an armful of lingerie to the dresser. You told me. Cholon. Cholet. Did you notice? It's funny. Almost the same name.

Destiny! he says.

Don't tease me.

She fills up a drawer of the dresser with her undergarments.

Oh, this is wonderful, she says. Look at all the room we have. And it's beautiful furniture. She runs her hand over the carvings of the wood.

He kicks the mosquito net aside with his foot.

Come, he says, come and lie down with me. You can do that later.

But she continues to empty her luggage, lines up her shoes in the closet, coils her satin sashes, and finally arranges her precious toiletries—brushes with boar bristle, powder puff made of swansdown, a manicure set with ivory handles kept in a case of blue Moroccan leather—on top of the dresser, all as carefully placed, she suddenly realizes, as they were on her rosewood bureau in Maillezais.

Antoine, who has tossed his clothes on a chair without even opening his own trunk and thrown himself naked on the bed, laughs as she busies herself.

Don't unpack everything, we're only staying here a few days.

I know, but it makes me feel more at home.

A very temporary home. Don't get too used to it.

We're not traveling anymore. Our trip is over. There! She closes the last drawer, then crawls onto the bed next to him and leans against the pillows, surveying the room with admiration.

Oh, you naive girl, you should know that traveling is never over in Indochina. With both his hands he spreads her hair over the white pillow.

Beautiful, he says. So beautiful.

I don't want to travel. I want to settle down, with you.

You do?

Yes. She runs her hand over his chest, his arms, his shoulders. You too are beautiful. Your skin is as brown as when you were on the beach at La Tranche.

He starts to unbutton her camisole, slowly, taking his time with each tiny button.

So you no longer have the regrets you had on the ship?

Regrets? How did you know I had—

Your eyes. They would become . . . hazy. As though you were wearing a veil.

I *did* wear a veil. For all that smoke. I was the veiled woman of the *Tonkin*! Thrilled, again, to have dared to come with him all the way here.

He moves his hand over her face as if checking if the veil is still there or gone. She blinks a couple of times.

I want to settle down too, he says. But nobody ever settles down completely here. You'll see: you have to be quick on your feet.

She follows the line of his chin with her fingertips, where a fresh blond beard is growing, paler than his skin.

You'll have to show me how to live here, then.

I will, he says. I will show you. He loosens her corset, slowly unlacing it hook by hook. This is how we are going to start. He slides the corset straps one after the other off her shoulders. Isn't it better without it? Feel it: the air on your bare skin. It's lovely, isn't it?

How do you know what it feels like? Have you done that to women when you came here before?

Shhh, he says, tossing the corset over one of the posts of the brass bed, letting it hang by a strap. Don't talk. Just feel the air . . . the heat, now. On your skin. He covers her breasts with his hands.

Yes, she says. Letting herself go into his hands, loose and soft where the corset was tight and rigid. She takes a long breath. She feels like a plant opening deep and wide to the sun.

Yellow stucco and green shutters: the colors of Indochina. She wonders if the bright yellow ochre dreamed up by the French architects and engineers will one day be smoothed and eroded and peeled by humidity. But now it has the luminosity of burnished gold, the dark green of the shutters has the high gloss of fresh paint. The majestic French villas, set back from the streets, hide behind a profusion of bamboo and mango trees. The municipal theater glares in the sun, a pale yellow biscuit catercorner from the hotel. The brand-new post office, a few hundred meters up on rue Catinat, was built by Gustave Eiffel, Antoine tells her when they take a walk later. Look at the wrought-iron work, look at the way it curves in curlicues, look at the columns, how intricately they are carved.

Art nouveau, Victorine says. I read about it in *Le Figaro*. The new neighborhoods in Paris are being built in that style; even the market in Niort was being redone that way.

It's already late in the afternoon, almost evening, they've missed lunch a long time ago, but the heat is less suffocating. The cafés on rue Catinat spread their tables and chairs on the sidewalks; the *colons'* wives are strolling up and down the street in their pale linens, their dresses cut in the latest fashion, their feet shod in stylish lace-up boots, their parasols bobbing. The horse-drawn cabs jam the street as far as Victorine can see, dropping off and picking up elegant couples. The store windows are more lavish than anything she's seen in Niort or in Cholet: straw and silk hats, linen and leather boots, perfumes, lingerie, fine wine and liquor, absinthes, Italian mineral waters, cigarettes and cigars, expensive stationery, exquisite trimmings, American toiletries, artfully arranged in wide and brightly lit-up windows. She remembers reading, in the 1889 World Exhibition Catalogue that Angelina had showed her, that rue Catinat is the rue de Rivoli of Asia. But in contrast to the opulence of the main street, the smells from the harbor drift all the way up here, the smells that she will forever associate with Indochina: frangipani and jasmine, overripe mangoes, dried fish, and the everpresent stench of mangroves and rotting meat and vegetables.

Look, Antoine says, motioning to the passing women. No matter how Parisian and elegant they think they are, look at the bottom of their dresses. Ha! Victorine, look at your dress.

The delicate pastel dresses are spattered with mud, their hems dark, dragging in the gutter. The rim of her own brand-new ivory linen dress she's bought in Fontenay before leaving is soiled black.

My God, she laughs. But she doesn't even bother picking up her skirts as she would have done in Vendée.

When they get back to the hotel, next to the shiny glass and brass of the front door, a young man is lying on his side, propped against the hotel wall, his golden brown chest naked, his skin caked with sweat and dirt, his eyes closed.

She flinches and turns her face away, not laughing anymore.

September 8, 1940
5:00 p.m.

THREE MONTHS EARLIER——it was on one of those late June evenings that are especially long on the Atlantic Coast around Saint John's day, when the sun lingers on the horizon until after ten——she had taken a blanket with her and walked to the ocean because she couldn't sleep. It was a couple of days after the armistice had been signed, the day de Gaulle had made his speech from London calling for resistance. Over the low roofs of the village houses the sky was still fully lit, a tender apricot. When she arrived at the beach the tide was pulling away. The dories rolled sideways. At eleven a pink glow was still illuminating the west. The night sky hovered overhead, hesitant, a dark fog of a sky, taking its time. She waited until the darkness engulfed the day, and wrapped herself in the blanket. After a while the coolness and the humidity penetrated her to the bones. For her aging body the hard-packed sand was painfully uncomfortable, and she tossed for hours, watching the cold disk of the moon rise up in the inky sky. To feel warmer, she gathered her knees in her arms and rocked a little inside the blanket, like a child.

At daybreak, a fisherman found her curled up in the blanket, her back to the reeds, her gray hair knotted with sand. She woke up with a start and sat up, embarrassed, picking bits of grass off her jacket and her hair. She recognized him; he had helped carry firewood into her house last winter. He squatted next to her and touched her shoulder, concerned that she might be sick, or worse . . .

You shouldn't stay out like this, Madame, he said, helping her up.

It will be a long time until she can spend a night on the beach again. Now that Germany has won, Hitler will try to suck the whole of Europe into the war. Everything is uncertain. The *Boches* are patrolling the shore day and night. It seems as though the years of peace since the previous war have been but a glimpse of time. In '14, she had decided to be a war "godmother." She remembers the packages of food she would send to the front, the books she carefully picked for the recruits, the gloves and scarves she knitted for them, the cheery postcards she sent her "godsons" to keep their morale up. Now, at seventy-four, she doesn't think she'd have the energy to do it again for another generation of soldiers. She doesn't believe in war anymore. So many million men died on both sides. And for what? To start all over again twenty years later?

The newspaper clippings stashed in her notebook are from *Le Courrier de Saïgon* and *L'Indochine Française*. She carefully unfolds the brittle, yellowed paper for fear it might rip. Boxed advertisements recommend newly opened shops: "Boucherie Parisienne Régnier, Quai de Saigon, across from the market" and "Madame Lejeune, seamstress, is pleased to announce the opening of her dressmaking and mending workshop near the new market." Under the headlines "The Pearl of the French Empire," "The Most Beautiful Jewels of Our Colonial Crown," float long-forgotten sentences and phrases: "Here, it's the real savage, you can see real mandarins, real pirates, real pagodas, real lepers, in other words, everything that makes up Asian savagery." "Women wear light dresses or long, lace dressing-gowns, without belt or corset." "Bewitchment." "Enchantment." "Steamroom fatigue, sponginess, flabbiness of the flesh, deceitful tan, languor, laziness." "A mysterious and sweet intoxication."

Well, yes, that last at least was true. In Saigon the summer never ended. It was dry summer followed by wet summer. The monsoon downpours didn't even cool the air. But every night, you forgot about the fevers, the stupefying heat, every night when naked shoulders blossomed like hothouse flowers, the soul dissolved into the tropical air.

Cholon

MARCH 1899. The Chinese landlord pushes the wooden door
that opens right onto the street, and in contrast with the bright
light outside they find themselves in a large room bathed in a kind
of steamy twilight, which makes the whitewashed walls look bluish. There are no windows in the room, only louvered shutters
which, even closed, let in the noises and smells of the market. The
ceiling is supported by solid columns of black wood. A thin mattress is resting on a low platform, above which hangs a torn mosquito net; the only other furniture is a pair of bamboo armchairs, a
table, and a Chinese trunk carved with dragons. Wooden planks
have been unevenly nailed on the earth floor. The legs of the
bed and those of the chairs, Victorine notices, are resting in tin
containers.

Vinaigre, the landlord says in his halting French. For the bugs.
If there's no vinegar, absinthe is very good! He laughs at his own
joke, showing his toothless gums, then points a finger at a narrow
open-air well at the back, where, next to a huge heap of decompos-
ing refuse, a pipe spits out a trickle of water. Then he picks up a
broom lying in a corner of the room and makes a show of sweeping the floor.

If floor is clean, no rats, he says. He puts away the broom and
seems to vanish from the flat.

Victorine drops down into one of the armchairs, kicks her legs up in the air, and bursts into laughter.

What's so funny? Antoine says, loosening the collar of his shirt and unbuttoning his sleeves.

Well, this is a change from Maillezais. All I can say is that I won't have to cook a *petit salé* or a *blanquette de veau*. I didn't see any kitchen!

There must be a wood oven outside at the back, Antoine says. But forget about French cuisine! We won't be living like Daumier who soaks up the gravy of his coq au vin with baguettes freshly baked by his boy.

With flour shipped from Paris!

I promise next time we move it'll be more comfortable and we'll have a cook.

He is standing in the middle of the room, surrounded by their luggage, their trunks, and her little suitcase—all covered by the labels of the different ports of call they've stopped at during their journey. His skin is darkened, his hair lighter than ever, disheveled, his eyes red, bags of fatigue under them.

She gets up and puts her arms around him and he presses her to him hard.

I didn't come here for comfort.

Where am I dragging you? he says. I can't believe you did this. That you came. That you're here with me, in this—

It's fine. She peeps at the street through the slats of the shutters. A young woman is walking by, carrying a basket of what looks like live eels. From where she is Victorine can see them curling and uncurling their long, snakelike bodies. Then she turns back into the room. I like it here. It seems more real than Saigon.

Don't fool yourself. The Chinese are not an open people.

Yes, she says. Impenetrable and treacherous. Isn't that right?

He smiles.

After Antoine leaves for Saigon the next morning—a short ride in the brand-new steam tramway—she unpacks the photographs, postcards, and letters that Angelina had sent from Indochina and spreads them on the mattress. The photograph of Angelina and Jules with their boy squatting in front of them doesn't look as jarring now as it did when she first saw it. French families, it seems, love to have themselves photographed with their domestics—showing them off, as it were. There were similar photos hanging in the lobby of the Continental. And the postcards: the card with the words *Delta du Mékong* spelled in white over the gray waters of the river. The one with the Saigon cathedral looking like Notre-Dame in Paris—but in reality, as she found out, it's much smaller and pinker. The one with the two Annamite girls wearing dark turbans and shyly looking away from the camera lens. The one with the Annamite mandarin sporting alarmingly long, curling fingernails. All pinned by the photographer like exotic species of butterflies. Here they are, now, those characters, walking past her window. It's her turn now, she thinks, to look like an exotic specimen to them. Certainly that's what it felt like when the *malabar,* one of the big horse-drawn carriages they took on their way over, dropped them off in front of the Cholon apartment yesterday, and all the Chinese women peddling their wares in the street got up and surrounded them in a respectful circle.

You forget Vendée as soon as you set foot at Cap Saint-Jacques, Angelina had written in one of the letters.

After you've seen the sunset at Nha Trang, your life will never be the same. Saigon is a beautiful town, but too hot. We are beginning to get used to colonial life. This is Cholon, the Chinese market near Saigon.

The cards from Hanoi had a decidedly morose and plaintive tone.

The skies are gray under "le crachin du Tonkin"—that's what they call the Tonkin's constant drizzle. Hanoi is cold. It's depressing here. We have no social life. Funny, Victorine, here it's as narrow-minded as a small town in France. Smaller, narrower-minded even than Fontenay!

That was the last one she'd received before leaving.

Victorine unfolds the map of Indochina and with her finger traces a long curvy line from the Mekong Delta to Hanoi. Who knows, they may not be in Hanoi anymore, they may have moved farther north, to Haiphong, where a few infantry regiments are now based as well.

How strange, unbearable even, to know that her sister is so close to her, and yet not to be able to see her. She wonders if Angelina knows that she is gone. Of course she must. Their parents must have written to her. But she wouldn't know anything else. The temptation to write to her is so strong that for a moment she forgets that even if they are closer geographically, the distance between them is much greater than if she were still in Maillezais. And if she wrote to her, her secret would be ripped open.

She puts Angelina's cards and letters away and opens the shutters a notch to let in some air. Across from their flat a row of open stalls with cloth awnings shade the alley from the sun. Under them women are sitting cross-legged, children playing at their feet, surrounded by baskets of dried fish. Other women walk barefoot, carrying baskets of fruit the color of bright radishes, which hang from poles balanced on their shoulders. She spends the afternoon watching them, afraid to venture out alone, yet unable to tear herself away from the sights of the street.

And then, so fast! It's nightfall. The light tips into darkness, the brutal heat of the day melts into balmy warmth, and the sharp daytime voices fade to a low rustling. She is still standing at the shutters, dizzied by the smell of charcoal fire mixed with a sweet scent she imagines might be that of opium burning when Antoine opens the front door, his presence suddenly filling the room.

You didn't go out, he says.

No.

He's brought two glasses, and a bottle of Martel offered by

someone at Customs, and a bowl of *pho* from the market, a delicate broth perfumed with ginger and lemon grass in a china dish. They devour it. He pours some Martel into the glasses and they raise them together and click them, but she can tell from his face that the bottle of Martel is not meant to celebrate, but to console.

What happened?

He nods without answering, drinks, then pours more into his glass. Those idiots!

And again she hears that slight twinge of Parisian accent— common, her mother, who doesn't trust anyone from farther away than Niort or Nantes, would say.

What are you talking about?

He pulls a cigarette out of a brand-new pack and lights it.

Ah, Victorine, he says, blowing out the smoke. You won't believe this. There has been a reassignment of the budget . . .

What do you mean?

Well . . . the position I was hired for . . . it seems to have evaporated. For now, anyway.

What?

I know, I know. I can hardly believe it myself. He lifts the bottle. More?

She shakes her head.

There are problems at the department, he explains. Some mix-up. Apparently they sent me a letter in France. Never got it. Assuming that the letter was sent at all. To make a long story short, the position was given to someone else who was there already. At least for the time being. It's total confusion over there.

What are you going to do?

He crushes his cigarette and takes her hand.

I don't know. Nothing is sure yet. There might be other options. But out of Saigon. He looks at her. I'm sorry. This is not what we expected.

No, she says slowly. Things must be run differently here. I'm sure it will turn out fine, one way or another. Contretemps are inevitable, I suppose.

He shrugs. Yes, you're right.

Out of Saigon, you said? Where?

Sa-Dec, Vinh Long, maybe.

Where is that?

He looks at her, and smiles, his frustration suddenly vanished.

In the Mekong Delta. Didn't I see you pore over the map of Indochina on the ship? I know you can find it again.

She did study the map, she was looking at it earlier today, she reels off the names to prove it: *Can-Tho, Ha-Noï, Me-Kong, My-Tho, Nha-Trang, Phan-Thiet,* all those halting, syncopated, bisyllabic words. But Vinh Long, no, that one, she can't remember.

The next day, she stayed in again while he went back to the Customs Department trying to find out what was happening. She still dared not venture out of their stifling room. Even though Cholon was barely five kilometers from Saigon, it was quite separate, another world altogether; very few Europeans lived in the Chinese town. She lay down under the mosquito net, which bellowed around her like the ripped train of a wedding dress, leafing through the books Antoine had brought with him about Indochina. One was called *L'Opium* and another was a collection of love stories set in Asia, *Amours Nomades.* But after a while her eyes closed and she drifted in and out of sleep, overwhelmed by the heat. When Antoine came back, it was night already. She felt disoriented, she listened to him talking about the bureaucracy of the Customs administration as though in a dream, while he touched her casually, taking his time. They made love, and when she woke up, hours or a few minutes later, she couldn't tell, she saw him standing at the shutters, a tall, solid silhouette motionless except for the red ember of his cigarette trembling in the dark.

Those early days in Cholon, trying to adjust to the heat, the humidity, the food, blur in her mind. Even the local dialect, this quick mix of French and Annamite words and even some English spoken by Annamites and *colons* alike made her feel foreign, out of her depth. She repeated after Antoine: *con gaï, boy, coolie-xe, chetty, ca-gna, chan-doo, nia-coue, choum-choum, pho.* Words she didn't understand but didn't ask him to translate. They sounded like incantations.

Their first reception at the Gia-Long Palace—the home of the governor-general of Cochinchina—made her think of those balls at Versailles under Louis XIV she had read about in her history books. Dazzling clothes and sumptuous food, but there were the droppings of rodents in the staircases and the corridors smelled dank, a mixture of mildew and the scent of too many heavy perfumes thrown together. All the newcomers to the various administrative departments had been invited. She and Antoine had shopped together to choose a dress for her, at Courtinat's and at Boy-Landry's, the most elegant boutiques in the French Quarter. It was the first time she had gone out to Saigon since their first days at the Continental. They had taken a *malabar* again—much more comfortable, Antoine had said, than the tramway, which he usually took to go to town. But when their carriage had been passed by the steaming and whistling engine, Victorine had longed to go for a ride on the tramway. The *malabar* had dropped them off at Quay Napoleon, and they had walked up rue Catinat, going from store to store, attended by exquisitely polite young women who, she thought, must have been amused by the sheer complexity of the French women's outfits—all those sashes and collars and ribbons and laces and layers of camisoles and shawls—while they glided along in simple wide-legged pants! Of course they were used to it, but the spectacle of the dressing rooms overflowing with piles of chiffon and the cries of a customer trapped in rows of minuscule mother-of-pearl buttons, trying to extricate herself from three layers of petticoats, made her laugh at the ridiculousness of it all.

The dress she had bought was in pale peach satin, with a guipure bodice buttoned up to her neck, and a bustle from which fell a cascade of peach taffeta. It was the most beautiful dress she had ever worn, and certainly the most expensive—it cost three or four times more than she would have paid in Niort. But she would never have found a dress like that in Vendée, Antoine pointed out. This was the kind of dress she could only have bought in Paris, so she couldn't really compare the prices. When she walked up the sumptuous allées of the Gia-Long Palace on Antoine's arm, toward the imposing mansion of yellow ochre, she felt as though they were on their way to their wedding, her true wedding, not like when she had stood by Armand at the altar of the Gué de Velluire chapel, her corset laced so tight over her budding stomach she'd almost fainted.

My wife, Madame Victorine Langelot, Antoine introduces her, to his future or potential superior, to his future or potential colleagues at Customs, to the owner of a rubber plantation and his wife, whom he's met himself a few days earlier. He seems already at ease, navigating the hierarchy of Saigon's small world with the same assurance with which he moved among the first, second, and third decks on the *Tonkin*.

Bonjour Madame, they answer back. Polite, unquestioning.
And every time her hand is held or kissed, she stands awkward and shy, the lie digging a little deeper, covered over by her new identity, like a splinter burying itself into the skin.

She takes refuge on the second-floor gallery, away from the crowd massed in the ballrooms. Dance music trails from the gardens, where an orchestra is playing fast-paced mazurkas and polkas. She leans over the banister, recognizing from the Continental Hotel the sweet scent of jasmine, when someone touches her arm.

Sorry to have startled you, says a small, redheaded woman, smiling engagingly. Don't you recognize me?

Oh, Victorine says, confused. I think so—but I'm not sure from where. The truth is that she has no recollection of the woman at all.

I was on the *Tonkin* with you and your husband, the woman says. On a different deck, but I saw you in the dining room. She holds her hand out. Madame Camille Désaunier. My husband is a senior customs officer.

Victorine Langelot, Victorine says, her heart racing.

Camille could almost be beautiful with her golden hair and gray eyes, except for her nose, which is a little too long, and her tiny mouth. Her milky skin is moist. From her reddish blond hair piled on top of her head a few strands escape, curling with sweat on her temples. Everyone around them, on the galleries, in the wide-open reception rooms, leans with a kind of studied languor, waving a fan or wiping their brow or neck, or standing close to one of the boys whose only job, it seems, is to wave huge fans made of ostrich feathers.

We've been here for three years, Camille says. This trip was our second visit back home. And you?

My first time here, Victorine says.

Mon Dieu! How exciting! And your husband is—?

With Customs, Victorine answers.

Oh, like my husband! What a coincidence! My husband is vice-director at the Régie. And yours?

It's not settled yet. I think, comptroller, Victorine says, hesitantly, well aware that Antoine's position puts him at a much lower grade in the Customs hierarchy, and that Camille knows it too. But Camille has already skipped ahead.

So how do you like our little town?

Oh, it's beautiful . . .

You know, Camille interrupts her, everybody says that after a couple of years it gets so boring here, so suffocating, with the heat, and everybody knowing each other and what not, that you can't wait to go home and breathe the good homeland air! But you know what? She leans forward close to Victorine's ear as if about to tell her a secret. I'm glad to be back. Don't listen to what people say about Saigon. It sticks to you, this place. After the first year, you really start to belong. Then you're never the same again. It's very hard to go back. Her eyes flash intensely, and then she laughs, as if mocking herself. Well, that's what I think, anyway.

Victorine takes a sip of champagne. Her flute keeps being refilled. An array of exquisitely dressed Annamite servants in black silk pants and wide red sashes float around armed with trays of petits fours and champagne.

It's the heat. That's what everybody says.

The heat? Victorine repeats.

A lot of people complain about the climate. It makes them sick. The sun is dangerous. It's too hot for us Europeans. But did you notice how it makes you feel—like in a dream—if you let yourself go? If you don't fight it?

Victorine nods, thinking about what Antoine had said, even on her first day, almost the same expression: let yourself go to the heat.

Yes, she says. I know what you mean. I like it.

Camille finishes her flute and hands it to a boy who quickly replaces it.

Her voice drops a little and she comes so close to Victorine their naked shoulders touch.

Oh, *pardon*, Camille says with a little laugh, but her surprisingly cool skin brushes slightly against Victorine's arm, making her almost shiver, in spite of the heat.

Victorine laughs too, but doesn't pull away. The smell of Camille's vanilla fragrance wafts around her. They both lean their arms against the banister, watching the couples dancing below.

These people are amazing, Camille says, pointing to the orchestra, which is composed in equal number of French and Annamite musicians. They pick up our ways so fast, our food, our language, even our music! I think they are extremely clever.

They are silent for a moment. There's a question Victorine has meant to ask since Camille has told her she's been here for three years, but it's a dangerous question, and she thinks maybe it's wiser not to say anything. But after the second or the third flute of champagne—she's not counting anymore—she takes a chance.

Would you, by any chance . . . would you happen to know a Monsieur and Madame Moreau? Angelina and Jules Moreau?

There, she's said it. If Camille knows her sister, then she risks being found out.

But Camille's face remains blank. She bites her lower lip, as if to dig into her memory.

Angelina and Jules Moreau, she repeats. What do they do?

He is an officer. She's a schoolteacher. At least she was, in France. They are in Hanoi now, but they were in Saigon until last year.

No, I don't recall . . . Friends of yours?

Yes.

No, I don't recall them at all. Oh, look at that woman over there. Camille suddenly points to a beautiful, buxom blonde, dancing with abandon in the arms of a uniformed colonel.

What about her?

Camille's voice drops to a whisper.

She's a *dégrafée*. Camille glances sideways to see if anyone is listening to them.

A what?

Camille is speaking so low Victorine has to bend her head toward hers, and now both of their arms are touching from shoulders to wrists and she feels a little uncomfortable, but pleasantly so, because here it seems that the distance between people collapses, everyone closer, hands on waists, hands in hands, hands around shoulders, men and women, and women between themselves.

You don't know what a *dégrafée* is? It's a woman who . . . you know . . . She points to her own chest. Unhooked. She laughs. Loose. No corset.

Oh!

Madame Berger, for instance. Camille points to a voluptuous brunette at the other end of the gallery. Madame Berger . . .
Is she "unhooked"?

No! Camille bursts into laughter. She is the wife of Berger, the head of Customs! But . . . She leans very close to Victorine again. She has a lover . . .

Victorine unfolds the fan she's brought with her, a small fan of rice paper decorated with cherry blossoms, and cools herself.

A lover.

Women like you.

Shameless women.

Loose women. Unhooked.

. . . with her boy, Camille continues then pauses dramatically, observing Victorine's reaction, and herself too. Hot, isn't it? She sighs. It's what they call the yellow evil. The flesh turns soft as a sponge . . . and the senses . . . Did you ever wonder why they say Indochina is so—bewitching? She pronounces the word with obvious delight, her eyes opening up like saucers.

No.

Camille darts a few more glances around her.

Well, think about it. She folds her fan back into her hand and points outside, toward the street, beyond the gardens. The outdoor cafés on the upper part of the rue Catinat are where you want to be seen before dinner, she continues cheerily, abruptly switching the conversation. Or else on the promenade, with your carriage. Let's go for a carriage ride, on the promenade, you and me, one evening.

Victorine doesn't tell her they don't have a carriage, that they are not even staying in town, but in a small room in the Chinese town.

Louis! Camille calls out to a man with ruddy cheeks and an imposing curling, black mustache, who suddenly appears on the gallery. Let me introduce you to Madame Langelot.

Enchanté. Louis Désaunier kisses Victorine's hand and bows. He smells of violet water and wears a gold ring on the small finger of his right hand. You look familiar, Madame. Have we met?

Victorine was on the *Tonkin* with us, Camille says.

Oh? Her husband looks at Victorine with renewed attention. That's not what I was thinking . . . No . . . Perhaps . . . Where are you from? If I may ask . . . His black eyes stare at Victorine so intently she lowers her eyes.

Cholet, she says, trying to stay calm, wondering if she should have lied, invented a whole other past in France.

Really! Louis Désaunier says. My mother's from Cholet. I wonder if I've seen you there. You have no idea how many people from Vendée we have here in Saigon. Sooner or later you're bound to run into someone you know from the mainland.

Victorine smiles politely.

Madame. It was very nice meeting you. *Chérie,* he says to Camille, I have to meet with the governor's assistant. Louis Désaunier takes Victorine's hand, kisses it again, and departs.

Your husband might be working in my husband's department, Camille says.

You mean, Victorine thinks, under your husband's orders. But she is relieved by the change of topic.

Do you have any children? Camille asks.

No.

Camille pats her stomach. I'm expecting a baby.

Oh. That's wonderful. Congratulations. Your first?

Just at that moment, Antoine rescues her, kisses Camille's hand, and steers Victorine away.

Who is she?

The wife of Désaunier. Louis Désaunier. He's vice-director of the Régie. Perhaps your superior, if—

The Opium Régie?

I suppose so.

He bristles. He wouldn't be my superior. The position I've been offered is in the department of imported merchandise, not at the Régie. Anyway, everything's still up in the air. What's wrong?

Nothing.

No, he says. It's "something." He puts his arm around her shoulder and pulls her to him. Tell me what it is.

Madame Victorine Langelot, she says, imitating a Parisian accent. That's what. It's not just that I am afraid to be found out. It's—I don't know.

There's a flash of pain in his face and she immediately regrets what she has just said. But his expression regains its calm so fast she wonders if maybe she imagined it, and his eyes stay on her pensively.

You could be.

What?

Madame Victorine Langelot.

Yes, I could be. She looks challengingly back at him. But I am not.

He nods.

I am not even sure about *Madame Victorine Texier.* She pronounces the name as though it was utterly foreign to her, even vaguely distasteful. Maybe I should introduce myself as *Victorine Jozelon.*

Maybe you should. We don't have to play by the rules. We decided to do it this way, but you can still change your mind. Do you know how many people have a double life here? We wouldn't be the first unlawful couple, as I understand. Does it matter to you what they think anyway?

She is silent for a moment. In Vendée, it would have mattered. But here . . . She looks at him. I don't know, she says. *Mademoiselle Victorine Jozelon,* she repeats, her tone becoming lighter, more playful. That would feel more like me. Yes, that is what I shall do. How about you? Would it matter to you what people think? Would it jeopardize your work at Customs? Or your business?

The familiar sardonic smile is playing at the corner of his lips.

Are you done, Mademoiselle?

She resists smiling back at him, picks up her taffeta train, and shifts her bustle in a little petulant, side-to-side sway of her hips.

I'm done.

Let's go then, he says, pulling her by the hand. And no, it wouldn't matter to me in the least. I couldn't care less what they think.

They walk down the grand staircase without bidding farewell to anyone. And during the time it takes them to reach the gate, Victorine feels a love for Antoine so intense, a gratitude so profound, that, as she steps with him over the fallen frangipani blossoms in the allées of the Gia-Long Palace, she doesn't care, she doesn't care at all at this moment about the life she has left in Vendée, and her children, and what anybody might think of her. The past is a locked door behind her.

The Customs Department is confused. The position which had been promised to Antoine was a desk job in Saigon monitoring tariffs on imported merchandise. That position has been temporarily filled by someone else, and they are reluctant to let go of the other man, who has a family of three to feed. There might be another position. It's all uncertain. More letters are exchanged, meetings arranged. It's maddening. But at least for now, the department agrees to pay Antoine's salary while his situation is being resolved.

Let me take you downtown, to the riverfront, and show you the neighborhood around the Customs Department, Antoine tells her, a few days after the reception at the Gia-Long Palace. Let's take advantage of this free time I have on my hands.

The Customs House—Cochinchina division is an imposing and elegant two-story building erected along the Saigon River, a dozen meters or so from the arroyo, or waterway, that links Saigon to Cholon.

I want to show you something, he says, looking up to the arcades of the second-floor veranda. See those flowers up there? He's pointing to the keystones of the stone arcades, each delicately carved with a flower.

Yes, very pretty.

Aren't they? Well, they are poppy flowers. The poppy is what is used to make opium.

The same poppies that grow in the fields behind the woods in Maillezais?

Same family. But those are a little different. You couldn't make opium with the French poppies. Something about the climate and the soil here.

And what's this? she asks, pointing to a tall, foreboding building whose entrance is guarded by a man wearing a blue uniform embroidered with the letters R and O.

That's the *bouillerie*, Antoine says, and she detects the pride in his voice, which makes her uneasy. *R* and *O* means Régie de l'Opium. This is where the raw opium is cooked into a paste that can be smoked. *Chan-doo,* they call it.

A hansom cab pulls up at the entrance. The officer inspects it and checks the papers of the driver and of a Chinese passenger.

It's a bit like a dungeon, isn't it?

Yes. I don't like it here. Let's go down to the riverfront, Victorine says.

I talked to one of the best Chinese tailors, Antoine continues, as they turn onto the Quay Napoleon. He's got a shop right here, actually. He shows her a sprawling warehouse that extends all the way to the river. If I give him a good price, he'd be interested in buying one or two hundred meters of white linen for suits; he's heard the Cholet linen is of such high quality.

She looks at him, surprised.

But the shipment won't get here until the end of the year.

I know, but why not start meeting other merchants and retailers now, while I have the time? Find out what can sell here? I might change my order in Cholet with the weavers. I've been told that I should have more bolts of white cloth shipped, fewer tablecloths and handkerchiefs.

After dropping Antoine off at Customs, where he has an appointment, Victorine walks back to the riverfront to watch the the crowds gather for the arrival of the *D'Artagnan*—the name of the ship is spelled in gold letters on the hull—on the run-down quay of the Messageries Maritimes. It is here that the two worlds, the Asian and the French, collide in a furious mix: the negotiations for the rides in *pousse-pousses* or carriages, the savvy ballet of the Annamites seeking customers, the upper-class French, dressed in white linen, the ones who take long afternoon naps and go to balls in the evening; and the others, the *petits blancs,* the small whites, who still cling to their austere and dark Sunday best and their cautious French habits. She figures that in the Saigon hierarchy Antoine and she would fit in the lower third, just below the middle. But nothing is that simple here. Antoine seems to be as comfortable drinking *choum-choum* with the sailors in a Chinese tavern on the docks as he is in one of the rue Catinat cafés. As for Victorine—a European woman alone—she attracts stares and cat-calls from the French sailors, already tipsy and loud in the after-noon. But she ignores them and loses herself in the anonymity of the harbor, thrilled by a feeling of freedom and lightness she never experienced in Vendée.

When she meets Antoine again, later, after his meeting, he takes her for an apéritif at the terrace of the Café de la Rotonde. That's where they go, the rich *colons;* sometimes accompanied by their wives, they drink Martel and absinthe at the sidewalk tables as they would in Paris. In the evening the weather becomes bearable—not just bearable, but sublime. Forget about smoking *chan-doo,* Antoine jokes, all I've got to do is sit at the terrace of the Select with you, in the evening, in front of a glass of absinthe.

She laughs, she feels her body melt, bones, flesh, senses run liq-uid gold. I am happy, she tells Antoine. I have never been so happy in my life. And he weaves his fingers through hers. Yes, he says, just to be here with you. That's what I wanted.

After that first day walking alone in Saigon, overcoming her shy-ness and initial fear, Victorine feels ready to explore Cholon by herself. The rank-smelling market is crowded, a maze of narrow, dark alleys in which she keeps losing her way. The Chinese and Annamite vendors all stare at her. At least she thinks they stare at her, but when she looks back their gaze is always turned away. She trips over baskets of mangoes, over buckets of eels. Her slen-der boots of glazed lambskin in buttery yellow soak up the mud that spills around the fish buckets, she slips in the gutter overflow-ing with goose blood, the bottom of her skirt is soiled black. *Madame! Madame!* the women cry after her, offering her little Chinese buns, pointing to heaps of dried, flat cuttlefish pungent with brine. *Madame! Madame!* She feels awkward, towering over them in her pale linens, her lace, her fluted cambric, with her umbrella the color of eggshells, even her strides are longer, more imperious. The Annamites move with tiny steps, so slim, narrow hips, thin wrists, all of them, it seems to her, men, women, children, their faces so delicately sculpted, their grace so exquisite, their language syncopated in breathless, halting monosyllables. Bird songs to her ears.

She asks Antoine to bring her an Annamite-French dictionary from Saigon, and, within a month, word by word, she learns the name of each fruit, each vegetable, each spice, each fish, each flower she buys in the market. She carries her notebook with her, the one she has started in Maillezais, and, instead of diary entries, she lists the new words she's learned, careful in copying the straight or curly tonal accents which dot the letters like grains of rice.

The gold-and-red façade of the Buddhist pagoda is tucked away between two Chinese merchants' houses at the end of an alley. A blue dragon with a fiery tongue stands guard at the gate, flanked by two frangipani trees in bloom. The smell is so enticing, the shade so refreshing that Victorine cannot resist walking in. The courtyard is quiet, and nobody stops her when she walks up the few steps leading into the temple. Deep into the shadows of the first room, a grinning Buddha with gold feet is sitting cross-legged on an altar surrounded by burning sticks of sandalwood and platters of shelled litchis, their pale flesh gleaming like pearls. Through a little door on the side she sees an old monk hunched over a wooden table, painting Chinese characters on red silk sashes. She observes him for a moment, not daring to walk away, afraid that the sound of her steps might reveal her presence. The monk's face is the color of one of the copper pots hanging over the fireplace in Maillezais. But she is mostly staring at his fingernails: they are the longest she has ever seen on a human being, at least twenty centimeters long, dark as if made of wood and curling and twisting like the tentacles of a strange beast. Suddenly he lifts his head. Too late to step back. He stands up and greets her with a deep bow.

Unsure how to respond, she bows back. He invites her to come in and sit down and shows her the banner he was working on.

Do you know anything about our language? he asks her in French.

She shakes her head, too intimidated to say a word.

He explains to her in soft, perfect French that he is painting Chinese characters, as they were used in the past, but are now rarely used by Annamites. Through the centuries, these characters, he says, have evolved until a script called *chu nom* was created. And then a French missionary by the name of Alexandre de Rhodes decided to transcribe that script into the Latin alphabet, in order to help the French missionaries learn the Vietnamese language more easily.

She listens, as repulsed by his fingernails as she is fascinated by what he is telling her. He notices her staring at his hands, and she blushes.

Well, he adds after a pause, *we* call our language Vietnamese, because we used to call our country Vietnam—at least . . . well, until the *Phap*, the French, came. But you call it Annamite. So you and I will call it Annamite. He smiles. And his eyes light up like those of a boy, mischievous in his old face. For you, this is *Indochine:* Cochinchina, in the south, here, in the delta, Annam in the center, and Tonkin in the north. Not for us. The smile hovers on his lips as he says those things, as though they were sharing a subtle joke. Here, would you like me to teach you something of our country? Listen.

She watches him silently.

Viet Nam, he says, accentuating both syllables after a short breath. Repeat.

And she does, two breathless, short syllables.

Good, he laughs. You have a good accent. Viet Nam. Means "Southern Viet." Now, repeat: An Nam.

She says it.

That means "Pacified South." He laughs again as if that was

another good joke, flashing a mouthful of shaky teeth. Pacified by the *Phap*! Maybe that's why you chose that name for our culture.

She doesn't laugh with him. She feels embarrassed again. She is a *Phap* herself, after all. But he doesn't seem to mind that she is.

Ah, he says, what was I saying? I was talking about that French scholar who taught us how to write like the Romans. He laughs again, heartily. And she smiles this time, sharing his sense of humor. Well, that was two hundred years of your calendar ago. It was a very complicated task. Let me show you. He writes a few words in the Latin alphabet and shows her the accents on top of some letters and under others that she is already familiar with. He pronounces each syllable slowly to illustrate the subtle, musical tones.

This script is called *quoc ngu,* he says. It's the one we all use here now. Only scholars and mandarins and the more educated Annamites still know how to write in the ancient manner with the Chinese characters. He looks at her for a moment, his eyes thoughtful, as though he was pondering his question. Would you like me to teach you how to write some characters?

He waits for her to answer, his thin fingers, prolonged by the alarmingly long and blackened curly nails, holding a brush sharpened to a very fine point.

Yes, she says. Teach me.

He traces the lines of a character with a speed and an astonishing sureness of wrist that makes her think of her father's swift and precise paintings of coats of arms.

Chiang, he says, pointing to the character with his curling nail.
Chiang, she repeats.
My name, he says. *Chiang.* Your name?
Victorine, she says, and he approximates her name in Chinese characters.

維克特琳

He gives her a scroll of rice paper and a brush, and carefully positions her fingers along the brush, as if it was a flute she was holding. *Vi-Ke-Te-Lin*, he says, pointing to each character. *Vi* stands for "unite," *Ke* means "to overcome," *Te* means "special," or secret," and *Lin* is "a fine piece of jade." This is you, in Chinese. "Beautiful piece of jade." She blushes. She painstakingly copies each character he has drawn, over and over. Each time, he corrects the angle of the brush. His name, *Chiang,* and then her name.

That afternoon she buys rice paper and a set of brushes with bamboo handles in a stall at the market not far from their flat. And from that day forward, every day, behind the half-opened shutters, she practices her strokes, the twist of her wrist, the heavy and light pressure, the speed. She repeats each character out loud, correcting herself, starting again, until she achieves an awkward but legible rendition of Chiang's characters.

You're really a schoolteacher at heart, Antoine says. She lifts her head. She was so absorbed in her task she hasn't heard him come in. He's watching her from the doorstep, smiling.

More like a very slow student, she laughs, carefully laying her brush away from the paper to avoid smudging it.

He moves closer and looks at the lines of characters she has drawn.

Beautiful. Not that I can tell, really. But they look—awfully authentic.

Chiang says I'm making good progress.

I'm impressed.

She gives him a look, not sure whether he is serious.

Very few Europeans can learn Oriental languages, let alone master them, he goes on. And let's face it, all you need to know is *pousse-pousse, tam-biet, chao, cam on, bao-nhieu, choum-choum . . .*

Choum-choum is what *you* need to know, she says, her face expressionless.

He laughs.

Everybody knows within two days of landing in the colony that *choum-choum* is the word for rice alcohol, although most *colons* only touch the local liquor when they're flat broke. Absinthe, Martel, vermouth, rum, though a hundred times the price, is what they favor.

I am going to learn to talk to the merchants in the market, Victorine says, getting up. I know a lot already.

Good for you. But the merchants are Chinese. If you can talk with them, that means your Chinese monk must be teaching you Chinese words, not Annamite words. It won't get you anywhere in Saigon.

She turns around at the door to face him.

Then I will learn Annamite too. I have plenty of time, don't I?

In the temple, Chiang waits for her. He bows in front of her, his hands folded into his wide sleeves. His expression is that of deference. He's rarely seen a *Phap* woman venture alone that far in the market, he's told her, and never past the first hall of the pagoda. The rice paper and the brushes are laid out for her. But this time, he has a little bound book next to him, written in *quoc ngu*, that he pushes toward her. She looks at him questioningly and he opens the book.

This, he says, is the most beautiful poem in Vietnamese literature. He pauses and looks at her. His eyes flash for a brief moment. The sly boyishness reappears in his face. Not Annamite. Vietnamese.

She nods.

It's a long poem, called *The Tale of Kiều*. A Vietnamese poet wrote it one hundred years ago. Nguyên Du. Have you heard of him?

No, Victorine says.

He runs his hands with the extraordinary nails over his balding skull and remains silent for a moment. The smell of sandalwood incense drifts to the little room. He leans toward her, his dark eyes shining.

I will tell you, then. His voice takes on a dramatic tone. It's the story of a beautiful young woman, Kiều, who became separated from her lover, Kim Trọng, by cruel circumstances. After years of suffering and humiliation, she became a prostitute. Many other things happened to her, she became the wife of another man, then she became so desperate she tried to drown herself in the river, but she was always thinking of Kim Trọng. And then, one day, finally, she was reunited with him. But . . . something happened when they saw each other again. You see, she had been with other men, she didn't feel she could be his lover anymore. Only his friend. Chiang pauses and looks at her thoughtfully for a moment, letting that notion sink in. She feels herself blushing. Satisfied with her reaction, he opens the book seemingly at random. Perhaps, he continues, after so many years, it was too late. The moment of their love had passed . . .

He looks up at her again. His face is intent.

Love, they say, is fleeting. Victorine looks away. Listen, he says. This is when she is prisoner in a brothel.

He reads, following the lines with a long fingernail:

Trước lầu Ngưng Bích khóa xuân,
   vẻ non xa tấm trăng gần ở chung
Bốn bể bát-ngát xa trông,
   cát vàng cồn nọ bụi hồng dặm kia.
Bẽ-bàng mây sớm đèn khuya,
   nửa tình nửa cảnh như chia tấm lòng.

This is what it means:

Locked in her spring at crystal tower, she lived
with friends—some hills far off, the moon nearby.

On all four sides her ranging eyes could see
the gold of the dunes, the ochre dust of trails.
With shame she watched dawn clouds, the midnight lamp—
the scene and what she felt both filled her soul.

I will teach you those lines, he says. If you'd like.

Sometime in April—it is still the dry season, she remembers—they start to spend evenings at the Café de la Rotonde with Camille and Louis Désaunier. Louis and Antoine have become acquainted at Customs and gone out on their own a few times. Now the two couples are meeting together for the first time. Victorine thinks it's a little strange, because Louis and Camille belong to a higher class, but that, perhaps, is Saigon, and Louis, she knows, has been helpful with Antoine. That evening, in her memory, is bathed in the yellow light of the gas lamps that illuminate the streets, and the passionate accents of a chanteuse from Paris accompanied by an accordion and a piano. Antoine holds her hand and leans toward her to kiss her.

You two look so happy, Camille says. You're still acting like newlyweds!

Antoine squeezes Victorine's hand.

We are, he says. We got married just before coming over.

She leans her head on his shoulder, like a newlywed bride. The secret inside of her lies dormant, doesn't even stir, the splinter buried so deep now that she doesn't feel it anymore. At this moment everything seems possible, their life in Indochina feels solid, happiness sweeps over her in warm waves.

I have news, Antoine suddenly says.

Victorine looks at him, surprised, while Louis signals to the waiter to bring them a carafe of absinthe.

You've been appointed? she asks.

Antoine nods and glances at Louis. Yes, I have been given a position, but—he looks at Victorine—it's not what we expected.

What, then? Victorine asks.

The Opium Office. He glances at her again, almost challengingly this time.

When did you find out?

This afternoon. It's only a six-month contract. But it's something.

Your husband, Louis says, taking the carafe from the waiter's hand and filling the glasses himself, two fingers' worth in each glass, and a splash of water. Your husband, he repeats, has agreed to help us, very generously, I will add, at the Régie.

Victorine turns toward Antoine, her eyes questioning.

A little smile floats on Antoine's lips, as though he was savoring a good mystery.

Apparently the Chinese gangs have started smuggling opium again, he says. And it's costing the colony a pretty penny. Did you realize, Victorine, that a third of the colony's budget comes from the opium tax?

Victorine doesn't answer. She sips her absinthe. The taste is so strong she has to catch her breath.

You need to water it down, Louis says, if it's too strong. Anyway, it's true we couldn't run the show without the opium tax.

Victorine looks at both of them, waiting to hear more.

Did they offer you a pipe to smoke when you went to the *bouillerie*? Camille asks.

We didn't go, Victorine says.

You should take her for a visit, Louis says, turning toward Antoine. Now that you are going to be working for us. You'd be impressed, Victorine.

When we first went it made me ill, Camille says. None of those delicious dreams they talk about. I got sick worse than on the *Tonkin*! She laughs. Louis had to carry me out and put me on a *pousse-pousse*. Remember, Louis?

Louis nods. Victorine remains silent.

Victorine thinks opium smoking should be made illegal, Antoine says.

Actually, smoking opium *is* illegal, Victorine says. Officially.

Louis gestures to the waiter for another carafe of water.

Well, for the Europeans, technically. Not for the Annamites.

But what about Daumier, and Fouron? You told me they go to smoke houses.

Antoine shrugs.

Between the law and the reality . . . He looks at Louis and laughs.

Have you been? Victorine asks Louis.

Yes.

She turns to Antoine.

You too?

Yes.

Did you like it?

Well . . . You sort of float between sleep and wakefulness. Camille is wrong. It's a sort of dream state.

Louis spent the whole night once, Camille says. When he came home the next morning, you would have thought he'd seen a ghost.

Not just once, Louis says, topping his glass of absinthe with fresh water. Anyway most people smoke at home. It's more comfortable. You can't live here and not try it. He looks at Victorine. Notwithstanding your opinion. You should try it, Victorine, you might like it . . . He picks up his glass and stirs it, making the greenish gold liquor shimmer in the candlelight like shot silk. You might learn something from the experience. It's just like absinthe. Or the little *con gaïs*.

Camille makes a face. Louis ignores her. After all, he says, the poppy is the emblem of the Régie. Antoine, didn't you show her the poppy flowers carved on the keystones of the Customs House arcades?

Yes, Antoine says, shooting a quick look at Victorine.

Anyway, Louis continues, what's the point of coming all the way here and living as you would in the provinces?

But aren't you from the provinces yourself? Victorine asks. Didn't you say you were from Cholet?

Antoine takes her hand, as if to warn her to keep quiet.

Madame, Louis says, we are a long way from Vendée here.

You can experience Cochinchina without trying opium, Antoine says. To each his own. Your way of life here doesn't have to be everybody's way of life, here or back home. Isn't it *that*, actually, the whole point of being here?

Louis doesn't smoke so much, Camille says. Do you, Louis?

Louis shrugs, and takes a drink.

Antoine, where will we go, then, Victorine asks, trying to bring the conversation back to where it started.

Vinh Long, Antoine says. It's the biggest post in the delta.

Vinh Long. Isn't it the town I couldn't find on the map the other day?

The very one.

It's on the first arm of the Mekong, Camille says dreamily. They say the river has nine arms, and they call them the nine dragons.

You were upset with Louis, Antoine says back in their flat in Cholon, weren't you? His tone is testy; she can smell alcohol on his breath as he lies next to her, trying to disentangle his feet from the mosquito net.

A little, she says.

You disapprove of the Régie, don't you?

Antoine, she says. It's not Louis. It's this opium business. But maybe I'm prejudiced, I don't know. And it sounds like a good job . . .

It's no paper and pencil–pushing life, that's for sure, he says with enthusiasm, no whistling on a bicycle on some French coastal road, let me tell you. No, here, I'd stand on the front line! He sighs. Anyway, it's just for a while. As soon as the shipment of linen arrives from Cholet, I'll either quit Customs or take a leave of absence.

The night is pitch-black without any breeze. The stillness is sweltering. She drifts in and out of sleep in his arms, tossing in the heat.

I have an idea, he says.

It's much later, already the night is fading, shadows of furniture and clothes merge in the darkness. She wonders if he has slept at all.

You could help me with the Saigon merchants.

Me?

Yes. We could work together. I bet you'd be very good at that. I bet you have a head for business. And clearly, with your knowledge of Chinese . . .

I'm just beginning to read and draw basic characters. It will take me a long time to say anything more than a few simple sentences. And anyway, as you said yourself, it's not Annamite.

But most of the local merchants are Chinese. I'm sure you can learn the language quickly. If you choose to.

She sees herself meeting Mr. Wang, one of the merchants she remembers him mentioning, in his warehouse at the docks, drinking glasses of tea in a dark back office, then pushing the shiny glass-and-brass doors of Établissements Denis Frères, or Le Bazar Saigonnais, or Richards', carrying a suitcase full of linen, wearing a smart little cambric dress with pleats down the front and short white gloves.

Feel my back, Antoine says, sitting up. His sweat drips down from his shoulders, soaking the sheet. You could keep the accounts. I'm getting a shipment ready. I'll stay in Customs just as long as the contract runs, and then we'll put all our energies into the linen. I want to be my own man. Am I boring you? he asks when she doesn't answer. His sharp voice yanks her awake.

No, but I'm tired. Let's go back to sleep.

I'm not tired, he says. He lights a cigarette.

Lie down with me.

On his breath the smell of absinthe mixed with tobacco repulses and excites her at the same time.

Why did you come here? he asks suddenly. For adventure? Maybe that's all it is and you were sick of your husband? This sudden confrontation confuses her. It's as though he were not really having a conversation with her, but pursuing some internal monologue that has suddenly surfaced.

What are you talking about?

He gets up, crosses the room. Already dawn is gleaming through the shutters' wooden slats, washing out the thickness of the night. In that light, standing by the window, he looks almost iridescent.

Antoine, why are you talking like this? I know why I came. You know it too. Her words are measured, soft in tone. Why are you questioning it now?

I don't know. He sits on the side of the bed, his back half turned from her, his hunched shoulders vulnerable. She presses her face against his back.

I came to be with you, she says. But even though the words are truthful, at this moment they are also meant to soothe, and they ring a little false to her.

He lies back down on the damp mattress, rounding his arms over his head.

He sighs. Maybe it's me. I'm restless. I don't know. Nothing's moving fast enough for me.

You need more patience. The test of strength is to be able to stay the course when things appear unfavorable.

Yes, you're right. I'm sorry if I was harsh before.

For a brief moment, with his anger, the fear has come back in her heart. This feeling of slow, free fall with nothing to hold on to. Like when she was with Armand. And then the feeling passes as he presses her to him, slowly, insistently, his hands on her breasts, on her belly. She opens her legs to his fingers, she sighs softly, he runs his tongue around her lips, deep into her mouth, she opens herself to him, throwing her arms behind her head, clutching the frame of the bed with her fists.

J'ai envie de toi . . .

.   .   .   .

When she wakes up at dawn to the sounds of chickens and ducks brought live to the market by peasants, she is thinking of her children. Perhaps she has dreamt of them. How thrilled Daniel would be to see the live birds, tied by the feet, hanging from long bamboo poles in clusters. How happily he would run from stall to stall, getting lost in the alleyways. How he would love the Chinese buns, with their faint taste of marzipan. And Madeleine? She imagines her standing at the shutters, as she did herself her first few days in Cholon, watching the street in silence. For the first time since she's been in Indochina, she has an urge to show them where she lives. She would pick a handful of jasmine blossoms and make them smell the delicious scent. Or even that acrid odor of a fire started with wet wood that drifts through the room in the morning. Or the incense wafting from the Buddhist temple behind the alley.

Antoine gets up and lights another cigarette at the window. The sticky heat already presses down in the little room. Against the soiled, white dawn, she now clearly sees his strong shoulders in the cutaway shirt, his profile, the strands of hair falling on his forehead.

Maybe you should write to them, he says suddenly, without turning. As if he knew what was going through her mind.

She says nothing. Six o'clock in the morning and already she can barely breathe. Full daylight now. The white, overcast sky outside. The white heat of the new day. The same day every day. She feels the sweat running down from her armpits. A violent headache bangs through her head.

There was a man her parents talked about in Cholet when she was a little girl, a father of three—the elder daughter was her age exactly—he had a farm at the edge of the bocage, she can't remember the name of the village. He left one morning to have his horse reshod and never came back. They talked about him for months after that. And then, one day, he was forgotten. That's exactly what she did. Now it's over. It's the past. The page is turned. Better never to look back. It's as though she had two lives, one here and one over there in Maillezais. What price was she paying to keep her two lives separate? So that no one—least of all her husband—would know who she was behind the tightly shut door? Not even her children, oh no, her children should never, never know who their mother really was.

If she wrote, even if she just sent one of those postcards with a photo of the Saigon River or a view of Notre-Dame Cathedral, it would be cracking a door open between her two worlds. The little house above the canal would appear smack in the middle of the rice paddies.

The next morning, in the dim light filtering through the openings of the roof, Chiang is waiting for her in the back room of the temple, *The Tale of Kiều* opened to a new page. He looks at her quizzically, perhaps noticing that she hasn't had much sleep, and starts to read:

> *Vầng trăng vằng-vặc giữa trời,*
> *đinh-ninh hai miệng, một lời song-song.*
> *Tóc-tơ căn vặn tấc lòng,*
> *trăm năm tạc một chữ đồng đến xương.*

Repeat, he says. And she does, without knowing what she is saying. When she knows it by heart, he translates the lines for her.

> The stark bright moon was gazing from the skies
> as with one voice both mouths pronounced the oath.
> Their hearts' recesses they explored and probed,
> etching their vow of union in their bones.

He nods. There is a flash of irony in his eyes. She turns her eyes away. Was Chiang trying to make her doubt her own feelings? But what did the old monk know about love?

September 8, 1940
5:15 p.m.

SHE SEES THEM again in the distance, two gray uniforms, one taller than the other, the same ones as this morning. Even from a distance she would never have mistaken them for two ordinary strollers, with the stiffness of their gait, their bean-shaped caps. They seem to be heading toward her. They've been checking identity cards lately. Not the S.S., the French cops. Still, she wonders if it's better to wait for them or ignore them and walk away. The seagulls take off in front of them, squealing with a plaintive wail, and alight a few meters ahead. Then they take off again and alight again, like a corps de ballet surrounding the principal dancers.

They are walking straight toward her, now a dozen meters away, at most. She hesitates. If she gets up and walks off it will seem as though she's running away. She doesn't move, only gathers the newspaper clippings and puts them back between the pages of the journal, and waits for them sitting on the sand.

The tall one touches his cap politely. His eyes are transparent. She sees them clearly now, an extraordinary pale turquoise.

Madame Texier, he says. Not with that strong Teutonic accent they all mimic behind their backs. Just a light touch of German. Her heart pumps erratically. How can he know her name? There are wild rumors that in Poland and Austria they are taking the rights of foreigners away. Well, she's not a foreigner, is she?

Oui, she says, forcing herself to stay calm.

Your home, the tall one says. You're moving, correct?

Yes. She can't figure out how they know that. She keeps her hands buried in her pockets, trying to stay very straight so that they don't see her fear. What business is it of theirs?

We've been told it belongs to Monsieur Erlanger, the smaller one reads on a folded piece of paper. Can you tell us how to find him?

Why? she says.

Just tell us, please, how we might get in touch with him, the smaller one insists.

She doesn't know what it means, that question. She doesn't trust them.

You can ask at the *mairie*.

His address, please.

The "please" is perfunctory, a simple, meaningless adornment that doesn't soften the command in any way.

But why? she asks again.

Madame! the short one says. And this time she is convinced she hears a threat in his voice.

I'm sorry, she says, I'm afraid I don't know his address.

The tall one, the one with the blue eyes, puts his hand on the short one's arm, and bows toward her, an old-fashioned bow. She almost expects him to take her hand and kiss it.

We were only inquiring, he says, in his formal, slightly stilted French, because the house might be available. To rent, I mean to say.

Then he touches his cap again.

Merci, madame. Another bow.

She watches them walk away. She has nothing to hide. She is French, Catholic, after all. It's the Israelites they're after, people say, and the gypsies. They wouldn't bother with a retired schoolteacher.

But what if they had asked her, with their icy politeness, looking through her journal with their hands covered in kid gloves: Madame, were you in Saigon in 1899?

Vinh Long

MAY 3, 1899. The boy is sitting on the staircase which rises in front of the blue façade in a double curve of delicately sculptured stone. He gets up, his long, bony arms hanging by his sides, and presses his back to the banister to let the *coolie-xe* carry their trunks up the stairs. He is a pale boy with transparent skin, his brown hair stiffly slicked back, wearing long white flannel trousers and a white shirt. He looks to be about thirteen or fourteen. He watches them without saying a word. When they reach the second floor, their floor, Victorine turns around and sees that he has sat back down on the same step and is still watching them.

The Vinh Long house overlooks the Tien Gang—the first "dragon" of the Mekong River, as Camille said. It used to belong to a rich Chinese merchant before being taken over by the French administration. They are going to share it with the family of the assistant director of Customs, who occupies the first floor. Their apartment is a suite of rooms tiled with a faded pattern of gray-blue-and-brown arabesques and filled with dark, heavy Chinese furniture.

One after the other, Victorine throws open the French doors and walks out on the balcony.

The heavy waters of the Mekong are rolling just a few hundred meters from the house.

Didn't I promise you? Antoine says. He puts his arms around her.

Yes, you did. It's beautiful, so beautiful. But speaking of your grand promises, Antoine, where is the cook?

He laughs. Not to worry, he says, we'll get the cook, a Chinese *bep*. They are the best. And a *con gaï* too, if you'd like.

She shakes her head. No *con gaï*. She's heard of the young, pretty Annamite girls who slink around on their cloth shoes, serving as maids or helping with the children, and who are a permanent temptation for the European men—according to Camille, anyway. Not that I wouldn't trust you, she says, looking at him with a seductive smile. Only a cook, she adds. And maybe a boy to do the errands. Look at me, she goes on, laughing at herself. Barely in Indochina for more than a few weeks, and I'm thinking like a spoiled *colon*'s wife!

He puts his arms around her.

So why don't you let yourself be spoiled a little? He kisses her in the neck. It won't turn you into a nasty *colon*.

Long, flat beans hang over the banister, the fruit of a tall, drippy tree called a flamboyant, Antoine tells her, and she loves that name, flamboyant, a tree bursting into flames. She reaches out and touches one of the elongated pods, which, to her surprise, feels like burnished leather. A melody rises slowly from somewhere near the river, melancholy and soulful. She tries to catch sight of a musician, but there's no one to be seen. A lonely barge glides on the river, heavy with produce, a *nia-coue* woman sitting at the bottom, moving the oars with her clenched toes.

The front door to the house is open. The brown-haired boy is sitting at a piano, his back to the door, picking out the first notes of a Chopin nocturne, or is it an étude? The melody sounds familiar. It's a nocturne, the same one, she realizes, Daniel was struggling over for weeks just a year before.

She stands in the courtyard, listening to the music. It was during the spring that Daniel was learning that piece, she remembers, just about the time she met Antoine on the beach. The boy looks nothing like Daniel, and yet his posture, leaning forward over the keyboard, his shoulders pinched, his shirtsleeves hanging on his wrists, is similar, even his manner of attacking the piece, his hesitation at the opening adagio, his pause, too long of a whole beat, after the first two measures. She is mesmerized. And when he starts the second movement, an andante, she is overwhelmed by pain and a feeling of guilt so intense it makes her gasp.

The assistant director's wife, at this moment, comes out to greet her on the patio, where the frangipani trees and the ferns growing in glazed pots are still glistening from the afternoon rain. She introduces herself as Madame Paulette Guérin, from La Rochelle, which is just south of Vendée. She is a thin and pale woman, as though the sun and the heat, instead of giving color to her skin, have drained it of life. Her hair is loosely pinned up, the same color and texture as her son's.

Charles, she says, this is Madame Langelot. She moved in with her husband in the upstairs flat this afternoon.

Victorine starts when she hears the name. For a moment she had become Victorine Texier again.

Charles stops playing and turns around but he doesn't get up. He just nods, maybe out of shyness.

I know, he says. His voice is deep. Maybe he's older than she thought.

With her hand Madame Guérin motions him to get up.

He walks languidly, as if the heat was exhausting him too, and holds his hand out.

You play well, Victorine says, shaking his hand.

He has the hands of a pianist, his mother says, picking up one of his bony hands and resting it on top of her own palm. Charles quickly withdraws his hand.

Victorine watches him stand awkwardly between the two of them. She looks at his skinny forearms, the skin so white, she sees the dark hair growing above his upper lip, not long or thick enough yet to warrant shaving. And for a moment she would like to hold him in her arms, this boy, she would like to ask him if a boy raised in the colony is different from a boy raised in France. I have a son too, she wants to say. He plays the piano too. He is a little younger than you are. Perhaps you would be friends if you knew each other.

You have no children yet? Madame Guérin asks, noticing how she is looking at Charles.

No, Victorine says.

It will come, Madame Guérin says. Charles made us wait too. She traces a finger across the back of his neck, then rests her hand over his shoulder. Didn't you, Charles? But the wait was worth it, believe me.

Paulette Guérin's gesture, her hand brushing the neck of her son before alighting on his shoulder, is almost sensual.

Let us know if the piano bothers you, Madame Guérin says. We'll try to be quieter when we practice in the evening.

It's fine, Victorine says. I enjoy it.

She hesitates for a moment.

Would you happen to know . . . that music we were hearing earlier, coming from the river? Do you know what that is?

Oh, that, Madame Guérin says. You hear it everywhere you go around here. It's the music of the delta, you might say. It's played on a sitar. A sixteen-string sitar.

During the monsoon months of the summer, the cottony heat of the morning air muffles the sounds and the afternoons provide the only respite, the pattering sound of the downpours more refreshing than the hot rain itself. In Vinh Long, which is even hotter than Saigon, Antoine exchanges his woolen suits for loose, white pants and shirts of pale linen. For a blond man, his skin is unusually dark. The French, Victorine has noticed, both the men and the women, don't let themselves tan, as a rule. They like to keep their skin white and soft, always carrying parasols or standing in the shade.

A young Annamite man named Anh who sleeps in a room at the back of the house appears every morning, dressed in flowing black pants and a long tunic, to clean, shop, and keep house. As for the cook, the Guérins have offered to share their *bep* with them. He brings up from the first-floor kitchen exquisite curried chicken or shrimp perfumed with ginger, coriander, lemon grass, saffron, and mint, a bouquet of flavors they've come to crave. The Guérins shun the traditional meals and the bread and butter heaped on most French tables. Too heavy. Antoine agrees. Eat like the people here, he says, otherwise you'll get sick.

Once he has settled into his work, Antoine offers to take her to the Vinh Long Customs House to show her where he works. It's a long walk, he says, would you rather take a *pousse-pousse?* But she would rather go on foot, to follow the path he takes every morn-ing, to see what he sees every day. From the house they walk along the riverbank, and on their way he tells her stories he has heard of Chinese contraband. Iron containers half filled with raw opium, floating behind junks—like this one, over there, see?—or hung under their hulls, *chan-doo* stuffed into bamboo sticks drifting on the arroyos, concealed in innocent honey or *nuoc nam* jars, even in the carcasses of dead fish.

Ugh! It must taste terrible!

Watch out where you're stepping. It's very muddy here.

The path they are following is narrow, invaded by puddles of murky waters, lined on one side by the grassy bank of the Mekong, and on the other by a thick vegetation of ferns and banana trees, heavy with green fruit.

Sometimes they hide it in fake chignons.

What do you mean, chignons? In the women's hair?

Yes, the *nia-coue* women, the peasant women. They pin fake hair on top of their heads and wrap the whole thing in a big turban. You can't tell they're hiding anything at all. It's very clever. Oh, here we are.

The Customs House is a brick building with a tiled roof and a veranda, set right on the river, the mangroves spilling at its feet, as though they wanted to reclaim it and swallow it into the river. She is surprised to see how ramshackle it looks, squalid, even, although it's evidently not old.

The humidity, he says. It peels off the paint, rots away the wood.

A hand-painted sign hangs above the door: RECETTES DES DOUANES ET REGIES—CUSTOMS REVENUE. Underneath is the translation in *quoc ngu,* the romanized script, which she spells out for him.

Inside, in the dark front office, porcelain and tin cases containing the different qualities of opium are stacked on wooden shelves, colored green, purple, and red, like rows of Elégantes or Boyards cigarette packs in a tobacconist's store in France. Victorine picks one up. A big *C* is punched underneath, next to a date and a number. The weight is marked on top of the boxes: 5 gr., 10 gr., 20 gr., 40 gr., 100 gr.

What's the *C* for?

Cochinchina.

And what's the difference between the porcelain and tin cases?

The porcelain cases are the best ones. He picks up a small one lacquered purple. This, for instance. It's called Benarès *luxe.* Cooked twice. Aged. Top quality. The best. Think about Armagnac, that kind of thing. For connoisseurs.

Have you ever tried it?

He nods. It's part of the job.

She tries to open it.

It's soldered, he says. Let me show you one that's already opened. He hands her another box, this one of red tin, and removes the lid.

She presses her finger to the dark paste and brings her finger to her tongue. It tastes sweet and something else too, a sharp, vaguely smoky taste that she cannot identify and which makes her wrinkle her nose.

Antoine laughs. I'll bring some home, if you'd like. Guérin's got a little den going at the back of the house. You can smoke it there. Not this, though. This is Yunnan. It's our cheapest *chan-doo.*

She shakes her head. No. You know how I feel. She hands him the box.

He fastens the top back on and fingers the case for a moment.

These tin boxes are no good. Look at this. It's all rusted already. Opium's acid's attacking it. Cheap stuff.

She looks around and takes in the whole room, the dingy furniture, the shabby shelves, the floor that would need a good sweeping.

So this is the fabled opium trade everybody's talking about.

Well, if you listen to Louis.

No, not just Louis. Look at this place. It says Customs Revenue in the front, but it has nothing to do with Customs. It's just a store to sell opium.

Well, it's true . . . He pulls out a cigarette from his case and lights it . . . and chase the Chinese junks carrying contraband down the Delta, he goes on, blowing out the smoke forcefully, don't forget that.

But it comes out to the same thing, doesn't it, in a way? What's illegal? A woman hiding opium in her hair? It's all so that we keep our hands on the precious opium. Sorry. *Chan-doo*.

Antoine props himself up to sit on the counter and crosses his legs. For a moment, the scent of his cigarette covers the damp smell of the Customs House.

We are doing with opium what we did with tobacco, he says after a silence. Think about it. Centralize the production and make it a monopoly.

She walks around the room, picking up the small porcelain cases and putting them back. They are pretty, like jewelry cases.

From France, all of this seemed to be happening in some far away, unreal world. It was . . . very abstract.

I know, but now, it is our world.

So this all comes from the Saigon *bouillerie*? She points to the shelves.

Most of it. There's another *bouillerie* in Haiphong, in the Tonkin, up north. And another one in Luang Prabang in Laos. But the best *chan-doo* comes from Saigon. A certain Monsieur Wang Taï is supervising the production. Apparently he knows what he is doing. He also happens to be the richest Chinese merchant in Indochina.

I see.

She goes to the window and lifts the wooden slats to look out. The heavy waters of the Mekong swell, flush with the grassy banks, beating against the brick wall of the Customs House.

So how will you go, as you say, chase after the Chinese junks?

Her tone, ironic and challenging, is not lost on him.

Victorine, does it upset you so much that I'm going to be working here?

She turns to face him.

Maybe I don't look at these things the way you do. She remains silent for a moment. Maybe—she hesitates—I'm narrow-minded?

Look, we couldn't stay here—he looks at her intently—I mean we, the *Phap*, the French, without the income from the opium tax. The Chinese and the Annamites are smoking anyway. We're just being realistic.

Antoine, it's too easy to say that. It's hypocritical.

Well, I guess we all are, then, including you, being here. And benefiting from it.

He slides down from the desk, crushes his cigarette and takes her hand.

Let's not talk politics. Come. Let's go back, shall we?

The stench of the mud and silt is overpowering outside, along the river, but Victorine prefers it to the smell of opium. At the bottom of a large barge moored at the dock, an Annamite sitting in the stern wearing a European-cut flannel jacket with the letters *RO* embroidered on the sleeve. He waves at them.

Antoine waves back.

We got a shipment this morning from Saigon, he says. This is Ngoe. He works with us.

Victorine waves to him.

They walk arm in arm for a while, following the riverbank back to the villa.

I agree with you, in a way, Antoine says, after a long, uncomfortable silence. That's why Customs doesn't like to hire us, the men who are fresh from the mainland. We have different ideas. They prefer to work with people who've been here for a while, already, who've come to accept things as they are, without question.

His face is thoughtful, but not troubled. Antoine, she thinks, is a realist, whereas she is still struggling to reconcile her fantasy of Indochina with its reality.

But the opium business is growing too fast, Antoine goes on. They need us. And I need them. So do you, Victorine, in order to live here.

Charles Guérin is playing the same Chopin nocturne when they enter the garden. His back is hunched over the piano by the open door as they pass by. A sudden feeling of guilt grips Victorine again, a chill running down her back, tightening her shoulders; then, after a moment, it passes, as suddenly as the rain stops in the afternoon and the sun dries up the puddles in the courtyard.

And you know, Antoine continues, lowering his voice as they walk up the stairs to their floor, Guérin, or even Louis Désaunier, if pressed, wouldn't disagree with me. It's the contradiction of the colony. For anyone with eyes to see it.

Every evening the assistant director's son practices his piano on the floor below. The playing is not technically skillful, but there's soul in it.

Every evening after dinner she waits for the scales to start. And after the warm-up, the first measures of the nocturne, she stops what she is doing, writing in her journal or working on some piece of embroidery. From the open windows the sound is clear. She hums the parts that will come before he plays them.

And after the boy has finished playing, almost as if in response, the melody on the sitar rises again, a plaintive *mélopée*. But no matter how many times she walks down to the riverbank, she can never find the player.

⌒

JULY 1899. They're sitting at the low Chinese table in front of bowls of *bun rieu,* a delicate shrimp soup just served by the *bep* from below. The evening breeze blows through the open windows. A sense of peace and contentment fills Victorine in such a sweet, overwhelming wave that she lets go of her spoon with a deep sigh.

He smiles at her. You know, he says, you look different than you did in Cholon.

Really?

He laughs.

Not just beautiful, but happy.

I liked Cholon, though.

Well . . . but there it is. Maybe it's the food. Or the weather. All that rain.

Yes, that must be it.

Or . . . He raises his eyebrows. Maybe you're with child . . . He picks her up in his arms and deposits her in the deep Chinese armchair by the window.

A wave of panic sweeps over her.

No, Antoine, I'm not. She playfully pushes him away with her foot. But what about the soup? she says.

The soup can wait.

He kneels next to her on the floor and buries his face into the folds of her skirt, gathering her legs in his arms. She caresses his head, the hair that he's let grow longer lately in Vinh Long, running her fingers through its silky strands, while he pulls her skirt up, his hands, then his lips on her bare skin, her breathing coming on faster and faster, barely muffled now. And she lets her head drop back, her eyes closed, her legs, thrown over the arms of the chair, opening up to him.

. . . .

From his expeditions upriver, Antoine brings her back presents: a silk sash, a tortoiseshell bracelet, an extraordinary bowl of gold and red Chinese porcelain, a china teapot decorated with delicate designs of faded cerulean blue. For her birthday, in August, he brings her a lacquered bowl that he has filled with frangipani and lotus flowers floating on water.

He places the bowl on a little table near their bed. Then he squats next to her and she pushes the white frangipani blossoms around the water with the tip of a finger.

They will turn to dust before rotting, he says. Frangipani blossoms won't dry. They have no fiber. They are to be savored in the moment, while they last, sometimes no more than a day.

The little Vinh Long chapel was within walking distance of the villa, in the center of the French quarter. It was more intimate than the huge Notre-Dame Cathedral in Saigon, where she had gone once, but just as devoid of warmth, with its whitewashed, unadorned walls. She asked Antoine to accompany her to mass. He wasn't much of a churchgoer, but he would go with her if she wished. She pinned a square of white lace mantilla in her hair. Monsieur and Madame Guérin and Charles nodded to them as they walked in. They sat on a back pew and left during the communion. In her state of adultery, she couldn't take the communion unless she first confessed and repented—which would mean separating from Antoine. The pew squeaked when they got up and several heads turned. She hoped it wasn't the Guérins. She kept her head down until they reached the portal. Mortal sin. She remembered how Bertha had said that, coldly cutting, in her expert's voice. When they were outside, she told Antoine how the three sisters would frighten each other with the litany of sins. And you still believe in that? he asked, taking her hand. She shrugged. It was irrational, perhaps, but the belief was too deeply stamped in her. She missed the atmosphere of a Gothic church, the echo of the flagstones under her heels, the burnished gold of the Renaissance paintings, the beams of light—on sunny days—flickering through the stained-glass windows and alighting on the floor like jewel-colored birds. The chapel seemed alien, almost fake. You don't have to attend mass, Antoine said, as they walked along the Mekong on their way back, if it makes you so uncomfortable. But she couldn't let go of the Church, the whole French colony gathered at the little chapel at eleven every Sunday. It would be worse not to go. It was part of her life, even if it brought her no peace of mind, but a weekly reminder of her guilt.

One day in October, she believes, although it might have been later, she isn't sure anymore—in her memory, the days in the Mekong Delta flow into an eternal present—she is strolling along the river after lunch, back from walking with Antoine a little way toward the Customs House. She decides to take a left turn toward the center of town instead of going straight home, and here it is, the school, a group of ochre buildings surrounding a bare court-yard under a pewter sky.

It's the after-lunch break, and the children—girls on one side in braids and navy blue pinafores, boys on the other in dark slacks and immaculate white shirts—are running and jumping rope or standing in clusters in the heat of midday. Victorine observes them for a few minutes. Then she impulsively walks through the court-yard, dodging the children, just as she used to do back home, goes straight to the back office, and introduces herself to the headmistress.

In the classrooms, the little wooden desks and benches are similar to those in the Vendée schools: dark wood scratched by years of use and porcelain inkpots in the corner. When she walks in with the headmistress, the little girls stand up without being told, as though it was expected of them whenever a French lady walked into the classroom, and sing *Alouette, Gentille Alouette* in her honor. A girl in the first row with her long auburn braids looks so much like Madeleine that she nearly jumps: the way the girl holds her-self, leaning on one leg and jutting one hip out.

Through the paneless windows, open on both sides of the

room, the bloated sky is turning purple, and the afternoon rain suddenly comes down. The girls keep singing, their voices barely covering the pounding of the storm. They sing *A la Claire Fontaine*, which Victorine used to sing to the children when they were babies to put them to sleep.

> *A la Claire Fontaine,*
> *M'en allant promener,*
> *J'ai trouvé l'eau si claire*
> *Que je m'y suis baignée.*
> *Dors, rossignol, dors,*
> *Toi qui as le coeur gai . . .*

A Caire Fonpaine, Madeleine would say, twisting her tongue and skipping the hard consonants, her voice fading fast into sleep.

It's a little tear in her heart, that song. A sharp tear that doesn't bleed. Just that tiny, dry crack. And all of a sudden it's the end of the song and the whole class is waiting for her reaction—the little girls standing stiff before their desks—and she applauds, softly, fingers of one hand tapping the palm of the other. She smiles and turns around while the girls sit back down on the benches and wait for the class to resume.

In the school office, where she sits, waiting for the headmistress, an enamel CINZANO sign hangs next to a calendar of the year 1899, depicting a couple of slender muses clad in flowing robes, their curly hair pinned with flowers and cascading past their shoulders.

The year 1900! In less than three months they'll be celebrating the new century in a country that still follows the lunar calendar. She remembers an article in *Le Figaro* she had read with Angelina just before her sister had left for Indochina. It was about the great World Exhibition already planned for the turn of the century. Dancers and performers and officials from the various colonies were going to be brought to Paris. Food from all over Asia would be served. And there would be a reproduction of a Buddhist temple and of the governor's palace in Saigon. You're going to be there, Victorine had said with a bit of envy for the journey her sister was about to make. You will experience all that firsthand. Perhaps you can go to Paris with Armand and see the exhibition, Angelina had suggested. Well, Victorine's life had taken another turn.

Now, here she is, in Indochina, in a French school lashed by the monsoon rains, waiting for the headmistress to tell her if she could work here, helping in the office or tutoring the children, anything to smell the familiar mixture of ink and fresh crisp notebooks that even here, in the tropical weather, pervades the classrooms.

The headmistress walks back into the office—Victorine sees her as if for the first time that morning—a woman barely older than she is, a woman she might easily have met back home, since she taught in Nantes before taking the Vinh Long post.

I'm sorry, but there's no way, madame, I can hire you, the headmistress is saying, since you haven't applied through the normal channels of the French Education Department. But you could, if you wish, come and help with the little class one or two afternoons a week. She has an apologetic smile. We can't put you on the payroll, however.

10 Octobre 1899

Chère Angelina,

This will be a shock to you, but I am writing from a house in Vinh Long overlooking the Mekong River. Yes, I've been in Cochinchina for more than six months, with Antoine Langelot— you must remember him from our summer at La Tranche when we were girls. I don't know what you will think of me, Angelina, but I am taking the chance to let you know where I am. Not a day has passed without my thinking of you, and yet I couldn't bring myself to write to you. Nobody in France knows I am here. I was—I am—afraid you will judge me harshly. But I would like to see you if we can arrange it, somehow. I will ask you—please—to keep this—the fact that I am in Indochina with Antoine—to yourself. I don't know if you are still in Hanoi, but I will send this letter there anyway, hoping they will forward it if you have moved. I love you dearly. I miss you.

Tender kisses.

Your sister, Victorine

It's way past midnight, the night after she has taken the letter to the Vinh Long post office, a simple brick building with none of the grandeur of the art nouveau post office in Saigon. She cannot sleep. What if she has set something in motion that she won't be able to control? She is alone, waiting up for Antoine, unnerved that he is not home yet, although he's warned her that he might not come back until morning. For the last three nights, Antoine and the men at Customs have been stopping all the barges and junks sailing down the river and searching them for smuggled opium. But they've been unsuccessful. The smugglers, they believe, are unloading opium a few kilometers upriver on the bank of the Co Chien River, across from An Binh Island, hiding it there, and then going back to pick it up later to carry it on foot a few kilometers downriver, past the customs post.

The mosquito net doesn't stir. There's a moment in the night when all breezes seem to die down, when the air is perfectly still and the heat weighs on you without respite, when sleep becomes impossible, the body laden, oppressed. She kicks the sheet off with her feet and walks out on the balcony. Under the full moon, great swaths of water gleam and surge silently, illustrating those lines from *The Tale of Kiều* she has read with Chiang:

Outside the window, squinting, peeped the moon—
gold spilled on waves, trees shadowed all the yard.

In the distance she can hear a murmur of Annamite speech, muted music in minor key, followed by silence. Then it picks up again, a barely audible whisper. It seems to be coming from the side of the house. She wraps a dressing gown over her nightshirt and walks down to the garden and round to the back toward the servants' quarters. Dim light escapes from a half-opened louvered door, indenting the shadows into slanted bands. Wreaths of smoke spiral out of the room, smelling sweet and heavy. In the opening of the door she sees two men lying on their side on a flat platform lit by a small porcelain lamp. A white, rumpled shirt is hanging by a nail on the wall. One of the men seems asleep. The other is leaning on his forearm and holding a long bamboo pipe in his mouth. He reaches forward to light it at the wick of the lamp. His smooth brown chest is naked. It's Anh, the young man who runs their errands. Eyes closed, he inhales the smoke from the pipe, then falls back on his side, letting the pipe slip out of his hands. Just then the other man draws himself up on his elbow to bring his pipe to the flame. He's not a man, but a boy. In the light of the small porcelain lamp she recognizes the blade of hair flopping over the forehead, the white, skinny shoulders of Charles Guérin. Charles's eyes meet hers blankly for a moment. He draws deeply on the pipe, then holds it out, offering it to her. She shakes her head without saying a word, and he lets his head fall back on a small pillow, his hips twisting sideways and his legs opening up with abandon.

She quickly turns and walks over toward the garden gate. The moonlight shimmers on the river. Charles, not much older than Daniel. Charles, coddled by his mother while his father is away on long trips to Saigon or to Hanoi. Pale Charles spending hours at the piano practicing Chopin. Charles, the love of his mother.

Antoine returns a little while after she has gone back to bed. He tears off his wet, muddy clothes and stands naked in the middle of the room, washing his feet and hands with water left at the bottom of the washbasin.

We've found the hiding place, he says, splashing the rest of the water over his head and over his chest and shoulders, it was loaded with *chan-doo*, already processed, not raw opium. Thirty kilos of *chan-doo,* hidden in the trunk of a longan tree, can you believe this? With a little luck, we'll be able to trace it back to one of the illicit boiling factories up north in the Tonkin. Finally some action!

He doesn't bother to dry himself and lies down, still wet, near her.

After all these weeks of waiting! Victorine, what do you think of that?

Good news, she says. But her voice is flat. She lies without moving, feeling the refreshing coolness of his body. She's happy for him, she would like to share his excitement, but she can only think of the two boys smoking opium at the back of the house. She doesn't tell him about the scene, as if it's a bad dream that will surely lose its power in daylight.

You're not saying anything, he says.

You know what I think, Antoine.

But this is smuggled opium! Victorine . . . His voice is still soft, but she can hear the tension, and that intonation—for lack of a better word she thinks of it as *parisienne*—which creeps up in his voice when he gets excited or angry. He presses his wet palm against her back. She shudders.

Feels good, doesn't it? Look, it wasn't my choice to work at the Régie. We are here so that later we can be in Saigon, so that I can work on the linen importing. You know that.

I know.

The scene behind the house lingers at the edge of her mind, Charles offering her the pipe with a half-smile, his legs spread out.

It was exciting tonight, Antoine repeats. Finding the balls of *chan-doo* in that tree. A stroke of luck. He lights a cigarette, inhales. The full moon helped us. The smoke, coming out of his mouth, sounds like a sigh.

It doesn't look the same from up close, he says finally. Not like the way they're showing it at home. "The French Empire." It's not very pretty from up close. But we all participate, in one way or another. Even you. He smokes silently for a while.

I'm going to work at the school, she says.

The school? Which school? To teach?

The elementary school. I would like to teach but at first—they won't hire me without a transfer from France. But I can help a couple of days a week.

He puts out his cigarette.

It's good, he says. I'm glad. He turns toward her and takes her in his arms. You were missing *your* work, eh?

When she arrives at the school the next afternoon, the children of the younger class stand up politely when she walks in. She is to help the regular mistress with the younger group of children. None of them know how to read yet. They've just learned the alphabet. She asks them to name five animals whose names start with the CH sound. Hands go up. CHAT is the first one. Then: CHIEN. She writes both words on the blackboard. Then a long silence.

What animal pulls a carriage?

Three hands shoot up.

Cheval!

She writes CHEVAL.

Two more.

An animal that gives milk?

They look at each other. There's hardly any milk in Indochina.

A little girl raises her hand shyly.

Vache?

Well, it gives milk and the *CH* sound is in the word. So I will write it down. But I was thinking of another one.

Chèvre, comes a voice from the older group.

She writes CHÈVRE.

One more.

Nobody can think of another one.

I'll give you a hint: an animal in the desert.

No answer.

She writes CHAMEAU. Camel, she says.

Chan-doo, says a voice, the same one, coming from the older group. Victorine ignores it.

By the time they've learned how to read the five words, it's almost the end of the hour and already the rain comes down in violent squalls, soaking the books of the children sitting by the windows. When the bell rings for recess a few minutes later, the children run out and gather under the veranda, waiting for the downpour to cease. The little girl with the red braids, who must be in the older class, is leaning against a pillar, reading a book. Victorine walks over to her.

Je m'appelle Marie, she tells Victorine. She is eleven, a year younger than Madeleine.

Victorine looks at the dark pink cover of her book: *Les Malheurs de Sophie.*

AND THEN everything happens at the same time.

First, in late October, they are notified that the crates of handkerchiefs, tablecloths, and bolts of linen are finally ready to be shipped from La Rochelle and are due to arrive in early December. The next day Antoine is notified of a promotion. "We are pleased to inform you that, in appreciation of the successful capture of the Chinese smugglers north of Vinh Long, you are to be promoted . . ." He is to become comptroller, which involves more responsibility and quite a substantial raise. But he's simultaneously informed—in another letter received the same day—that his six-month contract is not being renewed for the time being.

Would you believe the idiocy of the French administration? he says, tossing both letters to the ground. The left hand doesn't know what the right hand is doing!

Barely a week later, Angelina's postcard arrives, a photograph of Ha Long Bay with its limestone outcroppings shrouded in mist.

In the diagonal at the back of the card are just a couple of lines in her familiar curly handwriting:

> *Jules is being transferred from Hanoi to Saigon January 1.*
> *Perhaps we could meet in Da Lat for the New Year. We will be*
> *there from the twenty-fourth to the first.*

She shows the postcard to Antoine.

You wrote to her, he says, his face full of questions. Did you tell her about us? is the question he chooses to ask.

Yes.

She doesn't say anything about it? He is studying her face closely.

No. And she bursts into violent tears.

THEY ARE SITTING on the balcony of the Vinh Long house. It is dusk, that short, exquisite moment before the day sinks into utter darkness. The branches of the flamboyant tree have grown since they've arrived. The long, beanlike fruit hang so low they cover the floor of the balcony.

Since they are not renewing my contract, I suppose we should move back to Saigon for the winter, he says.

Not to Cholon?

No. We can find a more comfortable place in the French Quarter. I'll need to be in town to do the rounds of the stores. You can help me with the business, just as we'd planned.

She thinks of the little classroom in the Vinh Long school, where she was just beginning to learn the names of the pupils, and the office where she's cleaned out a desk for her papers.

He senses her hesitation. You'll get used to Saigon. You can work at a school there too. And won't you be relieved that I won't be working at the Régie?

Yes, she says. Yes, of course. She raises her hand. Listen.

What?

There is a silence, the hum of insects, then the soft notes of a piano.

Charles has started a new nocturne, she says.

They listen for a moment.

It is very like the other one.

Well, it's also Chopin, but this one is in a different key. Many of the nocturnes sound so similar . . .

They listen for a while to the crystalline notes, stumbling at first, then more assertive.

He's making progress, she says.

She waits for the nocturne to finish and the sitar to start. But it doesn't tonight. Only the cry of a bird that sounds like a seagull pierces the silence for an instant.

AND WHY ON earth would she be worried about two German officers finding out that she was in Saigon in 1899?

The question troubles her, as she watches the tall silhouettes fade into the ribbon of mist rising from the ocean. But then everybody's jumpy these days. The brutal arrival of the Germans is stirring intense fears and hatreds.

She slowly reopens the notebook and unfolds a clipping from *Le Cochinchinois*, the newspaper they used to read in Vinh Long, dated December 21, 1899, right around their move to Saigon. It is a list of recommendations to help the newly arrived settler to handle the climate: airy house, bamboo furniture, English-style kapok mattresses or Cambodian grass mats, flannel belt (to wear night and day), helmet or straw hat, and parasol.

The little house they rented in Saigon followed these prescriptions almost to the letter. It was in the European style, with a wrap-around wooden veranda and deck, at the edge of the French Quarter. A blood-colored bougainvillea climbed over the pillars of the veranda and a lemon tree grew in the back garden. They had bought bamboo-and-wicker furniture, and two rocking chairs made of curved wood, at the Bazar Saïgonnais. She doesn't remember about the mattress, only that the mosquito net billowed and cascaded all the way to the floor. It was like sleeping inside a cloud.

Antoine had made arrangements to rent the back of a Chinese

warehouse on the riverfront to store his crates of linen. The end of the year now blurs in her memory, the trips from the warehouse to the rue Catinat, the two of them carrying heavy suitcases of linen, loading them on a *pousse-pousse*. The stores vast and illuminated like ballrooms, the long wait in the antechambers, the brightly colored cloth spread on the counters, then folded, then spread again, the discussions, the negotiations, the sales, the promises of payments after the New Year ...

What she does remember of those last weeks in Saigon right before they left for Da Lat is how hectic the streets were, after the serenity of Vinh Long. The horses pawing the ground, the stop and go of the carriages, the entanglement of the *pousse-pousses*, the cacophony of the competing café orchestras at every street corner, and the flashiness of the outfits. An outburst of pleats, lace, guipure, buttons, bustles, ribbons, flounces, fringes, and silk flowers.

Da Lat

DECEMBER 24, 1899. The first thing she notices when the coach approaches the Da Lat station are the begonias—a flower that grows in temperate climates—bursting in a flurry of reds and oranges in window boxes, just as in a French village. And when she steps out of the coach, with her thin muslin frock, fit for Saigon weather, she shivers. Everybody jokes about the weather. Would you believe that you actually need a jacket here at night, that the beds in the hotels have blankets, and two blankets at that?

And then, sitting on a bench outside the station, a little way up the street, she sees Angelina and Jules, waiting for them.

They're here, Victorine says quietly, putting her hand on Antoine's arm.

Angelina stands up. Her hand comes flying up to her mouth. She spreads her arms wide as she used to do when she was little and she was afraid of a storm, or afraid of going out alone to the outhouse in the pitch black of the night, and she runs into her big sister's arms. Returning her embrace awkwardly, Victorine finds her heavier, almost matronly. But maybe she is the one who has changed.

Angelina, you remember Antoine?

Enchantée, Angelina says.

Antoine kisses her hand.

My God! You were a little girl, he says.

Angelina smiles.

You remember, on the beach? Victorine says. Jules, this is Antoine.

Pleased to meet you.

But it's obvious Jules, for his part, is not. He shakes hands coldly with Antoine, then takes a step back and rigidly stands a meter apart from their little group, his arms crossed over his chest.

The two men walk in front. Almost identical white linen suits, leather shoes with tan spats, only the hair color differs—brown for Jules, sandy blond for Antoine—and the demeanor. Jules is a short man who stretches himself upward, his head stiff above his neck, while Antoine, broad and tall, swings his arms and forges ahead with long strides. It seems unreal to her, a dream within a dream, this reunion in the hills of Da Lat. In the horse and buggy that takes them to their hotel, the women avoid any intimate talk, instead pointing out to each other the white villas of the French Quarter.

It's true, what they say, it does look like a little Paris, doesn't it? They laugh.

Don't they say that about Saigon too? Angelina asks.

No, Victorine says. Saigon is—making her voice low and dramatic—the Pearl of the Orient!

They burst into nervous laughter. Victorine leans back against the seat of the carriage and closes her eyes. Perhaps, if she let herself go, perhaps, then, everything would be as it was, as it should be? Maybe if they were alone it would be different. The horses trot on the cobblestones, shaking the passengers and throwing them against each other every time the coach makes a sharp turn.

I can't believe you're here, Angelina says. Her face, so similar to hers but more finely chiseled, is fighting to keep the tears back. Victorine wants to take her hand, but something in Jules's somber expression, staring at his wife, holds her back. Perhaps Angelina wouldn't want Jules to see her cry. Victorine exchanges a look with Antoine, then turns her head toward the window. Everything is not fine, she thinks. What was she hoping for, really? Did she want Angelina to be the one to forgive her?

She is standing at the dresser, her hair up, putting on a pair of tourmaline earrings he has bought her in Saigon before leaving, getting ready for dinner. Their bedroom is sumptuous, with similar brass and dark wood as in the Continental, and heavy velvet draperies that smother the light as though it has been deemed too crude to enter such an elegant hotel. She stands peeking between the draperies when Antoine comes up behind her.

Not now, she says, stiffening.

Yes, now. He squeezes her shoulders and kisses her neck playfully.

She moves her face away. They're waiting for us.

He kisses her on the right shoulder.

They'll wait, he says. His tone is light, happy.

She takes his hand and presses it. She doesn't want to spoil his mood. It is for her that they're here, after all, to begin to mend, if that's the right word, the tear between her and her family.

It's a bit . . . unsettling, she says. To be here with you . . . and with her at the same time.

Of course, he says. It would be, wouldn't it? After all that's happened. We have to let time do its work. For her as well as for you. Perhaps, he adds, you should be alone with her for a while.

She nods, grateful for his suggestion but not completely reassured. He takes her hand.

Let's go down, shall we?

Ahead of them, couples sweep down the corridor, the women's shoulders emerging out of the low-necked bodices like pale orchids over the delicate stems of their waists. A fire crackles in the huge fireplace in the lobby, aromas of venison waft through the hallways, crimson velvet ribbons are tied to Christmas trees (Christmas trees! Here!), bouquets of holly or holly-like branches hang in the doorways. Outside, the exuberant vegetation has been care-

fully pruned and shaped to frame the sweeping lawns, the manicured flower beds, and the water fountains, but the whole thing
looks more like a carefully designed theater set than the intended
French-style garden.

Everybody is so elegant, she whispers to Antoine. Do you
think my dress will do?

You're ravishing, he says.

That's what I thought, she says, and she pinches her skirts
between thumbs and forefingers, performing a full circle that ends
in a curtsy. Antoine catches her in his arms.

So why do you ask, then, Mademoiselle Jozelon?

So that you would answer, Monsieur Langelot! And you did!

But under the pleasantries, she feels that they too are part of a
show. And when they sit next to Angelina and Jules, at the table
reserved for them, out in the garden, the four of them will act in a
play entitled Family Reunion in Indochina.

In the gardens, the glass balls and angels and the gold stars
hung in the tamarind trees fight it out with the deep purple of the
hibiscus flowers and the pink of the laurels. The crib of carved wood
and the manger are, she thinks, comically incongruous, between a
guava and a mango tree, although pale Mary and half-naked Joseph
don't look so out of place in a climate as warm as their Palestine.
The whole scene looks to her like a pagan feast, jarring with the
glittery winterland motif of a traditional Christmas.

They're finishing dinner. One bottle of champagne and two bottles of Saint-Emilion—carried from across the world courtesy of
Les Messageries Maritimes—stand empty on the table. Balloon
glasses are still half-filled with Armagnac. Broken pieces of baguette lie in the breadbasket and rims of cheese in the plates.

Are they actually trying to make Camembert with milk from
the local cows? Antoine says, pushing his plate away. Admirable,
but inedible.

I thought the cows here didn't give milk, Victorine says.

The goats then, Jules says. That would explain the taste.

The goats don't give milk either, Angelina laughs. The Tonkinese don't drink any dairy, don't you know?

Cochinchinese, Angelina, Jules cuts in, we're not in the Tonkin anymore, we're in the South here, remember?

Angelina ignores him.

They call them Annamites, even in the South, Victorine says.

I know, Jules insists, but really the Annamites are only in Annam, the central region.

Antoine shrugs. These are all artificial denominations thought up by the French administration, he says. It's obvious he's getting exasperated with Jules's comments.

Well, Annamites or not, their cattle don't give milk.

Maybe the cows are shipped from Normandy along with the flour and everything else.

But that *bûche* . . . hmm, that *bûche*, on the other hand . . . Antoine wipes his mouth from the glistening chocolate cream.

Totally authentic, real butter cream!

From the same cows of mysterious origin.

They laugh. Even Jules loses his stiffness.

Jules and Antoine excuse themselves and drift off toward one of the parlor rooms to smoke cigars; Victorine and Angelina stay at the table, alone for the first time since they've been reunited, while a waiter comes to clear the empty dishes and sweep off the crumbs. A group of Annamite singers in long white robes make their way to a makeshift stage next to the crèche.

Almost midnight, Angelina says.

Remember midnight mass in Cholet? Victorine says. Her hands are lying flat on the table, the wedding band and the tourmaline ring Antoine has given her clearly visible. But Angelina doesn't seem to notice the rings. She is watching the choir.

I hear they are very good, she says. They sing *a cappella* at the cathedral of Saigon.

The singers try out a few notes, tuning their voices.

Victorine puts her hands on her lap, embarrassed by the rings. They are silent for a few moments.

Angelina . . . She glances at her sister and laughs a little. You look so different.

Fatter?

Hmmm. Let me see. No, but—healthy . . . Your cheeks are pink.

Angelina puts her hand on her stomach.

No! Don't tell me!

Yes! It will be the baby of the new century.

Ah mon Dieu!

The orchestra now gathers in front of the singers and tunes up: a cacophony of pinched violin cords and cello rumble.

I thought you said *a cappella*?

I thought so.

Maybe it's a dance?

It's Christmas. I doubt it.

Victorine takes a deep breath and deliberately brings her hands back to the table, encircling her glass of water. This time, she is sure of it, Angelina notices the rings, but she doesn't say anything. She wouldn't have forgotten her older sister's first engagement ring—a baguette solitaire. Victorine was, after all, the first Jozelon girl to marry.

Angelina. Be honest with me. What are they saying about me at home?

A violin squeaks. Angelina makes a face at the sound, then her expression changes and she looks Victorine squarely in the eyes.

Why didn't you write to them? Why didn't you at least tell them where you are? Why didn't you—I don't know—leave a note. Something, anything.

Angelina's voice is trembling, not just from her own anger, it seems, but from the whole family's anger. They must have exchanged letters and speculated and come to some conclusion, some judgment about her. Now it's as though they had reversed roles, Victorine becoming the younger sister, the one who's being admonished. She feels blood come up to her neck, her cheeks.

I couldn't. I know it sounds awful. It's a poor excuse . . . She wishes tears to well up in her eyes, but there's only that frightening lack of feeling.

Victorine, how did this happen?

Briefly their eyes meet.

He appeared on the beach one day out of the blue. That's all.

The singers, standing in a row at the front of the stage, begin a song, without the musicians.

They look as though they've just taken their first communion, Angelina says.

Maybe they have, Victorine says. After all, it's not enough that we hire them as our servants, we have to make them change their religion.

Angelina looks at her with surprise.

So you believe our presence here is not good. Don't you believe in the Church?

Well, yes, of course I do. It's just—well, they have their own religion. I've been studying with a Chinese monk—

Angelina interrupts her, singing along with the singers. *Il est né le divin enfant.* Remember? we used to sing it on Christmas morning.

Victorine nods and looks at Angelina. She seems older, older than her even. Her hair tightly pinned up, the way she leans back in her chair, all so familiar . . . of course, it could be because she is with child. And suddenly she sees it, the obvious resemblance. It's Marie-Louise, their mother! Same tilt of the head listening to the music, same expression of concern worn like an all-purpose mask, barely hiding reprobation. Or is she imagining it?

Angelina, she wants to say, my dear little sister, where are you?

But she doesn't say anything. She picks up her glass of Martel and brings it to her mouth, then realizes it's empty and puts it down. Angelina pushes her own glass, still half-filled, toward her.

Thanks. Victorine pauses for a moment. What . . . did they think happened?

Angelina sighs.

They figured it out eventually.

That I left with Antoine?

That you left with a man.

Victorine stays silent for a while.

Tell me. Give me, please, news from Daniel and Madeleine. Do you have any?

Yes.

From whom?

From papa and maman. Daniel passed his *brevet* with honors. Madeleine made it to the sixth grade.

And Armand? Her voice is blank.

He's fine, as far as I know. He's hired a girl to take care of them.

She can imagine her, a farm girl of sixteen or seventeen, barely older than Daniel. She would bet on it that she's already ended up in Armand's bed. She checks herself to see if she feels a twinge of pain, but no, nothing. An emptiness in her heart.

And what did our parents say about me?

They worried at first. Then they tried to understand. Papa said that you shouldn't have married Armand.

And Armand's family?

Well . . . They blame you.

Victorine looks at Angelina again. Yes, there is anger in her eyes, anger in the downward cast of her mouth, anger in the way one of her hands resting on the arm of her chair is closed in a fist, perhaps without her even being aware of it. Yes, she has changed. They have both changed.

And you? Do you blame me?

Angelina rearranges her napkin on her lap without answering. The carolers' voices are pure, light. They rise like froth in the open air.

I don't know. I don't know if I would have the courage to leave Jules if . . . something like that happened to me.

Courage! Victorine laughs in self-derision. It's not courage. It was—like that.

She stays silent for a moment. She wonders if the girl is braiding Madeleine's hair. She always hated anybody to touch her hair
except her mother. Victorine rolls a little bit of leftover bread
dough between her thumb and fingers.

I am a bad mother. She glances quickly at Angelina. Isn't it
what they all say?

What they say and what you are may be two different things.

Angelina has surprised her again. The grown-up mask dis-
solves from her sister's face, and the Angelina of their childhood
reappears, candid and questioning.

Is that what *you* think? Victorine asks at last.

But Angelina is looking over her shoulder toward the smoking
parlor to see if the men are coming back.

Do you love him? she asks.

Yes.

You were always a romantic.

Victorine wonders, is this sympathy or disdain she hears in her
sister's voice?

A romantic?

Well, even with Armand. I mean, the way things happened
with him . . . It's obvious Angelina is carefully choosing her words.
Do you think . . . perhaps you were in love with Antoine the
whole time?

When I saw him on the beach last year . . . Do you understand?

I don't know. It's a difficult situation you got yourself in.
Angelina reaches across the table and takes her hand, perhaps trying to soften her words.

Victorine pulls her hand away. You used to be on my side. Jules
hates me, doesn't he?

No. He's just . . . he doesn't talk much.

And you like that?

He's very even-tempered. You are more like papa. You want—
pfff! With her hand she cuts through the air. And then you do it.

Like papa! Victorine bursts out laughing. I hadn't thought
of that.

. . .

The photo was taken the week between Christmas and the New Year. Victorine was wearing the dress they had bought for the reception at the Gia-Long Palace, with the necklace of tourmaline and matching earrings, and Antoine the light-colored jacket with the stand-up hard collar most of the white men wore in Indochina. The back of the photo was stamped PIERRE DIEULEFILS— HANOI—1899, although it had been taken in Da Lat. Angelina had told them about the photographer, Dieulefils. He was very well established, apparently, in Hanoi, in the Tonkin. It was he who had taken the photograph of Angelina and Jules with their boy, the one she had sent to Victorine in Maillezais. Every year for the holiday season he came down to Da Lat and set up a small studio, not far from the palace, in a house overlooking the lake. The studio was installed in the front room of the house, open to a veranda flowered with begonias. They had changed into their fancy clothes, helping each other and laughing with anticipation. The studio was set the way it was for all the photos, with a swath of light blue fabric hanging as background, to simulate the sky, although of course you couldn't tell, since it came out gray, and a vase of silk roses on a stool. They had posed as Monsieur and Madame Langelot, their gold bands, which they always wore, and Victorine's tourmaline ring clearly in evidence on their fingers. That photo, she felt, was as close to a wedding photo as they would ever have.

What's wrong?

Antoine's eyes are on the mirror as he's unknotting his tie. He's watching her lying on the bed, her dark hair, unpinned, spread out on the pillow.

Nothing.

I know you, I know there's something. And you won't tell me if I don't ask.

He tosses his tie on the bed.

You talked with your sister for a long time while we were smoking. You looked upset when we got back.

He's right. She won't talk about certain things unless she's asked. She always thought it was because she didn't want to hurt anyone. But maybe it's because she doesn't want to be hurt. She watches him in silence. He unbuttons his cuff links, then his vest. He is focused on each button. He puts the cuff links on the dresser. He drapes the vest carefully over the back of the chair. Usually he tosses his clothes around carelessly.

She gets up from the bed and, without a word, starts brushing her hair in long, deep strokes, as she always does.

I don't know. I'm not sure she's that sympathetic.

She sits down next to Antoine on the bed, bends her neck a little, and parts her hair.

Can you tell me if the part is even and straight?

He pulls a strand of hair and moves it to the other side.

Perfectly straight, madame.

She brings one side of her hair over her shoulder and starts braiding it.

She gave you news of your children?

Yes. They're fine. Daniel passed his *brevet.*

And your husband?

She doesn't turn around, but deliberately starts braiding the other side.

He's fine, she says in a voice perfectly devoid of expression.

He takes her by the waist and makes her pivot and face him. His hands on her bare skin feel soothing.

Victorine. His eyes are warm, searching hers. Perhaps what I'm going to say is a bit harsh. But it's your silence that is poisoning your life. It's as if, in some way, what we have done has not happened. As if we were not really together. You're caught somewhere in between there and here.

She stares at him, surprised by his outburst. She looks away, unable to respond to the look in his eyes.

And I'd like to tell you something else.

What?

Until you face what you did, until you accept it, you're not going to be happy here.

The Christmas stars have been replaced by red and green Chinese lanterns for the New Year's Eve party. The program for the evening promises the *Réveillon du Siècle:* a chamber music concert in one of the indoor ballrooms, a chanteuse in the gardens, cannon fired at midnight, fireworks over the lake, promenades on Chinese junks decorated with multicolored garlands throughout the night.

She presses Antoine's arm against her. Her feeling of unreality has not abated the whole week they've been in Da Lat. And now another show is starting: the New Year spectacle. The guests are even more lavishly dressed than they were at Christmas, the women in long silk dresses, hair swept up, satiny shoulders, naked necks, and arms encircled with jet, pink beryl, and rubies, the men in black or white linen suits, the *gratin* of Saigon, as they say—Saigon's upper crust. She is wearing the same dress she had on at the Gia-Long reception, the one in the photograph, with the tourmaline earring and necklace set, and Antoine his suit of cream linen.

I want to go home, she says softly. Antoine puts his arm around her shoulders.

Tomorrow.

The cannon blast off. The fireworks shoot up over the lake, red poppies exploding into gold stars. Another salvo of cannon.

Vive le vingtième siècle!

They dance. The music is a quadrille, the same music they play in Vendée at country balls.

Bonne année, mon amour.

A third blast of cannon goes off. Champagne corks pop all around them.

Vive la France!

Angelina and Jules call out to them from their table and hand them each a glass of champagne.

Cheers!

Long live the twentieth century!

Exactly a hundred years, Angelina says dryly, looking again like Marie-Louise, sipping her glass of champagne. Neither more nor less.

And we will not see the end of it, Antoine remarks.

Even though it's an obvious fact, a veil of sadness falls on Victorine, as though the elaborate stage, the three cannon salvos and the firecrackers were harbingers of the end.

SHE WAKES UP with a start, dreaming that she is standing alone, still a child, in her father's workshop in Cholet, transfixed by the smoke erupting from a mound of leaves burning in the courtyard, threatening to engulf the whole building. She doesn't remember falling asleep earlier, doesn't even know where she is. Then she recognizes the smell of tobacco. Antoine is smoking in the dark, lying on his back.

You're up? she says. She can see the Chinese lanterns glowing between the curtains they forgot to close. The night is still dark, with barely a hint of gray in the sky.

I couldn't sleep.

Maybe it's the lamb from last night, or all that champagne.

He gives a dry, dismissive laugh. No, it's not that.

He pulls on his cigarette, blows the smoke out forcefully.

Antoine, what is it?

You're distant, he says after a couple of puffs of his cigarette. I don't know where you are. It's as if you're not quite here.

Since when?

I don't know, he says.

She remembers Armand telling her the same thing one day, pointing to his temple and saying, You're not quite there. But not like this, Armand's voice had been angry, confronting her. And he had been right, she wasn't there anymore, she had already left him, in her mind.

She turns toward him and puts her hand on his shoulder.

I'm here, she says. Let's go back to sleep.

He stubs out his cigarette, angrily, she thinks.

You go back to sleep, he says.

But she can't. She lies immobile next to him, her face turned toward the window, pretending to sleep, keeping her breathing low and steady. Gradually, the lanterns fade and a milky light fills the sky.

I've been awake at night, she starts to say suddenly, so low it's almost as though she is talking to herself. The last few nights. I've been thinking of them. I think of what they're doing. What they're going through because of me. I see other children pointing fingers at them. I see them younger than they really are now, crying at night because their mother has abandoned them. I think of what they're being told about me. That's what I've been thinking about.

He turns around and lights up another cigarette. I think about it too. That I made you leave your children behind. That's what's hurting you, isn't it? And it's my fault that it happened.

He takes her in his arms and she lies there, her head against his neck.

No, she says, it's not your fault. It's mine.

THE CITROËN pulls in front of the small row house on the main street of L'Aiguillon. The trunk, on the backseat, reaching almost up to the roof, looks like a small coffin. Maurice walks around the car and opens the passenger door to let her out.

You go in, Maurice says, unlocking the front door for her. I'll find someone to help me carry the trunk.

Her new house has three small rooms strung end to end. They smell dusty, but not damp like Villa Saint-Claude, which was so close to the ocean. She opens the windows to let in the air. They open right on the sidewalk at street level. She'll have to keep them tightly shut to protect her privacy. There will be no end-of-the-world horizon, only motor coaches and the occasional horse and buggy.

She leans out the window and watches Maurice and a man who was passing by helping him maneuver her trunk and slide it out of the car.

Where? they ask her, hesitating at the front door.

She points to the middle of the kitchen, which is the first room you walk into from the street. They let the trunk drop with a thud. Two or three dozen boxes are stacked high against the wall, and her furniture is piled in a corner.

The other man touches his cap with his fingers and leaves. She sits on one of the wooden chairs without removing her coat. Her tapestry bag is resting against the leg of a chair.

We have to buy you some food, Maurice says.

It's Sunday, she says. And besides, I brought what I had at La Faute. It's in that basket over there.

I'll make you some tea, maman, he offers. If you'd like.

Yes, thank you, she says. It got a little chilly, didn't it?

Night's coming. I'll bring in some wood and get a fire going.

There's a stack in the backyard, she says, I noticed it before.

He sets the water to boil in the kettle and carries an armload of logs and small branches through the back door. She watches him taking the teacups out of their newspaper wrappings and setting them on the kitchen counter. He picks up one of the newspaper pages and looks surprised.

Le Courrier de Saïgon, he reads. Who's sending you newspapers from Indochina?

She doesn't answer.

He looks more closely and whistles. Nineteen hundred! *Seigneur, maman!* You are a pack rat. Keeping papers from forty years ago! That was when Tante Angelina was there? Or was it Tonton René? He was something in the Department of Education in Saigon, wasn't he?

She ignores him—stupid of her to have wrapped the teacups with one of the newspapers she'd found in the trunk. He starts twisting the newspaper and methodically laying the twists along the stack of small firewood, then puts a match to them. The flames leap and engulf the paper. He crouches and pokes the wood until the flames lick one of the big logs. Then he stands up.

Nice. Very nice, *mon petit Maurice.* She leans forward and rubs her hands together, letting herself go to the warmth, to the smell of burning wood, the smell of fall. A wave of optimism fires up her spirit. Perhaps, after all, fall will be good here, in this new house, perhaps, somehow, the Germans will be beaten back. Men all around her are talking about resisting, taking to the woods and fighting. Organizing, getting weapons, following de Gaulle's call to arms.

She listens to him busying himself at the little stove, pouring boiling water in the teapot.

There's sugar in that suitcase, over there, she says, still staring at the fire, losing herself in the constantly changing pattern of the flames. The fire starts to crackle and spit.

The wood's dry, he says. It's good. It didn't get spoiled by the rain. Look how fast it's catching. It's not pine.

No, elm, I think.

What's that smell? he says suddenly.

What smell?

In the trunk. A kind of smoky smell.

Oh, she says, staying in her daydream. It's sandalwood. It's a tree that grows in Asia. It protects against moths.

I see.

He places two cups and saucers on a tray with the teapot and sets them on a folding table in front of her. Then he gets up again and when he comes back he pours tea for the two of them.

She sips at her tea, her eyes half-closed. The smell of sandalwood is stronger now. The smell of the Buddhist temple in Cholon. Tears come to her eyes. Chiang with his skin withered like old parchment and his long nails.

I found this in the trunk, he says.

She turns toward him and looks. On the tray is the photo album with the red leather cover.

She takes her time putting her porcelain cup down, making sure it doesn't spill.

He opens the album with care, as if he feared the pages would tear and turn to dust if he was too rough. There's a large picture slipped into the first page.

She glances at it. It's the photograph from Da Lat.

Saigon
I

JANUARY 2, 1900. The jostling of the *pousse-pousses,* the group of *coolie-xe* squatting in the shade of a *badamier* tree, the floating ceiling of the parasols, the tangle of masts on the river, the heat, like a fever after the coolness of the mountains. This time it isn't the strangeness that surprises her, but how familiar Saigon feels, how much like home. A feeling emphasized by the presence of Angelina and Jules, with whom they are chatting at the corner of boulevard Charner and rue Catinat, where the coach from Da Lat has dropped them off. Yes, home. And home also, later, with Phu waiting at their door, picking up their suitcases, his thin arms bulging from the effort, and serving them a Martel and soda water on the veranda.

They had rented the house a week or so before leaving for Da Lat. Victorine had fallen in love with it because it had some European comfort (whitewashed rooms, running water, a small kitchen with a charcoal stove) amid a lush setting. It was built at the edge of a little park, meticulously landscaped in the French manner—ruler-straight allées lined with trees and neatly tended flower beds. But the city gardeners must have given up on the back of the park and let it return to its natural state; it spilled over into their small backyard in a dense thicket of wild hibiscus, palms, and giant ferns, and monkeys balancing by their tails.

Camille had stopped by in her carriage to pay a visit soon after. With her white pleated dress, her creamy white skin, her red hair loosely pinned, her figure slimmed down since she had given birth to a little girl a few weeks earlier, Camille looked like a flirtatious *colon*'s wife, of which there were so many in Saigon. Standing at her door in her simple cotton dress, Victorine had envied her nonchalance, her brazenness. Camille had waved with her fan, which was coyly hiding one of her eyes, then she had leaned toward her driver, touching his naked shoulder with her fan. *Attends-moi,* she had said, using the informal *tu,* and jumped off the carriage. She had found the house charming, but when Victorine had herself brought a vermouth cassis on the veranda, she had insisted they couldn't live in Saigon without their own boy, and had suggested Phu, whose French employers had just gone back to France.

Victorine had thought Phu was a child who had wandered there by mistake when he appeared at their door, with his silk pants too large for his narrow hips, held by the wide sash that made his waist look absurdly thin, a voluminous turban overpowering his small face. They had stood awkwardly facing each other in the barely furnished dining room, Victorine, her hands clasped in front of her, unsure of how to treat him, and Phu, rigid, waiting to be told what to do. But he had taken over the household with confidence, heading off to a nearby market and coming back with a basketful to prepare a delicious beef *pho* with ginger and a dessert of bean paste. Later, he had emptied their cartons and trunks and tidied their three rooms. There was a simple wooden lean-to behind the house, the size of a small room, and Victorine had helped him make it as comfortable as possible, although she realized it was more for her sake than his, he didn't seem to mind how bare it was. And now here he was, welcoming them at the door, dinner ready, their bed turned out.

It was Antoine who had suggested inviting Angelina and Jules the following Sunday for lunch; weren't they family, after all? But Victorine was nervous. Nothing had been resolved in Da Lat—

and how could it be resolved, really? She still felt Angelina's mute reproach.

She went to mass with Angelina and Jules at Notre-Dame before lunch. It was worse than going to the little chapel in Vinh Long. Sitting between the two of them, without Antoine, who had stayed home, she felt like a child with her disapproving parents. She was back in Vendée, but in exile, in shame. The feeling was so crushing she couldn't imagine going back to mass after that, with or without Angelina and Jules.

In the *pousse-pousse* on the way home, she remained silent. The loud agitation of the French in the streets seemed futile and arrogant to her. All the joy had drained out of her. She could feel Angelina looking at her with curiosity, but she kept her head lowered.

Phu had cooked a *ca kho to,* a fish stew that he prepared exceptionally well, but Jules grumbled. How were they to drink the red wine he had brought if they were having fish? Anyway, he didn't trust these local dishes. That's how the Europeans got sick, eating that food.

Victorine humored him. Can't you give up wine, now that you live all the way across the world? Or loosen the rule about drinking white wine with fish? And they were yet to get sick in Indochina. The food in Saigon was the most delicious she had ever eaten. Jules shrugged. She wondered if she was beginning to sound like Louis Désaunier, extolling the virtues of the colony, and motioned Phu to uncork the bottle.

Angelina was showing now, her belly and hips heavy and her pale cheeks filled out. She waddled to the table, putting one hand on her lower back for support, overplaying the role of the expectant mother. Victorine regretted having invited them over.

They all drank the wine, and later emptied half the bottle of pear liqueur Jules had also brought along; by the time they had finished dessert, the collection of glasses reminded Victorine of the end of lunch at Cholet or Sainte-Christine. Her spirits were low again. It wasn't just the wine. It was the same feeling she had had in church: Vendée was invading the life she had created here in Saigon with Antoine, paralyzing her. And she had done it herself. She was the one who had brought Angelina back into her life.

Antoine smiled at her across the table. Perhaps he had noticed that she hadn't been talking much. She didn't smile back and got up to help Phu clear the table.

After the pear liqueur, Jules took out a deck of luette cards. It wasn't a game they played here. Antoine had forgotten the rules and they had to remind him. You had to make up a secret code of winks and faces to let your partner know which cards you held without the other team guessing. Gradually, her mood lifted, until they were all laughing so hard that Phu stood petrified at the door, clutching the coffeepot, not daring to bring it to the table.

I think your boy is scared, Jules remarked.

After Angelina and Jules left, they got ready for the night. During lunch, Antoine said, you seemed sad. But you laughed so much afterward. I haven't seen you laugh like that in a long time.

Really? She was surprised.

Yes, he said. Even Jules laughed. Unbelievable. This man looks like he's swallowed an umbrella most of the time.

Maybe Jules is homesick, she said, wondering why she was defending him. It's that card game that made us laugh. It's such a silly game. Didn't you play luette in Vendée?

Yes, he said. I did.

She thought of her evenings in Velluire playing luette with Armand that first summer. How much they had laughed then. It had been their best time together. How long ago that seemed now. Yes, the afternoon had turned out well after all. And yet now she felt dispirited again. It's as though the Victorine she had been before Antoine, the Victorine she had been in Vendée, moody, distant, silent, had come back and taken her place.

He sensed her unease but said nothing. He just took her by the hand to the bedroom and they both fell into the folds of the mosquito net. His hands touched her the way they always did, his kisses were as passionate as they always were, but she didn't feel them. She was watching their bodies move, their limbs fold and unfold, as though she was witnessing a strange, even ridiculous minuet performed by two actors.

THE SMILE that illuminates Chiang's face fills her with warmth. She hasn't seen him for nine months, yet he greets her as though he was expecting her. He bows, his hands tucked into his sleeves. His face has aged, she notices, but his eyes are shining, and he precedes her past the altar of the grinning Buddha, whose gold feet are surrounded by offerings of mangosteens, white flesh against deep purple skin, plates overflowing with *sapèques,* and burning sticks of sandalwood. In the back room they sit down at the table where they used to work together and he pulls out *The Tale of Kiều* from a shelf.

Do you remember? he asks.

She nods and begins to recite by heart:

> *Làn thu-thủy, nét xuân-sơn,*
> *hoa ghen thua thắm, liễu hờn kém xanh.*

Her eyes were autumn streams, her brows spring hills.

She hesitates for a moment, then the rest of the verse comes flowing out.

Flowers grudged her glamour, willows her fresh hue.

Good, he says, and she can see the pleasure and perhaps also the admiration in his eyes, that she can still remember and recite flawlessly, she, a European woman. But how emaciated his face has become, how sunken his cheeks and how prominent his cheekbones. Less than a year ago she had found his old face glowing, the skin taut, and now it seems to have withered.

Are you unwell, Chiang? she asks, wondering if the question is perhaps too personal. It must be tiring for you to be in the temple every day from morning to night.

He gives a small, dismissive shrug. Old age, he says. A young monk is due to come and help me soon.

But she wonders whether it is the opium or old age that is eating at him.

And when he picks up a brush to launch into the first stroke of a character—that moment of silent concentration makes her think of the pause before a runner starts a race—she sees that his hand is shaky, and his brush stroke not as firm as it was.

Your turn, he says, handing her the brush.

She copies the Chinese characters he has just drawn, then she reads an Annamite text written in *quoc ngu* and slowly translates it. Chiang corrects her, patiently.

After two hours, she sees the fatigue in his eyes, his hands tremble when he turns the pages of the book. The shadows are lengthening and it will soon be too dark, even with the candles they have lit up, to read or write.

I should go back, she says. It's getting late.

She places her hand on Chiang's hand, overcoming her repulsion at touching his long, twisted nails. With its hard claws, his hand feels like a bird, shaky and brittle. A wave of tenderness for the old monk comes over her. If she pressed the hand too hard, it seems, it might easily crumble beneath hers. He looks at her and nods with a shy smile, returning the pressure of her hand, accepting her sympathy.

The steam locomotive is puffing a cloud of gray smoke when she arrives at the tramway stop. She runs to it, feeling the passengers' eyes riveted on her. If she is to settle in Saigon, she will do it her own way, and not live this secluded life the French favor. She won't be afraid to mix with the Annamites and the Chinese. She will travel on her own in the wagons packed with women and children bringing their goods from the market, hens and pigs at their feet, and men going to work in Saigon.

Madame. A heavyset man with a black mustache, dressed in a dark suit, lifts his straw hat to salute her as she is about to board the tramway. She tries to remember if she has ever met him before and where.

This is the third-class wagon, madame, the man says. I think you'd be better off in first class. If you'd like to follow me. It's the first wagon behind the locomotive.

A line of Europeans, she can see from where she is standing, is forming in front of the first wagon—the "little whites" who can't afford to take a hansom cab but would rather not travel in too close quarters with the Annamites.

Thank you, she says, very kind of you. But I have a third-class ticket.

He places his hand on her naked elbow, right under the ribbon that keeps her short sleeve gathered. She shudders slightly under his touch, which feels too intimate.

Permit me, he says, to upgrade—this wagon is not for you— over here, if you please . . .

She pulls her arm away.

No. It's fine, she says firmly. Then manages: Much obliged.

He lifts his hat again and salutes her with a puzzled look.

As you wish. He shrugs disapprovingly, perhaps thinking she belongs to the class of those women they call unhooked.

THE WAREHOUSE where Antoine has rented space near the Messageries Maritimes Hotel is located on Quay Mytho, a few hundred meters from the opium-boiling factory. Victorine glances uncomfortably, as she walks past it with Antoine, at the poppy flowers carved inside the arches. But she is delighted to discover the vast and dark expanses Mr. Wang takes them through, filled

with huge piles of fabrics and precariously stacked towers of tea-
pots and china dishes. His ivory-colored skin, sunken cheeks, and
emaciated body suggest a great many pipes a day, and again she
thinks of Chiang. Their own corner, tucked away behind a half-
partition of rotted wood, is at the back of the spice warehouse,
among piles of canvas bags redolent of cardamom, coriander,
ginger, and curry.

Antoine cracks open the first crate, pulling out the nails with a
pair of pliers, and takes out a stack of white linen sheets. Victorine
lays them on a blanket they have brought with them. The sheets
are covered with a fine, brown dust, but otherwise undamaged.

The next day she helped him pack the finest sheets and tablecloths
and a few dozen handkerchiefs in her old suitcase, still covered
with its labels from the sea voyage, and they walked downtown
together. He was going to take the samples to Denis-Frères and
a few smaller boutiques on the Quai du Commerce that had ex-
pressed interest in placing orders. Meanwhile, she set out for the
Bazar Saïgonnais to buy some office supplies. In her cotton dress
and light canvas boots, her parasol casually hanging from her wrist,
she tried to ignore the sidelong looks the French administrators
and civil servants and the occasional sailors usually reserved for
unaccompanied women. She carried back home a big ledger of blue
Moroccan along with a case of pencils, spare nibs for her pen, and
a bottle of ink of a color called China blue.

In the afternoon she set herself up on the veranda, which was
cooler than the inside of the house, spread out the pieces of linen
on the wicker table, and opened the blue ledger. She made a list of
the various types of linen that had been shipped from Cholet, one
line for each category: red-and-white handkerchiefs, unbleached
linen napkins, tablecloths, sheets, pillowcases, the various models,
the different colors, the plain linen and the more luxurious, the
ones that were embroidered in Valenciennes or Venice stitches, or
the simplest ones in *point lancé*, and the bolts of fabric.

The hardest part was to settle on a reasonable price for each of the items. She spent a good deal of time converting the francs into Mexican piastres, the silver money that was used all over Asia. It was an interesting bit of information she had uncovered at the Saigon library: in the early days of the Asian trade, the Chinese insisted on being paid in silver for their spices and silk. So the Asian goods were shipped through Spanish America, that is, through Mexico, which was a major producer of silver, and the payments in silver would travel back across the Pacific Ocean from Acapulco to the Far East via Manila. The Mexican piastre had remained the trading currency of Southeast Asia. That monetary conversion was a difficult task requiring a lot of checking and double-checking, and when Antoine came back it was already late. Dinnertime.

She closed the ledger. He dropped the suitcase—it fell on its side on the floor and one of the locks popped open—and loosened up his collar as he sat down in one of the rocking chairs. His eyes looked tired, his face puffed. The clouds around his face were impossible to ignore. He cracked a match and lit a cigarette. Her eyes followed the red ember in the gathering dusk.

So, what happened? But she already knew the answer. She went to sit on the other rocking chair.

All this work—*your* work, our work—to prepare, procure introductions with the best shops—and how many orders do you figure were confirmed? Accepted, I should say.

He pulled angrily at his cigarette.

She looked at him silently.

Denis-Frères, nothing. Barron, Quai du Commerce, a dozen sheets and two bolts of unbleached linen.

She waited. He gave her a defiant look.

That's it. The others, nothing.

She ran the numbers in her head. They had hoped for five or six times that many orders.

It's only the first week, she said. She forced her voice to be strong and steady. We have to persevere.

He shook his head.

Of course. But it doesn't look good. Did you read in *Le Courrier de Saïgon* yesterday about Indian cotton and calico? The prices are unbeatable. Even lower than they were a few months ago. French linen is not worth the price difference. And now the stores are telling me linen is too heavy for the climate anyway. Only now are they saying this.

But they all said that the Cholet linen was of such superior quality the customers would pay the price difference. Remember? When we visited the stores before Christmas?

Yes, well . . . Phu! he called, without getting up. Phu emerged from the shadows of the dining room and bowed. Bring us absinthe and soda water, please. We'll have dinner later.

Oui, Monsieur.

Phu came back with the absinthe and poured the drink.

Just a finger, she said.

Antoine picked up his glass and took a long drink.

Victorine, I'm afraid you can't count too much on any form of stability here, with me.

She sipped a little of the absinthe and winced. Even watered down, it tasted like fire.

I don't care about that.

Are you sure?

She thought for a moment.

Yes. Why do you ask?

He put out his cigarette with his heel.

You seem moody lately.

But it's not because of that.

I thought maybe you were homesick.

She looked at him, surprised. How could he think that?

No, she said emphatically. I don't miss Maillezais. It was so oppressive.

I thought it was Armand you found oppressive.

She said nothing. She didn't want to talk about Armand.

Still, you keep trying to grow roots.

She wondered why he was insisting like that, challenging her, as it were. Digging in.

And you don't?

He lit another cigarette and smoked in silence for a while. No, he said finally. My roots are in Vendée, and perhaps also in Paris. I'm here to explore, to try to make a living. If we moved out of this house tomorrow, I wouldn't care.

It was too dark now for her to see his face. She had the impression he was talking to himself more than he was talking to her. Was he trying to provoke her? She drank more of the absinthe and put it down. The alcohol made her feel more closed in, almost angry.

We're deluding ourselves if we think we can build a comfortable little bourgeois life here.

What do you mean?

The reality of this place is this. He pointed with his cigarette toward the jungle growing at the back of their house, then flicked it off the veranda. To survive here, we have to understand that.

She got up.

I'm not interested in a little bourgeois life here, she said. You're wrong.

He called after her in the dark.

So what do you want then?

The next day when she came back from Cholon she found Antoine leaning over the ledger.

What are you doing?

Checking numbers. We're going to have to lower our prices. At this point, what do we have to lose? We have to get rid of the linen one way or another.

She sat down and leaned forward to unlace her boots.

I'll go to the college tomorrow to see if they'll hire me, she said.

He closed the ledger and looked at her with surprise.

You don't have to do that.

I want to, she said. I've meant to do it anyway.

. . .

There is a picture of them, not taken at the Dieulefils studio in Da Lat, but in the park behind their house, in the early weeks of 1900. A photographer used to set up his camera on a tripod on Sundays and offer his services to the families strolling nearby, the prints to be mailed later on. Antoine had thought it was a charming idea, and they had sat down on a bench. On that photograph, he has his arm around her waist, her head is leaning on his shoulder, and her white dress flows loosely, barely marked at the waist, showing a little of her bare ankle under the skirt. Behind them, just as she remembers it, the park forms a thick, blackish background of almost impenetrable vegetation. There is a softness, an informality in their clothes (her free-flowing muslin dress and his linen shirt worn without a jacket), and their pose (playful, openly affectionate) is strikingly different from the formality of the Da Lat photograph. Perhaps it was the distance, the climate, the immersion in another culture that was making them freer. She had had the photograph framed in delicate tortoiseshell by an Annamite craftsman down near the riverfront and set it on their dresser. It reminded her of the nymphs' flowing robes on the 1900 calendar that was hanging in their kitchen.

The same calendar hangs in the airy office of the Annamite school, the January page fluttering in a languid breeze, above a sign reading "Happy Year of the Mouse 1900," in French and in *quoc ngu*. A picture of a mouse has been drawn underneath by a child, looking rather like a rat with its formidable whiskers. The headmistress of the College Chasseloup-Laubat has given a letter of recommendation to Victorine for Madame Nguyen, the principal of the Annamite school, a small woman who wears the loose pants and tunic common among Annamite women and wears her hair tightly pulled back, elongating her eyelids. For a moment Victorine thinks she might be of mixed race, but she explains that she is French, from Bordeaux, and her husband is from Saigon. She seems astonished that Victorine has been studying Annamite and Chinese, and offers to hire her immediately to teach French literature three afternoons a week to the big class—especially poetry, Madame Nguyen says. They have fallen behind. Their regular teacher had to return to France because of illness. In the classroom, the girls stand up, just like the French girls from the Vinh Long school, and intone *Alouette, Gentille Alouette, Alouette, je te plumerai,* with their soft, singing accent.

They learn fast, the headmistress tells her. You won't believe how smart and eager they are.

And they are, they are. When Victorine sits down at her desk in the big class and opens the poetry textbook, they recite by heart the first lines of the Ronsard poem she meant to teach them:

> *Mignonne, allons voir si la rose*
> *Qui ce matin avait déclose*
> *Sa robe de pourpre au soleil,*
> *A point perdu cette vêprée,*
> *Les plis de sa robe pourprée*
> *Et son teint au vôtre pareil.*

> My lovely, let's go see if the rose
> Which this morning has opened
> Its purple robe to the sun,
> Has lost, tonight,
> The pleats of its purple robe
> And its carnation so like yours.

THE DÉSAUNIERS' new house is located near the Continental, a pleasant stroll after dinner past the illuminated cafés.

You'll see, Antoine says, their house is beautiful.

You've been there? Victorine asks, surprised.

I have, yes, a couple of times. Antoine sounds casual. But even in Saigon, it seems to her, it's odd that a simple customs comptroller would get invited to the house of the vice-director of the Régie for a private evening.

Louis Désaunier has been helping me, Antoine continues, sensing her surprise. He's invited me to his house to discuss the possibilities of another contract. I didn't want to tell you anything about it until something concrete developed . . . And you know, he adds, as they stop in front of an iron gate, they like both of us very much. You know how Camille is, always eager to make friends.

The house is two stories high, with a tiled roof, buttercup-yellow stucco, and green shutters. A *con gaï*, in attendance at the door, takes them through the veranda, inside cool, shadowy rooms furnished with iron-and-rattan furniture and smelling of cardamom and mint.

Camille appears in a cloud of perfume, carrying her new baby in her arms, a girl with a full head of copper curls, swathed in white.

She's so pretty, Victorine says.

You're our first guests, Camille says. We are inaugurating our new Chinese parlor. Victorine, I hope you'll forgive us.

It doesn't take long for Victorine to understand what she means. The small room Camille takes them to at the back of the house is fitted with flat beds of red lacquer, and the walls are hung with silk panels painted with traditional Chinese landscapes of lakes and mountains. Sandalwood incense sticks are burning in a silver dish. On a low table, slender bamboo pipes with ivory, silver, or horn tips and little bowls of clay are laid out near an oil lamp and long needles. Nothing but an elegant opium den. Victorine glances at Antoine, who picks up one of the pipes and weighs it in his hands, as though appraising it, making a point of ignoring her. He knew what the invitation was about. She is angry that he hasn't mentioned the purpose of their visit, and strangely excited by a sense of danger. Louis walks in, followed by a tall and handsome young man carrying a tray with a bottle of vermouth and one of blackcurrant liqueur and glasses. Louis bends to kiss Victorine's hand.

Enchanté, madame. Delighted to have you over.

Enchantée, monsieur.

At the same moment, the baby starts to wail, opening and closing her tiny hands against Camille's chest as though pumping the air.

Vermouth cassis, Mesdames? Louis signals to the young man to pour the drinks, and then clasps Antoine on the shoulder.

How about you, my friend?

Camille sits down on one of the low beds and invites Victorine to sit next to her. The baby keeps pushing against her breast with her hands. Victorine looks at her, pained to see the open mouth trying to suckle through the fabric of the blouse.

She's hungry, she says.

Trong, Camille asks the young man when he's finished serving the vermouth, would you call Lan and ask her to come and pick up the baby? A young woman—not the one who greeted them at the door, but another one, very young too—shuffles in barefoot a few seconds later and takes the baby from Camille's arms. The woman discreetly opens the front of her tunic and the baby latches on to her with the same avidity as she's tried to suckle her mother. For a brief moment, before Lan turns and walks away, Victorine sees the little hands rhythmically kneading the full, amber breast. In France also, women use the services of wet-nurses, for fear of damaging their breasts or to free themselves from the tyranny of the regular hours of breastfeeding, and yet here, in Indochina, the practice seems shocking to her, as though the milk of the young Annamite woman was bought too cheaply.

Camille, on the other hand, seems perfectly serene. She picks up her glass and raises it.

A votre santé!

Santé!

They all raise their glass and drink. The vermouth is smooth, softened just so by the sweetness of the blackcurrant liqueur, a delicious, slightly syrupy ribbon.

Louis squats near the table, opens a porcelain case, withdraws a tiny ball of opium paste, and begins to cook it over the lamp. Fascinated, Victorine leans forward, smelling the opium, watching the ball of paste bubble and sizzle at the tip of the needle. After a moment, when the paste has been reduced to a small bead, Louis drops it into the bowl of the pipe and hands the pipe to Antoine, who's sitting on a flat bed across from Victorine.

Antoine . . . , she says. He looks at her, his eyes defiant. She immediately stops herself. She may disapprove of opium, but they are guests of Camille and Louis, and it isn't her place to tell Antoine what to do.

Leaning on one elbow, Antoine steadies the pipe over the lamp and inhales deeply, his eyes closed. He blows the smoke and inhales a second time. It's obvious he's done this quite a few times before, that he's already something of an expert at it. And then he lies down and Louis turns toward the women.

Want to try? Victorine says nothing. Louis picks up another bead of paste and starts heating it.

Is this one for me? Camille asks. Her tone is coy, flirtatious.

Oui, ma chérie. Louis drops the sizzling bead of opium into the bowl of another pipe and hands it to her. She pulls on the pipe and coughs and has to catch her breath before inhaling another time. Louis points the needle toward Victorine, his eyes challenging her.

Sure?

Camille has already fallen back into her pillow next to her, and caresses her hand.

Try it, she says in a voice already hazy. One pipe . . . one pipe won't hurt you. It's a new sensation . . .

Across the room, Antoine is lying on his side, his legs folded against his stomach. His face looks like that of a child, his features slack, his eyes half-closed, a sleepy smile floating on his full, open lips. Victorine watches him, envious of him, of his daring. Perhaps she is the one who is close-minded, "small town," as Louis would say, fearful of new experiences. After all, opium smoking is an ancient Chinese custom, and Chiang himself has told her he smokes a pipe once in a while. Lie down with me, Camille whispers. She wears one of those new perfumes from Paris, heavy with musk and vanilla. Her hand caresses Victorine's naked arm. A shiver runs down her back. But it's Antoine she longs to lie next to, to curl into his arms, to kiss those open lips.

Louis has finished working a new ball of *chan-doo* over the little oil lamp until it's been reduced to a tiny black bead. How harmful could that tiny bead be? The smell, in the room, is troubling, intoxicating.

I'll try, she says.

Louis's eyebrows come up but he doesn't say anything. He leans over the lamp and drops the bead of *chan-doo* into the bowl of another pipe. She watches him intently, holding her breath.

A small pipe, he says. Very mild. Take your time.

She coughs with the smoke, then tries to inhale again. Camille squeezes her hand. Louis holds the pipe steady for her over the flame of the lamp. One more time, he says. He is solicitous, attentive, as though she was ill and he was administering a lifesaving remedy. Lie down, he whispers gently. But as soon as she leans against the hard leather pillow, her head swims as though she's drunk three or four glasses of vermouth cassis instead of just one, and a violent nausea brings her to her feet. Louis is already lying down.

Trong, he calls his servant in a weak voice, help Madame.

Trong takes her to the bathroom, with its brand-new shower Antoine had described to her, outfitted with British piping shipped from Calcutta. He wipes her brow with a cool napkin until she is steadier on her feet. His hands feel dry and smooth against her hot cheeks. When she is a little better, he helps her back to one of the flat beds. There she lies quiet, in a feverish daydream, for what seems like a long time. The silk painting hanging on the wall in front of her represents a waterfall cascading down a steep mountain and feeding into a lake. The waterfall seems to be animated, moving in a constant flow. The painting reminds her of those lines of *The Tale of Kiều*. How do they go again?

Her eyes were autumn streams, her brows spring hills.

She closes her eyes. She cannot remember more.

THEY WERE on their way to Mr. Wang's warehouse. Antoine had received a few more orders at the lower prices, and she had gone with him to help him pick out an assortment of linen. They stood for a moment on the quay before going in. It was early and the sky still had a freshness, a clear blue that would soon get muddied. A young Annamite woman was sitting in a big Chinese junk, her back to them. She was dressed in a white tunic, a white scarf tied as a turban around her head. She seemed to be resting in the early morning sun, or perhaps she was waiting for her husband. The dried-up shells of two huge crabs, in a mottled pattern of brown, were lying at her feet. Her unselfconscious pose and the simplicity of her dress and hair style—her hair only twisted under the turban—somehow made Victorine feel close to her. Of course, it was probably just her imagination, but the wall between colonizers and colonized seemed to have momentarily collapsed. She would have liked to step over the gunwale of the junk, which was swaying almost at their feet, sit down next to the woman, and exchange a few words with her in Annamite. But just then, Antoine pointed to the south of the river, toward the open sea, just as he had, so many years earlier, pointed toward the Atlantic Ocean.

It's over there, he said.

What is?

New Caledonia.

She remembered that name on the map, when they were traveling on the *Tonkin*, a thread of land in the middle of the South Pacific, east of New South Wales. Wasn't it the new penal colony, where the French convicts were being shipped?

Bravo! he said, and she made a pout, as she did every time she thought he was condescending toward her. But the new governor there has been recruiting *colons* to grow coffee. There's a new offer posted at Customs. Twenty-five hectares offered for free to any French citizen. Twenty-five hectares. Can you imagine?

She shot him a disbelieving look.

He laughed. I know it's a little far-fetched, but it's an intriguing possibility, wouldn't you say?

That idea was short-lived. Two days later, as they were eating the chicken broth prepared by Phu for breakfast—no more baguettes for them in the morning, they had switched to the local cooking at home—he announced in a mock-mournful voice they would have to give up their dream of growing coffee in New Caledonia.

You mean, *your* dream, she corrected wryly.

Whichever.

Why, then?

Because the land is only offered to those who have an agricultural background.

He gave her a teasing smile. She smiled back—just short of a smirk. Tomorrow, another opportunity would come and Antoine would explore it. And he was right. That was the way you had to live in Indochina. That was the life she had wanted with him.

FEBRUARY 14, 1900. It's the letter she notices first, because of the way he holds it by the corner, the envelope half-ripped, the heading, *Indochine Française, Douanes et Régies*, still clearly visible. She doesn't notice that he stumbles and almost misses the two steps of the veranda—or she has a vague notion that perhaps he's gone out for a drink and is a little tipsy. She doesn't notice that his suit is wrinkled and damp, and that it's midafternoon and he rarely comes home before dinnertime. She still stares at the letter when he drops it to the ground, and he says, pointing to the lemon tree, look at those lemons, have you ever seen so many lemons on a tree? So many, many lemons. They're going to be ripe in no time.

That's when she notices that his voice is weary, and that his body is sprawled in the chair, legs stretched out in front of him and arms hanging on the side and his head flung back as though he was extremely tired, about to go to sleep.

See for yourself, he tells her. Bastards!

She picks up the letter and pulls the fine onionskin paper—a carbon copy, it looks like—out of the ripped envelope.

> *Monsieur Langelot,*
> *Following our meetings with you on January 15 and Janu-*
> *ary 23, we regret to inform you that we are not in a position to*
> *resume your employment at this point in time. . . . The post you*
> *occupied in Vinh Long for a six month's contract. . . . Unfortu-*
> *nately the post in Saigon that you requested is not available at*
> *present . . . please be assured, however, that if, in the future . . .*

What convoluted language the French administration feels compelled to produce, like tropical flowers erupting from over-heated sap. She cannot bring herself to read every line all the way through. She looks at him. He's pulled himself upward and is fumbling to look for his cigarettes, striking a match.

Is it so bad that you had to go *touffianer* in the middle of the afternoon?

She's used the slang word on purpose, aggressively, that vulgar word they use for smoking opium. With that same accent he some-times has when he is angry. Her tone shows more disdain than she means to.

He shrugs. I'm fine, he says, and sits up higher, drops his jacket to the floor, rolls up his sleeves.

She picks up the jacket, hangs it on the back of a chair.

So those were the meetings that Louis set up for you? You didn't tell me about them.

He wipes the sweat from his forehead with the back of his hand.

I didn't want to make you hope for no reason.

But I wasn't worried. You told me that Louis was trying to help you out . . .

His face is closed, his eyes puffed. That is what worries her, as though he was slipping away from her. She's heard about these men who, after a few years or even just months in Indochina, spend their nights smoking and gradually losing touch with reality.

She says nothing.

There's something I haven't told you. He pulls his handkerchief out of his pocket this time and wipes his forehead and folds the handkerchief back slowly. God, it's so hot today.

What is it?

He gets up and steps over to the edge of the veranda.

I'm going to go to Port-de-France.

Port-de-France?

In New Caledonia.

I thought you had decided against it? That you had found out that without agricultural background, the French government wasn't helping?

It has nothing to do with coffee.

She looks at him, her arms folded on her lap, waiting. Standing up seems to have brought his energy back. He even seems to enjoy her puzzlement.

Do you know what nickel is?

Nickel? It's a—a metal, isn't it? Like copper?

Have you heard of the Société Le Nickel?

No.

If you'd been reading *Le Courrier de Saïgon* lately, you would know. Anyway, you're right, it's a metal, but not like copper, actually. It's a white metal that cannot be corroded—it doesn't rust—and it withstands very high temperatures. Very promising, they say, for the industry. There are nickel mines in New Caledonia. And

Société Le Nickel is the name of the nickel refinery over there. So, with my engineering degree, it occurred to me that— He glances at her. What?

She shakes her head. Nothing.

I know what you're thinking. But rest assured, the *bagne* is off-shore and the convicts are under high security. I hear Port-de-France is a rather charming little outpost.

I wasn't thinking about that, she says. I'm sure Port-de-France is charming. How long would you be gone?

It's a twenty-day trip. One way.

He crosses the veranda and sits down next to her. He takes her hand. Their arms stretch across the gap between the two chairs. She wants so much to respond to the warmth of his hand holding hers but her feelings are shut off.

It may seem preposterous, even a little crazy to you, but it's obvious we're not going to go anywhere with the linen. And . . . well, this seems worth looking into.

So you'll be gone . . . even with a short stay . . . She counts on her fingers. Two months. At least.

He looks at her, his eyes anxious, not at all vacant anymore, but searching hers.

Not much longer, I promise. Is that too long for you? You'll have Angelina here close to you, and your days at the school. And Camille who won't leave you alone. Perhaps you'll even enjoy being on your own . . . He weaves his fingers through hers, runs his thumb across her palm.

You really want to go, she says.

He smiles.

Yes. It's exciting. He uses his mocking, Parisian voice: Unex-plored virgin land. Sand as fine as powder. Blue lagoons. Would you rather come with me?

She pulls her hand out of his.

No, she says. You're right. I'll enjoy the time on my own. And anyway, we're in the middle of the semester. I can't leave the school.

. . .

Sometimes dreams reflect our deepest desires, the ones we are afraid to acknowledge, Chiang told her a few days later. They had been studying the last chapter of *The Tale of Kiều*, in which the heroine is about to be reunited with the love of her life, Trọng, only to realize she is willing to be his wife and his friend, but not his lover. It's too late.

> As Heaven shapes our fate we lend a hand.
> Renounce the world, reap joy—to lust spins grief.

> *Có trời mà cũng tại ta.*
> *Tu là cõi phúc tình là dây oan.*

Chiang's hand with its extravagant nails was holding the book open and his eyes were lost far away. She wondered if the poem held a special meaning for him. Had he known the love of a woman? Even a monk, after all, can know human love, perhaps even carnal love—she didn't know if Buddhist monks had to be celibate. His eyes focused on her again and he looked apologetic, almost embarrassed, as though he had just revealed something too intimate about himself. She blushed. He asked her if she would like to light incense for the Buddha and she said yes, and they walked out to the front room. She lit a fresh incense stick at the flame of an oil lamp and watched the coils of smoke spiral out, hiding the Buddha's golden grin for a moment.

Chiang accompanied her out to the courtyard of the temple, past the potted Chinese ferns, past the blue dragon with the red tongue. Instead of folding his arms into his sleeves to bid her goodbye, as he usually did, he took her hand and bowed.

But Victorine, it doesn't mean we should follow every one of our dreams, he said as an afterthought. He wasn't smiling with that gentle, detached irony he often had. He looked sad. She pressed his hand, that brittle little bird of a hand, into hers, turned around, and left. She didn't want him to see that she had tears in her eyes.

IT IS THE photo on which she is wearing the dress of peach taffeta with the guipure bodice buttoned up to her neck, and the necklace of tourmaline and matching earrings. Her hair is swept up in a loose bun pinned on top of her head, and a few strands flutter past her ears. Antoine has on the dark jacket with the stand-up hard collar the *colons* used to wear in Indochina. His short blond hair looks darker on the photo than it was in reality. Her hands are clasped in front of her and you can clearly see her tourmaline ring and gold band, although the right side of the photograph, where he stands, is partially blurred by a water stain and his gold band is hardly visible.

It's an old album, she says.

He pulls the picture out of its sleeve, glances at the back, then flips it over again.

It's you.

Yes. She rubs her hands together in the warmth of the fire. Then, after a silence: You should add some wood before the flames die down.

He says nothing. He gets up and walks to the window. The gas lamps in the street have been turned on, casting a yellow light. For a moment, his hand, caressing his shoulder, is clearly outlined. His hair, cut longer in front, is falling over his forehead, giving him the profile of a boy.

I should have told you long ago, she says.

He doesn't move from the window. Perhaps he hasn't heard what she said. But she doubts it.

Yes, maybe you should have, he says coldly, not looking at her. She wonders if she hears a trace of disdain in his voice. Perhaps she is imagining it.

He carries a couple of logs to the fire and pokes them to coax the flames into licking the fresh wood.

Push them over this way, she says.

Maman! I know what I'm doing. His tone, it's unmistakable, has a sharpness she is not accustomed to.

Pieces of dry wood crackle and sparks shoot out, landing on the floor.

Instinctively, she moves her feet away.

I knew about him, he says finally, replacing the grate in front of the fire and dusting the front of his pants, facing her. His voice is clear, cutting through the whoosh and fizzle of the fire, and yet she isn't sure she really heard him.

Saigon

II

MARCH 1, 1900. The night is eerily still. It's that short, silent hour when the evening noises have finally died down—even the monkeys in the nearby park are resting—and the early morning frenzy has not yet begun. He is sleeping on his back, one arm under her neck. She slides off his arm, careful not to wake him, and sits up. Her body is shivering in spite of the heat, not at all quiet as it should be. Her breasts are pushing against her night-gown, raw at the lightest pressure of the fabric. She gets up and squats over the china pot they keep under the bed. In her hands her breasts feel fuller, her belly heavier.

Tomorrow he is sailing for Port-de-France.

In the morning, the peculiar sensation seems to have vanished. And yet she wakes up with a feeling of deep contentment. One she hasn't felt, or hasn't known before, even when she was expecting Daniel and later Madeleine. She doesn't say anything to Antoine. They've never talked about having a child, and the precautions they have taken have kept her safe so far. Maybe it was a dream. She helps him pack and in the afternoon accompanies him to Quay Napoleon. His ship is smaller than the *Tonkin,* the shadow its gray hull casts is less monumental. It's a freighter carrying a cargo of tools, liquor, and tobacco to New Caledonia and due to bring back sandalwood, coffee, and nickel on his return trip to Saigon. The only other passengers are three Marist brothers on their way to join their mission in Port-de-France. Don't worry, he says. But she does. The trip lasts almost three weeks, and pirates are not unheard of in those waters. I'll miss you, she says. I'll be back as soon as I can, he says. I promise. He clasps her against him till she loses her breath, just this tremendous strength suffocating her, his lips melting against hers, his face in her neck, and then he abruptly turns around. She stays on the platform waving the red and white handkerchief he has brought her from the warehouse. He stands on the lower deck, one hand shading his eyes from the sun, not moving, his face too far up for her to read his expression. From a distance his body looks frozen. They both stand watching each other for a long time until the ship steams toward the open sea and she cannot see him anymore and all that's left on the river are the tangle of masts swaying between the mangroves.

At the intersection of Quay Napoleon and boulevard Charner, she makes her way among women balancing baskets of sweet potatoes on their long poles. A group of fortune-tellers, squatting under a tree, hail her, but she ignores them. The stench of the river and the sweetish smell of rotten fruit and fish, never completely cleaned up from the embankment at night, is turning her stomach; yes, a sure sign. She sits down on a bench next to a young *nia-coue* woman and her three children. One of them, a baby—almost a newborn—is sleeping. The older ones are elbowing her or trying to balance against the back of the bench, slipping and falling on her shoulder.

Pardon, madame. Pardon, madame.

And each time, she repeats, It's nothing. Don't worry about it. For a moment she feels the sensation from the night coming back, a subtle shift in her body, a jubilation of her senses.

What would it be like, having a child with Antoine? A tiny creature with a fine blond down curled into the crook of her arm, tugging at her breast. Alone in Saigon with Phu and perhaps a *con gai* while Antoine would travel between Port-de-France and Hanoi and Saigon. She wouldn't really be alone. Angelina and Camille would also have small babies. And then later, she would apply at the Education Department for a transfer to Saigon so that she could teach at the college. She would be reincarnated as a *colon*'s wife. Isn't it what the Easterners believe, that we can make up in a new life what we didn't achieve in the previous one? At least that's what she understood from Chiang's teachings. Well, she would have her next life in this life. And it would be a better one. And then in four years, in the summertime, the three of them would take their regulation trip to the *métropole*, the long voyage across three oceans, the return to the cool Atlantic coast . . . The steamer is pulling into the Bordeaux harbor, its huge hull overshadowing the same quay from which she and Antoine left a year ago . . .

One of the children, a girl of about four or five with delicately curled lips, pulls on her sleeve, interrupting her thoughts.

Madame! Madame! S'il vous plaît? the girl implores, holding her hand out.

Victorine's eyes fill with tears, and she takes out a handkerchief from her purse to dry her eyes. She looks for a few *sapèques* to give her, but the little girl pushes her hand away and pulls on the handkerchief.

Mouchoir, madame, mouchoir!

It's the handkerchief she wants.

It's wet, Victorine says.

Mouchoir, the girl repeats, pulling on it.

Victorine folds it carefully and puts it in the dirty little hand. The child's face blossoms in an ecstatic smile.

The same peculiar, tingling sensation in her breasts wakes her up the next morning. It couldn't pass for a dream this time, but she convinces herself she's been mistaken, that surely it's the sign of her blood being imminent, not of being with child. She doesn't know if it is disappointment or relief that she feels. To calm her confused feelings she decides to go to Cholon to see Chiang. But when she enters the back room she is surprised to see a young monk she has never seen before approach her. He speaks only a few words of French and introduces himself as Hué. After a few minutes of conversation, she finally understands with a shock: Chiang has passed away. He had been getting frail and emaciated, had he been ill without telling her?

But I just saw him the other day, she says softly.

He died in his sleep, two days ago, Hué says. It was very sudden. He put his hand on his chest, indicating his heart. He had planned to go north to his family, in Nha Trang. She remembers how small and childlike Chiang's hand had been when she had said goodbye to him. How gentle his eyes. Hué picks up *The Tale of Kiều* from the shelf above the table. Last week, he says, when I took my duties in the temple, Monsieur Chiang asked me to give this to you if you came by while he was away. Victorine opens the book. Chiang has inscribed it for her in Chinese characters.

She lights up a fresh stick of sandalwood at the feet of the Buddha and kneels down. Chiang had been her link with Indochina. Antoine, Angelina and Jules, Camille and Louis are like her, floating in a foreign land they only understand on the surface. She looks up to the Buddha. At this moment, his smile radiates more loving warmth than bleeding Jesus nailed to the cross with his crown of thorns. She places her head in her hands and weeps quietly. When she gets up, she is alone in the room. Incense fills the air; a gong sounds outside, each deep, throaty beat echoing for a long time, slowly fading into the next one.

The gong echoes for the last time. On the table where Chiang used to teach her Mandarin, Hué has laid out a red silk banner, a bottle of gold-colored ink, and a brush sharpened to the thinnest point. She sits down and traces the name Chiang in Chinese. Her characters don't have the dash of Chiang's own brush strokes, but her penmanship will have to do. When she is done, Hué hangs her banner next to the others overlapping one another on the wall.

March 15, 1900. There is no doubt. She is with child. All the signs are there, her breasts swollen and heavy, her stomach turning when Phu brings her coffee in the morning, and her blood hasn't come in almost six weeks. She doesn't write the news to Antoine. She doesn't tell anyone, not even Angelina. Certainly not Angelina. She couldn't bear imagining her sister's dark eyes resting on her face, with their mix of compassion, superiority, and, well—pity, the way she had looked at her in Da Lat on Christmas Eve. Since then they had tacitly dropped all mention of Armand and the children.

But how could she create a family with Antoine without having properly, openly finished with her previous life? Without first going back to Maillezais and talking to Armand face-to-face? Or writing to him at least?

Antoine is right. This silence is what's holding her back. And yet she doesn't know how to break it.

Her classes at the school are the only moments when the turmoil in her heart calms down. She sees the children's faces listening to her with rapt attention and she forgets how confused she is. She tells them about Rimbaud. They love "The Drunken Boat" and the stories about the boy genius who wrote most of his poems before the age of twenty and became a gun-runner in Ethiopia before dying at thirty-seven.

When she comes back from school, in the sultry afternoons, after her nausea has subsided, she lies down under the mosquito net and dozes off. Then her body finds a temporary balance, her secret buried so deep that she almost forgets about it.

But she can no more stop the growth inside of her than she can stop breathing.

THEY ARE GATHERED in the Désauniers' Chinese parlor, Angelina, Victorine, and Louis sitting across from Jules on the Chinese flat beds where, a few months ago, she smoked opium with Antoine. But the opium pipes have been removed and a porcelain oil lamp has taken their place on the low table. The pale blue tint of the china makes Victorine think of that line from a Chinese poem she has read with Hué: "The color of the sky after the rain."

You are the Jozelon sisters, aren't you? Louis asks, while Trong, the boy who had helped her to the bathroom that evening, lowers a tray of flutes filled with champagne toward them, his face expressionless, as though he doesn't remember her at all.

Yes, Victorine says. We are. She is surprised that he is asking, since it was Camille who insisted on inviting Angelina and her husband.

I finally realized where I knew you from, Louis continues, turning toward Victorine. Your father used to repair my father's carriage. Still does, I think.

Angelina looks at him with curiosity. Victorine carefully picks up her flute of champagne and sips from it.

I didn't realize both of you came to Indochina. When I met you at the governor's reception last year, Madame Langelot, I got you confused with your sister. He pushes a platter of petits fours in her direction.

Thank you, Victorine says. Well, we're both here.

She leans over and picks up a petit four. The less said the better. If she eats and if she ignores him, he might drop the subject. She drinks a little more champagne, angry with herself that she could still be so afraid to be found out.

Didn't you teach in a little village in the marshland, Louis insists—Maillezais, or Arçais, was it?

Victorine catches Angelina's eye. Can't he just let it go?

We're both schoolteachers, Victorine cuts him off quickly, putting down her glass. Angelina is about to say something, but Camille, walking in the room, interrupts her.

Good afternoon, everyone, she says. Giang is ready for us now. Trong appears behind her, carrying a tray of flickering candles.

What is this? Angelina whispers.

It's a séance, Victorine says. Camille said there would be a surprise. Her anxiety at having been recognized by Louis Désaunier as Victor-Paul's daughter is turning to mild panic. She's heard of these sessions when a seer guesses the future or brings a dead person back to life. What if Giang exposed her in front of everyone? She tries to think clearly. Well, what does it a matter, after all? Perhaps it's time for her to face what she's done.

Shhh, Camille says.

A slender young Annamite woman with a scarf twisted as a turban around her head, a necklace of big amber beads, and heavy gold rings is kneeling on a mat. A low, round table is placed in front of her. In the light of the candles her shadow leaps like a mushroom against the back wall. She tells them to place their right hands wide open on the table, thumbs and little fingers touching lightly.

Behind the glow of the candles, they can barely make out the young woman's features, only shadows flickering up and down her face. Louis sits on the floor next to Victorine, his little finger touching her thumb. She hopes that he won't feel how nervous she is. It's too late now to get up and leave the table unless she pretends to be sick, which of course she could, considering her so-called dysentery a few days before, but curiosity keeps her there. After a few minutes of Giang's incantations, Louis's fingers seem to shake a little against hers. On her right, Jules's hand feels more wooden. All of which, of course, could be her imagination. Meanwhile, Giang, on the other side of the table, is also touching hands with Angelina and Camille, and her singsong rises. Victorine and Angelina exchange a look. Angelina opens her eyes wide in mockery. Victorine stifles a laugh.

Man, Giang whispers, *chetty. Chetty, chetty.* Louis's hand feels shaky against Victorine's. Victorine tries to remember what the word *chetty* means, if it's similar to *coolie-xe.* Is it a driver? Or perhaps a moneylender? Oh, yes, an Indian driver. There is the sound of a foot scraping against the floor. And then total silence, even deeper than before. They all seem to fall into a kind of trance. Out of the silence, Giang's singsong rises again. It's impossible to know if she's addressing someone in particular, because her eyes are closed. *Personne ne sait,* Giang whispers. Husband doesn't know.

Now it's Jules, on the other side, who seems agitated. Victorine takes a deep breath. *Heart confused*. The chant dies down and starts again, almost with the rhythm of a child's lullaby. *Chetty, chetty*. Here, in the house, Giang continues. A woman's cough—Camille or Angelina, Victorine cannot tell—delicately caught in a throat. Husband doesn't know. Giang's delivery chokes and halts like an engine about to stall, then drops into a barely audible murmur in Annamite. Camille suddenly leans against the wall, eyes closed, mouth open, her head thrown back.

Camille! Louis cries, letting go of the circle.

Giang stops abruptly. A candle collapses on itself in a flower of yellow wax spreading around the candleholder and erupts in a high flame. Trong, who was standing at attention, hurries to blow it out.

Is she sick? Victorine asks.

But Camille opens her eyes, puts both hands on her cheeks, and smiles a pale smile.

It's the heat, she says. I'm sorry. I simply didn't feel well for a moment.

Victorine watches Louis bring her to her feet, Camille repeating in a light voice, I'm fine, I'm telling you, I'm fine.

What happened? Angelina whispers.

Victorine doesn't answer. She watches them leaving the room, Louis's arm holding Camille at an odd angle around her waist, almost as though he was the one leaning on her.

She picks up one of the flutes left on Trong's tray and carries it to the garden. The murmur of conversations fades behind her. A purple bougainvillea blooms against the back wall. A jasmine bush secretes its exquisite aroma. Under her feet, the path is covered with frangipani petals, their paleness already turning to a brown dust. The warm night seems both velvety and poisonous, an irresistible trap.

April 15, 1900. Easter. Angelina insists on Victorine's joining them at Notre-Dame for the Easter *grand-messe*. She remembers her mother telling Victor-Paul, you can miss every Sunday of the year that God made if you wish, but not Easter. Easter you must attend. So she does.

There's only standing room at the back of the church and Victorine, her back and legs tired, leans against the cool stone of the baptismal font. She crosses herself thoughtlessly, unable to concentrate on the service. At the Confiteor, she hits her chest like everybody else, with her closed fist, *mea culpa, mea culpa, mea maxima culpa.* It's my fault, my fault, my biggest fault. It was a mistake to go to church, she knows, but it's too late now. Every prayer seems a covert allusion to what she's done. She remembers Bertha's voice: remorse will follow you all your life. Only confession and repentance will bring peace of mind. Turmoil of the soul is the worst punishment.

She slips out the side door during the communion and walks out in the brutal midday sun. The rains are about to start any day now, and humidity saturates the air. Seeing her alone on the parvis, a beggar whose legs have been amputated, the stumps resting on a piece of wood mounted on wheels, drags himself all the way to her and stares up at her, his palm open, his face, ravaged by a malady that she cannot identify, shamelessly, perhaps provocatively, advertising his pain. She gives him a silver piastre and turns away, unable to sustain the gaze of his eyes, beautiful, a liquid black. Feeling the shame, as though she was somehow responsible for his state.

In the afternoon after lunch, the two of them, Angelina and Victorine, take a ride in the Saigon gardens.

They are moving at a walking pace, horses pawing the ground, coachmen chewing and spitting betel, one carriage behind the other, but at each step forward Victorine's nausea increases.

The carriage suddenly stops with a jolt. Victorine takes a deep breath. Angelina sticks her head out and taps the coachman's back.

What's happening? Why did we stop?

Everybody stop, Madame.

It's all these newcomers, Angelina says, fanning herself. All the junior officers' wives, all the customs officers' wives. They're barely off the ship, they have to come to the promenade just to be seen.

What is she talking about, Victorine thinks, isn't she a newcomer too? Aren't we all, really, just passing through here? She closes her eyes. If she doesn't see the sidewalk moving up and down like a wave with the movement of the horses, her stomach steadies itself.

Are you all right? Angelina asks. You look pale.

Victorine opens her eyes. It's nothing, she says. I'm fine.

Angelina searches her eyes.

Victorine, what are you going to do?

What do you mean?

You know what I mean.

I'm happy here, with Antoine.

Are you sure?

Why is she insisting like this? Victorine regrets spending the day with her. Perhaps it would have been better to be alone for Easter. The carriage starts again. They are approaching the lake and the acacia trees that border the wide allée cast soothing shadows.

But Daniel, Madeleine—don't you miss them?

Victorine's hand, the one that holds on to the side of the carriage, tightens. That is her answer, and Angelina seems to be satisfied with it.

I've been wondering . . . if you've thought of . . . a divorce? Angelina leans forward and taps their coachman on the shoulder again.

Here. We're getting off. Come back in an hour to pick us up near the lake, at this same place.

They walk in silence down a little path to the lake and sit on a bench, in the shade of a frangipani tree.

They never knew anyone who had gotten divorced. It was something people did in Paris, in certain circles. You heard about actresses divorcing, or such and such a countess. The word was always surrounded by a haze of scandal, fast life, gossip. In Saigon too there were divorces. Camille had a friend who was a divorcée. Victorine had met her at the Select. She was a petite, cheerful woman who had remarried with a customs officer. Secretly, Victorine had admired her courage. It was easier, simpler, to be Madame Langelot without going through all that trouble. Nobody had found her out. But that's not what she says to Angelina.

The Church . . . she says. The Church doesn't recognize—

The Church doesn't recognize the situation you're in now. And anyway, you told me you had stopped going to mass until this morning.

Yes. But don't you understand? It's not just the Church. It's the people we know. I would be ostracized.

Angelina looks at her with surprise.

I didn't think you cared what people thought.

What makes you say that?

Angelina shrugs. The way you're living here with Antoine. The liberties you take.

Victorine pushes a twig with the toe of her boot. That word "liberties," in the plural . . . The tone Angelina uses. She knows what it means. Under her apparent solicitude, there's the disdain again. She looks up at her sister, almost defiantly.

Maybe I care more than I thought.

But most people here—well, most of them wouldn't care.

What about at home, Daniel and Madeleine. Wouldn't they be—yes, singled out, fingers pointed at them?

Don't you think it's already happening?

Victorine gets up and smoothes her skirt.

Let's walk, shall we? I'd rather not talk about it.

But back home, that night, she can't stop thinking about it. Angelina is right in a way. The damage is already done. And now she is expecting Antoine's child. There is no way back. Or is there?

No matter what, she has to repair the damage. She has to have the courage to face what she has done.

> *Cher Armand,*
> *I am not writing to apologize. I couldn't ask for your forgiveness, nor expect you to forgive me. I am writing to ask you for a divorce. You might be shocked to hear that. But I think it would be better for our sake and the children's sake.*

She stops and rereads. The tone seems cold to her, too matter-of-fact.

She starts again.

> *Cher Armand,*
> *It must be shocking to you to receive a letter from me now, after all this time. I could not bear to face you after all the pain I have inflicted upon you and the children. I was afraid to face you and can barely stand writing to you now.*

The letter is torn into tiny pieces that float down to the floor.

> *Cher Armand,*
> *I am in love with Antoine Langelot. I want a divorce.*

This too is torn up. A snow of torn white paper surrounds her.

She lies awake under the mosquito net. Her body swells a little more every night. Once she dreams that she is an egg bursting with thick yolk, and then the yolk turns dark, the color of dried blood. Mostly she lies awake in dread. And the same questions twirl in her mind, endlessly. How can she start a new family when she's abandoned the first one? What would Antoine be like as a father and husband? Would he turn into another Armand? Would she, once again, feel a failure, a woman overwhelmed by the responsibilities of motherhood—the sheer immobility and oppression of it? And always, the most important question: how to face Armand?

In the morning, when she looks at herself in the swing mirror, it seems to her that her hips and breasts are expanding. But in profile she still looks flat as a flounder.

The letter from Antoine arrived at the same time as an envelope addressed to him from the Customs Administration. She put that one aside and opened Antoine's letter. There was a postcard depicting a small harbor filled with Chinese junks and a letter; the card read:

> *The seashore is beautiful, but Port-de-France, or Noumea as they call the capital here, is a sorry backwater of a place. There's no life, two cafés to speak of, no music, the food doesn't compare, the hotel—if you can call it that—rotten, fleas or worse in the bed, soiled linen; scorpions in the hallways. I miss you,* ma chérie.

The letter—dated three days later—was more upbeat.

> *Victorine chérie,*
> *Finally! Finally! This is what Cochinchina must have been like ten or fifteen years ago. Although the population here is quite different, another race altogether, darker and bigger, closer to the Negro race than to the Asian. I've met a fellow from Nantes who runs the Dumbea mine. He could help me find an engineering position at the nickel refinery plant. His name is Gustave Blanquin. His father is a banker. Don't think me scatterbrained, please! But when you come to the colonies, you have to explore all the different possibilities until you find the one that is the most profitable. I would love for you to come and see for yourself. The* D'Artagnan, *which will carry my letter, is returning to Noumea on the eighteenth. Book a passage on it as soon as you can and meet me in Port-de-France. Otherwise, I*

hear the Saghalien *is doing a special trip on the twenty-second.*
I know it's terribly short notice . . .

She imagined, that night, taking the *D'Artagnan* or the *Saghalien*, alone in a cabin for three weeks, plagued by a nausea worse than on her trip over from France. She imagined arriving at Port-de-France and telling Antoine: I am with child. Would there be joy in his eyes, or would he turn his face away? Did he love her enough to want a family with her? She wasn't sure. He too would talk about divorce, telling Armand and the children. No matter which way she turned, it came down to that. Wasn't that what she wanted? She felt trapped in the pitch-black room. The rains had started, and the nights were even more humid than before. She heard creeping sounds. She hoped it wasn't a scorpion. She had seen one on the veranda the day before and Phu had chased it away. She had felt trapped too when she had found out she was expecting Daniel. Was it something in her fate that made her so reckless with men? And then so scared of motherhood? Josephine Joliette: she suddenly remembered the name of the healer she had mentioned to Armand when she found herself pregnant. Well, there was no dearth of healers in Saigon if she needed one.

On the eighteenth she's not on the *D'Artagnan*. She's passing the porcelain dragon of the Cholon temple, with its tongue of fire. Hué has prepared the rice paper and her favorite brush, the one with the long bamboo handle and the wisp of hair as sharp as a blade. She dips it into the black ink, a mixture of pine soot, glue, and water, freshly prepared by Hué. She draws carefully, intensely, one row after another of characters. At first Hué points to the mistakes, the places where her hand has wavered, where the line, instead of curving in an elegant flight, pauses, hesitates, and awkwardly resumes its course. Hué is a tough teacher, tougher than Chiang was, she imagines him hitting his pupils' palms with a ruler at the least error. After a while he silently leaves the room.

She starts over, holding her breath. She thinks of the scales

Daniel used to practice, over and over, on the upright piano. For the scales too you have to gather speed, build a momentum, and then let them speed along. It's a question of rhythm. The text she is writing is long, the longest she has ever written. When Hué comes back to check on her progress, the rice paper she hands him is covered with characters. He stands above her, reading and rereading it silently, neglecting to correct the erroneous lines. The brush stays still between his fingers. Then he folds the paper and puts it into a pocket of his robe without saying a word.

The woman he takes her to lives in a covered alley in the back streets of Cholon behind the fish market, not far from where they had first stayed. The smell of dry cuttlefish follows them all the way into a passage so low they have to bend their heads. They reach a dark wooden door carved with dragons and snakes. A tiny Chinese woman with only three teeth left, black with betel, opens it. She invites Victorine to sit on a low bench, and sits down at a table with Hué. They speak Chinese together. Hard-breathing, nasal Chinese sounds. Two small tin boxes are placed in front of her on the table, looking like opium cases of the cheaper category, but they are filled with quicklime, and she occasionally dips a betel leaf in one of them and chews.

What does she say?

Ask if you married, Hué says.

Yes, I am. Victorine stares at the black betel juice trickling on the woman's chin, which she carelessly wipes off with the back of her hand.

Other children?

Yes. Victorine looks away. Two.

How long pregnant?

Four weeks.

She should be counting the days until Antoine's return, rather than consulting with a toothless Chinese witch doctor to bring back her blood.

On the wall she is facing, several portraits of older men and women stand on a kind of altar, as well as a saucer holding incense sticks and small offerings of fruit. Behind the altar, a French calendar hangs on the wall, illustrated with a diaphanous, sylph-like redhead. Next to it, an enamel plate advertises ABSINTHE SUPERIEURE 72 A. JUNOD. PONTARLIER (DOUBS). The words *absinthe supérieure* are drawn in curly letters. They used to have a bottle of that brand in Vinh Long. The Chinese words twirl around her in quick, syncopated syllables. She tries to understand them but gives up. The diaphanous sylph on the calendar has a long red mane flowing all the way down to her hips and a crown of forget-me-nots in her hair.

There are herbs, the monk translates, and Victorine's attention drifts back to reality. He uses several Chinese words she doesn't understand and then switches to French: But you won't need them.

Why?

The baby is weak. She doesn't think you'll be able to keep him. She wants to know if you would like her to tell your future instead.

The seers, Camille has told her, can tell your future in the palm of your hand or just by looking at your eyes. She remembers the way Marie, Armand's older sister, had looked at her when they had first met—had she guessed her future then? Victorine is afraid of fortune-tellers. What if the fortune-teller saw the shadow of dark foreboding on her face? What if she was told she was going to die young, or that all her dreams would be shattered, or to beware of accidents? The Chinese believe—Chiang told her—that you can avoid a wrong turn of events by consulting with a seer. But what if the future is tragic, a path closed by an inexorable fate? She'd rather not know and keep blind faith. Maybe she is a fatalist.

I came for the herbs, she says firmly.

The herbs are dangerous. She sees you are not sure you really want to take herbs.

She can't see that! But it doesn't matter. I want to take the herbs.

The Chinese woman chews her betel and shrugs, indifferent.

She fires up a few words to Hué, her inflection going up and down, up and down.

If you still want to, then you can come back in two weeks, Hué translates. She spits bits of betel and extends two pointed black nails toward Victorine. No sooner.

She lost the baby the next day, April 21, eight weeks after Antoine left. It simply slipped out of her, almost painlessly, an unformed mass of soft matter, mucus and blood, with no warning, into the porcelain pot with the blue Chinese dragon wrapped around its lip. By the time Dr. Berger, a native of Nantes himself, who had been recommended by Camille, was fetched, it was all over. He patted her cheek with a chubby hand.

Don't worry, he said. You'll be fine in no time.

The Chinese woman had been right. The baby had been weak. She hadn't taken the herbs. But was her sudden desire that day to get rid of the baby powerful enough to cause the miscarriage? She wondered. By the next morning she was overcome by remorse and weariness.

She wrote a letter to Antoine, saying that she had been ill with dysentery. She was recovering and he shouldn't worry, but she was too weak to make the trip to Noumea. She wished he would come home as soon as possible. She asked Phu to deliver the letter himself to the *Saghalien*, so that Antoine would receive it in Port-de-France when he was waiting for her to arrive on the ship.

Dr. Berger, called a second time two days later, as she was still feeling weak, promised that she would be coming around in a few days. The extreme climate was hard on women's bodies, he said. Women didn't recover as fast as they would in France. And she was alone, her husband away in Noumea, with only her sister in the colony. She should wait two or three months and resume. Then she'd be with child again. When she heard these words, by a perfectly illogical reversal, she felt exhilarated.

Phu brought her light broth and infusions in bed. He was especially solicitous, which made her wonder if he suspected anything. But then the French in Saigon were often suffering from one malaise or another. She sent word to Madame Nguyen at the school that she had a light case of dysentery and she couldn't attend to her classes for a while. When Angelina stopped by to see her she told her the same thing. Her sister had a worried look.

Is that what the doctor said? I heard—there've been cases of cholera in the last few weeks . . .

Victorine said Dr. Berger had given her ipeca and bismuth and she was already better.

Are you sure? Angelina said.

Victorine sat up and swung her legs off the bed.

I'm fine, she said firmly. Dr. Berger isn't concerned. Why should I be?

JUNE 3, 1900. The rain is pouring on Quay Napoleon. The French are huddled together under the awning of the Messageries Maritimes building; everyone else is outside, getting wet. Suddenly here he is at her side, weighted down by a heavy bag pulling on his shoulder.

You don't look sick, he says, putting the bag down and taking her into his arms. You look . . . wonderful. I was worried about you.

It was two months ago, she says. I'm all better now.

He is soaking wet, his hair in his eyes, his jacket wet under her hands. Rain streams down her face while they kiss, their lips are wet. I'm so, so happy to see you, he says, pressing her to him, and his eyes, paler now that his face has been darkened by the sun, probe hers. *Ma petite Victorine*. He pinches her cheek. All pink. He lifts her chin. Clear eyes!

She laughs. But her laugh sounds false to her. She has been hoping his arrival would erase the previous weeks of anguish. But no. She feels closed off. Perhaps she needs more time.

What? he says, feeling her reticence. Has my trip been too

long? Has it been really hard for you? He looks into her eyes, runs a finger along her cheek. I am back now, he says. I am with you. But she turns her face away. Instead of the joy she was hoping for, this dull emptiness.

Back at the house he carries her in his arms to the bedroom, and one by one removes the pins from her hair, one by one takes off her camisole, her skirt, her petticoats, and tosses them behind him all over the floor. No, she says, turning her face away from his kisses. She feels coiled around herself, unable to respond to him.

You've changed, he says, pulling the sheet over her, caressing her hair spilled over the pillow. Did something happen while I was away?

She shakes her head, unable to speak.

You're so beautiful, he says. His eyes are tender, but he doesn't press her. Perhaps she would like him to. But he doesn't. He is exhausted from his trip. He falls asleep in her arms.

When they wake up, later in the afternoon, she remembers the letter from the Douanes et Régies which she has kept on the dresser. He opens it next to her in the bed and right away, looking at his face, she sees it's good news.

It's that position I thought I could get three months ago, remember, but it wasn't available? They're offering it to me, with a higher salary.

Antoine, that's wonderful!

He throws her a glance, perhaps trying to figure out if she really means it.

Where, here in Saigon? Or back in Vinh Long?

In Saigon for the time being. In the main Opium Office. Later, perhaps back in the field. The letter doesn't mention that, but I know it's a possibility. It's good, Victorine, it's a good opportunity, he adds, guessing that she will need convincing.

Why now? She is trying to keep her voice neutral. Of course it's wonderful news, even if it means going back to work for the Opium Office.

He shrugs. I could venture to say that the capture of the pirate junk in Vinh Long may have helped, but the truth is that it's probably mostly due to Louis's pressures.

Louis has been a good friend to you, she says evenly.

He nods. He has.

What about New Caledonia?

The nickel can wait. This position will help us get back on our feet financially, and I'll be here in Saigon with you. Wouldn't you rather that we were together?

Yes, of course she would. Together here. They are, what is the expression, making a life here.

June 25, 1900. The rain is falling in sheets and the veranda is steaming. Antoine walks in from the veranda, his hair dripping and his shoulders and the back of his shirt soaked.

He puts the small stack of mail on the table. She notices, peeking out at the bottom, the green stamp of the French Republic and the familiar round postmark, half-smudged. Nobody writes to her from France. Nobody knows she is here. Without saying anything, she pulls on the envelope. Even blurred by the rain, there is no mistaking Armand's handwriting. A feeling of terror sweeps over her. She wipes her hands on her skirt and forces herself to slowly tear the envelope open.

He sits on the other side of the table, his chin in his hand. His eyes have that gray, cloudy shade.

It's from Armand, isn't it?

She nods.

> *Victorine,*
> *You will be surprised, no doubt . . .*

These long loops, the *t*'s crossed hastily. Reading the letter is like walking into their bedroom in Maillezais. The intimacy is thick, a little nauseating. She imagines whiffs of leather and rubber, Armand's smells.

She feels Antoine's eyes on her, hears the sound of the match he strikes. Read it, he says. His voice is neutral, neither harsh nor tender.

She glances at him and moves the ashtray a couple of centimeters to the side, toward him. The tips of his fingers, she sees, are yellow from smoking.

Did you write to him?

No.

How did he get the address?

I don't know.

Angelina, he says.

It is not so easy to disappear without a trace. It took me a while—a long time, as you can see—to decide to write to you. I was so angry at your betrayal that I didn't even want to hear from you. I am not writing to tell you that the children are miserable without you, or that Madeleine has been sick—some undefined illness that is making her unable to digest properly all her food, and that's leaving the doctors puzzled. Regardless of the reasons you left—which, I assume, have to do with the man you are currently with, and perhaps also with the possibility that I wasn't the right man for you—we are still married. Or are you perhaps suffering from a tragic case of amnesia? I can't force you to come back. I can't force you to do anything. But I can tell you that what you are doing is not right. That you cannot go on hiding for the rest of your life. It's been long enough now for you to know what you intend to do and let us know.

She pushes the letter toward Antoine. He reads it, then drops it between them on the table.

Phu enters to serve them the fish, placing a piece and a spoonful of rice dutifully on each plate.

It's not necessary, Phu, she says. You can take the plates away.

There's an inquisitive flash in his eyes, but he nods silently and just as silently clears the table.

It must be Angelina, Antoine repeats.

She wouldn't, Victorine says. Louis Désaunier tried to remember who she was; did he find out who she was back in Vendée?

Don't be so sure, he interrupts the thought. Anyway, sooner or later . . . He looks at her in silence for a moment. His face hardens. What are you afraid of?

She's surprised by the harshness of his tone. Again, the hint of the Parisian accent, a sign of anger. Common, her mother would have said. Yet this time she likes it, as though the toughness of his voice is the signal he is preparing to fight Armand. And perhaps that's what she wants, for him to claim her, for him to wrestle her from Armand.

I don't know, she says.

He looks at her coldly, she thinks, from across the table. You might be afraid of making a final decision. What do you really want, Victorine?

So he is leaving it up to her, after all. What she wants, not what he wants, or what they want together. But isn't this the freedom she wished for, to decide for herself?

Phu comes back with a dessert of red bean paste she is especially fond of. A branch of fresh mint is propped in the paste.

I thought, Monsieur, Phu says, hesitantly, that you might want to try this. It is Madame's favorite dessert.

Victorine is moved by his attention.

Merci, Phu. Bien sûr.

She leans over the table, picks up the branch of mint, and bites into a leaf.

Antoine lights up another cigarette. The *R* and *O* of the Régie de l'Opium are entwined at the bottom of the ashtray.

Did you hear what I said? he asks.

Yes, I did, she says. But she doesn't answer the question.

They remain silent for a long time, Antoine's unanswered question hanging between them.

The rain stops as abruptly as it came. The heavy drops fall off the roof of the veranda for a while, splashing lazily onto the railing. Then the sun starts to dry patches of the veranda. In a few minutes it will be entirely dry.

ANGELINA IS NOT her little sister anymore.

It's obvious to her when she walks in, umbrella dripping wet, lifting her skirt in a graceful sweep of her arm to take the two steps down leading into the veranda, where Victorine is arranging a bouquet of blood red hibiscus in a porcelain vase. The heaviness in her hips, the slowness, is getting more and more pronounced. Her belly is barely hidden by the shawl hanging down from her shoulders and artfully wrapped around her waist.

She sits down, cooling herself with a rice paper fan printed with a landscape of lakes and mountains.

Victorinette? Could I have a glass of water?

The letter is on the table, next to the vase of hibiscus.

Eau de Seltz, s'il-te-plaît, Angelina says when Phu appears.

Victorine hands her Armand's letter.

Look at this.

Angelina unfolds the letter and reads it without saying anything.

Phu places two glasses of soda water on the table.

Merci, Phu.

Is it you who told him?

Angelina deliberately puts the letter back on the table and looks at her. For the second time, Victorine feels that their roles have shifted. She has lost rank, while her little sister looks at her from her position of legitimate wife and mother-to-be.

What if I did? Her face is slightly defiant.

Victorine feels a huge wave of anger come up.

Then you would have betrayed me.

Angelina remains stone silent.

How could you have done that? I asked you specifically . . . You knew how difficult it is for me.

Angelina folds her hands over her round, now truly protruding belly—she looks like the Buddha from the Cholon temple.

I didn't write to Armand, Angelina says. Her eyes shift and look at Victorine with the same stony expression she had before, all her features held together with a slight backward tilt of her head.

You didn't?

Angelina shakes her head and looks away.

No. After a silence she says: I wrote to our parents.

You—

Angelina lifts her hand to interrupt her. I thought it was too cruel to know you were here, fine and well, when they were so tormented about you. Victorine flinches at the word *tormented*. I asked them not to say anything. Of course.

I can't believe you did that.

It was only to bring them some peace of mind. I should have realized . . . I suppose they must have told him . . .

It didn't occur to you that of course they would—

Don't talk to me like this.

Like what?

With that tone of voice.

—and that in any case you should have asked me before telling them?

It's that look in Angelina's eyes that makes her want to lash out at her, that look that has now come back, of a little girl lost and confused, as though her very grown-up façade has crumbled. But the flash of confusion is gone as fast as it appeared. Angelina was putting it on, apparently. And she looks at her sister steadily again.

If I had asked you, you would have said no.

So you did betray me.

I'm sorry. I thought I was acting for the best. Sooner or later they would have found out. How long can you stay like this, hidden here?

It was for me to decide, Victorine says. But her words sound foolish, defensive.

You're right, Angelina says after a long silence. I was wrong.

I'm sorry. She puts on her little-girl face just for an instant—Is she doing this on purpose? Victorine wonders.

Angelina leans heavily on the arm of her chair to get up. She picks up her umbrella which she had left open to dry in a corner of the veranda and pulls it closed.

I should go. *Au revoir.*

Victorine doesn't respond, doesn't look at her. She listens to her heels clap across the wooden floor, until she hears the front door open and click closed.

The rains don't stop. Every afternoon the light whitens and dulls, and the rain arrives like clockwork. Her second monsoon, her second summer. Fifteen months since they've arrived. The second year, you really start to belong, how had Camille put it? No, what she had said was: After the first year you really start to belong. But belong to what?

In the tramway coming back from Cholon, the peasant women pressed against her skirts, the children pulled on her sleeve, *Madame, Madame, un petit quelque chose s'il-vous-plaît,* begging for a few tin sapèques, and she gave them what she had. She looked at the sullied hem of her skirt, she felt the looks of the men on her chest. She felt embarrassed, not free. Maybe she had fooled herself.

JULY 3, 1900. He's home when she comes back, sitting at the dinner table, jotting notes in a little notebook. She sits down at the other end of the table and starts pulling off her gloves.

What's the matter? he says.

How do you mean?

He shrugs. I don't know—something in your face.

She drops the gloves in front of her on the table.

I brought back squid from Cholon, she says. For dinner.

He closes the notebook. When she raises an eyebrow to it, he says: Nothing. No, I'm just figuring some numbers, putting down some ideas.

She doesn't press him. He seems distracted, preoccupied with his projects. Life in Saigon going on.

Antoine . . .

Yes?

There's a moment of silence, which seems to fill up the room, absorbing the banging of pots coming from the kitchen.

He waits for her to go on, standing at the table, his hands leaning flat on the rattan top. His strong, capable hands. She feels as though she is moving on a narrow path along a cliff overlooking an ocean, and coming too close to the edge.

I wrote back to Armand. And you were right, by the way. It was Angelina.

His eyes open up. He seems unsure of what she's trying to say.

Maybe it's for the best. He pauses and looks at her thoughtfully. I didn't want to ask you . . . I didn't want to put any pressure on you.

In her mind she turns toward the open sea. She is standing right at the edge of the cliff. Her whole body tightens. One step forward and it will be too late to hold herself back. The smell of cilantro rises sharply from the kitchen, bringing her back to reality.

Antoine walks around the table and takes her hands, pulls her to her feet. Come, he says. Let's go to the veranda and rest there for a moment. It's beautiful at this time of day, after the rain.

Yes, she says. It's beautiful. She follows him.

Phu, he calls, bring us Martel and soda water.

They sit side by side on the rattan chairs. The lemons, she notices, have turned from green to yellow, they will be ripe within a few days. She'll have to remind Phu to pick them. But probably he'll have thought of that before she even gets a chance to mention it.

What did you tell him? he asks. Phu sets down the tray with two glasses filled with Martel and soda water and crushed ice. Antoine puts a glass into her hand. It feels wonderfully cool. She holds it for a moment, not drinking, then puts it down.

Antoine, she says.

She sees tenderness in his eyes, and also a watchful expectation.

I'm happy, he says. He takes her hand. Optimistic. So many possibilities, now, since Noumea. He lets go of her hand and lights a cigarette. Again, she notices how yellow his fingers are from nicotine.

You smoke so much, she says.

Which? He asks dryly. Cigarettes or opium?

I meant the cigarette. She can't help smiling. The spark between them is still there.

I enjoy it. It's calming.

She gets up and leans against one of the pillars of the veranda, the one covered with the bougainvillea which tumbles from its own weight, not having been properly attached to the trellis. She picks up petals that the rain has blown off the vine and gathers them in her hands.

So what did you tell Armand? Or would you rather not say?

It's too late now, the momentum pushes her forward, she will not stop herself. She comes back to the chairs and lets the petals fall onto a silver tray on the table.

They're lovely, she says. Aren't they?

She pushes the petals around with a finger until they cover the tray completely—like water lilies on a pond.

Antoine. She says his name this way, now for the third time. Breathes. I have to go back.

At first he doesn't understand. Then a mask grips his face, instantly clouding the loving attention. Whether with pain or anger she cannot tell. He has become unreadable, closed, in a single instant.

She puts her hand on his arm.

Antoine.

He pushes her hand away impatiently.

To France.

Yes.

He gets up, walks to the edge of the veranda. Another cigarette. Another struck match that he tosses out in the garden, that gets lost in the soil still drenched from the rain. His back is to her, his shoulders hunched. It's always his back that she remembers, the slope of his shoulders, the vulnerability of his nape, where the hair is cut shorter than in front.

I should have known. All those signs you gave me all the time, never happy . . . obsessed with what you left behind . . .

I have been happy, she says.

He looks at her.

You're happy when everything is going well. But when things are uncertain, Victorine, you get scared.

He's hitting where it hurts, where he thinks it will hurt. She tries to keep calm. Maybe if she keeps calm, they will trust each other.

I started teaching at the Annamite school because—

But he's not listening. He's too hurt to listen to explanations or analysis.

It's obvious. You couldn't do it. You came all the way here with me and you couldn't do it. He flips his half-smoked cigarette and takes one step off the veranda to squash it with his heel in the muddy soil.

That's not true, she says. You know that.

He turns around. His eyes have turned steel gray. I thought you had the courage, but no. I thought you could finally face him, tell him you're with me, that it's over between you two. But no. What did you tell him?

She shakes her head.

I can't talk with you when you're like this.

He takes one step on the veranda.

And how would you like me to be?

She feels the pleats of her pin-tucked skirt with her fingers. Her hands are sweating. She rubs them against the fabric.

She speaks softly. You're not even giving me the time to explain . . .

He leans against the bougainvillea. They've exchanged places, she notices. But it doesn't necessarily follow that they will understand each other better.

Explain, he says.

I do want to face him. I want to talk to him face-to-face.

You're going to take a ship across the world for thirty-five days just to talk to Armand face-to-face? His voice is sarcastic now, Armand's name spat out. I don't believe it.

I want to see my children—

Your children! They're almost grown. Didn't you tell me your son was going to boarding school next year? It's too late, now, Victorine! They barely need you anymore.

No, she says. They do. Because I want to explain things to them. I have to. I don't want to be a coward, hiding, running away, anymore. Do you understand? She doesn't like the plaintive tone her voice has taken. She is pleading with him instead of speaking calmly.

And then what? You're coming back two weeks later? This is crazy. You're fooling yourself. We could go back together, later—then, yes, I would understand. But this way, alone, like this? No.

He stays silent for a moment.

Like this . . . you're crushing me— His voice breaks.

Antoine . . . Please. Antoine . . .

No . . . If you go back, that's it. You're going back.

Don't say that. Please.

He lights up another cigarette. There's a circle of cigarette butts below the edge of the veranda. She starts to count them as if that mattered.

Look at me, he says, softly this time. Look at what you're doing. You did the same thing before we left. It's not courage, it's indecision. You just can't make up your mind, don't you see? He shakes his head. I'm sorry. Perhaps that was too harsh.

It's not true. Her voice is firm now. I'm not leaving you to go back to him. It's not like that. You always said that I should face him, contact them. That otherwise I couldn't really be happy here with you.

He blows a little puff of smoke without saying anything. After a while, he says: Yes, I did say that.

He hasn't shaved, she notices, and his growing beard makes him look tired, but also more attractive.

I need to go home for a while, she says, and—decide for myself. Then I'll come back.

You're fooling yourself, he says again.

Why can't you trust me?

He turns to face her squarely.

Because it's not just you, it's him too. And your family, and your village. I know Vendée. I'm from there too. Even if I moved to Paris later. I know what it's going to be like. He kicks a stone off the floor of the veranda. They'll reclaim you.

No. No they won't. You'll be here. There's you. There's our life here.

It will seem like a dream once you're back there.

Phu appears and discreetly clears his throat.

Dinner is served, Madame.

Antoine steps down from the veranda into the garden.

You can have your squid, he says. I'll see you later.

Please. Don't. Don't do this.

He stops by the hibiscus bush, the one with the blood red flowers that she picked the other day. He looks at her over his shoulder. His eyes are gray, not blue. If she got up at this moment, if she took the few steps leading to the edge of the veranda, if she went down the little path to the left of the lemon tree, if she walked toward him just now, she is sure of this, he would turn around and he would wait for her. If she got up now, the conversation they just had would be erased, it would just have been a mood, a flare of anger, a misunderstanding that they could clear. She would tell him the truth, which is that she wrote the letter to Armand but that she didn't mail it yet. She would tell him that she isn't sure she wants to send it, maybe there's another way, maybe she could wait, maybe, as he suggested, they could go back together. It wouldn't be too late to change the whole tone of what happened.

And perhaps, for a fraction of a moment, he is waiting for her to do just that. For a moment he remains in balance, there by the hibiscus bush. He is waiting for her to hold him back. And she doesn't. She doesn't move. Their eyes meet for that fraction of a second. His gray eyes are cloudy, his face crushed. And then it's over. His expression recomposes itself. His arm falls down to his side, and she only sees his back in the rumpled linen jacket, his determined steps toward the gate at the back of the garden, as he disappears behind the banana tree.

WHO TOLD YOU? She asks, in the same low voice. Daniel?

He is standing in front of the grate, his hands in his pants pockets, not looking at her.

Tante Angelina, he says.

Angelina. She had gone to say goodbye to her the day before she left. Her house opened right on the sidewalk, and she stood there, her belly like a balloon about to burst.

Aren't you going to ask me in? Victorine had said.

Angelina had nodded and taken her to the parlor.

I don't want to sit, Victorine said. I just want to say goodbye.

You're going home?

Yes.

Perhaps it's best, Angelina said. Will you come back?

I don't know. I'm leaving tomorrow on the *Peï-Ho*.

Angelina nodded. It was obvious she approved. She had pulled the string and Victorine was following. Victorine felt a flare of anger at her sister, and then it dissipated. After all, nobody was forcing her to go back. Our roots are in Vendée, Antoine had said. Is that what it was?

They kissed three times on each cheek, Vendée style.

I won't see you off on the quay, Angelina said. I assume you'd rather be alone with Antoine.

Victorine nodded.

She patted her sister's belly.

May all be well with you, Angelina.

They were at the door. Angelina took a step back and closed the door. The street was quiet, an Annamite boy was sleeping in the shade, his body curled against the wall. Victorine walked around him, careful not to disturb him.

She notices that Maurice has turned around and is looking at her. How long has she been silent?

What did Angelina say? Her words come from a great distance, she has to force them out.

Maurice sits on the chair across from her. His legs are open, he leans forward on his elbows, meets her eyes for a second, then turns his face away toward the hearth.

That it was true. That you left papa for another man and that you lived with him in Indochina.

The blush that she feels coming over her cheeks could have been caused by the fire. Even now, forty years later, these words are impossible to hear.

She pulls a handkerchief from her pocket, unfolds it, and covers her face with it.

Maman, he says.

She doesn't answer.

Maman, he repeats. His voice is not gentle.

Mmmm?

Did you love him?

The flames are engulfing the fireplace, whooshing and exploding.

She feels the tears gather in her eyes and doesn't bother to wipe them.

Antoine, she says softly. His name was Antoine.

Why did you come back then?

She still doesn't look at him.

I—I had to. I couldn't stay. After what I had done . . .

He gets up and stands in front of the grate, his back to her.

I went on seeing him, she says, when he came back to France. After your father and I separated. Every year he came.

Maurice leans over the grate and pokes the fire, which doesn't need any help. It's hot enough as it is.

No one knew. And then . . . one year he didn't come back. I waited for him. He would always come here in the summertime, while you were at Tante Emilienne's during the rainy season over there.

She stays silent for a long time.

And when I didn't hear, one whole summer, and still no news in the fall, no news, nothing . . . She takes a deep breath. I knew. And then months later I received a letter from his aunt. He had died. An illness of some kind, that he had caught in Indochina.

When? His voice is a murmur.

Fifteen years ago, she says. He was sixty-two.

The Peï-Ho

JULY 20, 1900. She is sitting on the side of the bed, her bare back to him. His hands cup her shoulders. She closes her eyes. For the last time, she thinks, pressing her hands on his. But he drops his hands and lets her go. She turns around. He's lying down now, his arms stretched above his head, looking at her, his face blank.

Don't you have to finish packing? he asks.

He points to her clothes, piles of them on the chairs, on the dresser, on the little rattan table. The trunk is open, not even half-filled. Her suitcase from Maillezais is upright on the floor, looking modest, the labels from the voyage out now faded and torn.

She slips the straps of her corset over her shoulders.

Would you help me? she asks.

He sits up and loops each lace one by one around the hooks.

It must feel tight, he says. You're not used to this anymore.

It's fine, she says. But she has to hold her breath when he pulls on the laces at the waist and ties them up.

There, he says. It's done.

She puts on her camisole and buttons it, pulls up her petticoat.

He watches her dress from the bed for a while, then he gets up.

I'll come back later, he says, and walks out.

She packs slowly at first, having a hard time deciding what to leave and what to take, because everything she leaves behind could be construed by him—and by her—as a promise to return. And perhaps it is. She leaves her Chinese slippers of black silk, an embroidered scarf, a couple of dresses of cambric, too light to be worn in Vendée. She packs with particular care the presents she has bought to take with her to France: pajamas of white silk for Madeleine, a jacket with the collar standing up for Daniel, and one for Armand, a bamboo and ivory pipe for Victor-Paul, probably not suitable for smoking tobacco, but as a souvenir, a teapot of white and blue china, perhaps for her mother, and paper fans, delicate porcelain bowls, silk banners drawn with Chinese characters, squares of colorful silks.

After a while it becomes too painful to pick each item so carefully, to question each of her choices. The packing would take all day, she would never be finished on time. She gathers the piles of clothes and arranges them in the trunk, the shoes on one side, the toiletries on the other. The little suitcase she will carry with her, it will contain her few personal necessities. A few books. Her notebook. She loses herself in the packing. It takes on a rhythm of its own. Her mechanical pacing through the room is soothing, it's a relief to be focused on the task at hand. She puts aside the dove-colored jacket and the pale blue dress she wore on her way over. She will wear them tonight. She tucks her matching gloves of gray leather in her purse. She walks out to the garden and picks a handful of frangipani petals that she stuffs in a pouch of quilted silk. They will die, they will not dry up but disintegrate. But their fragrance, she hopes, will remain.

At five o'clock he returns to the door of their bedroom. She has been packing all day, barely stopping to eat the lunch Phu served her on the veranda.

Are you ready? he asks.

Yes. Her heart tightens. It's worse, far worse, to leave a man you love. But her voice is determined, her gestures are smooth, controlled. They walk out through the front garden, he opens the gate for her. A couple dressed in elegant clothes walk by. Her skirt trails behind her and he's wearing a top hat—they must be going to a dance. A line of *pousse-pousses* has formed at the corner, waiting for customers. There's a pink glow at the end of the street, toward the west. She will not be here this evening, to have a Martel at the Select, or to stroll down rue Catinat with him all the way to the riverfront. They will not have dinner together. He will be alone, without her. But when the carriage he has ordered pulls up at the curb, its horse nervously pulling on his harness, when Phu carries her trunk out, her mood lifts unexpectedly. It will be her first real journey alone.

Bon voyage, Madame, Phu says. His arms are crossed in front of his chest and he bows. Hué, when she went to say goodbye to him, stood like that too, his eyes lowered. When he looked up, his face was smiling, but his eyes were sad. The same expression is in Phu's eyes now. She takes his hands in hers and presses them. She is banishing herself from Saigon, she feels a flash of pain through her heart.

Phu, thank you for everything.

Bon voyage, Madame, he repeats. I will take good care of Monsieur.

They are standing face-to-face on the quay, jostled by the passengers lining up to go on board. The luggage is piling up on one side of them, a wobbling pyramid of trunks and suitcases and cardboard boxes tied with twine. Over the Saigon River, the sun is setting, a perfect disk, the color of a blood orange, sinking into the rice paddies.

Be careful on the ship, he says. Don't forget to tie a handkerchief around your face for the soot.

I won't.

Do you have the Ricqlès for nausea?

Yes. She pats her purse. In here.

He takes both her hands in his. He circles her wrists. His hands might be touching her skin for the last time.

Be careful, he says again.

I will.

It will feel cold when you arrive in France, you'll have to get used to the climate there.

I know, she says. Don't worry.

He pulls her close by the waist. She leans her head against his chest.

We're still together, he says.

Yes, we are.

It's her turn to be the one leaving, to lean against the deck railing, to try to find him in the darkening crowd from the great height of the steamer. She recognizes him by his straw hat. She waves at him. She sees his hand come up for a moment. She is too far to read his eyes.

The *Peï-Ho* is being slowly towed away from the quay by the tugboats. She stays by the railing, her eyes holding on to the white spot of his hat until it is too dark and she is too far to see him anymore. And even after that she stays on the deck as the ship makes its way around the wide loops of the Saigon River. She watches the tugboats being let go, and then the ship starts vibrating and a huge puff of black smoke pours out of the stack and the noises of the engine become deafening.

A light breeze picks up as they approach the open sea. The lighthouse of Cap Saint-Jacques appears. The junks sway in Coconut Bay just as they had when they had first arrived.

After that they turn their back on Saigon.

The dream is played in reverse.

The first night she cannot sleep. She feels the vibrations of the engine in a way she doesn't remember feeling when she came over with Antoine. She listens to the pattering of small animals, terrified that a rat—those she remembers well—might jump on her bed if she falls asleep. She imagines Antoine being served dinner by Phu, sitting at the head of the dinner table. Although it's more likely that he went out and got drunk, or went *touffianer*—that word she hates.

. . .

She sits back in the chaise longue. She is not as sick as she was during their trip over. Perhaps living so near the water she has gotten used to the sea. Or perhaps, as Antoine had told her, it's the first time that's the worst.

When the water is peaceful and the wind blows the engine smoke away toward the open sea, the night is the best time. Out on the deck, it's like sinking into velvet, the blue-black of the ocean and that of the night sky blending with the balminess of the air like a caress.

Her memories become scattered. She barely remembers her journey back. There was a party when they approached the equator near Singapore. Heavy drinking. The older travelers recalled the rituals of passing the equator before the opening of the Suez Canal, in the 1860s. The first timers then were subjected to a series of practical jokes—they called it baptism of the line. An old sailor presided, disguised as Father Line, with a long fake beard. Everyone got very drunk. Now, of course, they didn't cross the equator anymore, they sailed north of it, through the Strait of Malacca, past Singapore. But there was still a lot of drinking.

The syrupy night. Far away, the sounds of a piano.

There was a couple, a couple she met at dinner, with whom she played whist in the evening. What was their name?

There it is, in the notebook.

Jean et Lena de Mareuil. Lena, née Roscoff, she had added.

It's funny, she would have thought . . . Her father was Russian, hence her name. She can't remember what Jean looked like. Lena was blond, her skin so pale it was almost colorless. And long, narrow, blue eyes. She wore a ring, a ruby set with diamonds. After she played her hand, she held her deck against her chest, her fingers fanned out, as if on purpose, to make her ring sparkle. There was a piano player and a singer in the drawing room, and sometimes Jean and Lena got up to waltz. Her tiny waist folded over Jean's sleeve with the grace of a reed. They were going back for good. He was with the postal administration. Watching Lena and Jean waltz was painful, like watching the end of a dream.

They made their way up the canal to the docks at Port Said, where they were able to get off. It was their last stop in the East. And then across from Cyprus the sky opened up and the sea got choppy and dark and they pulled out warm shawls and heavier jackets from their trunks and huddled at night in the grand salon. The waltzes seemed sadder, their tempo slower.

As they got closer to Europe, her memories of the little house by the canal in the marshlands of Vendée came back. Not what Armand or Daniel or Madeleine must look like now or what they must be doing. No. Just the house. The copper pots and cauldrons enflamed with the light of the sunset. The bedroom, the bottle of cornflower water on the rosewood bureau, the face powder in a bowl of blue china, the little box of mauve biscuit. She tried to remember the exact quality of the light in the late afternoon in the kitchen in the fall. The greenish cast of the canal in the pale morning.

One evening in the fall of 1899, while they were still in Vinh Long, on the balcony watching the Mekong River, she had asked Antoine: Do hollyhocks smell?

What did you say?

Do hollyhocks smell?

He had paused for a moment. Each of them closed their eyes and pictured the tall stems and large flowers growing wild in the villages of Vendée along the coast. Do hollyhocks smell? They were trying to remember. They couldn't.

It's raining in Bordeaux when the *Peï-Ho* casts its anchor. A gloomy, gray day on the Atlantic Coast. A porter brings her trunk to the coach. She carries her little suitcase of boiled leather herself. No more *coolie-xe*. No more *pousse-pousses*. She pulls out the roll of bills Antoine has given her to pay the coachman. She climbs up and sits at the back, alone.

She is exhausted and cold.

She doesn't remember anything else of the trip back home. There is a night in La Rochelle, in an inn near the seashore. She doesn't remember anything other than the sounds of the surf, and that milky light peculiar to the Vendée coast.

She is walking across the lawn toward the house, past the weeping willow, and pushes the door open. She is standing in the middle of the kitchen, at the foot of the stairs, holding her suitcase. She notices there's something missing . . . no doily in the middle of the table.

Qui est là?

She hears the floorboards creak the way they used to on the first step below the landing, and his steps coming down.

Qui est là? he calls again.

She is standing at the foot of the stairs in her winter coat— she's been cold since she's been back in France, two days before, though it's summertime—still holding her suitcase, and he sees her and keeps going down the stairs and stops in front of her without saying anything, without touching her. He just reaches out and takes the suitcase from her hand and puts it down on the floor next to them. And she doesn't know what goes through his eyes, only that there is no surprise, no anger, she can tell that.

I'm here, she says.

You're here.

His voice, she thinks, is like a perfume, a complex mix: irony and sarcasm as top note, a kind of rough burliness, and then, too subtle to pick out at first, but lingering behind, a reluctant warmth.

He puts his arms around her. Her head reaches his neck. He is a shorter man than Antoine, sturdier. He smells of leather and rubber, the same as her father, both men of the land, of horses and dogs, of wild game.

Tu es là, he repeats, and his hand gently touches her neck, strokes her hair, and then slowly, gingerly, searches for the pins holding her chignon up and starts to remove them. As if she had never been gone.

She pulls his hand away and takes a step back.

Are you back? he asks. Looking at her straight in the eyes.

She doesn't answer. She looks around. She has left the door open and gusts of wind make the curtains flutter.

Where are they?

At Sainte-Christine. With Adèle. A summer trip.

He looks at her again. His black eyes piercing. Waiting.

Are you back?

She sighs. The afternoon sun is flashing off the copper pots the way she remembers, the red glow contrasting with the cool light of the canal.

When are they coming back?

In two weeks or so.

She sits down at the table, still in her coat, the suitcase at her feet. With a finger she touches the wood surface. It feels dull and dry. It would need a good waxing.

You don't have anyone taking care of the house for you?

Yes, I do.

She nods.

That's right. You do.

If you come back she'll be gone.

She thinks about the long voyage back to the other side of the world. The slow adjustment to the different time zones. She will pick up the suitcase and walk out. She will take a steamer back to Saigon. The *D'Artagnan,* or the *Singapore.* That's what they talked about. The door is still open. Neither of them has bothered to close it. With the movement of the wind it squeaks on its hinges.

The door needs oil, she says.

He nods. He is still standing at the foot of the stairs, not leaning against the newel post, his legs solidly apart, his hands in the pockets of his trousers.

Where's Merlin?

Armand shakes his head.

He died?

He says nothing, looks down.

How? He was still young.

Run over by an automobile.

It's too bad, she says. A good dog, he was.

Under her hand the table feels familiar. She follows the veins and the cracks with a finger. An old Vendée table made of wild cherrywood.

Getting up and picking up the suitcase seems a huge effort. She's tired. So tired.

Give me a finger of port, she says.

He brings the bottle to the table with two small crystal glasses and sits across from her, filling the glasses. He picks up his and lifts it toward her.

A ton retour, he says. To your return.

She lifts hers too and takes a sip. The mellow, woodsy taste of the port surprises her. It is like nothing they ever drank in Saigon. He drinks his in one long gulp.

In the bedroom, nothing has changed. Her face powder in the bowl of blue china at the same place on the bureau, the bottles of ultramarine blue glass. The chest with the mother-of-pearl inlays full of discarded buttons and ribbons. The mauve box with the amethyst ring still in it. The silver crucifix nailed to the ivory cross hanging above the bed. The milky light filtering through the half-closed shutters. The cracks in the ceiling, the paint peeling.

I waited for you to come back, he says.

She lets him unbutton the coat, and the boots and her camisole of cambric. She doesn't look at him. It's Antoine who's still there with her, Antoine who unties her petticoat, unlaces her corset hook by hook.

. . .

She didn't have to stay. They could have just talked. She would have explained. And then she could have walked out again with her little suitcase.

The door was open. She could have taken the *D'Artagnan* or the *Singapore* back to Saigon.

And yet she did stay.

He pulled her to the bed. He smelled of leather and outdoors. His body was thicker, heavier than it used to be.

She didn't resist him.

TIME TO CLOSE the shutters, Maurice says, and he opens the window to reach out and pull the shutters in.

Don't. I'll do it later. Don't turn on the light either. He picks up the tea tray and carries it to the sink, runs the water and rinses the bowls and the teapot, leaves them to dry on the draining board.

The clicking of the cups, the splash of the water, the shuffle of his feet over the linoleum tiles by the sink are a mute reproach. His silence is almost more painful than his questions.

Well, he says, coming back to her, would you like me to prepare something for your dinner before I go?

No, she says, not looking at him.

It's as if he has opened a door and has walked away from it. And the door stands ajar between them, neither one of them making a move to cross the threshold.

She listens in the dark to the unfamiliar noises of the house and the street, the children's voices, right under her windows. For a moment, the smell of fresh paint on the white walls makes her think of the exciting smell of a brand-new notebook when it's first cracked open.

I should go back to Edmondina and Roland, then, he says. He's back at the grate, hesitant, facing her. His arms are behind his back. He's a big man, Maurice, with a fleshy face and thick eyebrows, and a benevolent cast to his mouth. But his face is closed, guarded.

Maurice, she says.

Yes?

They are both waiting for the other to say something. But then an engine sputters and speeds down the street.

The *Boches,* she says.

He looks out the window.

How do you know?

The cars they use, she says. Their engines sound different from ours. Maurice, she adds. It's a shame Pétain gave up so fast. After the way he fought at Verdun.

Maybe that's why. He didn't want to lose another million men.

You'll see, she says. We'll resist. We'll fight the same way we did in '14 to '18. De Gaulle is right.

He picks up the photograph from the table, the one taken by Dieulefils in Da Lat, and looks at it again.

If he was still here, she says, he would agree with me.

She moves her hands closer to the fire. It's chillier now, and damp. The wind has picked up. You can hear it howling even though they are on the bay side.

He was wounded at Verdun, she adds, aware that she is insisting more than she should, that he is not listening to her any more, but unable to stop herself. He came back to enlist, she says. He didn't have to. He was too old for that.

Maurice places the photograph back in the album and leaves the album on the table. She watches his hands. His gestures are precise, final.

I should leave you, he says. If you don't need anything else.

She nods without looking at him.

No, she says.

He leans to kiss her on the cheek.

Bonsoir, maman.

Bonsoir, mon petit.

. . .

After he left, she pushed and pulled, pushed and pulled the trunk closer to the fireplace. On top was a red silk robe printed with white chrysanthemums she didn't remember. Underneath was the peach satin dress with the taffeta bustle. She put it aside. She carefully picked up the dresses of light cambric and silk muslin. They came apart in her fingers. One by one she threw them into the fireplace. And then she tossed out the books, the Pierre Loti novels, the catalogue of the 1900 World Expo, the ledger of blue Moroccan. And then it was her notebooks full of Chinese characters. Antoine's letters. Menus from the *Tonkin,* from the *Peï-Ho.*

She tossed in every piece of paper, every article of clothing from the trunk, and threw away what she couldn't burn. Then she put the peach satin dress in front of her and looked at herself in the mirror over the fireplace. The waist was so tiny, she could never fit into it anymore. The satin was stained with long streaks of yellowish white. Maybe it was from the dampness at Villa Saint-Claude. She threw the dress into the fireplace. It took a long time to burn and gave off a bitter smoke.

She kept the notebook for last. It was almost completely filled in. The handwriting of her youth. The violet faded to sepia. Soon it would become illegible. She sat by the fireplace for a long time and read until she became too tired to stay awake. She considered putting it aside and giving it to Maurice. But she thought better of it. As the first gray of dawn lightened up the room, she tossed the notebook into the fire. At first it burned bright and tall, an explosion of sparks, then fell off to the side, half-consumed, the pages curled black on the edges. She picked it up with the tongs and pushed it back in the middle of the burning logs. This time it went up in flames in a few seconds. And then it was gone. It was only paper, after all.

NOTES ON VICTORINE

I met Roland Texier—the son of Maurice, the son of Victorine's return—and his wife, Nénette, on a cold and damp January day at the Angers train station where they had come to pick me up. They'd offered to drive me to Victorine's grave at L'Aiguillon, which I hadn't been able to find on my previous trip to Vendée.

In their house on the outskirts of Angers, they had shown me albums filled with postcards sent to Victorine, and some sent by her, all written in the loopy handwriting common in the early part of the century, all about news of vacations and trips. One of them, labeled *Souvenir de La Faute,* was a quaint montage, shot in black-and-white, of small postcards pinned among summer flowers (pansies and daisies) on a piece of weather-beaten wood. With the help of a magnifying glass, you could make out the casino the way it looked at the turn of the century, a simple structure with an entrance approached by two wooden stairways. On the beach, a row of wooden cabins had canopies of wood from which canvas awnings must have hung in the summertime, to shade the bathers from the sun. On a photograph entitled *The Harbor,* three teenaged boys sat, mussel nets stretched in front of them. The postcard was addressed to *Monsieur A. Texier, 19 rue Corbon, Paris, XVème arrt.* The text mentioned a rough sea and a successful fishing party: "We caught 30 liters of fish." There was a special greeting to Daniel and Madeleine. It was signed Maurice, your son and brother. He was sixteen years younger than Daniel.

There was also a notebook filled with recipes for treating illnesses and for the home manufacture of household products, from the cure of cancerous lesions to candles. We looked at it together, unable to decide whether it was Victorine's handwriting.

Earlier, in the car, while we were driving from the station, Nénette had talked about Victorine, whom she had never met. Roland was quiet. The twilight was gathering around us. I don't know if she left for another man, Nénette was saying, her face turned toward me over the front seat. Victorine's sister, Angelina, was married to a military man and they had moved to Indochina. Maybe Victorine decided to follow her sister. Nénette couldn't believe that Victorine had stopped loving Armand. He was a skirt-chaser, it was true. Everybody knew that. She must have been unhappy with him. Maybe she couldn't take it anymore. But still . . .

I had already gone looking for traces of Victorine in the French Overseas Archives—a euphemism for colonial records—which are housed in Aix-en-Provence. There, I had held many boxes of yellowed papers in my hands, brittle onionskin copies typed or handwritten in duplicate or triplicate—furious or poignant letters vividly evoking a world of bureaucracy and petty rebellion, long-winded feuds and inept disobedience, farcical entanglements that often ended tragically. Some of them concerned families named Texier and even a few Jozelons. But none of them was written by or addressed to Victorine, whether in the Indochina or in the New Caledonia section. So I could neither prove nor disprove Nénette's arguments.

During the ride from the station, Roland didn't say much. Nénette remembered a big box full of Victorine's personal papers and letters, which had remained for years in Maurice's wife's possession after Victorine's death. There was a letter written by Angelina, Victorine's sister, asking for money. Perhaps that letter had been sent from Indochina. That box had disappeared. The rest of Victorine's papers had been destroyed at her death, in December 1940, during the German occupation. She died in L'Aiguillon, where she had moved from La Faute, a few kilometers away, on the bay side, a few months before.

When we got ready the next morning for the drive to L'Aiguillon, it was still pitch black. There was hot coffee waiting for me in a thermos on the kitchen table, and a big loaf of Vendée *brioche*— not one of those small, individual, round-bellied *brioches* sold in Paris bakeries.

The alternatively flat and hilly landscape, desolate under a low, heavy sky, with its sleepy villages of gray stucco, was familiar to me by now. At every other crossroad a Christ agonized, carved of white marble or some other white stone, nailed to a tall granite cross. The winter had been wet, and the green marsh was bloated with water, the canals running high, flush with their banks.

In three or four hours—much longer than I had expected— we reached the shore. The cemetery of L'Aiguillon-sur-Mer was lashed with a bitter ocean wind. I walked behind Roland's burly back, my coat collar turned up, shivering. I remembered similar visits to Vendée cemeteries with my grandparents on All Saints' Day when I was a child. Tombstones worn smooth by centuries. The bristling of wet leaves under leather soles, a pungent smell of ripe, rich soil, a bouquet of gold chrysanthemums hastily arranged in the wrought-iron stand at the foot of the grave. Photos in oval frames, fading sepia. *A mon cher papa* carved in the grainy marble.

After a few minutes we stopped in front of a mound of earth sinking to one side, framed by a rectangle of granite. The burgundy-colored marble plaque was broken, half sunk into the ground. You could barely read the dates: August 11, 1866– December 27, 1940. The black marble cross on which a Christ was affixed was also broken. In contrast to the solid granite of Armand's gravestone, made to withstand the abuse of time, which I had seen in my previous visit to Vendée in the cemetery of La Jaudonnière-en-Pareds, Victorine's stone was already collapsing into the earth. Nénette apologized for the artificial flowers in the pots. She and Roland were the only people still visiting the grave. It was too hard to keep up with fresh flowers. Roland nodded and said nothing.

A few weeks later, Roland Texier sent me a large photograph of Victorine, twelve by sixteen inches, the one with the hair loosely piled in a topknot and the flounced collar curling at the neck, and the eyes looking away. He kept the original and mailed me a slightly grainy Xerox copy. Judging from the dress and hairstyle, it must date from the turn of the century. I taped it on the wall in my apartment in New York. The gaze is soft and dreamy, almost ghostly. There's an absence in the features. It is not the picture of a fully engaged young woman. And yet her absence has a density, a weight. I don't think she is simply a dreamer longing to escape. I see it as the picture of the woman who came home.